# The Dragon Forest III
## The King of Illiath

R. A. Douthitt

Author photo © 2018 Tom Becker

ISBN- 978-0692513293

*The Dragon Forest III* is a work of fiction. References to real people, events, establishments, organizations, or locales are intended only to provide a sense of authenticity and are used fictitiously. All other characters, incidents, and dialogue are drawn from the author's imagination. The perspective, opinions, and worldview represented by this book are those of the author and are not intended to be a reflection or endorsement of the publisher's views.

Printed in the U.S.A.

# DEDICATION

To Teresa and Sara.

The bravest warriors I know.

R. A. DOUTHITT

# What people are saying about *The Dragon Forest* books:

"The author does an excellent job at making you feel that you're part of the war. You can visualize the battle field and the enemy. You can feel the men fighting for king and kingdom. As you read, you can almost watch Peter grow into a man. Great read."

"*The Dragon Forest* is one of the most exciting stories I have read in some time. Douthitt really knows how to blend action with narrative. Her universe has a *Lord of the Rings* kind of feeling, but stands on its own. I would definitely recommend this tale to all fantasy readers and those who enjoy an exciting tale with loads of inspiration and hints at what is to come. I can't wait for book 2!"

"Read the book before the moves comes out. *The Dragon Forest* reads like a movie with the details of the entry into the mysterious forest to the battle scenes that take place between Good and Evil. The tension between these two forces will keep you turning each page to find out what happens next. You will find this book difficult to put down until you come to the last page and then you'll find yourself wanting more…"

"Very, very exciting sequel to The Dragon Forest!!!! In this book Peter goes thru trials that take him from boyhood to a man. He truly learns what his greatness is. The scenes are written so well that you feel like you are there helping Peter thru his battles. I love when a book is so well written that you can picture the characters in your head, the dragon, the owl and Peter are etched in my mind. I am really looking forward to the next Dragon Forest book."

"If you liked Dragon Forest, you will love it's sequel, Dragon Forest II: Son of the Oath. It's a coming of age story that takes Peter from childhood to manhood through a torturous path from slavery to human and dragon combat to fighting for his freedom and that of others. Besides this main theme, there are stories of other main characters like King Alexander and Peter's friend that are interwoven with it, all leading to the final battle that will be fought in the third installment of this amazing trilogy."

# ACKNOWLEDGMENTS

There are so many people to thank because writing this trilogy did not begin or end with me.

I'd like to thank my husband, Scott, and my son, Nathan, for supporting me on this insane endeavor that spanned over twenty years. Thank you for your patience and understanding as I researched and discussed my little story and beloved characters with you over countless dinners. I could not have completed this project without you.

I would also like to thank my editor, Christopher Moore, whose advice, meticulous editing skills, and constructive criticism helped make me a better writer with a thicker skin which is necessary in the writing business.

For my assistant editor, Wayne Purdin, whose excellent suggestions on plot and characters made *The Dragon Forest II* more descriptive and detailed for the reader.

Without Beta Readers, a writer's job is almost impossible. So, I'd like to thank all the beta readers who have taken the time out of their busy lives to read the rough drafts of my books. Christian Peterson, Jake Murphy, Andrew Walma, and Cora Woods: I thank you for your thoughtful suggestions and comments on *The Dragon Forest II* and *The Dragon Forest III*. With your help, my books are now more enjoyable for my readers.

I'd like to thank author Stephen Biesty for his book, *Cross-sections Castle*. This book helped me to visualize life within and around the medieval castles of long ago. As a result, I was able to create the fantastical lands of Théadril, Vulgaard, and the palace at Illiath in great detail for my readers.

I'd also like to mention Master Merlin and Dugald A. Steer for their book *Wizardology* which helped me with some terminology and ideas about spells.

Without Dr. R.C. Sproul's little book, *The Truth of the Cross*, I would never have been able to accurately understand the theme of salvation and the redemptive act of Christ in order to show those themes in my story. This book also helped me understand sacrifice and covenant. These are also prevalent themes in my story.

After I read *The Count of Monte Cristo* by Alexandres Dumas, I was moved and reminded of the story of Joseph in the book of Genesis. Both stories inspired the storyline in *The Dragon Forest II*. I wondered how Peter would respond to being innocently imprisoned. Would he seek to escape in order to enact revenge like Edmond Dantes? Or would he be able to endure imprisonment with integrity and honor as Joseph did? These books left an enduring impact on me and have influenced my writing.

A big thanks goes out to my school, Valley Academy Charter School, in Arizona. I truly appreciate the support of staff, parents, and students. Every time I see a student reading one of my books at school or hear about students checking my books out of the library, I am reminded how blessed I am to be a published author. Not only am I privileged to have my books at this fine school and others, but I am privileged to teach such amazing students.

I'd like to thank my original publisher, Ramona Tucker, for believing in my story from the start. Thank you for giving an unknown writer a chance way back in 2008. I cannot begin to express how exciting it is to see my stories in print.

Finally, I'd like to thank my Lord and Savior, Jesus Christ, for giving me this story so many years ago. There were times when I felt He had taken over and wrote through me. Because of Him, I am able to share this little story of a young boy's life forever transformed. Because of Him, I live and breathe and have life everlasting.

"Bring me the swords," the man said. He waved his hand as though the Elf would magically obey.

"And why should I do that?" the Elf asked. He stood defiantly with arms crossed. "I was told he would come for them."

The man shook his head. "You fool," he said. Then, he turned his body to reveal a second man standing behind him. This man wore a heavy coat made of wolf fur with a hood that hid his face. He came forward and removed the hood.

The Elf gasped, stepped back, then turned to his assistant and quickly sent him further back into the cave. The two men waited patiently. The Elf returned followed by three helpers carrying a large wooden box carved with a strange pattern along its cover. They placed it atop a table made of rock and then stepped back. The two men slowly opened the box. One reached in and removed one object from inside. He raised it high.

"The Sword of Alexander," he whispered to his companion.

"Put it back!" the other man said. "Are you mad? There are spies all around."

The two men took the box and rode off into the darkness.

"Was that really him?" the Elf asked his superior.

"Indeed," he replied. "That was the King of Illiath."

# PART I

# 1 IN THE BEGINNING

The wind was so frigid that if his skin were exposed for only a few seconds, it would turn hard as stone. But that didn't stop him. He continued climbing the snow covered mountain as though on a quest. His determination kept him going even though all he had was a pick ax he'd made from a piece of iron and wood for the handle.

His hands, wrapped in strips of cloth, had blackened fingertips. The flesh had died, so the pain had stopped. He inhaled as much thin air as he could and turned around to continue on. He reached up and felt a rocky mantle then securely gripped it with his frozen fingers. With all the strength he had left, he pulled himself up and looked around. Finally, he'd reached the last precipice. He struggled to stand. He leaned into the icy wind that almost blew him over the edge. And that's when he saw it.

The cave.

The mountains of Vulgaard had several caves that hid the precious loot of the dragons. Known for many millenniums, the dragon caves could make a Man, Elf, or Dwarf very wealthy. If they made it out alive.

But this man, half dead from the biting cold, entered into the cave without hesitation. It was as if he had known no dragon resided within. He walked into the cave entrance that was several feet taller than his head. He ambled in as he unwrapped the strips of cloth that covered his face. He removed the makeshift eye protectors that the old wizard had constructed for him. They worked. He squinted his eyes, and then rubbed them with his numb hands. Finally, he focused on the innards of the cave.

Illumined only by a single torch, the cave went deep into the mountain. The man used the rock walls to guide him toward the light. His final destination was not the bounty of precious gemstones and gold, but what lay amidst the stones and gold: a single dragon egg.

When he saw the egg resting on top of the stack of gemstones, he almost fainted. The altitude mixed with his exhaustion began to take its toll on his body, but the sight of the egg indeed took its toll on his psyche.

*Could this be it?*

He carefully approached the nest. The setting was just as he was told it would be: No dragon was nearby. He leaned down and studied his treasure. It was more beautiful than he had ever imagined. He slowly reached out to touch it. As his finger almost made contact with the surface of the egg, it jiggled.

The man jumped back at first, and then he remembered it was just an egg. He grabbed it and placed it inside the bag strapped to his shoulder. He quickly wrapped his face and hands in the cloth strips and headed out of the cave. He stood in the entrance leaning into the wind again.

*Hadn't thought of the trip down,* he thought. *Not sure how this is going to work out, but I must try.*

§

"He's here!" the boy shouted. "He made it!"

The servant boy ran down the corridor until he felt a strong arm grab his shoulder.

"Quiet now," the voice said.

The boy looked up into the kind eyes of the King.

"My Lord," the boy said. "He's here!"

King Aidan, known for his brown eyes and hair, unusual for an Elf, looked up and saw a half dead man covered in ice standing in the entrance to the palace of Vulgaard.

The icy man reached into his bag and held out his treasure. The King, eyebrows raised, methodically walked toward the man never taking his eye off the dragon egg jiggling in his palm.

"Your highness." The man's voice was barely above a whisper. "For you."

The King looked into the man's iced covered eyelids and slowly took the egg from him.

"Constable!" the King shouted.

An older Elf ran into the entrance hall.

"Yes, my Lord," he replied. Then he gasped at the sight of the man thawing out right in front of him.

"Take this man to the apothecary. Get him warmed up, fed, and rested," the King ordered while examining the egg. "Then bring him to me."

"Yes, my Lord." The Constable reached out to take hold of the man who then collapsed in his arms.

§

The two stood staring at the large egg stirring in front of them. They laid it on a table covered with a velvet cloth.

"What do you think?" the King Aidan asked.

Before him stood an older man, tall and thin with a long white beard and spectacles resting on his angular nose. The man's name was Theodore Sirus III. A wise old wizard, Theodore was an advisor to the King of Vulgaard and had been for many years. He bent down and examined the surface of the egg intently.

"I have never seen anything like it before," Theo replied. "A diamond encrusted surface."

"I've seen red ruby, green emerald, and even sapphire encrusted eggs." The King rubbed his bearded chin. "But never in my thousand years have I seen this."

Theo looked up at his sovereign.

"You know what I am asking," the King said and turned to his desk.

Theo removed his spectacles and cleaned them with his sleeve. He did not answer.

"Well?" The King poured a cup of ale. "Can it be?"

Theo placed his spectacles back on and walked toward the King.

"Can it be the one?" the King asked as he handed Theo the cup.

Theo took the cup and swirled its contents.

"Answer me!" The King grew impatient.

"It is without a doubt the prophecy fulfilled," Theo said. Then he took a gulp of ale.

## 2 THE DRAGON PROPHECY

The old Dwarf waved to his assistants and they all gathered round the pit where the egg rested. His young son, with hair as red as his father's, ran over to the edge of the pit and dangled a string over it. A bone was tied to the end of the string.

"Your boy is doing it again." An older Dwarf chuckled. He picked up the little boy and took him to the corner of the room. "You keep doing that and we'll have to call you Dangler."

The Dwarves laughed.

The boy's father walked over to his son. "Dangler," he said and touched his son's chin." I like that."

He turned and walked toward the pit. "Now son, pay attention."

The boy nodded.

All the Dwarves, dressed in linen tunics but wearing their leather breastplates, stood by the pit when Theo entered into the room. He motioned for everyone to step aside as he approached the pit and looked in. At the bottom was the diamond encrusted egg, still jiggling.

Theo leaned over and watched as the egg cracked. He looked back at the King who stood in the entrance of the room. Theo grinned, turned his head, and continued watching as the tiny dragon pushed its way out of the egg. All the Dwarves came to the edge of the pit to watch the sight.

Finally, the head of the dragon appeared. Then one wing followed by the next, until its entire body rested outside its shell. It blinked its tiny eyes and wailed for its mother.

Theo looked over at King Aidan and grinned.

"A Draco," Theo said.

The King clasped his hands together, closed his eyes, and exhaled.

§

"Here, here, what is this meeting about, King Aidan?" One guest sat with arms crossed and eyes squinted.

King Aidan, King of the Elves at Vulgaard, walked up to the large round table carved from quartz that stood in the middle of his grand dining hall. On his arm was Queen Ragnalla in a long silk gown of the bluest blue. Her white hair was braided and rested to the side on her shoulder. They approached the table then stopped. He held out the chair for his wife then sat down on his throne. Each of his ten guests waited patiently for the announcement.

"Gentlemen," King Aidan said. "The prophecy has been fulfilled."

The men took in what was said then looked at one another. Some seemed as bored as before the announcement while others understood immediately what the King was speaking of.

Theagan, a young man and knight to King Aidan dressed in his silver armor, stood and leaned on the table. He cocked his head as though confused.

"You mean the dragon is here?" he asked. "*The* dragon of prophecy has arrived?"

King Aidan nodded. "Yes and I have seen it for myself."

Theagan turned to Glenthryd, a ruler from the valley below. He stood with eyes wide open. Glenthryd and his people had long battled the fierce dragons. The prophecy was well known in his valley.

"And what did the White Dragon say?" he asked.

"Ask him yourself." Aidan motioned for his guards to open the large double doors at one end of the hall. When they did, a beautiful and lithe white dragon appeared in the entrance. Its talons clicked on the polished floor made of stone inlayed with diamonds. The Wyvern paused and studied its reflection in the floor. And then, in an instant, transformed into an old man wearing a white robe with a rope as a sash.

"Sir Theodore Sirus III," Olrrig said as he made his way around the table. The leader of a mountain people, Olrigg, trusted in the counsel of the White Dragon.

Theo checked his reflection in the shiny floor once more before addressing the group.

"Is this true, Theo?" Olrigg gestured to the King. "Has the Dragon of Promise been found?"

Theo slowly grinned with a sparkle in his eyes. "Yes, this is true," he said. "I have seen the hatchling myself."

And with that, the entire group began shouting and talking with one another. Some of the leaders approached the King while others demanded to see the hatchling. Others questioned Theo.

"When will we know?" Olrigg asked. "When will we know its wisdom and counsel? My people have suffered enough from the mountain dragons."

"Yes!" Another leader named Thordin slammed his fist on the table. "We need the terrorizing to stop once and for all!"

King Aidan raised his large hands to try and silence the group. "Friends," he said calmly. "Please, listen to me. We shall have our answers soon. Theo here will work with the dragon masters and let us know all that we need to know."

Theo nodded in agreement. "Patience." He raised his hand as the men sat down in their chairs. "We must wait and see how the dragon grows. But I must tell you, I have never seen a dragon of this form in all my years. It is unlike any other dragon."

"What do you mean?" Glenthryd leaned forward with a raised eyebrow.

Theo hesitated as though trying to select the right words. "Well." He walked around the table and dragged his hand along the smooth surface. "Its scales. I have never seen such scales on a dragon before."

All the men looked at one another for clarity.

Theo used his hands to try and help them understand. "They glisten in the firelight. They are iridescent. It is difficult to describe. One must see it to understand—"

"Let's go!" Olrigg pushed aside his chair and began walking toward Theo.

Theo looked to the King who nodded. Then, he noticed all the guests present had the same desire to see the newly hatched dragon.

"Very well then." Theo rubbed his bearded chin. "This way."

# 3 THE HATCHLING

One of King Aidan's guards led the excited guests through a corridor deep inside the mountain home of the King and his family. The torch shed its light on the winding corridor as the men squabbled some more about the dragons and their villages.

"This had better be the one, King Aidan," Glenthryd threatened.

"You mean to say *your majesty*." The Constable corrected him as he walked behind the King. He shot Glenthryd a harsh look.

"Pardon me, *your majesty*," Glenthryd said.

Finally, the corridor opened into a room with a large pit in the center. Several Elves and Dwarves stood around. They hastily came to attention once their King entered. Each bowed and kept a distance as he moved about the room. Every once in a while, the wailing of a newly hatched dragon could be heard coming from the pit. Theo walked over to the King and motioned him to look inside.

The King indulged him and peeked over the edge of the pit. Instantly, he was shocked by a thin line of fire coming from the hatchling below. He moved away in time to have his beard singed by the fire.

"My apologies, your majesty," Theo said as he moved the King away from the pit. Theo shot the Dragon Master a stern look of disapproval.

"He's a bit temperamental." The Dragon Master chuckled nervously.

"Here, let's have a look," Olrigg said as he rubbed his hands together. He quickly made his way to the edge of the pit and peered over. His face changed as soon as his eyes saw the sight. With wide eyes, he turned his head to Glenthryd. His mouth fell open. Intrigued, Glenthryd walked over and stood next to Olrigg.

He peered over the edge as well.

"Astonishing," he whispered.

There, at the bottom of the pit, stood a tiny Draco with glistening scales and glowing yellow eyes. It squawked and spread its leathery wings. Its tail swished back and forth along the dirt. Then, it hissed as it looked into the eyes of its intruders.

"Back off," Olrigg said. He used his arm to push Glenthryd back. "I know that hissing sound all too well."

Another line of fire came from the pit below. All the guests stepped back.

"Well?" King Aidan spoke with pride in his voice. He nodded toward Theo. "Is it not the Dragon of Promise?"

One by one, the other rulers came toward the pit and inspected the prize dragon below. And one by one, each of the men agreed the promise had been fulfilled.

"Amazing, King Aidan." Thordin walked over and placed his hand on the King's shoulder. "In our lifetime, the prophecy is fulfilled. I never would have thought—"

"King Aidan!" a shout from the corridor interrupted Thordin. All the men turned to see several Elfin knights come running down the corridor toward the King. Many of them had bloodied wounds that needed attending. Some of them were pale as they leaned against the wall, trying to catch their breath. King Aidan's eyes grew wide.

"What is this? What happened?" He reached out to help one of the Elves just as he collapsed.

"Sire, we have been attacked." The Elf gasped. "There are many soldiers coming. We…we tried to stop them, but—"

"Ñien nothriel," King Aidan ordered the Elves. "Ëioen niuen thëiriel ulrienden!" He waved them on.

The Elves nodded and helped the injured. The sound of approaching soldiers was heard by all.

"What is this?" Thordin said as the uninjured Elfin knights moved into position.

"We've been found out, I'm afraid." King Aidan frowned. Thordin removed his sword and watched the darkened corridor.

Each of the guests struggled to remain calm as they heard the commotion in the darkness.

"How could this have happened, Aidan?" Glenthryd shouted. "I thought you said your scouts made sure that none of us were followed—"

King Glenthryd was interrupted by the soldiers as they stormed in and surrounded all the men including King Aidan. Their swords still dripped blood. Thordin stood ready with his sword drawn. Theo stepped back to the wall of the cave. He leaned on the wall and listened.

And waited.

One soldier pushed through the guests and rudely stood in front of King Aidan. He inspected the wounded Elfin knights nearby, still bleeding. Then, he nodded to Thordin who lowered his sword once he realized they were outnumbered.

"What do you want here?" King Aidan demanded of the soldiers. He stared at the blade pointed at his chest. "Leave my palace this instant."

The soldier turned and made his way to the pit.

"Gladly, King Aidan," he hissed through the visor of his helmet. "We all will leave at once, just as soon as I have the dragon."

Theo pushed on the wall behind him.

"What nonsense is this?" King Aidan began to approach the soldier but was stopped by a blade across his chest. He could feel the weight of the metal. Olrigg drew his sword, but three soldiers pointed their sword tips at his throat.

"No nonsense at all, King," the head soldier replied casually. "All we want is the dragon. Nothing else."

Aidan looked at Theo who had nothing to say.

"Never!" King Aidan said. "You must be mad to think we would let you take the dragon away from here!"

"Give us the dragon now, and everyone lives." The soldier slowly approached the King. "Everyone will live, oh good King Aidan. The villagers, your family, these rulers...all will live if we take the dragon now."

King Aidan swallowed hard.

"But if we do not take the dragon now..." The soldier turned his head and made eye contact with Olrigg. "Everyone here dies. Every villager will die and every village will burn. I promise you this, each and every ruler will surely die in a fortnight"

"You fool!" Olrigg shouted.

"If we give you the dragon we all die!" King Aidan said. "Yes, even you! Don't you understand? This dragon is the One."

Theo felt the wall behind him open.

"Don't you see?" King Aidan raised his hand and pointed to the pit. "Without this dragon, the beasts out there will devour all of us soon!"

The soldier jerked his head back and laughed. "Yes, well, that is a dilemma isn't it?"

Theo quietly and quickly disappeared into the wall. It closed without anyone noticing.

"I have warned you, King," the soldier said. "Now, give me the dragon and everything will remain as it was."

The room grew silent. No one moved as eyes shifted back and forth from King to soldier to Elfin knight. No one dared to move.

Suddenly, from the pit came a high pitched squawk that startled everyone. The soldier looked into the pit in time to see Theo grab the tiny dragon and shove it into a linen bag. Theo looked up and saw the soldiers watching him. He grinned at them, and then disappeared into an opening in the wall of the pit. It closed behind him.

"No!" the soldier shouted. He turned to King Aidan.

"Kill them all!" the soldier ordered. Then he lunged forward and thrust his sword into King Aidan's chest. He withdrew the sword and watched the King fall to the ground. A pool of blood formed around the dead body. The soldier turned to his men and watched them kill the rest of the rulers.

§

Theo took the bag carrying the hatchling and ran through the secret passage until he reached the opening. As he stood in the opening of the cave, he quickly transformed into the White Dragon and flew off over the cliff with the bag in its claws.

The dragon soared over Vulgaard swooping low over the river and valleys until it reached a small cabin on the edge of the woods. It flapped its wings and landed. Three Elves ran out to meet the beast with swords and spears in their hands.

The White Dragon roared then took the bag from its claws with its mouth. The elder Elf noticed the bag and dropped his sword. He motioned for his companions to do the same. With arms spread out as a gesture of kindness, the Elf cautiously approached, never taking his eyes off the dragon. Finally, he stood before it and began to take the bag. The dragon lowered its snout and transformed back into the wizard, Theodore Sirus.

"Don't touch it!" Theo ordered. The Elves fell back at the sight of the shape shifter.

"You are that wizard!" the elder shouted. "What magic have you brought to this house? What do you want with us?"

Theo took a few steps toward the Elves, two of whom still held the swords up in defiance.

"Lower those weapons, you fools," he said as he hastily walked passed them and entered into their cabin.

They stood together trying to decide whether to follow Theo or not.

"He is under a spell," the elder said. "He is from a long line of wizards."

"Should we trust him?" the other Elf asked.

The elder shrugged. "I feel we had better follow him."

He entered his cabin where he found Theo standing near the table.

"What do you want with us?" the elder asked.

"Close the door." Theo pointed behind the Elves. The younger one closed the door as ordered. "Come close."

The Elves hesitated then obeyed more out of curiosity than fear.

"Again, what do you want with—"

"Hush you fools!" Theo said. "Now, listen carefully to every word I say. I am Theodore, the wizard to King Aidan, who was slain this very day by the Knights of Ranvieg."

The Elves gasped when they heard the news.

"What will become of us?" the younger one asked. He covered his mouth as tears formed in his eyes.

Quiet!" Theo ordered. "I am the White Dragon of old." He held up the bag.

"The White Dragon," the elder whispered. "You are under a spell!"

"Yes." Theo gestured toward the Elf. "So it would be wise for you to listen to me now."

The Elves looked at one another. "What evil is this! What evil is this!" the elder cried. His hands trembled.

"Quiet! Within this bag is the very Dragon of Promise." Theo slowly opened the bag. The Elves leaned in to see what Theo was talking about. A squawk came from inside and the Elves jumped back.

Then, suddenly a small dragon head appeared, then two legs, and then the body of a tiny Draco.

"Look at that," the elder said to his companions. "A Draco hatchling."

All gathered round the table and studied their new guest. The little dragon sniffed the table and took a few more steps out of the bag. A wisp of smoke rose from its nostrils. It lifted its head and looked deeply into each one's eyes as they stared back in wonder. Like a flash, it spewed fire from its mouth, sending each Elf back a few feet.

"Alright," the elder Elf said. "What is it you want us to do?"

Theo took out several gold coins from a pouch attached to his belt and tossed them to the Elf. "Take these as payment. Watch over the dragon for a few days. I will return for it."

Theo started to leave the small cabin, but the Elf stopped him. "Will they come for it?" he asked.

Theo sighed heavily as though not wanting to answer. He turned around slowly. "Yes," he said.

All three Elves looked at one another then turned to the tiny Dragon chasing its tail on the table. "Any advice?" he asked Theo.

"Take up sword, spear, anything." Theo opened the door. "But whatever you do, do not let them take that Dragon. Understand?"

But before they could answer, he transformed back into the White Dragon and flew off into the sky thick with clouds. Thunder could be heard in the distance and a few raindrops pelted the ground. The younger Elf grabbed the door and searched the skies for intruders before closing it.

# 4 THE WAR OF RANVIEG

Once news spread of the surprise attack on King Aidan and the rulers, war began in the regions surrounding Vulgaard. Glenthryd and Thordin survived the attack along with Theagan, but Olrigg perished with many of Aidan's men that night in the hidden corridor deep within the palace.

The valleys were set afire by the dragons of Ranvieg. Sheep and cattle were pilfered and the Ogres took advantage of the chaos in the skies to take what was left. The villagers ran into the woods for cover from the flying beasts and from the Knights of Ranvieg, but it was no use. Many men and women perished in the fires. Through their spies, the Knights of Ranvieg knew the Dragon was being hidden away somewhere nearby.

Theo returned to the palace to assist the Queen in any way he could, but her task was monumental and it weighed heavily on her fair shoulders.

"There's been no time to mourn my husband," she said as she paced her chambers.

"Yes, your Majesty," Theo said.

"And now the Dragon is missing yet these monsters will go on attacking until it is handed over to them." She covered her face with her hands. "Oh, Theo, I don't know what to do."

He came to her and placed his hands on her thin shoulders.

"One more day," he said. "One more day and I shall return with great news. I promise you."

She removed her hands to reveal eyes weary with tears. "But can we last another day?" She turned away. "Can my people last one more day?"

"They must," he said. "We have waited too long for this moment to give up now. All is not lost even though it may seem that way. Trust me."

Theo approached the large window in the Queens chambers and gazed below. He could see the fires in the hamlets below glowing in the twilight as the dragons flew back and forth searching desperately for the One. He opened the glass door and stepped out onto the balcony. Instantly, he transformed into the White Dragon. The Queen met him on the balcony. She stroked its long neck layered with white scales.

"Go, my friend," she said as she looked down on the burning villages. "Bring it back so this may all come to an end."

With that, the White Dragon took flight and the Queen returned to her chambers.

§

"Follow it," the knight commanded as he nudged his dragon forward. It glided through the air not far behind the White Dragon.

Swooping low along the river and over several smoldering hamlets, the dragon finally came upon the little cabin in the woods. It flapped its wings sending sticks and leaves flying everywhere. The three Elves came running out the front door to meet their guest.

The dragon shook its head and nodded to the men. Then, it transformed into Theodore Sirus once again, and the four hastily made their way into the cabin.

"Theodore!" the elder Elf shouted. "You must come!" He took Theo's arm and began dragging him toward the back door of the cabin. But Theo did not budge.

"Perhaps a beverage first?" he insisted. The elder Elf motioned for his son to bring out a cup of ale for their guest.

"Drink it down and then come with me. Hurry!" the Elf said.

But Theo took his own time gulping down the warm beer. He even sat down on a rickety old chair for a second or two.

"I've come a long way," he said. His host nodded but nervously paced the room. Theo noticed the three Elves had changed much over the course of just a few days. And he knew why.

"So, do you all have names?" he asked.

The elder Elf placed his hand on his chest. "I am Thuriel."

Theo nodded toward him.

"And this is my eldest son, Eliel." The Elf bowed his head.

Thuriel pointed to the boy. "And my youngest son, Oliel. He has become very attached to the dragon." The young Elf smiled.

Theo grinned politely at each one. He drank and then slammed down the cup onto the table. The foam flew about. Finally, Theo stood. "Alright then, show me what you are so anxious to show me," he said.

Thuriel threw open the door and grabbed a torch from a barrel out back. He lit the torch and made his way down a path toward the woods. Theo, who wore a long white robe with a rope belt around his waist, hoisted up his robe so as not to trip as he made his way down the path. When the path ended, the deep woods began.

Thuriel stood at the edge and stared into the woods. He raised the torch high as the sun was too low in the sky to provide much light. Theo walked up and stood next to him.

"Well?" he asked. "What is—"

He was interrupted by a low ominous growl coming from within the trees ahead of them. Then, several trees began to shake. Some trees snapped in two and fell to the ground. Theo balanced himself as the ground began to shake. The growl grew louder and, shockingly, closer to the four bystanders.

Thuriel turned toward Theo with eyes wide open and a grin on his face. He even hopped up and down. Theo raised his eyebrows at the sight of this elder Elf, who must have been over one thousand years old, acting like a small child at holiday time.

And then that's when Theo saw what caused the Elf's giddiness.

In between the trees, Theo saw two large yellow eyes glowing from within. They blinked and focused on him like they were looking into his soul. He took a few steps back, but the Elves ran toward the eyes as though familiar with the source. And once the torch in Thuriel's hand illuminated the area, Theo saw the reason for the excitement of his hosts.

There, in the midst of the trees, stood the Dragon of Promise, in all its glory. The Elves stroked its enormous snout causing it to close its eyes with comfort. It was as though the beast enjoyed the petting.

"How can this be?" Theo took a few steps toward the sight. "It has only been a few days. This creature is full grown."

"We noticed it was growing faster than we thought after you left. By the next morning, it was as large as the cabin! So we hid it out here in the gorge," Eliel shouted.

"Astonishing," Theo murmured under his breath. He stood face to face with the Dragon, now moaning as the Elves stroked its neck and scratched under its chin. It slowly opened its eyes. Theo thought he'd take a chance, so he reached out his hand to touch the snout, but the beast began to growl.

Theo retracted his arm and took a step back.

"It won't hurt you," Thuriel said as he scratched the Dragon's chin. "Have you ever seen such scales before? Magnificent!"

Theo studied the eyes of the Dragon and noticed they became fiercer. The nostrils opened and closed. "Yes, magnificent," he whispered while he stepped back.

"I've lived a long time and have seen many a dragon, but never like this!" Thuriel said.

In that instant, the Dragon raised its head and roared ferociously causing each to cover their ears from the pain.

Theo, without thinking, transformed into the White Dragon and roared back. It reared back and flapped its wings as protection, but then it noticed the Dragon wasn't roaring at them, but at something behind them.

The White Dragon turned its body in time to see a row of knights riding up to the edge of the wood with torches, bows and arrows, and swords. Then, the dragon turned to see how the Dragon of Promise would respond.

The three Elves ran deeper into the woods behind the Dragon's tail and waited.

"Attack!" The same head knight who killed King Aidan, raised his arm then lowered it causing the archers to send fiery arrows into the air. The White Dragon took flight and hovered over the scene sixty feet above. As the fire spread, it could see the Dragon in its entirety. *It could easily measure seventy feet in length*, the White Dragon thought. *And forty feet in the air.*

Satisfied with setting the forest afire, the knight then ordered his archers to send their arrows into the chest of the beast. He raised his arm again and lowered. The archers obeyed, sending their arrows directly at the Dragon.

"No!" Oliel shouted. He ran out from behind and placed himself between the arrows and the Dragon, as though trying to protect it. Several arrows pierced his flesh and he fell to the ground dead.

Thuriel ran to try and save his youngest son. He knelt next to him and noticed dozens of arrows all around. He gazed up at the Dragon and saw no arrows had penetrated its scales. The Dragon lowered its snout, sniffed the dead Elf, and then turned its head toward the soldiers and archers.

When he saw the arrows had no effect on the Dragon, the knight ordered his men to rush the beast to slay it. But the White Dragon sensed the futility of this act once it saw the enormity of the Dragon. It circled above to see how this attack would end.

The men galloped down the gorge shouting as they came, but then their horses reared up and threw the men to the ground. The Dragon raised its head higher and higher above the trees until it stood up on all four of its legs and spread its wings out sending more trees falling to the ground. It inhaled deeply.

"Retreat!" The Head Knight yanked the reins of his horse to turn it around.

But it was too late. A stream of fire came forth from the mouth of the Dragon of Promise, incinerating all the knights, archers, and soldiers that tried to attack it. In mere seconds, the woods were quiet again. Then, it spewed out a strange blue flame that extinguished the fires around it. The White Dragon felt it was safe to land once again.

Eliel ran out and joined his father by the side of his dead brother. The White Dragon transformed into Theo yet again.

"I am sorry for the loss of your youngest son." Theo placed his hand on Thuriel's shoulder. Then, he gazed up at the Dragon. Smoke rose from its nostrils. Theo stared into the glowing eyes of the majestic beast. "Your son must have loved the Dragon to have sacrificed his life for it in such a way."

Thuriel sniffed and wiped his tear stained face. "Yes," he said in a voice barely above a whisper. "It was sort of a pet to him. He fed it and watched over it."

Theo motioned for the Elf to follow him. "Come now, lift him up, and carry him to the cabin," he said. Thuriel obeyed and lifted his son's body over his shoulders. Together, he and his Eliel made their way up the path. Theo watched solemnly.

"This will not be the last death in this battle," he sighed. "I'm afraid it is only beginning."

Theo turned around and studied the Dragon as it stood panting.

"It is you," he said. Then, he, too, reached out and stroked the snout of the Dragon. The scales were smooth. They lined the long neck and chest growing larger as they reached across its back. The wings folded in again and the claws dug into the dirt. "The Dragon of Promise."

"We have waited for so long," Theo said. "It is time to go."

The Dragon began to follow Theo out of the gorge.

"But where are you taking it?" Thuriel shouted from atop the hill. "Not far from here, right?"

"To the Queen," Theo said as he marched up the path toward the little cabin. "She is waiting."

# 5 THE OATH

The dragons continued to sweep over the hamlets, setting them on fire, sending the men, women, and Elves running for their lives into the forest where they were forced to watch their farms and livestock burn. The destruction continued until, finally, the Dragon appeared before them all.

High on a hill near the White Forest, the Dragon landed. As the sun rose behind it, its scales shone brightly causing all to pause and listen to its calming voice.

The dragons landed at the base of the hill in stunned silence as the Dragon spoke. Using the secret language of the dragons, it explained the details of the Oath between man and dragon, between the Elves and dragons.

At first, the dragons roared in disapproval, clawing at the ground and hysterically flapping wings at the idea of any Oath with man or Elves. Their fire lit up the new sky. But the Dragon continued to explain why the pact was imperative.

"To live in peace with one another, we must come together and end this destruction," the Dragon said. "The Elves have learned our ways and our language. We must believe man can learn as well."

"Never!" shouted one dragon. A lithe Wyvern with shiny black scales and eyes that glowed red in the dawn, arrogantly approached and hissed its disapproval. "We will never bow down to man! They slaughter us for our scales to use as trophies, they grind our bones and horns to use as medicine, and they destroy our nest for the precious gemstones. And now you ask us to live in peace with them?"

Behind this black dragon stood several others that roared and spewed fire to show their allegiance.

"For I am the Dragon of Bedlam," the Wyvern continued. "And I will never enter into any pact with man!"

The Dragon studied the Dragon of Bedlam carefully as though it could see the intent of its heart. "You must do what you must," it said. "But know this. There will be consequences of your actions. And these consequences will be great."

Bedlam snorted.

"And costly." The Dragon squinted its eyes.

With that, the Dragon of Bedlam turned to its followers. "Come with me!" it shouted, reared up, and flapped its wings in defiance. "And together we will make our own peace. We will rule the lands and defeat all who stand in our way. Together, we will live forever!"

The dragons roared their approval, took flight alongside Bedlam, and soon disappeared into the sunrise. The Dragon watched with a sorrowful heart for it knew the results of such rejection of the Oath.

It turned to the remaining dragons at its feet and examined each one's heart. It could sense that they wanted peace and a life of ease as well. The Dragon could see the deep scars across their snouts and bodies from years of battling and years of fruitless attacks. It sensed the weariness in the eyes of each one. These intelligent beasts had lost many hatchlings and watched their nests be destroyed by wicked greedy men, yet here they were, willing to listen and enter into a pact to end the hatred. The Dragon admired them.

Once the dragons listened to the Dragon of Promise, Queen Ragnalla approached the hill with her Elfin soldiers and archers. King Glenthryd and Lord Thordin, brave survivors of the attack by the Knights of Ranvieg, marched forward with a garrison of nervous soldiers. High on the hill before them stood the Dragon. Unsure of what to expect, the soldiers marched with swords drawn and eyes on the beast.

When the rulers of men met at the bottom of the hill, they gripped forearms as a gesture of goodwill and brotherhood. Then, they turned to face the Dragon. Glenthryd raised the visor on his helmet.

"I have never seen such a dragon," he said as his eyes studied the scales.

"Nor I," Thordin said as though in a trance. He knowingly grinned. "What a magnificent beast. With this creature on our side, we can be invincible in any war!"

"No!" came a shout from behind them. Both men turned their heads to see Theo calmly approaching them with his hand raised. "No."

"Theodore." Glenthryd sighed. "Are you still around?" He chuckled.

"Still," Theo said. He ambled up the hill making his way to the Dragon where he stopped and turned toward all who stood at the base.

He raised both hands. All stood silent.

"Listen one and all!" Theo said. "We stand here this new day to enter into a pact with the Dragon of Promise. A pact of peace that was promised to us thousands of years ago when the prophecy was first revealed. A Dragon, unlike any dragon before, would come to usher in a time of peace between man and Elf and dragon."

Thordin squinted and smirked.

"An oath of *peace*," Theo continued. "*Not* of war."

The dragons wailed and clawed at the ground in approval. Thordin looked away with a red face of embarrassment.

"No more wars!" Theo shouted. "No more battles!"

The men and Elves joined the shouts and appraisal this time.

"A time of peace," Theo finished.

Queen Ragnalla and the rulers of men made their way up the hill to stand next to the Dragon. As they came closer, Ragnalla's eyes grew wider and wider. In an almost hypnotic state, she lifted her hand to touch the sparkling scales. When she touched them, she quickly withdrew her hand and giggled like a child.

"They are so smooth," she said. "So lovely."

The Dragon lowered its snout for her to touch. Instantly, their eyes connected. She petted its snout and rested her head near its left eye. She closed her eyes and exhaled.

"The time has finally come," she whispered. "I have waited for this moment all my life."

The Dragon once again raised its head to examine the entire scene: The rulers of men standing with the ruler of the Elves alongside the Dragon of Promise. It was later told, that the roar of the dragons and applause of the soldiers could be heard for many miles.

"As we have seen here, there are many who do not desire this pact and when word of it is spread throughout the lands, many more will object," the Dragon said. The crowd grew silent. "But it is up to us to preserve it, defend it, and, if need be, perish for it."

"The scales of the Dragon are more powerful than any weapon forged by man," Theo said. "So many men will come to destroy it in order to have those scales."

He turned to look at Queen Ragnalla, Glenthryd, and Thordin. "But as long as we work together to learn the ways of the dragons and respect each other," he said, "together we can ensure this Oath will endure."

And when he finished speaking, he transformed into the White Dragon and flew off into the morning sky followed by all the other dragons. They circled above for a while, and then headed to their homes in the mountains, seas, and forests.

§

Deep inside the Mountains of Ranvieg, the Dragon of Bedlam conspired with its followers about how to defeat the Dragon of Promise.

We will fight in the air as well as on the ground, but we will fight no matter what!" Bedlam hissed. And so the battle ensued with many a fierce fight in the air above the villages and over the seas. But the Dragon of Promise met its enemies on all fronts, defeating them over and over again sending them falling from the skies.

The men and women of the villages would discard the remains of the dead dragons in bonfires. For legend said that the horns and scales of evil dragons caused a slow and painful death if they became part of the soil or if ingested. No one wanted to take a chance.

The battles continued until Bedlam's dragons were no more. Soon, it stood alone on a mountain ledge, scarred and bleeding, watching as the Dragon of Promise circled high above Vulgaard as its guard inspecting the land until satisfied. Then, the Dragon of Promise flew to meet Bedlam where it stood.

"Your time is over," the Dragon said.

"Never!" Bedlam hissed and spat blood at the feet of its nemesis.

"And now you will suffer the consequences of your actions," the Dragon said.

"Go ahead!" Bedlam reared back and flapped its wings exposing its chest. "Strike me down. Kill me!"

But the Dragon remained pensive and calm.

"What are you waiting for?" The Dragon of Bedlam panted and nearly collapsed from exhaustion. "Do it! Or are you too much of a coward?"

"Your punishment is not death," the Dragon explained. "For the Queen and the rulers of men are merciful."

Bedlam narrowed its eyes as though confused about what it had just heard.

"No, they have instructed me to inform you that your punishment is banishment," the Dragon turned its body and flew off the ledge. It hovered there as it continued to speak. "You shall remain exiled here in the Mountains of Ranvieg never to show yourself again. All men, Elves, and Dwarves have been instructed to slaughter you if they see you in any region off this mountain. Your head will be brought to the Queen for a prize."

"A death mark?" Bedlam's eyes grew wide.

The Dragon rose higher. "It is as you say."

"No!"

The screams of Bedlam could be heard as the Dragon flew on toward Vulgaard.

"No!" Bedlam roared. "Kill me! I want to be dead! You cannot leave me..."

But the Dragon flew on, ignoring the evil dragon's pleas.

"...to die alone in these mountains! I cannot bare this! You cannot do this to me!"

The Dragon of Promise continued gliding on the mist toward Vulgaard where it landed on the green pastures near the glistening palace of Queen Ragnalla. She met it there with her guards.

"We have not heard the last of Bedlam," she said as she approached. She gracefully lifted the hem of her dark blue linen gown as she made her way through the damp grasses. Her white braided hair was pulled back tightly revealing the elegant features of her face and her pale blue eyes. On her brow rested a thin crown made of silver.

The Dragon shook off the moisture from its head. "You are correct. Bedlam will try to find a way to escape."

"But we will be ready," she said. "Now, Theo tells us you must go?"

The Dragon nodded and turned its head toward the north. "Yes. I will go to a place of rest and peace where I will wait until the appointed time to assist man with the settlement of the land to the north."

"But why north? Why not the sea or here in the White Forest?" She spread her arms out wide.

The Dragon returned its gaze to the lovely Queen. "There is a land, untouched and unspoiled, that calls to me. There is a forest with a calm clear lake in the clearing. This is where I will make my home. The Dragon Forest."

It turned its large body and began to walk off. The Queen walked alongside.

"And all who live near it will live in placidity so long as they keep the Dragon Forest in their sight, so long as they do not disturb my woodland realm..."

Suddenly, the Dragon spread its wings and began to flap them. The Queen stepped back and protected her face with her hand as she watched it hover over her.

"...and so long as the Oath is never forsaken," the Dragon said to her, its yellow eyes glowing.

And with that, it turned its body and flew off to the north with the sun on its back. The green grasses on the hills danced in the breeze as the Dragon flew over. The Queen's gown flowed behind her as she strained to watch the Dragon fly until it finally disappeared from sight.

# 6 LADY LAURIEN OF GLENTHRYST

Over one hundred years had passed since the departure of the Dragon, and the promised peace had spread throughout the regions surrounding Vulgaard.

The rulers of men, King Glenthryd and Lord Thordin, settled in the villages near Vulgaard. Each man married Elfin women and had children who married into the Elfin family of Queen Ragnalla. These children grew in wisdom and stature and bore children of their own.

They learned the ways of the Dragon.

They respected the Oath.

The land thrived.

One autumn afternoon, a young girl with long dark hair and green eyes was born to the ruler Glenthryst, son of Glenthryd. Half Elf, she was admired in the land for her exceptional beauty, as most Elfin women had white hair and pale skin. As she grew, she was found to be inquisitive and loved learning. It was decided she would move to the palace at Vulgaard and study under the great tutor, Theodore Sirus III.

As was her daily habit, she wandered through the palace of her great aunt, the Queen, looking for her dearest friend.

"Theo!" she shouted. "Where the devil are you?"

She stomped down the corridor past sculptures of great elfin warriors and tapestries depicting life at Vulgaard. Peeking into each room she came upon, she found them empty or full of servants preparing food.

"What do you want girl?" asked a perturbed servant.

"I cannot find my tutor," she said as she looked past the servant and searched the room. She exhaled loudly and went on to the next room. "Theo!"

"A lady doesn't shout, my dear," said a soft voice from behind.

The girl stopped with wide eyes as though she recognized the voice as one of authority. She slowly turned her body around. The Queen stood with her hands folded in front of her and her long white gown glistening in the torchlight.

The girl curtsied and bowed. "Sorry, your majesty," she said in a tiny voice barely above a whisper.

"A curtsy will do," the Queen said as she continued walking down the corridor. "You certainly do not have to do both."

"Yes ma'am," the girl quickly followed behind her great Aunt. "But I cannot find Theo, I mean, Professor Theodore, Auntie. Do you know where he is?"

The Queen chuckled. "How old are you now, child?"

Laurien stared at the ground. "I am nearly one hundred years old in Elfin years. Only thirteen years old to man."

The Queen raised an eyebrow. "Well, that explains your behavior."

Laurien frowned.

"You mean after all these months of working with him, you didn't think to look in the Dragon Master's cave?" the Queen asked.

She stopped walking and placed her hand on her forehead. "Oh, no," she sighed with frustration. "I completely forgot!"

Then, she turned and ran off in the opposite direction.

"A lady doesn't run down halls, either!" the Queen shouted after her niece. But it was no use, Lady Laurien continued on down the hall, through a set of glass doors, and down some steps outside that led to a set of caves alongside the palace where most of the dragons were kept.

A servant walked up to the Queen carrying some cloth. "She reminds me of someone," the servant, an older woman with a scarf over her head and tied under her chin, said to the Queen.

"You couldn't possibly mean me," the Queen turned to the older woman who chuckled. "Why I never ran down halls yelling and—"

"Ahem," the old woman raised an eyebrow and looked directly at the Queen. "I seem to recall you running down the halls a few times calling out after your father." She turned and made her way toward the sewing room.

The Queen crossed her arms over her chest. "Well, that was entirely different."

§

"Theo!" Laurien cried. "I finally found you." She bent over and

36

tried to catch her breath. Her tutor stood near the entrance to the dragon caves. These caves were carved out of the mountains and filled with newly hatched dragons for training with the Dragon Master.

"And why were you looking for me, my dear?" Theo looked up from his book with his spectacles on his nose. He thumbed through the book while awaiting her answer. "Aren't you supposed to be doing your lessons?"

"My dragon egg." She made her way deeper into the cave, still panting. "It hatched this morning! It finally hatched!"

"Really?" he turned and closed his book.

"Yes! It looks like a Draco, Theo." She smiled a proud smile. "A beautiful Draco with purple scales that glitter. I've decided to name it after you. Theodore Sirus IV."

Theo removed his spectacles. "Well, I couldn't be prouder. Except, didn't I ask you *weeks* ago to bring that egg to these caves?"

"What book is that you're reading?" Laurien started to reach out for the book Theo had in his hands, but he quickly turned away.

"Excuse me." He cleared his throat. "Answer my question. You know how dangerous it is to keep dragons eggs out in the open. And now it has hatched. That invites even more danger."

Laurien frowned and looked down at her feet.

"So, where is this hatchling?" Theo rocked back and forth on his heels.

Laurien sighed. "In my bedchamber."

Theo raised his eyebrows. "What?"

Laurien cringed.

"Are you telling me that you have a newly hatched Draco dragon in your bedchamber at this very moment?"

Laurien nodded.

Theo placed his hand on his forehead as if it ached. "You there," he called to an Elf working in the stables. Please go and retrieve the newly hatched dragon out of Lady Laurien's bedchamber and bring it here to the caves, please."

The Elf's eyes widened when he took in what Theo had asked him to do. He looked at Laurien then back at Theo, and then he quickly searched for a linen sack. When he found it, he inspected it to make sure it was usable. He looked at Lady Laurien who stood with the proud grin on her face again.

"You'll find it sleeping on the tiny bed I made for it underneath *my* bed," she said.

The Elf looked at Theo, shrugged his shoulders, and then headed off toward the palace.

"Good luck," Theo said with frustration in his voice.

"Now, did you complete your lessons yet?" he asked.

Laurien reached for the book in his hand again. "What book are you reading?"

"Did you hear my question? I'm beginning to think you need to have your ears washed." He turned and headed deeper into the stables.

"Oh Theo, you know how I love the dragons." Laurien followed him. "I found that egg! It belonged to me. Had I brought it here, it would be just another dragon used for battle."

"Still," Theo said. "It's dangerous."

"And I firmly believe dragons are more than that," she said. "They shouldn't be used only for battle. There is so much we can learn from them."

Theo walked on until they reached the dragon pit.

"So, what book are you reading?" she asked again.

"What book are you talking about?" he said as he turned toward her.

She smirked. "The one in your hands." She peeked over his shoulder, but he slammed it shut and placed it on a small wooden table.

"Oh, it's nothing of interest at all," he said as he removed his pipe from a pocket in his robe.

"Then, you should have no problem showing it to me." She reached for it, but it disappeared into thin air. "Oh, you old wizard!"

"Now, now." He lit his pipe. "Temper."

"Bring it back!" She crossed her arms and stared at Theo. But a noise interrupted her thought. It came from the pit behind her. It resembled a tiny growl. She carefully made her way over to the pit and slowly peered over the edge. There, at the bottom, were three newly hatched dragons playing with an acorn someone had thrown in.

"Aren't they adorable?" She clasped her hands and jumped up and down.

"Hmm, yes, I suppose." Theo puffed on his pipe.

She spied their bejeweled eggshells.

"Sapphires!" she said. "How beautiful."

"Here now, get away from there!" a scruffy voice startled Laurien and she moved away from the pit. She turned her head and saw a thick waisted Dwarf walking toward her with three Elfin guards not far behind. They were very handsome in appearance compared to the Dwarf. Laurien backed all the way to the wall of the cave.

"Yes, Dragon Master."

"Hmmph," he said. "That's more like it." On his face was a thick rust colored beard that reached to his mid-belly. On his arms were scars caused by burnt skin healed over. He was even missing a finger on his left hand. He frightened Laurien.

"Lady Laurien," one Elf said to her with a slight bow of his head. "Good day."

She bowed as well, then quickly smoothed her hair and wiped her face with the sleeve of her gown when he turned away. Then, she watched as the Elves inspected the tiny dragon hatchlings.

"Wyverns. Small wings, long bodies," one Elf said with some disappointment in his voice. "I suppose they are sea dragons?"

The Dragon Master nodded.

"Alright. Not what we had hoped for, but we'll take them," he motioned for his companions to collect the tiny creatures and cage them. They leapt into the pit and disappeared from sight, but the entire pit lit up as the dragons spewed fire at the intruders. Yelps of pain could be heard from below. Laurien giggled and the Dragon Master turned his head. He shot her a harsh look.

"Come, my dear." Theo reached out and gently took her arm. "The dragon cave is not the place for a Lady."

Laurien rolled her eyes and went along with Theo. Suddenly, the Elf Theo had sent to retrieve the newly hatched dragon appeared. His face was red, his hair was singed, and so were his hands.

Theo chortled. "I take it the hatchling has learned to spew its fire?"

The Elf sneered. His eyebrows were also singed and he huffed past the two with the baby dragon squirming inside the linen sack.

"Oh, do be careful with it!" she ordered as the Elf walked toward the caves.

She chuckled until she saw darkness and felt her feet leave the ground. Her stomach turned the way it did when she rode the dragons in a downward spiral. That's when she knew Theo had transported her to another place. Her feet landed with a thud and she opened her eyes.

"I hate it when you do that without warning." She straightened out her gown. "Scares me to death."

Theo was already sitting at his desk in the palace library. He thumbed through a book and puffed on his pipe.

"Theo, when will you teach me the ways of magic?" Laurien ran her long fingers over the rows of books on the shelf. "And I've shown you that I know some things already. Why won't you show me more?"

He looked up from his book. "Come here, my dear."

She turned her head and smiled. She plopped down on a wooden chair and scooted it over to Theo's desk. He turned the open book around so that she could read it and slid it over to her across the table. Laurien carefully examined it through narrowed eyes. But her eyes widened when she saw what it was.

"The Dragon Chronicles," she said. She gently picked up the page and turned it over. "The ways of the dragons."

Theo puffed on his pipe.

"I've always wanted to read this book," she said as her eyes darted all over the pages.

"Yes, I know," he replied with a grin. "And I figured it is time that you read through it now that you know the language of the dragons and you've worked with the Elves in training them...and you've hatched your very own dragon egg." He leered at her.

But she was only half listening as she turned page after page. "Potions from dragon horns, healing salves from dragon scales," she mumbled. "Dragons that live in the trees, mountains, oceans..."

"Your father, King Glenthryst, asked me to teach you the ways of the wizards," Theo said,

She looked up from the book. "Really?" Her eyes widened.

Theo nodded then set his pipe down. "But, my dear, the time of the wizards is coming to an end." He stood and walked over to a bookcase.

Laurien frowned. "But how can that be?"

Theo removed a book and brought it to the table. He set it down near Laurien then sat back down in his chair. "Because magic is...well, it is *limited*," he said.

She squinted. "Limited? Whatever can you mean?"

"My Lady, years ago, in these mountains, I, as a White Dragon, was lured down and transformed into a man by a wizard named Theodore Sirus II. Soon, he taught me how to shift shapes so that I could become a liaison between man and dragon. A brilliant idea, really," he said. "But an idea with its limitations, I'm afraid."

"Please explain," she said.

"You see, the magic spell is not forever." Theo leaned in close. "And what this means is that one day, I will either remain a dragon...or a man."

Laurien's eyes grew wide. "You mean, you won't be able to shift shapes any longer?"

Theo shook his head no.

"But I so love that about you." Her face was crestfallen. "So, which shape will you choose?"

"It will not be up to me, I'm afraid. It will just happen," he said. "You see, all magic is only temporary." He sat back in his chair.

"Well, which shape do you prefer to be?" she asked.

He grinned. "Which shape do you suppose?"

Laurien laughed. "A man!"

"Yes, and not a wizard," he reached for his pipe, but before his hand took it, the pipe began to float and glide over to Laurien. Theo nodded. "Very good, my dear."

"I've been practicing." She opened her palm and the pipe fell into it. She closed her fingers around it. "I do so enjoy magic, how can it be that I cannot learn from you? Oh, please teach me before…before it's too late and you are no longer able to."

Theo's face suddenly looked saddened. "I have received my orders from the King, so I will teach you the ways of magic, but…"

She reached over and touched his hand. "But what?"

Theo's eyes gazed across the room, but Laurien knew he was looking into the future.

"What do you see?" she asked.

"Pain," he said without hesitation which scared Laurien. She furrowed her brow then sat back.

"I see war, pain, and death…" he was mumbling now. Laurien knew Theo was there in the midst of it all. His eyes were distant. "All caused by one magic spell."

"What? We are at peace, how can this be?" she asked. "What magic spell? Whose?"

"A very powerful magic spell will be cast while you and I live," Theo said. "And a great number of rulers will succumb to its temptation."

Laurien shook her head as though trying to rid herself of what was heard.

Theo was back with her so he took her hand. "My dear, all magic is…"

"What?"

"Evil," he said. He stood and walked over to the large picture window that overlooked the Queen's gardens.

"But surely not *all* magic." She followed after him. "I mean, look at you! You are here as a result of a magic spell. You are not evil!"

Theo turned his face toward hers and placed his hands on her shoulders. "Laurien," he said. "Magic is temporary. It isn't real. It comes from without not within." He looked out the window. "It is not like the power of the Dragon of the Forest."

"What do you mean?"

"Magic uses what we see and knows how to fool us into thinking what we see is real," he said. "I appear to be a man. But we both know I am only a dragon under a magic spell that one day will come to an end."

She nodded.

"What if you discovered tomorrow that all you knew to be real, wasn't?" he asked.

She squinted and searched Theo's face. "I would be…well, I would be *devastated*," she said.

Theo nodded and gently touched her cheek.

"Exactly," he said. "And that, my dear, is magic.

# 7 THE MOUNTAINS OF RANVIEG

On most afternoons, young Laurien would take walks along the mountain paths near the palace. She grew weary from the palace at Vulgaard and all the tutoring with Theo. Learning her role as Lady grew wearisome as well, for she was betrothed to a young man, a prince, and would be married in years to come.

After her conversation with Theo, she felt like being alone to think. She saddled her favorite dragon, Avalon, mounted it, and flew off into the late afternoon sun. The wind in her hair helped clear her mind and the beautiful views of the green valleys and farmlands began to assuage her fears. *War could be coming to the land,* she thought. *It cannot be true.*

She squeezed the saddle with her thighs and pulled the reins to turn her dragon toward the north, but it resisted.

"What is it?" she asked. In dragon speak, it told her it heard the sound of a wounded dragon crying out.

Together they glided trying to hear from where the sound came. Suddenly, Laurien sat up. "Yes," she exclaimed. "I hear it too."

She searched the valley below but only spotted a few sheep grazing in the pastures. She and her dragon then swooped by and caused the sheep to scatter. After a while, the dragon climbed several feet higher into the sky until her dragon abruptly turned toward the mountains.

"Wait," she said. "The mountains of Ranvieg. We cannot go there!"

She pulled on the reins.

"Yes, I know. I hear it, too. But we are forbidden to go there," she said. The dragon continued to resist her. She heard the cry again. "Oh, alright."

They approached the shadowy mountains and the dragon found a ledge to land upon. It glided in to a bumpy landing.

"Ouch," Laurien said. She dismounted and rubbed her behind. "That was a lousy landing."

The dragon shook its head and began searching for some grass to nibble.

"Stay here," she ordered. She turned toward the sound and removed a small knife from the belt around her waist. Looking all around, she could see why the mountain range was feared by the villagers. The jagged black rocks rose out of the earth, blocking out the sun. The mountains seemed to leer down at her.

She swallowed.

The violet sky brushed with smooth clouds made her relax. She breathed in the cooler mountain air and carefully made her way around the ledge. Her dragon had successfully found a tiny patch of grass. It nibbled freely.

Laurien noticed some small white flowers had made their way through the cracks of the rocks. She bent down and gathered them. She made a small wreath out of the flowers and placed it on her head like a crown.

"I can't believe I found flowers growing in this dark forsaken area," she said. "The Ranvieg Mountains. I have to admit, it is quiet and peaceful up here. No wonder the dragons prefer to live in these mountains."

She walked on. "Dragons should be free to fly off and wander the lands as they wish," she sighed. "So should I."

Her dragon growled in its language. "Yes, I know. I'll be careful," she said to it.

Nearby, and unbeknownst to Laurien, was another dragon hiding behind a very large rock watching her every move. It watched and waited, hating the girl with every step she took. It narrowed its red eyes, despising her and all that she represented, until she raised her face up to the sky and started singing.

The dragon noticed her long dark hair against her fair skin, the white flowers crowning her head, and her large green eyes. She sang her Elfin song in a gentle voice. The dragon's eyes never left her form as she approached the rock it hid behind.

"Oh, I don't remember anymore songs." Laurien sighed. She bent down to admire a set of yellow flowers growing between some stones. Then, she heard a noise.

A few small pebbles fell off the side of a rock. She stood and inspected the area, clinging to her knife. And from between the mountain and the large rock, she noticed a pair of red glowing eyes: the eyes of a dragon.

Startled, the wreath of flowers fell off her head. She stepped back, forgetting the language of the dragon for a moment. She could feel the fear rise deep inside her. The dragon moved again. She raised the knife.

"Stand back!" she ordered.

The dragon paused for a moment.

"I heard a cry...a cry from a wounded dragon. Are you *hurt*?" she asked in its language.

The dragon tilted its head, impressed with how well she spoke dragon. A growl came from deep within its throat.

Laurien began to raise her hands. "I've, uh...I've come to help you."

The dragon focused its eyes on the knife in her hand. Laurien noticed this and lowered the weapon. The dragon slowly made its way around the rock revealing its size.

Laurien gasped and backed off using the mountain as a guide. With her back to the mountain, she began to slide away.

"No, don't leave," the dragon said. It bent its head low and sniffed the ground. "I've been admiring your beauty."

And the dragon meant it. The beast truly did admire her even though it longed to gobble her up.

Laurien cocked her head. "You mean my scent. You're wondering if I'll taste good!" she raised her knife again.

The dragon chuckled. Laurien wasn't expecting that reaction. A kindness swept over its eyes and its countenance changed.

"I'll ask you again, are you hurt? We heard the sound of a wounded dragon."

"No, I am not hurt." It sniffed her feet. "You have come from the palace at Vulgaard?"

She nodded.

"I can smell the scent of grassy knolls on you." It took a step toward her. "And of Elves. I used to live in that region."

Laurien felt her body relax as she gazed into the creature's red eyes. "Really? Vulgaard? You are not from this mountain region?"

It shook its head no, and then continued to sniff the air around Laurien. "Those white flowers," it said. "you had them in your hair."

Laurien reached up and awkwardly fingered her hair. Her face became warm. "Oh those," she said, embarrassed. "Silly little flowers."

"They are as lovely as you are."

Laurien smiled. She always loved how polite most dragons were and thought them much more polite than most people. But she gripped the knife just in case.

"Thank you," she said. "You are kind...for a dragon."

"And yet you cling to your weapon," it said.

Laurien looked at the knife in her hand and then at the dragon's eyes. Its nostrils flared.

"I know the ways of the dragon," she said. "I have been taught by the Dragon Masters of the palace."

"Never to trust?" it said as it turned away.

"Exactly," she said with a sense of defiance. "Trust must be earned."

"And what is your name, child?" it asked.

"I am Lady Laurien," she said, "of Glenthryst."

Upon hearing that name, the dragon retracted its head and snorted because it remembered her grandfather, King Glenthryd. "Your grandfather, Glenthryd," it hissed, "I knew him well."

"You did?" Laurien raised an eyebrow. The sudden return of anger in the dragon's eyes when it spoke her grandfather's name shocked her. "You despised him, didn't you?"

The dragon squinted its eyes. "I despise all men."

Laurien backed up and began to step toward her dragon still grazing nearby.

The black dragon edged toward her. "My dear, do not be afraid."

"Why not?" She gestured for her dragon to come to her, but it continued to eat as its leisure.

"I could never gobble you up," it said. "The world is a much better place with a young songstress like you gracing all living creatures with your gentle voice."

Laurien turned her head and saw the gentleness had returned to its eyes. "Thank you," she said softly as though flattered.

The dragon sighed heavily. "But I do long to fly off this mountain and enjoy the freedom I used to know."

"What happened? Did you injure a wing?" Laurien took a few steps toward the beast inspecting it.

"No, child. I'm afraid I have been banished here atop this cursed mountain for the rest of my life," he exhaled. Some smoke rose from its nostrils.

Laurien's eyes grew large. "How tragic," she said. She looked over the cliff and saw the green valley below. "It's so beautiful all around here. You should be able to enjoy it."

"No, my punishment is to suffer here alone, forever," it said.

"Well, what was it that you did to deserve such a punishment?" she asked.

But the creature, knowing it could not tell her the truth, decided to twist the truth instead. "I never shared my talents, my gifts, with others.

Instead I was selfish and cruel. I kept all my talents to myself when I could have been using them for the greater good."

Laurien listened intently to what the dragon said. "Oh, I understand."

"If only." The dragon turned around and looked out over the edge of the mountain. "If only I could have another chance to make amends and show everyone how repentant I am."

"I see," she said.

"Do you?" It turned toward her. "Do you *really* understand?"

She nodded.

"Because you can help me, you see." It looked into her eyes.

"I can?" She put her hand on her chest. "Are you sure *I* can help?"

"Why yes," it said. "You know someone who can help me...change."

"I do?" she squinted. "Are you sure?"

"Yes!" The dragon snout came dangerously close to Laurien's body. She stepped back just to be sure. "You know the White Dragon!"

Laurien stood straight.

"You know that Theodore Sirus III is also the White Dragon? And that he knows the spell that can help me. Well, he can help me change!"

"Yes, I know Theo. He is my tutor." She noticed the beast almost smiled. "He told me of the black dragon exiled here forever by the Dragon of Promise,"

The dragon recoiled upon hearing the name.

"Are you that dragon?" she asked.

The dragon thought for a moment, turned to her, and spoke. "Yes. I am the dragon exiled forever."

Laurien raised her chin. "Then why should I trust you?"

"Because I have seen the error of my ways, child," it answered.

"I am not a child," she said. "I know more than you know."

The dragon grinned. "Do you know of the spell?"

Laurien gazed deep into its eyes and felt a calm sweep over her body. "No, but Theo does."

"Exactly! Imagine you return to tell him that you have met the dragon in exile and it now vows to help all men. To make peace with all men and Elves is now its cause! Imagine how thrilled the rulers will be to know this," it explained. "And imagine how happy they will be that you showed mercy on a dragon. Your kind heart has made me long to change and use my talents and gifts to help others."

Laurien thought for a moment. "I suppose I could ask him..." She tapped her chin with her finger, thinking carefully about the request.

"Don't you see? Theodore can help me become a man, just like he is. And then, as a man, I can make peace. I can use my talents and gifts to help all mankind!"

Laurien looked at the dragon. "I guess so, but—"

"And I will, Lady Laurien. I *will* make peace with all men. I will use my talents to help others, you'll see," it said with a faraway look in its eyes. "Because of your good heart, because you showed me kindness when no one else did, because you know my language, I have changed in my heart. Go! Go now and talk to the White Dragon, I mean, Theodore. Ask him if he will do this good deed!"

But Laurien remained hesitant. She remembered all that Theo had told her about the magic spell. Yet, she didn't say anything to the dragon about the spell's limitations. She turned and walked toward her dragon.

"Yes, that's it! Go and tell him what I said. Tell him he has a chance to help a poor dragon make peace with its past. Go on! Bring me the good news. And hurry! Please hurry!"

Laurien took the reins of her dragon and climbed on its back while the pleas of the dragon could still be heard in the background. She nudged her dragon forward and away they flew off the mountain ledge. She turned to see the black dragon flapping its long wings as though urging her on. Then, she turned and leaned forward with her dragon as it dove down toward the valleys below with Vulgaard in the distance.

§

The next morning, Laurien sat at the long wooden table in the dining hall using her finger to push a strawberry around her plate.

"My dear, do not use your fingers to play with your food," Theo commanded as he paced by a window.

Laurien rested her chin on her hand as she then used her fork to push the strawberry.

"And you might want to consider eating your breakfast instead of only pushing it around your plate." He made his way over to the table.

"I'm not hungry," she said.

Theo crinkled his brow as though concerned. "Are you not well?" he asked.

She exhaled heavily. "I am fine."

But she wasn't fine. There was something bothering her and it would continue to bother her unless she did something about it. She knew there was a connection between herself and the dragon she met on the mountain. There remained an unspoken connection. They both were separated from the life they once knew. Laurien was sent away to Vulgaard to undergo instruction from Theo, but she left behind her loved ones. She couldn't help but feel she was sent away because she was a half-breed, at least that's what the other children her age called her. Her mother was an Elfin female, but her father a human male. Her sisters were from another woman, a human female. That set her apart from them all. That's what made her different.

Laurien thought of what the dragon had said and how he had wished he could repent by becoming a man and making peace. She sighed. Across her mind came images of home. The luscious green grasses that grew around her father's estate, the baby goats and sheep that fed on the grasses, and her family gathered in the fields playing games together.

And yet, there were times when she loved being at Vulgaard and learning about the dragons and her fellow Elves. She loved being able to speak to the dragons and ride them across the sky. Living at the estate with her father would mean leaving all this behind.

"Well then, since you are not going to eat breakfast, we might as well begin today's lessons. Come along." He turned and headed toward the library.

"But Theo." Laurien stood up to follow him. He turned to her with a raised eyebrow as though concerned.

"Yes, what is it?" He noticed a strange look on her face; one he hadn't seen before. He took a few steps toward her. She looked directly at him, yet through him at the same time. He knew her thoughts were elsewhere.

"What do you know about…" she hesitated.

He cocked his head, "about what?"

"About the Dragon of Bedlam?" She paused for his reaction. It did not disappoint. Both eyes widened and even glowed with a hint of blue revealing his true dragon nature.

He squinted then approached her. "I have told you enough about this dragon. Why do you want to know more?"

She stepped around him and walked toward the bookshelves on the far side of the room. There stood a table with several chairs. She sat down and motioned for him to follow. Theo sat with some apprehension.

"Theo, I met the dragon," she said. "The Dragon of Bedlam."

Theo shook his head and rubbed his forehead with his hand. "My dear," he sighed. "You never fail to surprise me." He exhaled heavily.

"I know." She winced as though in pain. "I know I shouldn't have, but—"

"And what were you doing in the Ranvieg Mountains?"

"I was riding my dragon over the hills." She leaned forward. "And this time, we heard a noise. It was the sound of a wounded dragon. We just had to stop and search for it."

Theo smirked.

"Honestly," she insisted. "It's true."

"Oh, I don't doubt it," he said. He adjusted his wire rimmed spectacles. "I know dragons and the sound of the wounded is a classic maneuver in drawing in one's prey."

She frowned. "I am not his prey."

Theo leaned forward. "Tell me," he said. "Why did you speak to this creature knowing it is in exile? Why would you bother me with this information now? Do you realize I must inform your aunt, the Queen, about all this?"

He stood to leave.

"No! This must only be between you and me for now," she urged.

"Why?" He walked away.

"Because I want to bring it here," she said rather sternly. Theo stopped. He slowly turned to face her.

"What? Are you insane?" He began to storm off. "Don't be a ridiculous child."

She rose and hastily followed him out of the dining room and down the hall lined with tapestries and guarded by statues of elfin kings of the past. Theo walked on, ignoring his student. Finally, he stopped directly in front of the statue of King Aidan, pushed it, and watched the wall open.

"Won't you hear me out?" Laurien shouted after him.

"Come this way," he said as he disappeared into the darkened passage way. "I will not  speak of this out there in the open for all the servants                              to                              overhear."

# 8 THE ANIFORNUM SPELL

Theo removed three books from the bookshelves of his personal library and slammed them down onto the table in the center of the room. Laurien stood by and watched. She could feel his frustration.

"I know what I am asking of you," she said.

"No," he interrupted. "No, you do not."

She looked up and sighed. "Please, let me finish."

She walked over to the table.

"My dear child," Theo began.

"Please." She banged her fist onto the table. "I am not a child!"

Theo's eyes narrowed as he studied her for a moment. Then, he sat down in one of the chairs surrounding the table. He raised his hand and said, "Please, continue."

Laurien turned and paced the room as she spoke. "You don't understand, but I do. I know what the dragon is feeling."

Theo listened.

"I know what it feels like to be exiled. To be away from everything one cares about is the hardest thing imaginable. I know what it means to be despised."

"How so?" Theo asked.

"I know I am a half-breed." Laurien gazed down at the floor.

Theo cringed at the sound of those words. "And who has ever called you this horrible name?"

"The other children," she whispered. "I know what they call me and why."

Theo stood and walked over to her. "My dear, you are no such thing. You are Lady Laurien. The daughter of the King."

Laurien looked at her tutor with her large eyes that sparkled green in the firelight. "It doesn't matter. I know what others say about me."

"Is that what this is all about?" Theo took her chin.

"No." She jerked away. "I want to help the dragon. It asked for my help. There must be a reason it came to me."

Theo turned around. "Yes, I am certain of that." Theo's voice dripped with sarcasm. "And must I remind you why this dragon is exiled into the mountains?"

"I know," she said, "but I don't care why."

"*Now* you are talking like a child." He approached the table, picked up a book, and opened it to a chapter.

"Please, you must help me help it." She leaned on the table looking fiercely at her tutor.

"We have much to do," Theo said without looking up from his book. "I still have to show you the art of blending metals. This is what your father has asked of me. I do not have time for games."

"Please, just listen to me," she begged.

Theo sighed and carefully closed the book. "And what is it you want me to do, exactly?"

Laurien stood straight, unsure how to answer the question. She pulled at her dress. "Well, I want...*it* wants...uh, well, we want..."

Theo looked at her. "Speak up. We have a lot of work to do today."

She wringed her hands as though nervous. "I know it's going to sound like madness, but..." She pulled at her dress again.

"Oh, do get on with it," Theo said.

"I want you to turn the Dragon of Bedlam into a man," she said. She waited for the reaction.

Theo gazed at her over his spectacles. He slowly reached up and removed them, then carefully placed them on the table before he spoke. "You want me to do *what*?"

"The Anifornum spell," she said. "You know, the transformation spell that—"

"I know the name of the spell, my dear." Theo interrupted her with a stern look.

"Well, I want you to perform it on the Dragon of Bedlam."

Theo gave her a look of someone who had been asked to kiss the corpse of his worst enemy. But then his countenance changed. Suddenly, his eyes had a faraway look. He grew strangely silent.

"I have been reading about this spell. I can see you are thinking about it," she said with excitement. "You see, the dragon desires to repent of its evil ways. It longs to help man and forge a connection between man and dragon just as you have done. It longs to teach man the ways of the dragon and make peace. Oh please, Theo. You can help this poor dragon achieve its destiny. It has been exiled for so many years. Nothing good has come of this exile. The dragons still attack, the people still do not understand the ways of the dragon, yet we have the chance to truly make a difference. Won't you help us? Please?"

Although he appeared to not be listening, Theo heard every word that was spoken. He knew the Anifornum spell very well because it had been used on him so many years before. He had been the lucky one. The transformation had worked and he had survived. Others had not fared so well. Theo stood and walked off toward a door on the adjacent wall. His hands rested behind his back.

"Theo, are you listening to me?" Laurien followed him. "I know how you are when you are deep in thought."

He stood by the door in silence.

"I know you do not wish to do wizardry or cast magic spells any longer, but this one time could truly make a difference," she continued to speak at his back. "What are you thinking? Please tell me."

"It has been foretold," he whispered.

She leaned in to hear. "What?" she asked. "What did you say?"

But all that Theo did was reach into his robe pocket and pull out a key. He inserted the key into the door and opened it. He picked up a lit candle and motioned for Laurien to follow him into the dark passageway.

§

"What is this place?" she asked as they walked down many narrow steps. Water dripped down the coarse brick walls and a few rats scurried out of their way as they stepped. But Theo did not answer.

Finally, they stopped in front of another wooden door. Theo pushed it open and swatted away the cobwebs from the entrance. He raised the candle high into the air and a few more cobwebs dangling above them caught on fire and immediately burned away. Theo walked over to a sconce on the wall and lit the candle. He then lit the candles resting in each sconce. Soon the entire room was illuminated.

Laurien stood in the middle of the room in awe of what she noticed.

Along the walls, hung several dragon skins of several types and colors. The scales glistened in the candlelight. On the round table in the center of the room were books covered in dust, dragon scales the size of dinner plates, and shells of dragon eggs. Above them hung a chandelier crudely made of dragon horns and covered with a thick layer of cobwebs. Stacks of leather bound books stood all around the room.

Dragon claws and teeth lay scattered on the floor and several glass beakers filled with malodorous fluid sat along the wooden bookshelves against the walls. The fluids were different colors. One beaker had a dragon claw soaking in it. Another had many dragon eyes floating in it. There were even some glass jars filled with dead frogs, newts, and bats. Laurien grimaced. Finally, in the corner, stood a large black cauldron made of cast iron resting on a pile of burnt wood.

She looked at Theo with eyes widened with fear. "What...is this place?" she asked again, nervously rubbing her forearms.

Theo ran his thin hand over one of the tomes on the table, removing years of dust from its leather cover. His mind raced to the time when he had worked alongside the wizard Goyle as his apprentice. He could still hear the orders from his master as he assisted him in potion making and scribbling down the spells that worked and blotting out the ones that did not.

"This is the secret room off the dungeon of the palace," he said. "This is where the wizard Goyle had worked for many years."

He looked up with worried eyes. "This is a wizard's workshop."

"The wizard Goyle." Laurien's eyes were wide with wonder. "That's right. You were his apprentice, weren't you? This is where he created his potions and spells?" she asked as she studied dead creatures floating in the fluids inside the beakers.

"Yes," Theo said. "He worked hard to create potions that healed and others that induced sleep. He even created potions that aroused love while others caused death."

"What does an apprentice do for a wizard, Theo?" Laurien asked. She slid her hand along the dusty table.

"Oh, well, let me see if I can remember..." But Theo could remember every detail of his time in the workshop. It would forever be ingrained in his memory. He only hesitated before bringing all the memories to his mind because some were painful to recall. "I laundered the many robes that my master wore. I remember that." He chuckled.

He made his way to the stack of books. "I helped prepare the ingredients for the many potions," he said. "I researched the spells and recorded them inside these books."

"This is where I learned that wizards used all parts of the dragon to make their potions." Theo picked up a dragon's tooth off the table.

Laurien turned to inspect the books on the shelves. She let out a small scream when she came upon a rather large dragon skull sitting on the shelf. She covered her mouth.

"A place of horrors for a dragon." Theo grimaced and set the tooth down.

Laurien continued to inspect the books on the shelves.

"The Wizard's Code," Laurien read the title of one certain book. "What's this one about?"

Theo jerked his head around when he heard the title. "Stay clear of that book, my dear. Inside that book are all the reasons why I should not cast the Anifornum spell on the Dragon of Bedlam."

"So, this is where it happened, isn't it?" she asked with intrigue as she walked over to Theo. "Your transformation?"

He nodded.

"Well, what is the Wizard's Code?"

"You see, for millennia wizards have discovered many spells and cast them all the while recording the successes and failures of each one. However, wizards over time discovered the limitations of magic, as I have," he said.

Laurien remembered his warnings about magic.

"These limitations included attempts to recreate certain spells. Once a wizard begins to experiment with a spell in order to make it his own, that is when the spell turns against him with horrific results."

Theo gazed into the dark liquid still resting inside the cauldron. Inside his head, he could hear the roars of the dragons as they were being tied down. "This is where the White Dragon became the man, Theodore Sirus III."

"I was brought here at the request of King Aidan to meet with Goyle. He knew the Elfin wizard had made a breakthrough. He had developed a way to use the Anifornum spell in order to transform a dragon into a man." Theo stood by the black cauldron. "I was one of a clan of rare pale dragons with light eyes. This clan hailed from the outer regions. Because we were so rare, Goyle felt he would try the Anifornum spell and transform us into Elves, but the Elves refused. They knew the cost of such a spell."

"The cost?" Laurien asked.

Theo glanced at her. "There is a certain economy to magic, my dear," he said. "Remember? All magic comes at a cost."

Laurien listened.

"So, Goyle decided not to experiment with the spell," Theo sighed. "He did not go against the Wizard's Code."

"And it worked!" Laurien exclaimed. She looked at her tutor and smiled. "So, does this mean you will do it?" she asked. She reached out and touched his arm. He looked at her hand then into her eyes.

"Hmmm...I am not sure yet," he said again without moving his eyes from the liquid.

She spun around and clasped her hands together as a young girl does when she is happy.

"But," he interrupted and raised his hand. "First, I will seek counsel with the Dragon of the Forest."

Laurien stopped her celebrating and noticed the seriousness in Theo's face as he walked to the door. "The Dragon of the Forest?" she asked.

"Yes," he said. "And then I shall also meet with Queen Ragnalla, since this decision greatly affects her and her kingdom."

Laurien watched Theo blow out several candles before he opened the chamber door leading to the stairway out. She ran over to him. "I understand."

"Oh, Theo, thank you so very much," she said. "I cannot thank you enough. I know you will see that this is a wonderful thing you will do. The Dragon of Bedlam has promised that it will help bring peace to all regions."

"And you believe this?" Theo asked.

Laurien thought for a moment. "Yes," she said.

Theo merely closed the door, turned the key, and locked it.

"You'll see!" Laurien said. She ran up the stairs. "You'll see! This will be wonderful!"

§

Theo stood on the balcony off the vast palace library. The balcony overlooked the mountain precipice with the Vulgaard River flowing below. Only a sliver of sunlight cut through the clouds as the sun set.

He thought back to his time with the wizard Goyle.

*"You serve me and will assist me until I deem you ready to be a wizard," Goyle shoved his finger into Theo's chest.*

*"I refuse!" Theo pounded his hand on the table. "I will no longer remain here watching you slaughter dragons!"*

*"All wizards use the beasts and many others," Goyle insisted. "You know this."*

*Theo winced. "But other wizards are not also dragons!" He transformed into the White Dragon, turning over tables and sending books to the floor. He snarled at his unmoved master.*

*Goyle reached into his sleeve and removed his wand. He raised it high above his head. "You will cease this behavior immediately, or I will be forced to defend myself!"*

*Theo knew Goyle could instantly strike him dead with a death spell. He returned to his human form.*

*King Aidan entered into the room surrounded by his guards.*

*"What is going on in here?" he shouted. He could see the two men had been arguing.*

*Goyle replaced his wand inside his sleeve and bowed. "Your majesty."*

*Theo also bowed. "May I speak my mind, sire?" Theo asked.*

*"Of course," the King said.*

*"Your majesty, I am honored to be in your service here at the palace," Theo began. "But I can no longer participate in the capture and slaughter of my own kind."*

*King Aidan glanced around the room and saw the dragon parts scattered about. He sighed.*

*"Your work as a man has been impeccable, Theodore," King Aidan said. "Your potions and anodynes have helped my people for years."*

*Theo bowed.*

*"We have used dragon parts mixed with nature or the parts of other creatures to create these potions for years," King Aidan said as he made his way to a table.*

*"Yes, sire," Theo said. "But my potions do not require the use of dragons."*

*Goyle squinted his eyes and shot Theo a hateful look.*

*King Aidan looked surprised.*

*"And you yourself said my potions have helped your people." Theo waved his arm over the table that held many bottles of his concoctions.*

*"And so I did." King Aidan smiled. "Theodore, I will honor your request. I believe you have proven to be most useful in bringing Elves and man together with the dragons."*

*Theo closed his eyes and sighed with relief.*

*"I do believe there is work for you elsewhere in my kingdom."*

*King Aidan led Theo out of the Goyle's workshop.*

Theo grinned at the memory of the kindness of King Aidan, but he knew it was time to revisit the Anifornum spell once more.

In seconds, Theo transformed into the White Dragon and spread its wings. The warm air rose underneath them as the White Dragon dove off the balcony and flew toward the northern region.

As it flew, it passed over desert plains and the Blue River as it cut its way through the gorge toward the grassy hill country. There, to the north, the White Dragon approached a serene forest that stood out from the amber plains.

The trees that stood on guard in the forest were nothing extraordinary in appearance with their deep green hue. What made this forest unique was what lay within. The White Dragon landed, panting from exhaustion, but it did not enter at first. Instead, the creature approached with caution.

It squawked two times, scattering several sparrows from the trees. Suddenly, a low ominous growl came from deep within the trees. The dragon proceeded to enter the forest through the path until it reached the clearing in the middle where a calm lake appeared. A mist covered the surface of the lake and on the other side a pair of glowing yellow eyes emerged from within the trees.

The White Dragon froze and watched the eyes rise until the mammoth head of the Dragon of of the Forest broke through the trees. A front leg followed, then another leg, wings, and finally, its large body burst forth followed by the long tail swishing along the ground. The ground shook with each step. It had been years since the White Dragon had seen the Dragon of the Forest.

"Why are you here?" it hissed in the dragon language. Smoke rose from its nostrils.

The White Dragon bowed its head with respect. "I have come to seek counsel," it said.

"I thought so," the Dragon said.

It ambled its way to the edge of the lake and motioned with its head for the White Dragon to follow. Images appeared in the lake. Startled by what it saw, the White Dragon flapped its wings and stepped back.

"Do not be afraid. The images you see are of the future," the Dragon said. In the lake, the White Dragon saw dark clouds rising behind the palace of Vulgaard. Next, an image of a mysterious man in a black cloak appeared. In his hands was a cane with a dragon head carved in ivory at its end. The man's long thin fingers, adorned with rings of silver, grasped the cane. After that came many images of dragons attacking villages with people screaming and running for their lives into the woods.

"There is a darkness coming," the Dragon said. "The Dragon of Bedlam has been found. I fear this is why you have come?"

The White Dragon looked into the large glowing eyes of the great creature before it. "The Dragon of Bedlam," it said, "He knows of the Anifornum spell and requests to be transformed into a man in order to bridge the gap between man and dragon. It seeks to repent of its past deeds."

The Dragon turned its head toward the White Dragon.

"This deeply concerns you," it said.

The White Dragon nodded. "This spell has not been performed in many years, with good reason."

The Dragon listened.

"I fear the transformation of this dragon will only cause disaster." The White Dragon lowered its head and peered into the lake once again. An image of ten swords appeared. The swords had intricate designs on the blades. Then, Lady Laurien's face appeared with her dark hair flowing. The White Dragon gasped when he saw the image of her young face in the water. She and the man in the black cloak stood before ten rulers of men.

"You have foreseen this," the Dragon said.

"Yes." the White Dragon lowered his head as though saddened by the vision. "Unfortunately, I have seen this in a vision."

The Dragon of the Forest raised its head high near the tops of the trees. "This must come to pass."

The White Dragon turned its body to prepare to depart. Its head hung low.

"Cast the spell. Do as you must. All this…this plan must come to pass," the Dragon said.

"But the Wizard's Code," the White Dragon said as it turned its head to face the Dragon of the Forest. "What if…?"

"Cast the spell one last time," the Dragon said.

"But why must all this happen? Why must the peace end and this darkness reign?" the White Dragon asked. "Why must I be the one to usher in this time of uncertainty?"

"That the true meaning of the Oath and the purpose of the Dragon Forest can be made known, evil must be defeated." The Dragon turned its head around and grinned slightly at its guest. "For evil to be defeated once and for all, it must be allowed to rise."

The White Dragon tilted its head in confusion.

"Even if I told you everything, you wouldn't comprehend it all," the Dragon said. "You must trust that there is a plan. And this plan must come to pass."

The Dragon of the Forest began to head back into the trees, but stopped and spoke without turning around. "No one will understand now," it said. "But one day soon, you will understand. Everyone will know and understand."

The giant Dragon of the Forest disappeared between the trees. A few white doves ascended out from the treetops into the night sky. The White Dragon stood still, silently admiring the tranquil place for a moment before departing. All that could be heard was the rustling of the leaves and an owl hoot in the distance. The White Dragon did not want to leave. It wanted to somehow cherish the serenity of the Dragon Forest before heading back to Vulgaard to usher in a time of uncertainty.  A time of war.

# 9 TRANSFORMATION

Laurien paced along the balcony of her room that overlooked the lake. She wrung her hands over and over again as she paced. Her hair was pulled back in a sloppy bun.

"My dear," said the seamstress as she worked on a new dress for Lady Laurien at a table in the center of the room. "Please stop with all this incessant pacing."

"Yes, ma'am." Laurien pulled out a chair and sat down. She began tapping her foot as she craned her neck to see out the window. The tapping grew louder.

"Laurien!" The seamstress, a portly woman, had a needle between her pursed lips.

The tapping stopped.

"I'm sorry, but I am nervous," Laurien said. Stood and began pacing again.

"About what?" The seamstress continued sewing.

Laurien turned to her and opened her mouth to tell her about Theo, but then changed her mind. "Nothing in particular."

"Good, then fold these pieces of cloth." She pointed to a pile of different pieces of fabric.

Laurien sighed and began to do as she was told when she heard the sound of wings flapping. She threw down the fabric and ran to the window. There she saw the White Dragon approaching the palace. Laurien ran out of the room, down the staircase, and across the hall.

§

There, standing in the grand entrance hall, stood Theo. Several elves approached then led him to the Queen's chambers for a private meeting.

Laurien raced over to him. "Well?" she asked as he turned to walk down the hall. "How did it go?"

But Theo ignored her and continued on with the escort. Laurien realized it was no use asking him as he walked away. She knew she would have to wait. As Theo disappeared around the corner with the Elfin escort, Laurien turned and began pacing the grand entrance hall, back and forth, wringing her hands.

The Queen approached her throne. "I respect your opinion on the matter, Theo, however…"

"Your highness," Theo interrupted. "We have no say in this. It must come to pass."

Queen Ragnalla sat on her throne in the entrance to her chambers.

"But why?" She leaned forward.

"In order for the true meaning of the Oath and the purpose of the Dragon of Promise to be known, this evil presence must rise," Theo said and approached her. "It must rise in order to be defeated."

She ran her long ringed fingers over the arm of the chair as she took in Theo's words. "It must come to pass," she sighed. "We should have killed this beast and all its followers when we had the chance."

Theo understood what she meant. "Your Majesty, no matter what, a dark Lord would have risen to usher in the time of war regardless of our actions," he said.

"The Dragon of Bedlam has been chosen for this moment," Theo said. "The fact that it is Bedlam is most beneficial since we know its limitation. We would be foolish to try and fight this."

The Queen studied her guest, stood, and adjusted her long dressing gown. She lifted her hand. "So be it," she said as she turned to leave. "Do what you must."

Theo bowed and started to leave when the Queen turned toward him once again.

"I never thought…" she began. "I never thought my reign would be the one to usher in this time of darkness."

"Yes, your majesty," Theo said.

"So much pain…and suffering is coming. But, hopefully, my heir will be the one to put an end to it all." She gazed up at Theo with eyes moist with tears.

"Yes, your majesty," Theo said. He tried to display some encouragement in his demeanor.

"One *can* hope." She tried to smile, but turned and closed the door to her bedchamber.

§

Theo maneuvered down the myriad of steps leading away from the palace to a wide open garden landing. The area was darkened by the shadows of the nearby Ranvieg Mountains. "How fitting," Theo mumbled as he gazed over to the ominous mountain range. He ordered the elves to light quickly the torches that lined the grassy area. As they did, they heard the sound of wings flapping. In the dark sky, illumined by only a touch of moonlight protruding through the clouds, was the Dragon of Bedlam quickly approaching the landing.

Theo motioned for the elves to leave and they obeyed, taking their torches with them. Laurien hesitated at first, but then she made her way to the grassy area. The torch flames flickered in the breeze and Laurien's gown flowed behind her. She stood next to Theo.

The Dragon of Bedlam landed with an abrupt thud. Its wings quickly folded under and its tail swung around. The beast lowered its head and growled a deep throaty growl that did not seem friendly to Laurien. She backed up. Theo moved his arm out from his side and motioned for her to get behind him. Wearing his long dark blue robe over his linen night clothes, Theo came toward the dragon. Its eyes glowed red in the darkness. The scales reflected the torch light near where it stood.

As Theo approached, the dragon snarled and revealed its sharp teeth. But Theo was not afraid of the show of strength. He knew Bedlam's ways far too well to be intimidated by them. Theo raised his hand and Bedlam's eyes twitched. Laurien came onto the grass, but Theo jerked around and motioned for her to stop. He shook his head, his wide eyes filled with concern. She understood his look, so she backed off.

The Dragon of Bedlam clawed at the ground.

"Get this over with," it hissed in dragon language.

"Oh yes, I am certain you've not much time to waste." Theo took out a small leather pouch and jiggled it.

"Hurry, you fool," the dragon growled and gurgled again. Smoke rose from its nostrils. It spied the girl standing in the shadows. "What is she doing here?"

"She is not your concern," Theo said and removed a vile of blue liquid from the pouch and removed the cork that kept it sealed.

"I don't want her to see this," it said.

"Why not?" Theo shook the vile, mixing its contents. "She's the reason you are here."

The Dragon of Bedlam lowered its head again and snarled.

"You should be grateful. You successfully tricked her into thinking you are a sincere humanitarian now." Theo lifted the vile to the torchlight, inspecting the mixture.

"Quiet, you pathetic subservient of man!" Bedlam said. "Get on with this."

Theo took careful steps toward the mouth of the beast. "Know what I say is truth. She is the only one here you have fooled."

"I care for the child," Bedlam said.

Theo raised an eyebrow.

"And because I do, I do not want her to see this…to see me this way," the dragon said.

"In agony?" Theo said. He chortled and lifted the vile. "Now, open your mouth, swallow this, and take heed for my instructions."

But the dragon raised its head and made eye contact with Laurien.

"Are you…alright?" she asked the dragon.

"Yes, child," it said in a much softer tone. Theo noticed its eyes no longer glowed. "But you will soon see me in much pain. I do not want you to be frightened. This is how it must happen."

"She will be fine, now drink." Theo began to pour the liquid.

"Turn away," the dragon said to her. Laurien obeyed.

Then, the dragon opened its mouth and allowed Theo to pour in the entire vile of blue liquid. He stepped back and watched the creature swallow. Theo raised his arms and began uttering incantations in a strange language that Laurien did not understand.

She waited with her back turned, listening to Theo continue with the strange mutterings. "Analythrién," Theo said with arms held high. "mathrath Bedlam duriénthen!"

But nothing happened. So, Laurien slowly turned her head to watch the scene in time to see the strangest sight.

There, in the torchlight, stood Theo with arms still raised and the dragon lying on the ground. At first, Laurien thought it was asleep, so she turned her body around to watch. But then, it happened. The creature roared out in agony and began convulsing on the ground as Theo uttered more sayings. Laurien gasped and covered her mouth. She turned away, unable to watch the scene. But listening to it wasn't any better. The dragon screamed a high pitch scream that caused the dragons in the caves of the mountains nearby to howl and roar. The terrible sound continued.

"Illiëthren mathrath, ünden nien iriénden Bedlam!" Theo shouted.

The dragon's screams echoed all around her. She covered her ears, but the screams could not be muffled. It was as if the beast was being tortured to death.

"Stop," she said.

Theo continued to shout more words in the strange Elfin language and the dragon roared, slamming its tail on the ground. Laurien turned to see it standing, shaking its head back and forth as the wind picked up all around it. Leaves and twigs circled in a type of cyclone sending Theo's robe flowing. Laurien's hair blew into her face and the wind was so strong, she could barely stand. She blinked through the debris, desperately trying to see what was happening, but the wind blew out the torches so all she could do was listen.

"Stop this!" she screamed, but her voice could not be heard in the wind.

The roars of agony continued as Theo shouted out even more incantations.

"Uthvääs niénthan ë iel!" He pointed to the dragon writhing with pain.

Laurien felt her body fill with fear. "What have I done?" she shouted. She knew the creature could only take so much pain. She never thought to ask Theo if any dragon had died from this spell. Her heart beat faster and she felt faint. The thought began to take over her mind. She raced to Theo's side and yanked on his arm.

"Stop!" she ordered. But he ignored her. "Theo, please stop this! You're killing it!"

She tried to shout above the intense wind, but Theo stepped away and continued waving his arms.

"Theo, no!" she felt tears running down her face. "You must stop now. You're killing it!"

And instantly, the wind stopped. The screams and roars stopped. And, finally, Theo stopped. He lowered his arms and, panting from exhaustion, turned toward the girl.

Laurien wept openly, "Theo, you're killing it. Please, please don't hurt it…"

Theo shook his head and removed his robe. "No," he said, shaking off the dust from his robe. "You are mistaken."

She crinkled her brow and tilted her head in confusion.

"Not *it*," Theo said, turning to the place where the dragon once stood. "But *he*…".

Theo took his robe and walked over to the naked man hunched down on the ground drenched in sweat. Laurien's eyes grew wide as she gasped.

Theo quickly covered the man with his robe and helped him to stand. He tried, but his legs were too weak. Theo insisted and allowed the man to lean on him for support. Finally, the man stood and turned to Laurien.

"My Lady…may I present to you, Lord Bedlam of Ranvieg," Theo said with no emotion.

"Lady…L, Lady, Laurien," the man stuttered. He stood well over six feet tall, and though robed, she could tell he was of muscular build, but thin and angular. His hair was dark and so were his eyes. No longer did they glow red. She noticed his hands were thin with long fingers. His face seemed chiseled out of stone, but when he managed a smile, Laurien warmed to him and ran over to assist him as he walked with Theo.

§

While the man rested on the large couch in Theo's chambers, Laurien rinsed a small towel in a basin of water, wrung it out, and placed it on the man's forehead. He looked at her with gentle eyes as she wiped the sweat from his brow. He shivered.

"Is he ill?" she asked Theo. "He shivers."

Theo sat nearby at a table reading a book. He looked up for a moment, and then continued reading. "No, he is fine. His body is reacting to the new cell formation. It will fight it at first, but soon all his cells will come to accept the change…for a while."

Soon, the man fell asleep. Laurien came to where Theo sat reading. She pulled out a chair and joined him.

"I can't believe it's real," she said as she leaned forward. "I can't believe you did it!"

"Hmmm…" Theo kept reading.

"I honestly am shocked," she grinned like a young girl with a crush. "He's wonderful."

"He's not a toy, my dear," Theo said and turned the page of his book. "Nor is he some project you completed for one of my classes."

She frowned.

Theo slammed the book shut and turned to face his student. "And he is not what you think he is."

She looked into Theo's face. She saw that fierceness in his eyes. "What do you mean?"

"Remember what I told you, about this spell, about magic?" he said. "I need for you to remember."

Laurien raised her eyebrows and nodded.

"All magic is limited," he said as he turned to watch Bedlam sleeping. "And all magic is evil."

"But he wants to change all that," she insisted. "He longs to be good, Theo. He longs to do good, as you have done."

Theo turned to her and slid the book over to her. She looked at its cover.

"My dear," he sighed. "I was a good dragon, of noble birth. I was chosen for a purpose. Yet as I told you before, the spell I am under is temporary. One day, it will cease."

She understood.

"I am capable of doing only what I was capable of doing before, as a dragon," he said. He leaned back and pulled out his pipe. Carved from white marble, the pipe resembled a white dragon with sapphires as the eyes. It was a most beautiful creation. "Technically, I am still a dragon."

He held up the pipe so that Laurien could see it. Then, a thin stream of controlled fire came from his mouth and lit his pipe. He grinned and took a few puffs. The smoke rose up and encircled his head then dissipated. "Therefore," he looked over at Laurien. "I am *not* a man."

She studied the dragon pipe with the sparkling sapphires as eyes, and then she looked over at Bedlam.

"Neither is he a man," Theo explained. "And my dear, as with all magic, there is a cost."

She turned her head. "You mentioned that before. I still don't understand what you mean?"

Theo looked down almost with regret. "This deed I have done..." He rubbed his chin. "Well, it has come at a great cost."

She narrowed her eyes.

"There are consequences to all our actions, my dear," he waited to see if she comprehended what he was trying to say, "Including magic. Do you understand?"

She looked down at the book he slid to her and read the title: *The Time of Man.* "No, I don't know what you are saying."

Theo puffed on his pipe again.

"No, I didn't think you would. Not yet," he said, "But soon, my dear. Soon you will understand everything."

"Good!" she said as she stood. "I hope so."

# 10 THE DAWNING OF BEDLAM

Laurien approached the large wooden door with caution. She straightened her shoulders, ran her fingers through her hair, and raised her hand to knock. She hesitated. She didn't know what to expect on the other side. Finally, she took a deep breath in and knocked. Then, she turned the knob and opened the door.

She slowly peeked around the door and saw Bedlam sitting on a cot with his back toward her. He was nude except for the suede trousers he wore. He was sweating profusely, yet shivering at the same time. A an old servant stood in the corner mixing some herbs together to make a tea. He wore a cotton shirt, brown trousers, and an apron around his waist.

"He...hello?" she said.

Bedlam barely turned his head. When he did, Laurien could see his eyes glowed red. Along his spine appeared the ridges of a dragon, but they quickly disappeared beneath the skin.

"Come in, child," the servant said. He waved his hand. "Just making our guest some tea to settle his nerves."

She smelled the scent of rosemary in the air and heard the spoon hit the side of the ceramic cup as the servant stirred the mixture. Then, he walked to the fire and retrieved the small ceramic pot of steaming water. Laurien took a few steps toward the guest as she watched the servant make the tea.

"I'm cold," the guest said. The servant quickly put down his spoon and gathered up a long sleeved tunic to put over the man. Laurien rushed over to help with the sleeves. As she raised his arm, Bedlam's skin rippled like water. Some scales appeared then disappeared under his skin and his eyes returned to black.

"There," she said as she forced a smile once the tunic was over his torso. "Isn't that better?"

But the man Bedlam simply stared into the fire pit before him. His eyes remained dull and distant. Laurien sat on a stool nearby watching him.

"I know it is strange, this new form," she said. "But it will get better."

Bedlam blinked a few times. His features were striking, like a statue lining the grand halls of the palace.

"Soon, you'll be on your feet, making friends, and finding things to do, and—"

Bedlam slowly stood, interrupting her pep talk.

"There's no time for that foolishness," he said. He turned and struggled to walk.

Laurien frowned. "I understand."

"I've got to meet with the leaders and talk some sense into them," he clumsily paced the small room lit only by the fire, using his arms to help balance on two legs. "There's so much to be done."

Laurien turned to face him. "If there's anything I can do to help..."

"Here," the servant said to Bedlam, "Drink this."

Bedlam took the cup and gulped down the contents immediately. He bent over in pain for a few minutes.

"What is this?" he finally asked.

"A tea to help your innards heal," the servant took the cup and returned to the table in the corner. "Your body has been through much. It takes time for it to heal from the inside out."

Bedlam raised his hand and turned it over as though inspecting it. "I feel weaker," he said.

"And you will be," came a calm voice from the doorway.

"Theo!" Laurien turned her head. She ran to him and embraced him, very pleased to see him.

"What do you mean?" Bedlam asked with a furrowed brow.

"A man's body is considerably weaker than a dragon's," Theo said, his grey beard fell over his dark blue tunic. "When you are in the form of a man, you will be weaker in strength, but, at times, stronger in intellect." Theo tapped his temple with his thin finger.

Bedlam bent over again as pain raced through his new body. He hastily made his way to the cot and sat down, panting.

"It won't be long before you are strong enough to move around without pain," Laurien said from the safety of Theo's side.

Bedlam nodded, but he still hadn't made eye contact with her. Laurien felt an odd distance between them.

"Well, come along Laurien," Theo said. She turned to leave with him. "Let us leave our guest in peace."

"No, wait," Bedlam said. He stood and reached out his hand. "Please, Laurien, stay with me," he implored, finally making eye contact. She squeezed Theo's hand and looked into the dark eyes of her new friend. Instantly, she felt warmth flow through her. Like a quivering child, she slowly let go of Theo's hand and stepped toward Bedlam.

"Are you certain, my dear?" Theo asked.

"Yes," she said and reached out her hand to Bedlam. As soon as her flesh met his, a strange warmth raced through her. She helped him sit back down on the cot. "I am certain."

"Sing to me," Bedlam said as he lay back on the cot, "As you did on the mountain that day. Your voice soothes me."

"Alright," she smiled.

"And then, if you would be so kind as to read to me," Bedlam asked as he raised his hand to touch her chin. He gently traced her face with his long finger. "I want to hear stories in your language."

"Of course!" She motioned for the servant to bring her books off the shelf near the table. "What a wonderful idea!"

"Your presence calms me," Bedlam sighed.

Theo could hear them conversing as he closed the door behind him.

§

Many months later, Theo stood on the balcony of the palace that overlooked the gardens below. Since the rain had stopped, the flowers bloomed and covered the garden paths. King Glenthryst stood alongside Theo.

"Well?" he asked. "Any new developments?"

Theo stood with his arms crossed. His linen robe flowed in the breeze. "He has learned much these last few months."

"And he has followed through with his promise to meet with the dragons," Queen Ragnalla said. She sat at a table playing a game of cards with one of her ladies in waiting. "I must say, the villagers have noticed fewer attacks."

"How long has it been now?" King Glenthryst asked.

"Nine months to be exact," Theo answered. He turned and paced the room.

"My scouts tell me he prospers greatly in the land," the Queen laid down a card, causing a frown to appear on her opponent's face. The

Queen smiled and turned toward Glenthryst. "What do your scouts relay?"

"The same." Glenthryst entered the room and poured himself a goblet of ale. He reached up and scratched his bearded chin. It had become more speckled with grey. "The leaders of men have bestowed great gifts upon him. They have provided him the funds to build a grand estate at the base of the Ranvieg Mountains. They have provided him jewels from dragon eggs and elegant clothing like robes of a Lord."

He turned to Theo.

"And they will continue to bestow gifts upon him as long as he comes through with his promises," Theo said. "He learns more and more magic, creates weapons of power to use in battle, and creates peace with the dragons. What more could the leaders of men want?"

Glenthryst tilted his head. "And Laurien?" he sighed. "Does she continue to meet with him?"

Theo nodded. "In between her own studies, she tutors him on man's language, sings him her songs, and, well…"

"What?" Glenthryst asked. He swallowed more ale.

"Well, your majesty, she…*comforts* him." Theo selected his words carefully.

"Comforts him?" Glenthryst's face became flushed.

"Only through her music and her presence, my Lord." Theo bowed. Glenthryst exhaled as though relieved.

"Exactly." Queen Ragnalla stood. "And that's what worries me."

"Your Highness," Theo said as he approached her. "Her presence brings comfort to many. You know this. It is part of why we brought her here. It is the royal Elfin blood in her veins that does this remarkable thing to all who come into her presence."

The Queen made her way across the room to King Glenthryst.

"I understand, but…" The Queen turned to her friend. "I am very concerned."

Glenthryst titled his head with confusion. "With what?"

"Their continued meetings. I don't like it," she said frankly.

Theo gazed down as though he knew what the Queen meant.

"I sense something else is happening…" she said.

"Go on," Glenthryst said.

"I sense Lord Bedlam is, well," she hesitated and rubbed her hands together. "I feel he is…well, he is in love with the girl."

Glenthryst frowned and looked at Theo.

"Theodore?" he asked as he slammed down the goblet onto the table, splashing its contents on the parchment paper nearby. "Could this be true?"

Theo approached.

"From what my scouts relay to me, I believe this is true," the Queen interjected. "She is only a young girl, but her beauty and poise makes her seem older. Perhaps Bedlam sees her as a woman."

Glenthryst listened intently. Then, he turned back to Theo. "Well?"

"Bedlam is incapable of loving anything or anyone. His heart is completely darkened. It is as black as night," Theo explained. "One must always remember; Bedlam is not a man and, therefore, he cannot feel as a man feels…for a woman."

"But my scouts—"

"He admires her," Theo interrupted and raised his finger. "He appreciates her…beauty, her purity and innocence." He turned to enter the balcony again. "In a way, he envies her."

"Envies her?" Glenthryst said.

Theo nodded and leaned on the wooden railing. He peered over the edge and watched the Vulgaard River flow beneath them.

"Yes," he said. "He can admire the beauty around him. But most dragons have envied man at one time or another. We envy your determination and intellect. Yet we see your gentleness of touch with a newborn or with the land. We envy your skills as a craftsman and envy that power to create. We can only dream of creating a palace such as this. And beauty? Well, a woman's beauty is rare, indeed. Bedlam knows he can never have love nor give it. He envies her youth, her desire, and her future."

He turned to Glenthryst. "He knows his future is limited. Hers is not."

"I see." Glenthryst eyes were distant.

"But envy leads to coveting," Theo said as he rubbed the nape of his neck. "Which leads to greed…and ends with violence."

Glenthryst quickly turned his head to Theo.

"And that is what I fear most of all." Theo looked into Glenthryst's eyes.

"What do you mean?" The Queen approached.

Theo inhaled. "Lord Bedlam is using her for now. He needs her to teach him the ways of man. He relies on her comfort as his body deals with the painful change. But as he becomes greedy for more power, for more prestige, he will grow tired of her."

"And?"

"And, I'm afraid his feelings for her will change," he said. "Especially, when he discovers her betrothal to Aléon's heir."

Glenthryst took in Theo's words. He turned with that faraway look as though imagining his daughter's future nuptials.

"We must be prepared for what can happen," Theo said and walked away. "All I envisioned is coming to pass already. There is much more to come."

Theo motioned for the Queen and Glenthryst to sit at the table. They acquiesced and sat at the table as she dismissed her servants. Theo leaned in to ensure he was heard.

"As we all know, the Elves of Vulgaard are more pure in heart and intent. But the heart of man is desperately wicked and difficult to know. As a result, one must go by their actions rather than mere words. This can be difficult at times, when the actions of man are hidden or disguised," he said and then took out his pipe and hammered it on the table. "But my dragon scouts have provided me with pertinent information that sets our plans into further action."

"What is it?" Glenthryst asked.

"Bedlam is growing in power. And the more men join him, the more powerful he becomes," Theo said. The queen slowly closed her eyes and leaned back in her chair.

"And?" she said with a weary look.

"And so, he has recruited many wizards to assist him in his work." Theo's hand searched through his pocket for a match.

"I suppose a good smoke is something you dragons also envy?" Glenthryst asked.

"Indeed." Theo held up his dragon pipe. "Oh and thumbs." He wriggled his thumb and chuckled.

Glenthryst produced a match for him and struck it. Theo took the match and blew it out. "I'd forgotten, I do not need a match," his eyes twinkled as he spewed a thin line of fire and lit his pipe, but some sparks caught the nearby papers on fire. The Queen's servant rushed to the table to extinguish the small fire.

The Queen smirked as did Glenthryst. Theo frowned.

"Please, from now on, Theo, use a match." Glenthryst handed him another one.

"Aye, perhaps I'd better." Theo puffed on his pipe. "Well, I suppose we knew this day would come. The Dragon foretold it and so did the prophets of old. Bedlam has been made into a man to serve his purpose. Now it is time to test the ways of man. We shall send them out to the lands, one by one, and there they shall establish their kingdoms. Some will choose wisely, while others…" he sighed, "will remain foolish and trust in brute strength to rule their lands."

The Queen continued to gaze downward. Theo watched her as he smoked.

"Bedlam will continue to seduce them, some rulers will betray their people for a piece of the pie," Glenthryst said and rose from his seat. "Yet I am certain some will remain true."

"Pie," Theo sighed. "Can we have some brought in?" He nodded to the servant standing near the door. The servant nodded back then exited the room. The Queen shook her head.

"And sugary sweets," she sighed. "Another way dragons envy Elves and man?"

"Precisely," Theo grinned. "As I was saying, this is our time of testing," Theo continued. "It is our time to divide the wheat from the tares."

"Do you mean the chaff?" Glenthryst asked.

"No," Theo explained. "I mean the tares; the worthless and noxious weeds that can destroy the wheat...the useful portion of the harvest. We must know who is on our side and who must be destroyed."

"But will we be sacrificing Laurien in the meantime?" the Queen asked.

"No," Theo said. "She will be informed of everything before the wars. She will make her own choice."

"And you have seen this?" the Queen asked with the desperation of a loving aunt.

"I have," Theo said. He studied his carved pipe in his hand. "She will make her choice completely aware of the consequences."

"And you will tell her this?" Glenthryst asked.

Theo looked up at the King. "You and I together." He grinned.

The Queen shook her head. "I feel as though we are using her as a pawn in this game."

"No. Not at all," Theo said. He jabbed his finger onto the table for emphasis. "She has been chosen for this time...as have you, as have I."

"But..."

"And what shall come from her choice shall be the reward for all the enduring and faith," he smiled and touched the Queen's hand reassuringly. "What she shall produce shall be the answer to all our woes."

The Queen's eyes shone with tears as she remembered. "Yes. You are so right." She wiped a tear away. "You are so very right."

# 11 THE APPROACHING DARKNESS

Many years had passed and the Elfin Queen met with the rulers of men to discuss her concerns with the growing darkness. Each ruler decided to leave Vulgaard and discover a region of land where they could live away from the darkness. The people packed up their lives and one by one headed over the mountain pass to the north near where the Dragon Forest stood.

In those early years of Théadril, ten leaders arose and divided ten regions. Boundaries were set and laws established. As news of the early settlements returned to the Queen, the Elves of Vulgaard prepared for what was to come.

As more years passed and Lady Laurien grew in wisdom and in beauty. Because she had Elfin blood within her, she did not age as quickly as her human father. The Elves were more pure and therefore lived longer than men. She remained a young woman in appearance.

Laurien knew she was betrothed to marry the heir of King Aléon who had settled successfully at Illiath. The young man she would one day marry had been knighted on the battlefield during the war with the Edonites in the Cornshire near Illiath. Her father had told her of the young prince's courage and skill on the battlefield.

Laurien's heart grew fonder of her future husband and king. As she waited for the time to journey to Illiath, she continued her tutelage under Theo, learning the ways of the blending metals and the teachings of the Elfin wizards. But she no longer wanted to learn in order to use magic. She wanted to learn in order to know the real from the counterfeit. And as she learned, the darkness spread over the lands. The Queen and her Elves of Vulgaard knew the time of Lord Bedlam was upon them.

§

Lord Bedlam had also grown in strength and power over the years. His ways of effective communication gained him credibility among the rulers of men and they bestowed great gifts upon him in exchange for his impressive metal blending skills in weaponry. As his wealth accumulated, he successfully bewitched his advisor Lord Caragon into betraying King_Illiath's trust by joining with the Edonites in attacking the people of Illiath in the Cornshire. Caragon blocked off access to the Blue River and supplied the enemy of Illiath with weapons from his estate at Hildron. King Illiath (Alexander's grandfather)exiled Lord Caragon to Hildron in the Black Hills where he continued to serve Lord Bedlam until the appointed time.

With his new found wealth, Bedlam built for himself a grand estate carved out of the Mountains of Ranvieg where loyal dragons joined his cause of trickery and deception. He continued to learn the ways of magic and successfully cast spells upon the land. But his desire to conquer the Anifornmum, or transformation spell, grew in intensity. In order to build an army more potent than any army of men, he knew he would have to create his own dragon soldiers possessing of both dragon power and man's intelligence. Yet, the success in magic he longed for continued to elude him.

§

"Bring them here!" Lord Bedlam shouted to his workers. He ordered captured wolves, bears, and dragons be brought into the dungeons of his estate carved out of the Ranvieg Mountains. Bound in chains and caged, the animals were rolled into the dungeon where Bedlam conducted his bizarre experiments on the animals using the Anifornum spell he tried to perfect. He had almost memorized the incantations Theo used for his own metamorphosis all those years before, but the wizard's code forbade experimentation with existing spells, especially for the transformation spell which could lead to painful death. Theo had warned Lord Bedlam of this code, but Bedlam ignored the dire warnings.

"My Lord, the dragons," one worker said as he approached Lord Bedlam. "We have secured their mouths shut with leather straps, but I fear they won't hold for much longer!"

Bedlam nodded and waved the men on. He seemed unconcerned about the dragons or any of the animals.

"Bring me one wolf," he ordered.

He made his way to a large black cauldron with steaming liquid inside. Bedlam watched as his men struggled to bring the wolf near their master. He raised his arms and halted them.

"When I give the order, release it!" he shouted above the roars of the animals and the whips of his men.

They held onto the chains that held the beast down, but it almost wriggled free. Its mouth, bound by leather straps, leaked drool onto the dirt. Its fur was matted with sweat. Bedlam stared into its frightened eyes, waved his hands, and began his incantations.

"Release it!" he shouted. His men obeyed and ran aside as their master began the spell.

The wolf writhed in pain as the whirlwind rose all around it. All the men in the cave hid their faces from the flying pebbles and dirt. The wolf howled and groaned from the pain. The leather straps fell to the ground, torn in two.

Finally, when finished with the spell, Bedlam approached the beast lying on the ground, heaving from exhaustion. His men slowly removed their hands from their eyes and witnessed the results of the transformation. Lord Bedlam knelt next to his newest creation: a large wolf-like beast known as a Zadok. He stroked its neck and whispered into its large ears. When it stood, it was now twice the size of the wolf with thick black fur and a large bear-like snout that contained many teeth.

"Well done, my pet," Lord Bedlam said to soothe the animal. It stood panting and drooling. Bedlam waved one of his men over. "Give it something to eat."

The servant nodded and began to take the chain to lead the beast away into the caves, but as he did, the Zadok turned its head and sunk its large teeth into the man's neck, slowly draining the life out of him until his body went limp. And then the beast feasted on the dead servant as Lord Bedlam watched.

Bedlam walked along the corridors lined with men captured from local villages. They were bound and chained. He inspected each one then ordered one to be brought to the cauldron.

His servants took the man off the chain and dragged him before Bedlam. Then, Bedlam ordered the dragon be brought over. Once the man and dragon were in place, Bedlam began the incantations yet again. The servants ran away and hid behind stacks of stones as the whirlwind rose in strength making it impossible to see anything. They could hear the screams from the man and the roar of the dragon. When all was quiet again, the servants peeked over the stacks to find the man lying on the ground and the dragon dead. Once the dust settled, they saw the naked man was yet another creature mutation like previous other failed attempts before. Bedlam's caves were full of his Baroks, failed attempts at shape shifting. Lord Bedlam knelt next to the grotesque mutation of man and dragon and ordered a chain be fastened around its neck. Then, Beldam helped the creature stand.

As his servants helped the creature limp off to the caves, Bedlam squinted and pursed his lips in frustration. "Another attempt has failed," he said. "This won't do."

"Next!" he shouted and waved for his servant to bring him the next animal.

More men joined Bedlam in his pursuits, all the while falling for his seductive lies and promises of immense power. With time, Bedlam's magical prowess grew as he continued with his grotesque experiments with magical spells. Every wizard under his command failed to produce the same spell Theo had used to transform a man into a dragon. Bedlam's frustration grew. He changed his tactics.

§

"My lady," Moriah said as she peeked around the door. "I have another gift to bring to you."

She giggled and then approached Laurien as she sat by her dressing table. One of her servants worked on her hair while others applied perfumes to her skin.

Laurien smiled. "Bring it here," she waved to Moriah, her favorite lady-in-waiting and friend. "Let's see it!"

In her hands rested a red velvet box. Moriah curtsied and slowly raised the lid to reveal a diamond and ruby necklace. Laurien's eyes widened at the sight of the necklace sparkling in the candlelight.

"Oh, it is so beautiful, isn't it, my lady?" Moriah sighed, "With gems from the Ranvieg mines!"

Laurien nodded and carefully reached for it. Her fingers traced the large gemstones surrounded by delicately cut diamonds. She lifted it up and brought it to her neck, staring in the mirror at her reflection.

"Here, my lady," Moriah said. "Let me help you clasp it around your neck."

Laurien watched as the necklace was placed around her neck. It fell gracefully onto her bosom and matched the long red velvet gown Bedlam had given to her to wear for the evening's special occasion.

"There is a card!" Moriah held a small envelope sealed with the black wax and Lord Bedlam's signet.

She handed it to Laurien who opened it and silently read the words…

*A special gift for my very special guest. I count the hours until we see each other again. I cannot describe to you in man's words what your presence means to me. So I hope my gifts express my love for you in a more satisfying way.*

"What does it say?" Moriah gleefully asked. Laurien smiled at her girlishness.

"It is from Lord Bedlam." Laurien placed the note onto the table. "It is a thank-you gift for the tutoring I have done for him these last months."

Moriah looked at the servants and smirked.

"That is one very special thank-you gift," she said.

Laurien frowned. "Yes, it is." She fingered the necklace for a moment and then stood. "I suppose we should leave now."

Moriah followed Laurien down the hall. "You know, my lady," she giggled. "I do believe Lord Bedlam cares deeply for you."

Laurien simply listened as they walked.

"And I wouldn't be surprised if," Moriah continued. "…if he asked you to be his—"

"Enough!" Laurien stopped her. Moriah stood still. "Come, let us not speak of such things. We must be off now. We are already late."

Moriah curtsied. "Yes, my lady."

§

"Enter, my dear." Bedlam waved his guest of honor into the grand entranceway of his estate. Lady Laurien, accompanied by Moriah, entered the regal yet mysterious estate. She wore the long red velvet gown stitched with gold thread. Tiny crystals lined the bodice and neckline. They sparkled in the torchlight as she walked. Her long dark hair cascaded down her back in waves. The sides were braided, revealing ruby earrings dangling from her ears and the ruby and diamond necklace around her neck. Bedlam grinned when he saw his gift resting against her fair skin.

"You look more beautiful every day," Lord Bedlam said and he gently took her hand and kissed her fingers. Moriah giggled. Laurien turned to her and gave her a stern look.

"Come this way," he ordered. "It is finished and hanging in the dining hall."

He took her hand and led her through the grand hall. She noticed several sterling silver rings on his long fingers; gifts from the rulers. On the walls hung large tapestries also given to him by many rulers. The intricate stone tilework in the floor intrigued Laurien. It resembled a puzzle she and Bedlam had worked on together. She gazed up at the ceiling with its mural of the night sky painted across it. Finally, they arrived at the dining hall where a framed portrait hung covered with a black cloth.

"Here it is," Bedlam said as he turned to his guest and smiled. His dark eyes reflected the candlelight nearby. He was dressed impeccably in a burgundy suede tunic cut to fit him snuggly. Around his thin waist he wore a belt of braided leather and at his side was a sheath holding an ivory handled knife. His black suede trousers were offset by black leather boots. The monochromatic look made him appear even taller than he was. Finally, around his ample shoulders was draped his usual black cape, secured at the neck by a diamond brooch in the shape of a dragon's head. His dark hair slicked back revealing his strong facial features.

"You look dashing tonight," Laurien said with a genuine smile, for she meant it. Bedlam made a very handsome man.

He grinned and nodded. He seemed unaware of how to handle such a compliment by a woman. So, he changed the subject and grabbed the cloth with his thin hand.

"This, my dear, is my gift for you," he said. "A tiny gesture for all that you have done for me."

"Really, you don't have to give me yet another..." Laurien blushed and tried to stop Bedlam, but it was too late.

He yanked hard on the cloth and it fell to the ground, revealing the portrait of Lady Laurien of Glenthryst. Moriah gasped and covered her mouth.

"Oh...how beautiful, my Lady," Moriah said as she lowered her hands.

The painting, framed in a gilt frame carved in detail, showed Laurien dressed in a flowing dark green gown with her pale shoulders bare. Her brown hair rested over one shoulder and around her neck lay an emerald necklace. It was yet another recent gift Bedlam had made for her.

Laurien stood before her portrait unable to speak. In the painting, she looked far older than she felt. The Laurien in the painting was a grown woman, not the clumsy girl running through the palace. She realized she had grown in stature over the years. Could this be how Bedlam saw her? As a beautiful woman?

"I don't know what to say," she said and gently touched her neck. Her eyes never left the portrait. "I remember posing for it, but never in my mind did I think…"

"That you were this beautiful?" Bedlam said as he turned to her. His eyes moved over her form. He slid behind her and placed both hands on her shoulders and gently squeezed them. She could feel his warm breath on her neck. Together, they stood gazing at the painting.

"Leave us," he said coldly to Moriah who curtsied and hastily left the room with a red face.

"Is that *me*?" Laurien asked incredulously.

Bedlam chuckled. "Of course it is. You see? You are *that* beautiful." He turned her around to face him. "Didn't you know?"

Embarrassed, she lowered her green eyes and gazed at the floor. He carefully lifted her chin with his finger until her eyes met his.

"Now I can look at you whenever I wish," he grinned.

He held her chin there for a moment then cautiously leaned in toward her waiting lips. With their eyes so dangerously close together, Laurien felt the blood leave her head. She closed her eyes, parted her lips, and waited.

"So beautiful," Bedlam whispered. He caressed her face then pressed his lips to hers. He wrapped his arms around her waist and pulled her toward him.

Laurien gasped and stepped back. "I feel faint."

Bedlam smiled and steadied her. "Come," he said, "sit down." He took her hand and led her to a waiting chair.

Laurien sat, trying to catch her breath. Before she could speak, a servant entered with a crystal pitcher of wine. Bedlam poured his guest a glass and made her drink. "This will calm your nerves before the other guests arrive."

She nodded as she drank and some wine ran down her chin. Bedlam took out his handkerchief and gently wiped it for her. "Don't worry. None fell to your gown."

He lifted her ruby necklace. "I see you wore my latest present tonight?"

She nodded and continued to look deep into his eyes as he spoke. She watched his lips move and studied the details of his face as he spoke of the jewels and how the necklace was made. Laurien sat amazed at what she saw. Bedlam had truly mastered the art of being a man. Or had he only mastered the trick of fooling the eye into thinking he was a man? All Laurien knew, was that his magic had grown more powerful than she could have imagined. His touch was gentle, yet strong, and very real. His voice was deep and masculine, yet comforting, and not in any way threatening. He spoke with eloquent words and nothing vulgar or crass. *How could this be?* She thought. He seemed more like a man than the men she had met.

Soon after, the rest of the guests had arrived and were meandering through the large estate after dinner conversing about this and that. Laurien continued her tour of the rooms, inspecting the artwork that hung on the walls and the books on the shelves, all the while feeling Bedlam's eyes watching her as she navigated through the crowds and around the room. Once in a while, she would look across the room and catch him staring at her even as someone was speaking to him. He would grin and nod to her as though telling her he was aware of her every move.

She awkwardly nodded back and continued on her way and as she did, she began to understand what Theo had meant when he warned her about magic so many years ago.

Moriah approached Laurien's side. "You know, my Lady," Moriah said.

Laurien turned to her.

"His eyes never leave you," Moriah nodded to Bedlam, who continued to stare with intensity. "I believe he is in love with you."

"One would believe so," Laurien said. "One would believe so."

## 12 GREAT PROMISE

As more years passed, the darkness spread. More and more people feared for their lives and headed for the new settlement north of Theádril. Here, the pact with the dragons was tested.

With Bedlam's power growing in strength and scale, his magical spells began to affect more than just the land. His wicked Baroks, the result of many failed attempts at the Anifornum spell, were mutations of men and dragon. Their sickly gray skin was grotesque and warped beyond recognition. They pillaged the smaller farms and slaughtered the flocks. Bedlam continued to betray the wizard's code of recreating spells with his experiments on animals, creating more fierce, wolf-like Zadoks. These mutants took pleasure in destroying any life found in their path.

Finally, Bedlam's dragons began attacking the villages yet again. The lush farmlands of Théadril were not exempt from this violence. And as the attacks grew in number, the rulers did not know where to turn for relief. But the Dragon of the Forest, in its cathedral of trees to the north, honored its role in the Oath by destroying the Baroks and dragons while instilling reverence into the hearts of every living creature. As a result, the ten rulers met with the Dragon for counsel and peace began to spread.

Lord Bedlam, watching from his perch atop his estate in Ranvieg and gathering details about Théadril from his many spies, took advantage of everything that occurred in the lands for his own power and control. The vanity of man did nothing to hinder Bedlam. Instead, vanity and desire only increased his potential for deception. For his ultimate goal was to defeat the only one that could not be defeated.

§

"He has sent for you." Theo stood alone in the doorway of the smith's workshop outside the grand palace walls. It was here that Laurien worked on blending metals as an apprentice to the elder Elves. She excelled in making fine swords balanced to perfection. Elves, Dwarves, and men from miles around came to purchase her elaborate creations. Queen Ragnalla awarded her niece in the art of sword-making for which Laurien was honored.

Laurien stood at the anvil with hammer in hand, banging on the blade of her newest sword, and, as a result, she did not hear Theo.

"My dear!" he shouted above the roaring fires in the pits and the clanging hammers.

Laurien finally looked up at her friend and smiled.

"He has sent for you," Theo said. The smile disappeared from Laurien's face. "Come meet me in my library." She nodded as she wiped sweat from her face.

Laurien washed and soon made her way to the library where she saw Theo standing alone on his balcony enjoying the sunlight as it streaked down. In his hand, he held a piece of parchment paper folded and sealed with black sealing wax. Laurien approached.

She took the envelope and inspected its seal. "Lord Bedlam," she sighed.

"Yes."

"You disapprove?" she asked as she opened it. But Theo remained silent as she read. "I don't understand."

Theo turned around and walked past her.

"He asks for your assistance," he said. He motioned for her to follow him into the library and she obeyed.

"How did you know? He wants my assistance with what?"

Theo pushed on a bookcase and it opened like a door revealing a secret passage. He removed a candle from the sconce and began stepping down the staircase.

"Theo?" Laurien followed him, "Assistance with what?" But her tutor remained silent as he made his way down to the last step, removed a key from his robe, and opened the door to the wizard's room.

Once inside, Theo replaced the candle into a sconce and waved his arm. When he did, a fire ignited inside the fireplace and instantly lit the room. He walked to the cauldron in the corner of the room and waited for his student.

"The time has come," Theo said.

"Speak plainly." Laurien tossed aside the note. "I grow tired of the riddles and platitudes."

"Very well then." Theo waved his arm over the dark liquid resting inside the cauldron and it began to stir. "Watch closely, pay attention, and learn something."

Laurien stood by his side and peered into the liquid. She winced and turned away from its foul smell. But a flicker of light forced her to return her gaze. Inside the liquid, she saw images of herself working alongside Bedlam inside his hideaway.

"What is this?" she asked.

"It is you and Bedlam at his estate," Theo explained.

"I've been there many times and have never seen this place," she said.

"This is his newest hideaway." Theo looked about the room where they stood. "Much like this one here."

"You mean, he has a wizard's room as well?"

"Precisely," Theo said. "And he has been very busy there and at Hildron."

"Busy with his magical spells of weapon making and mutations?" Laurien raised an eyebrow with a look of disgust. "He has told me of all this. Is this what he wants me to assist him with? Developing the shape shifter spell? Well, he can forget it. There is no way that I—"

"He thinks he has discovered a way to forge a weapon so powerful, it will penetrate the Dragon's scales," Theo interrupted her.

Laurien let out a small laugh. "I'd like to see that." She walked away and adjusted her cloak. "Doesn't he know that is impossible?"

Theo joined her near the fire. "It is all a ruse, my dear," he said.

She furrowed her brow. "But, how do you know?"

"My dragon scouts have told me that Bedlam plans to create ten swords to bestow upon his greatest clients, the ten rulers of Théadril."

She looked down at the letter on the table. "And that's why he needs my help?"

"He has been told of your skills in metal blending and sword making. Your reputation precedes you."

Laurien thought about it for a second, and then turned away. "He's using me again."

"Exactly," Theo moved about the room.

She exhaled heavily and sat down near the table. "I am so very tired of this game he's playing."

"As am I," Theo sat down across from her. "And I am happy to say that the game is almost over."

She looked up at her tutor. "Say again?"

He smiled. "You have grown much these many years, my dear. You have grown, not only in stature and beauty, but in wisdom and intellect.

I have seen it, the Queen has seen it, and Bedlam has seen it. The Elfin masters have taught you much in the art of sword making. Now that skill will assist us in claiming our prize once and for all."

"I still do not understand," she said.

"You will assist Lord Bedlam with this task. And in doing so, you will help forge the secret message of the Elves into each sword," he said.

Laurien listened.

"A message has been developed that protects the Oath made between the Dragon and men. When the swords are together inside the Dragon Forest, the spell of Lord Bedlam is destroyed and he returns to his dragon form...forever."

Laurien's mouth fell open.

"That's right," Theo said. "Our chance has come. He has called upon you because you came through with your end of the bargain."

She squinted her eyes, thinking about something else. "The swords," she said. "And if Lord Bedlam succeeds in deceiving all the rulers, what shall become of the swords?"

Theo sat back and slid his hands across the surface of the wooden table. "That cannot happen."

Laurien inhaled. "But what if it does? Then what?"

Theo hesitated. "Then Bedlam wins this warped game of 'capture the flag' and if he gathers all the swords together ..."

"Yes?"

"He will destroy them at Hildron. Subsequently, the Oath will be destroyed, followed by the Dragon Forest..." he said. "And the Dragon therein."

Laurien looked away. "He has become *that* powerful?"

"Not yet," Theo said. "But the time is at hand. More and more join his cause. He seeks out the weak minded and, unfortunately, there are many willing to believe his lies. The more who join him, the more powerful he becomes."

Laurien stood and paced the room. "Who will be the one?"

"The one?"

"Yes. Who will be the one to take the swords into the Dragon Forest?" she asked in a voice quivering with desperation. "Who shall it be?"

Theo turned in his chair to face her. "It must be your heir, my lady."

She stopped and stared at Theo in silence.

"My dear?" Theo asked. "Are you alright?"

"For such a time as this," she murmured with eyes wet with tears.

"I beg your pardon?" Theo asked.

Laurien walked over to him and wiped her face with her shaking hands. "I suppose this is why I was brought here?" she asked. "To Vulgaard?"

Theo sighed.

"For such a time as this?" she picked up the letter. "Is that all?"

Theo reached over and took her hand into his. "Sit, child. You're trembling."

Laurien refused.

"Very well," Theo said. He stood and took both her shoulders. "My dear, when you were born over one hundred years agon, it was decided you would be the one. You were betrothed to the son of a King who hadn't even been born yet. You were tutored for this purpose. Bedlam selected you for your skills alone. And finally, when he was given the sight...he selected you for your heir."

A steady stream of tears fell from her eyes as she listened. "So this is all that my life will be? Sword making, marrying a man I do not know, and giving birth to a son who will probably die in battle saving the land from this evil I helped create. Is that all there is?"

She jerked her body away, crinkled the letter, and threw it to the ground.

"No." Theo took her into his arms and held her as she sobbed. "Quiet now."

When she stopped trembling, Theo sat her down and continued her education about her future. "You have been chosen to save not one kingdom, but *two* kingdoms. You have been chosen to marry a noble King who will love you more than he loves himself. You will live in a grand palace and build a life together in peace and harmony. Then, one day, you will have a son, a beautiful precocious little boy. And this son will be the one to deliver these two kingdoms from an evil presence not seen before."

Laurien smiled through her tears. "I, for one, am excited for this time," he grinned. "And so very proud of you, my dear."

Laurien wiped her face. "You know," she giggled. "You're pretty good at this counseling stuff...at least, for an old dragon."

§

Now that Laurien understood the purpose at hand, she sought out guidance from the elder swordmakers at the palace. She knew the swords had to be glorious in appearance and fit for the royal hands that would hold them, yet they would also hold a secret spell that would serve a most valuable purpose.

A rare spring storm blew outside making the fires inside the smith's workshop harder to stoke. Satisfied with her work, Laurien stood over the ten swords made of the finest metals blended to perfection. But each blade was plain with no carvings. An elder Elf entered and stood next to her.

"I will speak the message and you will carve it according to my instructions, understand?" he commanded as he made his way around the table.

Laurien nodded and put on her gloves.

"I am ready when you are," she said.

# 13 DELIVERING THE SWORDS

When Laurien completed the task of creating the swords of Bedlam to his exact specifications, she had each one placed into its own wooden case, stained and varnished to a shine. The swords were unlike any other swords in all the lands.

It was at this time Queen Ragnalla, ruler of the Elves, and King Glenthryst, ruler of men, came together to announce the great news of Laurien's journey to Illiath in order to marry the son of King Aléon. The people from the outer regions came to hear the great news, as many saw this marriage as a sign of the end of the darkness. For the son of King Aléon had proven himself to be strong in battle yet fair. He ruled with dignity and lived in the palace facing the Dragon Forest.

Lord Bedlam did not receive an invitation to the grand celebration, much to his disappointment. Instead, he waited inside his estate at Ranvieg for the arrival of the swords by his beloved friend, Lady Laurien.

After the celebration when the people had returned to their villages, Laurien knew it was time to visit Bedlam. She brought with her Moriah, her lady-in-waiting, and two of her father's guards. The entourage landed outside the estate and dismounted their dragons. Laurien stroked the snout of her favorite dragon, Avalon.

"Stay here, my friend," she said gently. The dragon blinked its large amber eyes, shook its head, and snorted.

The entourage was led down the stairway to the master of the house, waiting inside his hideaway underneath his palace.

The walls dripped with water and the air was incredibly damp. When she entered, Laurien saw Bedlam hunched over a table littered with papers—drawings of buildings he planned to build. The room had many fire pits lit. Tables were scattered around, each covered with stacks of papers and ink-stained quills.

"What is it?" he asked without looking up.

"The swords have arrived, my Lord." his servant announced with his head bowed.

Bedlam looked up and saw Laurien. She wore a long ivory gown made of linen. Around her neck hung the ruby and diamond necklace he had given her before. He winced as though in great pain at the sight of her elegant beauty contrasted against the blackened walls of his dungeon. She could see his skin glisten with sweat. He wore only a thin undergarment over his taught torso and black suede trousers tucked into his riding boots. The heat from the fire pits made the room unbearably hot. He was pale and thin from lack of sleep and food.

"At least you had the decency to bring them to me yourself," he said, mockingly, "How thoughtful of you."

Laurien motioned for her entourage to step back. She made her way over to Lord Bedlam. Her face turned down with sorrow.

"I...of course I brought them," she said. "I...I wanted to say goodbye."

"And how was the celebration?" He breathed heavily and tapped his chin with his long finger. "No doubt you'll be heading to Théadril soon?"

"Very soon," she answered with no emotion in her voice. She wondered if he only asked as a formality. She raised her arm and the guards carried the boxes of swords over to the table and laid them out one by one. "They are finished." His eyes ignored the boxes and never left her as she spoke. She could feel the weight of his stare.

"Please." She closed her eyes and sighed. "Take them."

"So that's it?" He stepped toward her. "After all these years together? After all this time we have spent together, it is to end like *this*?"

She lowered her gaze, refusing to look into his eyes. "Yes."

"No!" he shouted and slammed his fist onto the table. Laurien jumped and the guards grabbed the hilts of their swords. She turned to them.

"Stop!" she ordered. "Seize your swords. Put them back!" She knew Bedlam could kill every one of them in an instant, but her father insisted that they escort her.

The guards obeyed, but stood by with caution.

"This is how it has to be," she said with gentleness. "You know this."

He looked away and shook his head.

"You're not well." She finally looked at him. "You haven't been sleeping, have you?"

He ignored her.

"You cannot lock yourself away like this, night after night, working. You have to take care of yourself." She could see he wasn't listening to her.

So, she lifted her hand in a gesture of kindness. Bedlam looked at it. Beads of sweat formed on his brow. He carefully took her hand into his. His face contorted as though fighting back tears as he squeezed her flesh.

"Goodbye," she said. "It is time for me to leave." She started to turn.

But before she could reach the others, Bedlam did what he could to keep her from leaving. Instantly, he transformed into his dragon form and roared so loudly the building shook and dirt fell from the rafters. Laurien covered her ears from the ferocious roar. Moriah screamed and fell to the ground. The guards helped her up.

The Dragon of Bedlam spewed a stream of fire along the ceiling and faced Laurien with his glowing red eyes.

"Don't leave me!" Bedlam said to her in dragon speak.

"How could I stay? Look at yourself! This is who you really are!" she shouted to him. "Full of anger and hatred!"

He transformed back into his human form and leaned on the table for support. The act of transforming took too much energy out of him so he did it less and less. Laurien ran to him.

"Are you alright?" she cried. He pushed her away.

"No," he murmured. "I…am not alright. *I hurt!*"

His scream startled Laurien.

"Don't you understand?" He turned to her with black eyes and a tightened jaw. "The very sight of you *hurts* me."

Laurien cringed.

"Because I cannot have you," he panted.

"You have believed the lie," she said and reached out to stroke his hair. "You believed the spell. It is so real, that you have deceived yourself into thinking you *are* a man."

When her hand touched him, he trembled. She took a step back realizing it was a mistake.

"How do you think it feels?" he said. He walked over to her and stood inches away from her face. The sweat poured down his neck. His eyes traced the details of her face and he slowly raised his hand to caress her, but stopped himself. "How do you think it feels to never have…what *he* will one day have?"

Laurien closed her eyes. Bedlam stepped around her and stood behind her.

"To never touch what he will one day touch?" His hands touched her arms and softly followed them up to her hair. He took it into his hands and breathed in her scent. Tears welled in Laurien's eyes as she remembered the times they spent together reading, talking, and playing games as friends. She closed her eyes.

"To never feel what he will one day feel." He gently lowered her hair. She could feel his hot breath on her neck. His hands slowly slid around her thin waist. "To know that he will give you the greatest gift that I could never bestow upon you..." He quickly stepped away from her with contempt and overturned a table nearby. Its contents scattered all over the floor.

"A son!" he shouted and slammed down his hand onto another table. He turned to her. "*A son!*"

Startled, Laurien's eyes widened in shock. "How did, how did you know this?" she murmured.

He walked over to the table with his plans laid out and leaned over it. She could see from his heaving shoulders that he was weeping.

She felt the warmth of compassion overwhelm her. She ran over to him and caressed his head, burning with fever.

"I'm so sorry," she cried, "please forgive me. I'm so very sorry. I did all this! This is all my fault. I was so stupid. I had no idea what I was asking so many years ago."

She gently rubbed his back. "I was a young girl and so foolish. I had no idea the pain I would cause," she cried as the tears streamed down her face. She took his face into her hands. "Please forgive me!"

He took her hands and kissed the palms.

"Please forgive me," she wept.

Bedlam fell to his knees and wrapped his arms around her waist. He buried his face into her bosom. "Please don't leave me," he cried.

Laurien stroked his hair, wet with sweat, as he cried.

"I am nothing without you." He looked up at her. "I cannot do this alone. Please, don't leave me."

Laurien cried, but as she looked into his eyes, the thought overcame her: she was believing the lie. "No." She shook her head and began to pull away, but he resisted. She could not believe how real the spell was and that she was being deceived yet again.

"We can build a life together here," Bedlam implored. "We can stay together forever, just the two of us."

"No, we cannot." She shook her head and tried to pull away from him. He tightened his hold on her.

"You don't need to leave and flee to that other land. Please, I know we can do this together," he said. "There is still time. I need you here with me!"

She yanked his arms from around her and stepped away. "No!"

Bedlam remained on his knees before her.

"You've changed." She shook her head and wiped her eyes. "You said you would do good deeds as a man."

"I have!" he rose to his feet.

"No, you haven't." She swallowed hard. The intense heat made her throat dry. "You have deceived men, and you said you would unite them!"

She could see the hardness return to his face.

"You said you would work with men, but your dragons attacked them and they had to flee to other lands!" she cried.

He shook his head and turned away from her. "I am working with men!"

"To do what? Wage war?"

"If that is what they desire!" he yelled.

"But how can that be the good you promised?" She stepped toward him. "War is nothing but death and destruction!"

"They desire war, so I made them weapons of war." He made his way behind yet another table and waved his hands over the scattered papers filled with drawings of weapon designs. "I have given them what they wanted."

"Only to deceive them…to *destroy* them!" She pointed at him. "And now I know that was your plan all along: Vengeance. No, I won't be a part of this." She turned to leave.

"You are already a part of this, my dear," Bedlam said.

Her guards stood nearby with Moriah.

"My lady, we must go now!" Moriah waved her hands.

Laurien wiped her forehead as Bedlam slowly stepped around the table. She knew what he meant. When she begged Theo for the spell to be cast, she became a part of the entire plan. Laurien felt the regret rise within her.

"I have finished the job you asked of me," she said as she caught her footing. She waved her arm over the swords. "My task is complete. Now I must go."

Bedlam stood panting, his hands formed into fists.

"But be warned, Lord Bedlam," she said and looked over at him. "These swords…as grand as they are…will *never* penetrate the scales of the Dragon."

Bedlam chuckled. "It doesn't matter, my dear…nothing matters anymore."

"Then, my work here is done." She waved her arms in front of her.

A stern look came over his face. "Go then," he hissed. "Leave me…*Queen* Laurien. Marry this fool Alexander, the one they call the defender of men," he said with sarcasm.

Laurien narrowed her eyes. "I see you now for what you truly are." She turned away from him.

"Wait!" he yelled and reached for her.

"What is it?" she asked.

"But this Alexander...he's just a young man."

"And I am a young woman. Besides, he will prove to be a noble man and a great King," she said with certainty. "And I will be there for him, by his side through it all. He will be my King and I will be his Queen."

Bedlam squinted his eyes and shook his head. "You're a fool, then." He wiped his face with his sleeve. "And what will you tell him of *us*?" he smirked.

The question shocked her. She had never considered it before.

"*Us*?" she said. "I suppose I will never speak of it." Her voice was cold.

Bedlam closed his eyes and staggered as though an arrow had pierced his heart. Images of a young Laurien giggling to him as she read her stories raced across his mind. "Just like that?" he said as he slowly opened his eyes. "All those years together, laughing, reading, singing to me...*gone*? Forever?"

"That's how it has to be," she said. Her voice cracked. She reached up, unhooked the ruby necklace from around her neck, and laid it on the table. She raised her eyes to him and turned to leave.

Bedlam ran over and picked up the necklace. He gripped it tightly in his hand, the fire's reflection danced in the rubies' glare. He growled as he watched her walk off.

"Leave then, my Queen! Forget me!" He threw the necklace across the room and shouted after her. "Forget all this if you can!"

She ignored him as Moriah hugged her.

"But know this, Queen Laurien."

Laurien stopped and turned her head. Bedlam approached her with eyes as black as death itself and a grimace filled with rage.

"I will not rest," he hissed and jabbed his finger at her, "until everyone close to you..." He pointed that same long finger at Moriah and a shot of green fire struck her dead.

"No!" Laurien shouted and knelt by her friend's motionless body on the ground. She turned to Bedlam with wide eyes filled with horror.

"I will not rest until everyone you love dearly..."

Another shot of green fire pierced the chests of the two guards with her, killing them instantly. Laurien was aghast.

And only then Bedlam finished his horrible promise. "...dies."

"No! Stop!" Laurien screamed as she reached for the dead guards.

"And I will not rest until every*thing* that you hold dear to your heart..." He lifted his arm and the green fire rose to the ceiling.

"Suffers as I suffer," he finished.

Laurien knelt beside her dead friend and wept hot tears of hatred as she watched any semblance of kindness and goodness drain from Lord Bedlam's eyes.

"For as long as you live, my Queen," he said. "Your suffering will be my task, my goal, my *purpose*."

She slowly stood to leave, using her arms to balance.

"I hate you," she whispered through pursed lips, "And I do feel sorry for you."

Bedlam's expression did not change.

"Good," he said. "This is how it has to be." He coolly turned away.

Laurien ran up the stairs, out the entrance, and to the waiting dragons only to find her beloved Avalon lying dead on the grass. She ran over and tried to lift its head, but it was too late. Bedlam had struck it dead from within his lair. Laurien mounted another dragon, heeled its ribs hard, and ordered it to fly.

*"This is how it has to be,"* she remembered Bedlam's last words to her.

Together, they flew toward the palace at Vulgaard, but as they flew, the wind seemed to not only cool her hot skin and dry her tear-stained face, but also clear her mind. And for the first time in her life, her purpose for living was absolutely clear to her: She was to spend the rest of her days preparing.

First, she would prepare herself, and then, prepare her son.

As a result of her last meeting with Bedlam, Laurien knew what she needed to do. First, she met with the Elfin builders and asked them questions about how they build. "What do you begin with?" she asked one Elf.

He thought about it for a moment, and then kicked the rocky ground on which they stood. "A strong foundation is always best, my Lady."

"A foundation?" she asked.

"A solid foundation of rock," he bent down to show her. "A foundation of rock is essential. It doesn't matter how grand a palace is...without that foundation of rock, it will crumble."

Laurien took in everything he had told her. She bent down and ran her fingers along the rough surface of the rock. "*Petras*..." she sighed. "Peter. The rock."

She smiled and picked up a small rock. "One day, I shall bring forth a son who shall be called Peter," she handled the rock in her hand. "And he shall be the foundation on which to build the kingdom."

Next, she visited with the Elfin warriors and asked them how they find their way home when there are no stars in the sky. The leader took out a brass compass from a leather pouch he kept on his belt.

"I use this," he said, opening it. "It will show me where I am and then I will know how to get home."

As time passed, Laurien continued in her preparations.

She worked with the Elfin masters who showed her how to construct a special compass made of finest gold. She began to thoroughly read *The Dragon Chronicles* and study the ways of the dragons and the dragon masters.

"This book will help anyone learn what they need to know about the many types of dragons," the Dragon Master said.

"Thank you, Dangler," she said as she closed the book. "The preparations are almost complete."

§

In the end, Laurien used her final time at Vulgaard wisely preparing herself for the final task. But then the day came to depart for her future home in Théadril. With her life packed into wagons pulled by horses, she sat on her horse and waved to Theodore knowing she would see him soon at the palace of Illiath where her future husband would be crowned King Alexander.

Queen Ragnalla stood waving alongside King Glenthryst and Theo.

"Well," the Queen said. "She is off to begin her new life as a Queen."

The King nodded. "I will join her soon."

"Why on earth is she riding a horse? She should have flown on a dragon," the Queen said.

"Well, when I asked her, she told me she needed to see the land and map the journey in case her future son needed to know what the terrain was like from Illiath all the way to Vulgaard," the King said.

The Queen shook her head in disbelief.

"She told me she will spend her days preparing her son for his time as King," Theo said.

"And the swords?" the Queen asked. "What do we know of the swords?"

"Bedlam has already presented them to the ten rulers. Only Aléon has used wisdom and hidden his away for the appropriate time. He has never trusted Bedlam and he continues to suspect Lord Caragon."

"I see," she said and turned to walk away.

"All is not lost, Queen Ragnalla," King Glenthryst said. "My son, Baldrieg, shows great promise."

The Queen nodded as she departed.

"Yes," the King sighed "Great promise."

There on the balcony, he watched his daughter ride off into the mountains as the Elfin guards road high above them on silvery dragons.

"And so it begins," Theo said.

"Yes," King Glenthryst agreed. "You must go to Illiath and offer your services to the King."

"I will," Theo said as his eyes followed Laurien on her horse. He placed his hand on King Glenthryst's shoulder. "I will. And you must prepare for what is to come."

"Yes," the King said. "All of us must prepare for what is to come."

# Part II

## 14 THE REUNION

Queen Laurien did arrive at Illiath and married King Alexander there at the palace of his father. Years later, as Laurien had hoped, they had a son whom they called Peter. He became the leader and fighter his mother had dreamed he would be. After brashly entering the Dragon Forest as a young boy, Peter discovered his destiny and what it means to be king. But his true test came when he was abducted and taken to Rünbrior prison. There he learned the ways of the dragons and fought in the Great Arena with Sir Nøel, a knight captured while on the quest for the swords. As was promised, the Dragon of the Forest remained faithful to the Oath and looked after Peter even by helping him escape from Rünbrior prison.

Now, as King Alexander makes his way toward Vulgaard, the quest for the swords continues, and Annika, Simon, and Crispin wait for Peter's arrival. Although Prince Peter would never forget his time in the Dragon Forest or in the prison, he would need to move on and join in the fight to stop Sir William and Lord Bedlam's power from taking over all of Théadril. He would need to finally be ready to rule as King of Illiath.

§

"Hold steady," Sir Roland said. "If they spot us, the plan is ruined."

Two Elves, dressed in the leather battle armor of Vulgaard, stood ready to attack alongside Sir Roland. They hid behind large boulders near Hildron Castle. The female Elf, Eris, aimed her bow and arrow at one of the Barok guards twenty-feet away. Her counterpart, Elric, aimed at the other. Sir Roland, a Royal Knight on the quest for the swords, had led them to this place once his scouts had discovered the last of the swords was inside the castle walls.

"Say the word, and we go," Eris was not a tall Elf, but was muscular for a female. Her braided white hair was pulled back tightly away from her face. She aimed the arrow and held the bow string with strong arms. She whispered as she aimed. Her fingers began to tremble.

Sir Roland, unkept and weary-eyed from many days of travel, brushed aside his dark hair from his face. He watched for any signs of other Baroks approaching. When he saw it was clear, he touched Eris's shoulder and she released her arrow. Her aim was true. The sharp arrow pierced the neck of one Barok and it silently fell to the ground. Before the second Barok could react, Elric's arrow pierced its skull.

"Now!" Sir Roland leapt from behind the boulder and ran by the dead Baroks. The two Elves followed him inside. He heard the buzzing of an arrow fly by his ears. "Get down!"

They fell to the ground as more arrows flew past them. They could hear the grunts of Baroks approaching from behind.

"Well, they're on to us. Now what?" Eris asked.

"Run!" Sir Roland took off down the darkened corridor toward the main hall of the palace.

Eris and Elric obeyed and ran down the corridor, dodging arrows along the way. Finally, all three came to an opening where they separated and prepared to fight the oncoming Baroks.

"Stay here and fight them off. I'm heading to retrieve the sword!" Sir Roland shouted and  took off around the corner with sword drawn. "Meet me back at the hiding place!"

Elric nodded and loaded his bow with two arrows. Eris did the same.

Then, they waited.

"Now!" Elric shouted once a Barok entered the open space. His arrows pierced the creature, but it still advanced. Eris let go of her arrows. One hit the creature right between its eyes. It collapsed a few feet away.

More Baroks followed. Elric drew his sword. "No time to load! Now we must fight!"

Eris dropped her bow and removed her sword in time to slice the throat of an oncoming Barok. Its hot blood splattered across her face. She spit on the ground and wiped her face.

Elric swung around and sliced the leg of another Barok, but it still advanced and sliced his arm. He screamed from the pain then thrust his sword into the belly of the creature, kicked it back and began fighting with another Barok.

Sir Roland ran along the railing of the once beautiful palace of Hildron, but now he could see it was just another place for Bedlam's experiments with magic spells. Below, on the first floor where the grand dining hall once was, he could see Bedlam and all his grotesque creatures working in desperation on armor and weapons. The sound of many hammers clanging and fires roaring made it difficult for him to hear the orders Lord Bedlam shouted to his servants. He leaned in closer and saw what he had hoped to see.

The Sword of Niahm, the last of the ten swords that had been lost.

Lord Bedlam was studying the blade of the sword and comparing it to his own weapons. He shouted at his servants to bring him other swords. His face was contorted with anger and Roland knew Bedlam was frustrated because he had not been able to create the same masterful blade as Laurien once created. He tossed aside each sword his servants brought to him until they formed a large pile next to his feet. He kicked them away and shouted for more to be made.

"That's the one," Sir Roland murmured to himself. "The last sword. Now all I need to do is get down there and take it. Easy enough."

Before he moved, Elric and Eris approached him.

"I didn't expect to see you two again so soon," Roland said.

"We've not much time. More Baroks will come," Elric huffed. He and Eris were drenched with sweat. The heat inside the palace was almost unbearable.

"What is this place?" Eris asked. She studied the happenings below. Rays of fire shot from Bedlam's fingertips to the blade of the Sword of Niahm, but the blade reflected the fire.

"There it is," Roland said and pointed. "Bedlam is trying to destroy the blade, but isn't having any luck."

Eris and Elric saw the sword on the table before Bedlam.

"Are you certain this sword, this *one sword* is worth all this trouble? Is it worth risking your life, Sir Roland?" Eris asked.

He looked hard at her. "I have lost many friends in this quest. Great knights, all of them," he said. Then, he turned to leave. "I owe them this. I owe them more than I could ever repay."

"Alright then, let's go get it." Elric began to leave, but Roland grabbed his arm.

"Wait here," he said to Elric. "Cover me."

The two Elves watched the knight disappear into darkness. They knew he was heading downstairs to the fire pits below.

Elric drew an arrow from his quiver and loaded his bow. "Keep watch for approaching Baroks."

Eris turned and aimed her bow at the corridor opening, waiting for any sign of the enemy. Below, Sir Roland carefully made his way down the stairs with a knife in his hand. He quietly came up behind a guard, covered his mouth, and slit his throat. He gently lowered the guard to the ground so no noise could be heard. He managed to make his way to the ground level where the madness was. The sweat in his eyes burned, but he knew he had to keep going.

"He made it." Elric could see Roland hiding in the shadows on the first floor. He turned to Eris. "I have an idea."

Suddenly, Roland heard a loud commotion coming from above where the two Elves were hiding. He heard it and so did the others. Bedlam pointed and ordered Baroks to attack the Elves. Elric release two arrows that hit the guards protecting Bedlam. He waved his hand and fire rose to where Elric stood. He ducked out of the way in time to avoid the flames. Eris turned to see if he was alright, but as she did more Baroks came from the corridor. She released her arrows and quickly loaded more.

Roland saw Bedlam motion for more guards to fight the Elves, then, Bedlam grabbed the Sword of Niahm and left with it. Roland followed after him.

§

Peter, his brown hair matted to his sweaty forehead, squeezed the dragon with his thighs and held on tightly. It had been so long since he soared through the air on the back of a dragon. Certainly, he had never ridden one so small and fast. He remembered his ride on the back of the Great Dragon of the Forest so many years before. Its massive body had all the power and control. The speed of the smaller dragon caught him off guard and he could barely catch his breath.

He sat atop the saddle, gasping for air as the dragon soared over the tall grasses. But Peter managed a laugh as the cool air stung his face. The air smelled clean and fresh…the air smelled like *freedom*. All those months inside Rünbrior prison began to fade. He gazed toward the green hills where he had spotted Annika, Simon, and Crispin waving to him moments before. They had run down the hill to where their dragons awaited them. Peter pulled on the reins and motioned for his dragon to land. It obeyed and as soon as Peter felt its legs touch ground, he leapt off and ran toward his waiting friends.

He felt the sting of tears in his eyes but he didn't want to cry. He was too happy for tears. He laughed heartily instead. It was Simon who met him first there on the hill in a strong embrace.

"Peter!" He yelled as he grabbed his long lost friend securely. Peter's eyes grew large and he could barely breathe in Simon's embrace.

"Simon," Peter said as they parted. "I can't believe it's you here, right now, here with me on these hills of Vulgaard!"

"Peter!" He heard the voices of Crispin and Annika as they ran toward him. They embraced him at the same time, nearly knocking him to the ground.

"Oh, Peter!" Annika said as she wrapped her arms around his neck and squeezed. Her short blonde hair covered her eyes. The only thing Crispin could do was laugh.

When they parted, Peter looked at each of them standing there, staring at him with incredulous eyes. "What are you doing here?" he asked with a chuckle.

Simon looked at Crispin who looked at Annika. It seemed as though no one knew how to answer, so they laughed again. Peter inspected Annika's new look.

He reached out and touched her short hair. She recoiled in embarrassment.

"Oh, I know," she smirked. "Short."

"Yes," Peter said. "But why?" He inspected her clothing and breastplate, too. He reached over and touched the hilt of the sword attached to her belt.

Simon laughed again. "Our little girl is now...well, a *warrior*," he said.

Annika straightened as though proud of the new description.

"Impressive," Peter said. He placed his hands on Simon's and Crispin's shoulders. "And you? Tell me, what are you doing here so far away from home?"

"We were going to ask you the same question," Crispin said. "Last we heard, you were heading to Knight Training and then..." He hesitated then looked down.

"Peter." Annika stepped in and grabbed Peter's shoulders. "We thought...I mean, we'd heard the worst. I can't even bring myself to say the words." Her eyes welled with tears.

"We heard you'd been killed, Peter." Simon completed her thought.

"What?" Peter looked past them. "You heard what?"

"Yes, it's true," Annika said. "We went to your funeral and everything. It was unbearable."

He imagined his father's shock. "So, that's why no one was sent to rescue me."

"All of Illiath mourned," Simon said. "And that's when Theo…"

"Professor Theo?" Peter said.

"Yes, Theo!" Annika said. She couldn't help but laugh. "He helped us. He was the one who sent us on this journey to come find you."

"To come find me?"

"Well," Crispin said. "It was more of a journey to Vulgaard, now that we know everything."

"What do you mean?" Peter asked.

"They mean to say that they were sent on a journey to escape the Duke of Illiath," came a familiar voice from behind him. Peter turned and immediately smiled.

"Theo!" he shouted and then ran to his former tutor and embraced his tall thin frame. As he did, his mind became flooded with memories from his time with Theo at the palace. "Professor! You're really here!"

Theo patted Peter's back. "It's alright, my boy," he whispered and held Peter. Annika wiped the tears from her face as she watched the scene.

"Yes, we are all here with you now, Peter," Theo said. He pulled away and looked into his sovereign's weary eyes.

Peter smiled and nodded. "I remembered," he said. "I tried to remember everything that you taught me while…while I was in that awful place."

Theo placed his hands on Peter's shoulders.

"I did my best," Peter said and he reached into his pocket and pulled out the golden compass. "I listened to what you said. And I tried to remain faithful to the Oath," Peter continued.

"And you did well, Peter" Theo said. "We all are very proud of you."

Peter nodded. "And my father, Theo?" he asked as he placed the compass back into his pocket. "Where is he? When will I see him again?" He looked around and saw Elfin soldiers speaking with men and Dwarves, but he did not see his father, the King, anywhere.

"Where is he?" Peter asked his friends. "I was told he lives." His face took on a look of desperation. "This is true, isn't it?"

Theo turned him around toward the dragon. "It is true. Your father is safe and on his way to Vulgaard. He will arrive very soon."

Peter closed his eyes and sighed with relief.

"But first," Theo said as he walked Peter to his dragon. "There's something we need to finish."

Peter understood and mounted his dragon. He gazed over at his friends and used his sleeve to wipe sweat from his eyes. "Yes, Theo, you are right. Valbrand will gather more fighters and attack again. We must meet him where he is, kill his remaining guards, and then head to the palace."

"Of course." Simon ran to his dragon and Crispin followed.

Annika smiled with shiny eyes as though proud of her friend. Then, she too ran and mounted her dragon.

"Follow me! Together we will attack!" Peter shouted.

§

Sir Roland crept down the corridor leaving the commotion behind. He followed after Lord Bedlam, with his black cape flowing behind him. He held the last of the missing swords in his bony hands.

"Guard!" Bedlam shouted. Soon, an armored man approached. "Take this and lock it up. Then go and find out what is happening up there."

Bedlam pointed behind him just as Sir Roland ducked behind a stone column. He saw Bedlam hand the sword to the guard and then turn down another hall. When all was clear, Roland followed after the guard making sure to be quiet. When he spotted the guard, he aimed and threw his knife striking the man in the neck. When the guard reached for the knife, he dropped the sword and it fell to the ground with a loud crash.

Roland quickly ran to the guard, retrieved the sword and took off down the corridor unsure of where it led.

"Sir Roland!" Elric called after him. He turned in time to see Eris and Elric trampling down the corridor. He could see that Elric was limping.

"Are you hurt?" he asked as they approached.

"Never mind that." Elric winced. "You have the sword now let's get out of here."

They turned to run, but felt a cold wind around them. The wind grew in strength and surrounded them with an impenetrable cyclone.

"What's happening?" Eris shouted through the wind. Her hair flew around her face, blocking her vision.

"You fools," Lord Bedlam appeared before them. He raised his hand and the sword flew to him. He grasped it and laughed at the sight of the knight and two Elves trapped.

Elric reached back to grab an arrow from his quiver, but the wind was too strong. Soon, Baroks and guards surrounded them with spears and sword tips pointed at their throats. The wind stopped.

Bedlam admired the sword in his hands then looked at Roland with those black eyes. "You have failed yet again, knight," he hissed.

The Baroks roared.

"Take them and feed them to my dragon," Bedlam ordered then turned to walk off.

Roland's eyes never left the sword still in the grasp of the evil Lord. He shifted his gaze to Elric. "On three," he said. Elric nodded.

"One…"

"Come on, let's go!" the guard grabbed Sir Roland's arm and yanked him hard.

"Two…"

"You, too, let's go!" another guard grabbed Elric who screamed from pain and fell to the ground. "Get up! Come on, get up now!"

"Three!"

Elric reached up and took the sword in the guard's hand, crushed the man's nose with his elbow, then used the sword to stab a Barok. He spun around and finished off the guard with the sword.

"Go now!" Elric shouted to Roland and Eris. They took off after Bedlam and when they saw him, Roland threw a sword at the evil Lord's arm slicing it through. When the sword fell to the ground, Eris ran up and grabbed it. She ran on before anyone knew she had it.

"After her!" Bedlam shouted as he held his wounded arm. Several Baroks growled and ran off, but Roland turned and punched one in the face with his fist, knocking it out cold. Another Barok ran up and thrust its sword into Sir Roland's back. He spat blood into the air and fell to his knees. Elric tried to assist, but the wound in his thigh slowed him down and, soon, three Baroks stabbed him through with their spears. Bedlam laughed at the sight of the deaths. Then, he raised his hand to draw the Sword of Niahm to him, but his wounded arm prevented it. He winced with pain. "Bring back that sword!" he ordered his Baroks.

Eris ran as fast as she could with the sword still in her grasp. She could hear the growls of the Baroks as they followed close behind her. She finally saw the entrance to the grand hall and staircase. She ran up the stairs two at a time, slid the sword into the sheath attached to her belt, took the bow from her back and loaded three arrows. Then, she aimed.

She released one arrow at a time, hitting each Barok in the face, sending them backwards down the stairs. She lifted her head and yelled out words in a strange language. Another Barok ran up, but covered its ears. She noticed the creature struggling with the sound, so she sent an arrow into its chest to relieve it. She yelped the words again. Suddenly, a dragon roar was heard from outside the castle. A few more Baroks ran up the stairs, but Eris jumped up on a window ledge, kicked out the panes of glass. She leapt out of the window just in time to miss the spears thrown at her. As she fell through the night sky, the cold air shocked her after being inside the inferno that was Hildron. Before her body hit the ground, her dragon swooped in. She hit its body with a thud, gripped the saddle horn, and mounted it and, together, they flew away from the shouts of Baroks aligning the castle walls. Many transformed into crows and flew after her, so she loaded her bow once again and shot a crow through with an arrow. The others flew off in defeat. Eris grinned. She turned and patted her dragon's neck.

"Thank you, my friend," she said in dragonspeak. "Now, let's get this sword home."

# 15 THE PALACE AT VULGAARD

As Peter's dragon swooped low over the grassy hills, he spotted the garrison of Valbrand's guards taking positions to attack. He raised his sword into the air, signaling the commencement of the battle.

Below him, he saw General Aluein and his men riding horses into the fight with swords drawn.

Next to him, he heard to whoops and calls of his friends as their dragons caught up. All four of them flew together. Peter's heart leapt with excitement. Then, he squeezed his dragon's ribs and the beast dove toward the guards. As it did, Peter easily swiped them with his sword sending arms flying in a blood splattering mess. He pulled on his dragon's reins sending it high into the air for another turn. Together, they turned and swooped in low for another attack. Each time, Peter's innards rose inside him and he felt a bit nauseous. Several archers sent their arrows flying into his path, almost striking his dragon's chest, but the beast wore a breastplate that blocked several arrows.

"Brilliant!" Peter shouted. Then he swiped at more guards with his sword, ending their lives there on the battlefield. He searched the area, but saw no Valbrand. *The coward,* he thought. He knew Valbrand made his escape somehow. Peter felt a sudden surge of revenge flow through him, but then he remembered his mother's words. He exhaled deeply and turned his dragon back around. That's when he saw General Aluein fighting with two guards at once. Peter swooped in low to assist his father's dearest friend. He came up behind a guard as he raised his sword to strike. But Peter plunged the end of his sword deep into the back of the guard, saving the General.

"Yes! Peter!" He heard Simon shout. Peter looked over his shoulder to see Simon atop his dragon, flying alongside him.

"Once more!" Peter motioned for them to turn around and attack again. But when they did, they saw the Elves had finished the job. Every guard was dead. Peter cheered the victory.

But their celebration ended quickly. In the sky before them, Peter saw dragons approaching.

"Look!" He pointed. Simon and the others immediately saw what alarmed Peter. More of Valbrand's men flew into the battle atop the remaining dragons from within the mountain prison. Peter felt the rage build within his chest. "Those dragons deserve to be free!"

He yanked on the reins and nudged his dragon forward. Simon and the others followed. Below, General Aluein could see what was happening. He shouted to his men and the Elves. "More fighters are coming! Get ready!"

Thætil ordered his Elves into battle formations alongside Aluein's men. They marched forward ready to clash with Valbrand's fighters. Peter gripped his sword, pulled back on the reins of his dragon, and the beast spewed out a stream of fire that caught the approaching fighters off guard. Peter watched one fall to his death, and then looked up just as a fighter sliced at Peter with his sword. Peter tugged at his dragon and turned it into a dive just in time. As he dove low to the ground, he could see Aluein's men fighting hard against Valbrand's fighters. He saw the dead bodies of Elves and men littering the hillside. Peter pulled back hard on his dragon sending it soaring up toward the battle in the air.

"Enough!" he shouted. "This ends now!"

He and his dragon flew fast into the oncoming fighters. Peter sliced at the dragon wings and limbs of Valbrand's men. Blood splattered everywhere. His dragon spewed fire while out maneuvering the fire coming in from other dragons.

"Tell them!" Peter shouted to his dragon. "Tell those dragons they can be free!"

His dragon squawked. "Tell them they no longer have to obey Valbrand's orders!"

His dragon squawked and Peter could see the other dragons twist their heads as though listening. The fighters yanked the reins desperately trying to get the dragons to obey.

"Yes!" Peter shouted. "It's working! The dragons are fighting against Valbrand's men!"

"Come on, Peter!" He heard Simon shout. He turned to see his friends victoriously soaring through the air. That's when Peter noticed no more dragons approaching him. But he did hear a few arrows whiz by his ears. Then, he felt the jolt of his dragon's body as two arrows pierced its side.

"No!" he shouted. He pulled on the reins to turn his dragon toward the grassy hills again. When it landed, he dismounted, and checked his dragon. It labored to breathe. An Elf ran up to him.

"Help it!" Peter urged.

"I will try." The Elf called some other Elves to assist him, but to no avail because the dragon had been hit by poisoned arrows. Peter stroked its neck and looked into its eyes.

"Hang on," he whispered to the dragon, but it was no use. The beast closed its eyes and breathed its last. "No!" Peter shouted. He saw a helmet nearby and picked it up. He yelled and threw the helmet away in anger.

The Elves expressed their sympathies as they walked off.

"I am so very sick of death!" Peter shouted into the sky. Then, he turned and ran to the top of the hill in time to see Aluein and his men riding back as one. The sight of all the men riding with Thætil's Elves running alongside sent a chill up Peter's neck. It reminded him of the battle against Lord Caragon in the desert plains. He raised his hands and shouted as the horses thundered past him.

Simon, Crispin, and Annika landed nearby. They dismounted their dragons and ran over to Peter.

"Peter, are you alright?" Annika shouted.

"We saw what happened," Simon said.

"My dragon." Peter shook his head.

"Peter!" General Aluein shouted. "Well done! The fight is over." He frowned when he saw the dead dragon.

"I'm so sorry," Annika said.

"Come now," General Aluein said. "We've no time to weep or mourn. We must depart soon for Vulgaard."

Thætil ordered his Elves to help gather the wounded and dead from the battlefield. Peter waved to his friends to assist. Together, they brought healing paste, water, and bandages to the wounded. Peter also helped bring in the dead. He grabbed the hands of one dead Elfin fighter. Peter looked into the dead Elf's face and noticed how young he was. He reached down and removed a silver chain from around his neck.

"I'll make sure your mother receives this," Peter whispered to the Elf. "I wish I had known your name."

Then, he dragged the body to where the dead were lined up. He dusted off his trousers and turned to leave, but something stopped him. "What will happen to them all?" he asked.

"They will be returned to their families for burial," Theo said as he walked up to Peter.

"So many of them are young," Peter said.

"Yes," Theo nodded. "And they fought valiantly. As did you."

Annika ran up. Her eyes blinked slowly from weariness. "We are finished assisting the wounded."

Simon and Crispin walked over. "I suppose we had better get back to the palace before dark," Crispin said. His reddish hair was matted to his forehead from sweat.

"Well, we are dragon riders now," Annika said.

The four of them embraced there on the grassy hills. Theo chuckled and walked off.

"We're more than that," Peter said to his friends as he pulled away, "We're warriors now."

"Who would have thought?" Crispin said as he wiped his forehead. "The four of us...warriors!"

They each laughed as they spoke of the last time they had seen each other. Peter realized how they were once students getting ready for what they considered to be "adventure" yet, only now, as they reminisced, did they realize how foolish they had been in their thinking. He remembered how they once thought they knew what adventure was, yet only now were they about to embark, together, on the grandest adventure of their lives.

§

"And my father, he will meet us there?" Peter asked as he walked with General Aluein as the day turned to evening.

"Yes, Peter," Aluein said. "We have word that he is on his way. When we arrive at the palace, the Queen will be there to greet us." He patted Peter's back.

Peter ran his fingers through his hair. "I still cannot fathom all this."

Aluein laughed heartily. "I know," he said. "So much has happened in this short amount of time."

Just then, an Elf wandered over, guiding a dragon with him. He handed the reins to Peter.

"Now we must be off. I fear more of Bedlam's men will come out of those dark mountains very soon." Aluein looked concerned. "And when that happens, all hell will break loose."

Peter took the reins and mounted his dragon. He saw that his friends were already high in the sky circling above as the sun began to set. It didn't take much effort to get his dragon to soar into the air. The air felt much cooler as the sun lowered behind the mountains. Peter's skin chilled as his dragon sped through the air over the White Forest. Peter's dangling feet touched the treetops as they whisked by. He could smell the fresh pine scent and hear the howls of a few wolves in the distance. Then, his eyes widened when he saw the sight.

There, in the distance, glistening in the last slivers of daylight, was the palace at Vulgaard carved out of the mountains. Its walls shimmered along with its stained glass windows. Peter grew intrigued with the castle, wondering what it was made of. Its spires reached ever upward. When he gazed below, he could see many Elves running down a myriad of stairs as they realized Peter and his friends were arriving. He watched as they made their way to a set of tall gates. Peter tugged on the reins of his dragon, ordering it to land at the entrance, but the beast resisted and flew over the palace instead. Peter looked behind, confused as to why his dragon was taking him up and over the palace.

"Where are we going?" he shouted.

Simon turned and waved. He pointed to the ground where Peter noticed a landing area behind the palace. The area consisted of green grass spread out across the precipice of a mountain overlooking the valley below. It was a magnificent sight. His eyes followed his friends as each of their dragons landed effortlessly on the grass with Elves nearby ready to take the reins.

Peter's dragon landed with a thud. Peter dismounted and rubbed his backside while grimacing from the pain. "I suppose I'm not used to riding."

Simon and Crispin both chuckled at the sight of their friend. They approached him.

"Don't worry," Simon said. "It will all come back to you soon." He ran over to assist Annika as she dismounted her dragon. She took his hand.

"Thank you, Simon," she said and she made her way to Peter.

"Absolutely," Simon said with a smile.

"Come on, you two! Let's get Peter something to eat," Crispin put his arm around Peter's shoulders. "Come this way for all the fantastic food that you can possibly imagine, Peter. It's incredible!"

Peter smiled and his mouth water as he imagined food again. Real food.

He looked up at the castle before him as they walked to the back entrance. "I don't think I have ever seen anything like this before."

"I know," Simon said from behind them as they walked. "It was constructed from diamonds and limestone."

"Diamonds?" Peter asked. "Is this a dream?"

"Diamonds mined by Elves," Annika said as she pointed to the

Ranvieg Mountains nearby. "There are many precious gems inside those mountains."

Peter frowned, gazing at the silhouette of the mountains to the west. "I know all too well about mountain mining."

Just then, his friend from the prison came to his mind.

"What of my friend, Jason? Where is he?" Peter asked.

"Don't worry, Peter," Simon explained. "He's been taken to the infirmary. I'm sure you'll see him very soon."

"Come! Let's go eat!" Crispin tried to change the subject back to food. "Hurry or we'll miss everything."

§

As soon as Peter entered the palace, a trumpet sounded, startling him. His friends stood next to him.

"What is it?" he asked. A garrison of Elfin guards marched into the grand space. Peter could see their reflections in the mirror-like floor. "What's happening?"

"The Queen," Annika whispered. "She's coming."

Just then, Peter looked to his right as a set of very tall doors opened, revealing her Highness, Queen Thordis, in all her regal splendor. Peter had only heard of her existence from Theo's stories. He never imagined the beautiful sight of such a room and such a presence, especially after the death and darkness he had recently experienced. She was escorted by her son, Thurdin.

Simon and the others bowed, so Peter followed suit, still unsure if he were dreaming or not. When Peter stood straight again, the Queen stood only a few feet away. Her white hair was pulled back revealing her soft face and crystal blue eyes. That's when Peter remembered how dirty and sweaty he was from the prison and the battle. He felt a rush of shame come over him as he imagined what he must look like. He lowered his eyes.

But the Queen reached out her hand and gently touched his chin. She raised his face until his eyes met hers. She smiled a warm smile that melted Peter's heart. He had never seen eyes like her eyes before. They sparkled like pools of cool water. For a moment, he stood hypnotized until Simon tugged at his tunic, rousing him from his daydream.

"Your Royal Highness." Simon bowed again as though hoping Peter would imitate him. Peter did.

"Finally," she said to Peter. "At last I get to meet the young man I have heard so much about."

Peter swallowed hard.

"My mother spoke often of you, your mother, and your father," she said.

Peter cocked his head.

"Your mother lived here among my people for many years before she embarked on her journey to Illiath to become Queen," she explained.

Peter nodded.

"I was just a young Elfin girl when she left so many years ago," the Queen said as she smiled and motioned to the large open doors nearby. "When she left, my mother took me to the balcony of my room and pointed to your mother riding off into the White Forest. She told me that a son would come along and he would be the one to save our people from the darkness."

Peter's face grew warm.

"And now I am face to face with that promised son," she said. She took his hand and looked into his eyes. "The Son of the Oath."

Peter searched for the words to say, but none came to him.

"The future King of Illiath." She grinned. "And here you are. Safe at last."

"And starving, might I add," Crispin interjected.

"No doubt you are starving," the Queen said. She waved over a servant and began to walk toward another room. "Come this way and we will make sure you are never hungry again."

Her gown was made of deep blue velvet stitched with silver thread. Her braided hair ran down her back. When she walked, she seemed to float along the floor. She was quite the contrast to his appearance, dark with dirt and dried blood from Valbrand's fighters.

"Would it be possible if I could," Peter asked. He didn't want to ruin the moment, but he felt he must, "...change my clothes first and wash?"

"There will be plenty of time to bathe and change into clean attire. But first, we must get you fed. I am certain your father will be joining us very soon." She led him through the grand hall.

"My father?"

She nodded. "We have word he will be arriving very soon."

When they entered the banquet room, Peter instantly smelled fresh flowers, wine, and food. He looked around at the feast, eyes wide open and nostrils flaring. Crispin leaned over and nudged Peter.

"See?" he said. "I told you so!"

# 16 THE RETURN OF THE KING

"Quickly!" Valbrand climbed over the rocks, scraping his knees in a desperate attempt to make his way into the mountain. Only a sliver of sunlight remained on the horizon. "We must hide!"

A few of his guards managed to move along with him, but they each were wounded from the fight.

"Hurry, you fools!" Valbrand turned to see his guards struggling to climb over the large boulders. "We must get to the dragons and escape before—" The caw of several crows circling above interrupted him.

His guards were sprawled out over the boulders, panting as though relieved they had a chance to rest. "What is it, my lord?" one guard huffed.

But Valbrand only watched the crows circling above. "Oh no," he said.

A bright flash of fire appeared before Valbrand. He shielded his eyes.

"And where do you think you're going?" came a familiar voice out of the smoke.

Valbrand slowly lowered his hand from his eyes only to find Lord Bedlam, his master, standing before him with many of his Baroks landing nearby on dragons. Sir William also stood nearby.

Valbrand attempted to bow, but lost his balance. "My lord," he said. "I was just making my way over to the—"

"Silence, you idiot!" Bedlam shouted.

Valbrand lowered his head.

"Because of you, I have lost millions of gold coins, most of my gemstones, and access to the dragons inside that mountain fortress!" Bedlam pointed to the mountain that once housed the Great Arena, Rünbrior prison, and his mines.

"Yes, my lord," Valbrand said and bowed even lower.

"And now because of your ineptness, I have also lost the Prince along with my dragons!" Bedlam shot a line of fire near Valbrand's feet. The warden leapt out of the way and landed hard on the rocky ground.

"I know, my lord, but it wasn't my fault. You see, I was only..."

"Silence!" Bedlam shouted and raised his hand. "You have burdened me one too many times, you old fool. I let your deceptive ways go on too long and now it has cost me much. Take him!"

Three Baroks ran to Valbrand who screamed for his guards. When they moved to assist, Bedlam shot them with his fire and killed them instantly. The Baroks grabbed Valbrand and bound his hands and legs with leather straps. Once they had finished, they ran to their master's side.

"Your guards were lucky. Their death came quickly," Bedlam said as he leaned on his cane. "But you, you old miscreant, will die slowly." He waved and a roar could be heard in the distance as a mammoth black dragon flew in from the south and landed in front of Valbrand, who shook with fright at the sight of the beast. He could smell the stench of sulfur in its breath and its eyes glowed green like emeralds.

"No!" he screamed and tried to wriggle free from the leather straps.

Lord Bedlam stroked the snout of his dragon. "You must pay dearly for the loss of my beloved Scathar. This is one of its offspring. I know it will enjoy eating you as much I would enjoy it," he hissed and his eyes glowed red. "That is, if I were a dragon."

Valbrand's eyes grew large as the black dragon opened its jaws and lunged toward him. Will turned away from the gruesome sight. Then, he watched as Lord Bedlam mounted his dragon with his Baroks following.

"Come, Sir William," Bedlam said. "We will want to miss this scene. We're not barbarians, after all. It's time to see what we can salvage from my fortress."

§

The brightness of the room instantly filled Peter with cheer. He inhaled the scents deeply. Then, Crispin led him over to the banquet tables filled with delicious fruits, pastries, savory meats, and thick puddings. Peter stumbled as though he felt faint.

"Imagine," Crispin said with a mesmerizing voice as he waved his hand, "All you can eat, right here before your eyes. Everything is for you."

Peter nodded, picked up a plate, and made his way to the bounty. *I hope I never wake from this dream*, he thought. *Nøel, I'm sorry you aren't here to see this, my friend.*

Once his plate was full of fruits, meats, cheeses, and pastries, Peter sat down at the table between Simon and Crispin. Annika sat across from him with her bright eyes gleaming. Peter took a moment to observe the people in the banquet room. He spotted General Aluein speaking with the Queen and with some Elfin warriors. Aluein's men conversed freely with other Elves all while sharing the wine and food. Peter leaned back taking in everything he could see. He looked above and saw a crystal chandelier sparkling from the glimpse of daylight coming in through the large windows. He rubbed his eyes as though trying to wake up, but it wasn't necessary. He was already wide awake and his life was back. He lifted a piece of fruit to his mouth and sunk his teeth deep into the skin. When the juices hit his palette, his eyes closed with delight from the savory flavor.

"Delicious, isn't it?" Annika said.

"There are no words," Peter sighed. Simon and Cripsin both patted his back and laughed heartily.

At that moment, the air in the room changed. The murmuring stopped and everyone turned. Suddenly, everyone in the room stood at attention, including General Aluein and the Queen. Then, the other warriors turned and stood at attention. Peter remained seated and continued to chew his food. He looked left and right, watching the scene with curiosity.

"Peter?" He heard a familiar voice coming from behind him. He swallowed. Before he could turn, he saw Simon, Annika, and Crispin staring behind him with wide eyes. It was as though they were seeing a ghost.

"Peter," the voice cracked. That's when Peter felt the hairs on his arms and neck stand up. He inhaled and turned around. When he did, he slowly pushed his chair back and stood. For the first time in many months, Peter gazed into the teary eyes of his father, King Alexander.

Without a word, Peter ran to his father's waiting arms. When the two embraced, Annika wept quietly.

"Father," Peter whispered. He breathed in his father's scent and held onto his body, not wanting to ever let him go. He felt his father's arms tighten around him as he pulled him in even closer. Tears welled up in his eyes.

King Alexander rubbed his son's thin back and wept tears of joy as well as tears of anger at the thought of his only son held prisoner at Rünbrior. He pulled away and looked into Peter's eyes.

"You're alive," he said as he brushed aside Peter's bangs from his eyes. "You're alive and you're here with me now."

Peter nodded. "Yes, Father," he choked back tears.

"You're safe with us now," Alexander said. "My son." He pulled Peter close to him again.

"Yes, father." Peter closed his eyes. "But…father, I'm so sorry."

King Alexander winced and pulled away to look into Peter's face. "Peter, why? Why would you say such a thing? Why are you sorry? None of this was your fault."

Peter looked down. "But I'm sorry that you had to go through all this."

Alexander smiled. "What I endured was nothing compared to what you went through."

For a moment, Peter remembered the time in the forest with the Dragon.

"I should have told you," he mumbled. His eyes looked away. "I should have told you what the Dragon said to me, but I didn't. Instead I chose to go to Knight Training. I chose to ignore what the Dragon said, and—"

"No." King Alexander interrupted. "Don't do this to yourself, Peter. It's over now. You are here with me and you are safe."

Peter embraced his father again. He knew deep inside that his father was right. None of it mattered to Peter. He was with his father again. Nothing else mattered to him.

Together they laughed through their tears.

"You've grown. You're taller now than I remembered." Alexander chuckled. "I'd almost forgotten how much you look like your mother," Alexander said as he closed his eyes.

"I missed you, father," Peter sighed. "I miss our home."

"Your Majesty," General Aluein interrupted. He approached the two. Aluein took Alexander by the shoulders. "So glad you made it safely to the palace, my old friend."

King Alexander gripped Aluein's forearm in a gesture of friendship, then walked to the Queen with Peter at his side. "Your Highness." He bowed. General Aluein remained one of King Alexander's most loyal soldiers and friends. They had fought together in battle and now they were ready to fight again.

Queen Thordis curtsied.

"Welcome, my Lord," she said. She quickly took Alexander's arm. "We are so pleased that you made it out alive and well. Welcome to Vulgaard. My home is your home."

King Alexander, dressed in battle armor, looked into the eyes of all the loyal men and Dwarves present in the room along with the Elves surrounding him. He briefly smiled, but then the smile left his face when he thought of what awaited them.

"I am honored to be here." He placed his hand over his heart. "I am honored to be among all of you." He walked over to the center of the room. "I thank you for being part of this historic moment. I thank you for helping to save my son's life. As you know, we are yet again on the verge of war."

The men nodded.

"But I know, with your help, together we can rid all our lands of this evil dark presence forever."

"Hoorah!" One soldier raised his cup and shouted. The others joined him in raising their cups and drank. Then, everyone applauded enthusiastically at the sight of the King together with his son, Prince Peter. The two embraced yet again. Annika, Simon, and Crispin grinned and clapped enthusiastically.

"To think, just a few short months ago, we thought they were gone forever," Annika said with misty eyes. "And now…"

"Hope," Simon said. He put his arm around her shoulder. "There is hope once again."

Annika nodded and wiped her tears.

§

Queen Esmeralda, her auburn hair pulled back revealing her hazel eyes, stood by the table wearing her dressing gown. Her servants had awakened her in the middle of the night with news of an approaching rider. One female Elf.

"Bring her in." She waved to her servants then leaned on the table as the doors of her chambers opened. "Enter, quickly!"

In the doorway, stood Eris pale from exhaustion.

"Come, sit down before you fall down." the Queen waved to her servant to assist the Elfin girl. "Now, my servants woke me from a sound sleep to tell me that you have arrived with urgent news. What is this news?"

Eris, her leather breastplate still caked with splattered dried blood, blinked a few times as she sat in the wooden chair. Her face was splotched with dirt and grime. She wiped her face with her sleeve, then stood and swiftly removed the sword from the sheath attached to her belt. When she did, the Queen's guards removed their swords and rushed toward her. Eris stopped and turned to them with a look of anger.

"Please," the Queen said to her guards. "Stand down." She looked at the sword in the young Elfin girl's hand. Eris gently laid it on the table before the Queen.

In a voice still raspy from exhaustion, Eris said, "The Sword of Niahm, your majesty."

Queen Esmeralda, daughter of the late King Eulrik, leaned over the sword then looked back at Eris.

"Are you certain this is *the* sword?" she asked.

Eris simply nodded.

The Queen slowly reached out and picked up the sword with both hands. Its heavy weight surprised her. "The Sword of Niahm...the last of the missing swords," her voice cracked, "finally found."

Eris turned to leave. "Wait!" Queen Esmeralda stopped her. "You must rest and eat something. Quickly! Bring her some water and some fruit."

Eris shook her head no. "I must return to the palace at Vulgaard and report to my Queen the news," she said.

"But you are exhausted, please you must—"

Eris shook her head.

"And what of Sir Roland?" the Queen asked.

Eris blinked her weary eyes and lowered her head. "I...I alone survived."

Queen Esmeralda placed the sword on the table and ran her fingers along the hilt. "So tragic, this quest has been so very tragic," she said as she thought of her brother, Sir Ryek. "So many lives lost."

"He died doing what he was called to do," Eris said with defiance. "They all died in the service of their King...or Queen. They would have it no other way. That's what it means to be a knight or a soldier."

"Yes, of course, I understand," Queen Esmeralda said. "I will be sure to inform his father, Lord Algrin."

"Yes, your majesty." Eris bowed then turned to leave. The Queen watched her depart her room then returned her gaze to the sword. She waved her Constable over.

"The last of the missing swords," she said. "Do you know what this means?"

"Yes, your Highness," the Constable said.

Queen Esmeralda had heard of the quest many years before from her father, King Eulrik. The orders from King Alexander angered her father. He never agreed with the quest nor did he swear allegiance to the Oath. She remembered the hurt and despair in her father's eyes as his son and knight, Sir Ryek, rode off on the quest for the missing swords never to be heard from again.

"What to do," she said and began to pace the room. As she did, she saw that the windows were opened. "Quick! Close all the windows and draw the curtains. There are spies everywhere. Lord Bedlam will not rest until he destroys the swords and those who hide them."

She watched as her servants obeyed her orders. "Now, we shall hide this one in a safe place until Isleif arrives. No one can know about this, understand?"

Her Constable nodded.

She took a nearby blue velvet cloth and draped it over the Sword of Niahm. "No one can know," she whispered.

# 17 KNIGHTED

*"I told you I would win,"* Damon hissed and spat as he stood over Sir Nøel's dead body. Peter tried but couldn't move his arms. He knew he was bound by chains with armed guards to his left and right. All he could do was watch Damon stand in victory over his friend's body.

*"You leave him alone!" Peter shouted.*

*Damon approached. "Or what?"*

*"I'll kill you!" Peter's jaw clenched.*

*Damon threw his head back and laughed heartily. "Take him and give him ten lashings," Damon ordered the guards and they grabbed Peter.*

*"I'll get you for this!" Peter shouted as he tugged against the chains that restrained his arms. "I'll get you!" The guards grabbed his arms and turned him around. Then, one guard raised the whip high into the air.*

"Peter." King Alexander shook his son's body, trying to rouse him from sleep.

Peter sat up and looked around the room with frantic eyes. He sat panting and then he tasted blood in his mouth.

"Peter, are you alright?" Alexander asked him with concerned eyes. "You were shouting in your sleep."

But Peter didn't speak. A trickle of blood came from between his lips. Alexander leaned over, took a cloth off the table, and gave it to Peter.

"Your lip is bleeding," he said to Peter, who reached up and felt the blood. "You were having another nightmare."

Peter nodded. "Yes," he said as he wiped his mouth.

"These nightmares continue each night, Peter," Alexander said. "You need your sleep. Perhaps the apothecary can give you something to help."

"No." Peter slid out of the covers. "I'll be alright."

"Are you certain?" Alexander studied his son's face.

Peter nodded.

"Well, it's over now," Alexander said. "Time to wake up and

prepare for your big day."

Peter leaned forward. "Yes, father," he said with distant eyes.

"Come, get washed up and meet us downstairs for a wonderful breakfast." Alexander walked toward the door. "Alright?"

Peter gazed out the large window near his bed in silence.

"Son?"

Peter turned to his father. "Yes father?"

Alexander narrowed his eyes. "Are you sure you're alright?"

Peter threw off the covers and hopped out of bed. He took the robe that lay on a nearby chair and put it on. "Yes, I'll see you downstairs."

"Good." Alexander opened the door. "Today is a day I have waited for since you were born. I am very proud of you, son."

Peter forced a smile. "Thank you, father. I am looking forward to this. I have always wanted to be a knight."

Alexander tilted his head. He seemed to notice the lack of true enthusiasm in Peter's response. When his father left the room, Peter walked to the window overlooking the gardens surrounding the palace. He pictured Damon's face and Nøel's body on the arena floor.

"I'm so sorry, Nøel. I should have stopped Damon. I failed you, my friend." Peter grimaced with pain. He placed his hands over his eyes as though trying to erase the image from his mind.

"I failed you," he sighed. "I hope I don't fail again."

§

The servants waved each guest into the grand hall lit by sconces adorned with candles. Glittering light reflected off the polished floors and walls creating a luminous world for the guests to enter.

Peter stood near the throne wearing his new set of royal armor provided to him by the Queen's smiths. The silver armor was polished to a shine and covered most of his body, making him look years older than he was. Peter stood upright and tall with pride as he awaited his father.

The guests murmured when they saw him, each with eyes wide with excitement and wonder. So many of them had heard the horrific news of Peter's death, now they stood a few feet away from this "ghost" boy who had saved so many lives with his skill and determination. No one present questioned his right to be knighted.

Simon and Crispin entered the room dressed in their new tunics and brown suede trousers. But this time, Annika did not wear the boyish clothing. Instead of trousers and a tunic, she was once again dressed in a fine gown of bluest silk that reached to the floor. Her hair, still shorter than she'd like, was brushed to a shine and atop her head was her silver crown with one large sapphire in the middle.

"You look beautiful," Simon said to her. Crispin rolled is eyes.

When Peter saw her regal form enter the room, he inhaled quickly as though trying to catch his breath. His reaction did not go unnoticed and many of the guests gestured and commented. Peter felt his face grow warm with embarrassment. He swallowed hard and gathered his composure as Annika made her way to the front. When her sparkling blue eyes met Peter's eyes, she winked playfully. Peter felt himself smile, and, for a moment, he felt like himself again.

And then, the trumpets announced the start of the moment in Peter's life that he knew he would never forget. Although this moment was not at the Crow Valley Knight Training camp nor was it in his father's palace at Illiath as he had imagined it for so many years, it was still a momentous occasion that would live in his memory forever. He only wished his mother was there. And, deep down, he longed for his horse, Titan, to be with him.

The large wooden doors swung open and King Alexander entered. All his knights and soldiers stood at attention when he walked by. Peter couldn't help but stand at attention. His father's presence demanded it.

Before he knew it, his father was before him wearing his polished armor and scarlet cape. On his forehead was the crown of Illiath once worn by Peter's forefathers. Peter's mind raced and he grew dizzy from the excitement. He found himself gazing around the room, realizing it was the same room where his mother once stood when she was told the news of her betrothal to his father. He looked up at the ceiling painted with detailed scenes depicting the day the Dragon swore the Oath with the rulers of men and Elves. Peter closed his eyes for a second or two, trying to remain calm amongst the history and pomp.

At that moment, the Queen was led into the hall by her son, Thurdin. Both wore silk attire and silver crowns on their brows. Once Queen Thordis sat on her crystal throne adorned with gemstones, the ceremony began. Peter turned and followed his father with his eyes as the King stood before the throne. The crowd grew deathly still as King Alexander placed his hand on Peter's shoulder.

"Kneel," he said.

Peter obeyed and, with his head bowed in humble adoration before his father, he knelt on the small stool before him.

*This can't be happening*, he thought. Sir Nøel's face came to his mind. He wished his friend could be with him. *Am I dreaming, Nøel? If so, don't wake me.*

Peter exhaled.

*I always dreamed of being a knight,* Peter thought. *But now I know I am meant to be more than just a knight. I am meant to be King.*

Queen Thordis spoke first. "Do you, King Alexander, affirm that Prince Peter of Illiath has grown in virtue, honor, and chivalry, the hallmarks of a knight of the royal realm and lineage to the throne?"

King Alexander turned to her grace. "May it please this court and your majesty that I am able to affirm that Prince Peter of Illiath has achieved virtue, chivalry, and honor having heard the counsel of his peers and through my own certain knowledge."

King Alexander then turned to his son kneeling before him.

"Why so regal?" Crispin whispered to Simon.

"This ceremony is different because Peter is not only to be a Royal Knight, but he is heir to the throne," Simon answered. Crispin nodded and continued to watch the scene.

"His achievements and conduct while held prisoner at Rünbrior have revealed this affirmation to be true," Alexander said and smiled at his son.

"This court thanks you for your counsel, King Alexander," the Queen said. She raised her hand. "Sword bearers, bring forth the Sword of Alexander."

Peter raised his head to spy the Sword bearer. He approached carrying a sword draped in red velvet. Another chill ran through Peter's body.

"What's this?" Annika asked Simon.

"This is the sword that the King will use to dub Peter a knight in his realm," Simon whispered. "It is draped in red to symbolize the blood shed by previous Knights of Alexander's Realm.

"So moving." Annika smiled and clasped her hands together.

Alexander removed the cloth and reached for the sword of his fathers. He raised it high as the light reflected off the glistening blade.

"Prince Peter," he began. "You have been deemed fit for this high rank of knighthood that many others have held with honor, chivalry, and virtue in the service of their King, and in defense of the Oath between rulers and the Dragon of Promise. You have been deemed fit by your peers, this court, and by myself, King Alexander of Illiath."

Peter swallowed hard.

"Prince Peter, do you swear by all that you hold sacred and true to honor the service of your King and to uphold the Oath sworn by your fathers?"

Peter inhaled. The words from his father hit him like fire from a dragon when he realized what was being asked of him and what had been asked of so many other men who came before him, men like Nøel who had willingly sacrificed their freedom and lives in service to the King. Peter raised his eyes.

"I will," he swore knowing in his heart that he truly meant it.

"That you will be honorable to your peers in all lands far and near?"

"I will." Peter thought of his friends.

"That you will conduct yourself with honor drawing your sword only for a just and noble cause? That you will fight for the honor of the weak and defend the defenseless for the benefit and greater glory of the throne?"

"I swear." Peter swallowed as he watched his father hold the Sword of Alexander out in front of his body. It hovered over Peter.

"Then, having sworn these solemn oaths in the presence of your peers, this court, and your King, with the powers bestowed upon me, with right of arms," his father said with shiny eyes, "I, King Alexander of Illiath, do knight thee, Sir Peter, Prince of Illiath, Knight of the Royal Order of Illiath, and future King."

Peter bowed his head as his father tapped his right shoulder with the blade of the sword. "Once for honor," Alexander said and then touched Peter's left shoulder, "Twice for duty."

Peter smiled when he realized the ceremony was almost over.

"And thrice for chivalry. Rise, Sir Peter," Alexander ordered. He grinned and choked back tears. "My son."

When Peter stood, Queen Thordis approached him. She waved over her servant who carried a silver tray. The Queen reached over and took a chain from the tray, then placed it over Peter's head. It rested on his new tunic right over his heart.

"Accept this chain passed from knight to knight. Each link in this chain symbolizes a knight who has served. For each knight is a link that joins the kingdoms together in honor and truth," she said.

Peter bowed before the Queen.

"May you always endeavor to be that link, Sir Peter," she smiled.

Next, his father waved over a servant who carried something covered with a purple velvet cloth. Alexander removed the cloth to reveal a magnificent sword with a long thin blade decorated with an intricate filigree design and a gold hilt. Peter's eyes grew wide.

"What a sword!" Crispin said and tugged Simon's arm.

King Alexander took the sword and held it in front of Peter whose eyes studied every detail in the weapon.

"In the name of King Aléon, King Illiath, and the Oath of our fathers, guardian of the realm, sworn to protect all who live within its borders. Now that you have sworn allegiance to the Oath, and are willing to die for it, if need be, it is time you had your very own sword."

"Father," Peter whispered as he took the hilt into his hand. He turned the weapon over in his hand admiring its beauty. "Is it really mine?"

"Now that's a sword of a king!" Simon nudged Crispin who nodded enthusiastically.

Peter felt a shiver run through his body.

"Sir Peter, Prince of Illiath, and future heir to the throne," King Alexander said. "My son, my only son. I present to you the Sword of Peter."

Peter looked into his father's face, a face he knew so well. He remembered back to his time in the prison when he wondered if he would ever see his father again. All his life, his father was his hero. He had longed to have his father's attention so much so that he had risked his life to enter the Dragon Forest to slay the Dragon. And now, just over three years later, he stood before his father as a new knight in the Royal Realm of King Alexander. His dream had finally come true.

Peter held the sword and bowed his head respectfully to his father. And then, he embraced his father as the guests roared their approval.

"I'm so proud of you," King Alexander whispered into Peter's ear.

They parted and laughed heartily with joy. Peter realized he had never known true happiness until that moment. He turned to face the crowd as they applauded and cheered the scene. Simon, Crispin, and Annika rushed toward Peter. Simon shook his hand as Crispin patted his back. Annika wrapped her arms around his neck nearly sending him to the ground.

"Hey!" Peter chuckled. "Watch the new sword."

Annika giggled and Peter gently touched her chin.

"Can you believe it?" she laughed. She picked up the gold chain around Peter's neck and admired it. "It wasn't too long ago we were all enjoying our graduation ceremony thinking we'd never see each other again. And here you are, a Royal Knight!"

"Yes, here we are," Crispin said. "Together again. This day makes all those times we rode for our lives through the forest without food on those painful saddles almost worth it." He shook Peter's hand. They all laughed.

Each guest approached Peter to congratulate him. Alexander watched the celebration for a few moments, then made his way over to Theo who watched the scene from the entrance. He leaned on a wooden staff with a pensive look.

"Hello my old friend," Alexander said. "Why won't you come in and join us?"

Theo smiled a thin smile, but in his eyes Alexander could see concern. "The time has come, Alexander," he said with a more serious tone. "The darkness waits for no one."

Alexander looked away and nodded.

"We knew it would come," Theo said as he leaned on his staff.

Alexander exhaled. "Yes, indeed," he said as he watched his son celebrate with his friends. "Tomorrow morning we will meet and discuss recent events."

Theo understood. "Yes, in my chambers, first thing in the morning." He turned and quickly ambled down the hall out of sight.

"But tonight, we celebrate," Alexander said. He blinked back tears. "Talk of war can wait." He sighed heavily before he joined the rest of the celebration.

§

Sir William leaned forward on the table taking in everything that was told to him that night. His fingers gripped the marble tabletop until the knuckles were white. His arms shook as the anger rose within him and he overturned the table. His chiseled jaw clenched. He squinted his eyes and his brown hair was matted to his face with sweat.

"What did you say?" he asked through clenched teeth. A vein in his forehead bulged.

"Sir, our spies have relayed the news that Prince Peter was knighted in the palace at Vulgaard," the soldier said with eyes far off.

Sir William, once a newly dubbed knight in King Alexander's realm and Peter's dearest friend, became the proclaimed Duke of Illiath by Lord Bedlam as a way to steal the kingdom for himself. While under the same spell that once bewitched Sir Peregrine and Lord Caragon years before, Will had succeeded in taking over the kingdom at Illiath. He began to breathe heavily as though the oxygen had disappeared from the room as he thought of Peter's potential rise to power.

"No!" He overturned the table, sending maps and papers flying to the floor. The soldier backed away from the fury.

"How can this be?" Will shouted. "He was supposed to die in that prison!"

The soldier remained silent.

Will turned away and strode to the window overlooking the

courtyard of Hildron. The black rock below was lit only by the fires burning from within the two towers near the castle.

"How can this be," he murmured to himself again. "I was told that boy would remain in Rünbrior forever!" Beads of sweat rolled down his face.

"Yes, sir," the soldier said.

"Was this part of the plan?" Will said to himself. "Bedlam must have known of Peter's escape."

Will ran out of the room and headed downstairs to his master's dungeon. He could feel the heat from the fires even before he reached the cave entrance.

There, in the dungeon at Hildron, Will watched the scene of Lord Bedlam casting yet another magic spell on a poor captured creature. Will raised his hand over his face to protect it from the intense winds and debris. Once the spell was cast, Will watched the soldiers chain the Zadok beast and dragged it away to its cell in the cave. Nearby, Will watched the Baroks hammer the blackened metal swords into a crude shape with jagged edges. More weapons of war lined the cave floor by the Baroks as they feverishly worked. Shields, spears, and swords, along with helmets and breastplates made of the same black metal, piled up inside the dungeon.

Lord Bedlam wiped his brow with a handkerchief he kept inside his breast pocket. He turned to see Will admiring the thorough work of the Baroks.

"Leave us," Lord Bedlam ordered his workers. They hastily exited the premises without making eye contact.

When he heard the voice, Will turned to see his master staring at him.

"How can this be?" Will shouted at him. "You told me Peter would—"

Bedlam raised his hand and silenced Will.

"Enough," he said. He meandered over to a table littered with half-finished swords and placed his dragonhead cane on top of it, then he methodically turned to Will. "All is happening as I have planned. I have no time for your complaints or questions. Trust, Will. You must learn to trust."

"But how?" Will shouted again. "You planned Peter's escape?"

"I knew it would occur, yes," Bedlam said as he inspected his sharp nails. Then he looked intently at his impatient protégé. "Everything is happening as I knew it would, Will. You must trust me."

Will continued to breathe hard. He smirked as though struggling to believe his master.

"But he was knighted!" He slammed his fist down on the table. "He is now a Royal Knight!"

Bedlam shrugged. "And this concerns me because…"

Will turned away as though disgusted. He ran his hand through his hair and growled.

"Jealous, are you?" Bedlam chuckled.

Will shook his head.

Lord Bedlam squinted as though trying to understand Will's reaction to the news. "What does it matter? He is the Prince. Of course he would be knighted by his father. It is of no concern to us whether he becomes a knight or not. What does concern us is preventing him from entering the Dragon Forest. We are to continue preparing for battle. King Alexander made his way to Vulgaard and now the preparations begin. Understand?"

Will stood with his back to his master. His shoulders heaved.

Lord Bedlam lifted his cane from the table and admired it. The red ruby eyes glistened. "I need to know that I can count on you, Will."

Suddenly, the air in the room grew excessively cold. Will could feel the cold on the back of his neck. He rubbed it and turned to his master. Bedlam's eyes glowed red. Will gasped then composed himself.

"Yes, my Lord," Will said. "You can count on me. I will continue to prepare for the battle."

Just then a roar could be heard from deep within a large pit. The earth beneath his feet trembled and Will leaned on the table for balance. The roar was unlike anything Will had ever heard before.

"Good." Bedlam turned, his black cape flowing behind him. He stopped at the entrance to his chambers off the dungeon. "I need you, Will. You have a major part in all of this. And you will be greatly rewarded for your hard work."

Will nodded.

Bedlam turned and gave Will one last glance.

"Patience," he said as he exited. "You will have your time in the sun, I promise."

Will's eyes lowered.

"I am a man of my word." Bedlam disappeared into his chambers.

When Will returned to his room again, he made his way to the bookshelf. He ran his fingers over the tomes as though searching for a specific title. He stopped at one book and removed it.

"Théadril," he read.

He opened the book and turned to a familiar page. Then, he closed it, tossed it onto the table, and returned to the large window.

"When will it be my time?" Will said to no one there.

# 18 SECRETS REVEALED

Two days after the ceremony, Peter lay sleeping on a large roomy bed covered with blankets. His breathing was deep, but his limbs jerked from time to time as though he were dreaming.

King Alexander quietly entered the room and drew back the thick curtains, letting in streams of warm sunshine that filled the room. Peter's eyes blinked as he returned from his dreamscape to the reality of the moment. When his eyes opened, his entire body jerked awake and he sat up with wide frightened eyes, panting as though trying to breathe. The sudden movement startled Alexander.

"Where am I?" Peter asked with wide eyes. "Where are the guards? Nøel?"

Alexander came to his son's side and rested his hand on his shoulder. "Son," he said. "You're safe. You're with *me* now."

Peter, still unsure of his surroundings, continued to breathe heavily.

Alexander sat on the bed and tried to make eye contact with his son. "Peter," he said. "You're in the palace at Vulgaard."

Peter finally looked at him and his breathing slowed.

"It's alright, now," his father smiled.

Peter nodded. "How long have I slept?"

"Almost an entire day," Alexander said. He walked over to a chair. "We let you rest."

Peter rubbed his face with hands, trying to remove the sleep from his eyes and the nightmare from his mind.

"Here are some clean clothes. Get dressed and come eat some breakfast. We have a lot to discuss today." Alexander made his way to the door.

"Am I safe now, Father?" Peter asked with concern in his eyes.

Alexander cocked his head as though confused by the question. "Of course," he grinned. "All is well."

Peter looked away with listless eyes.

"Come, get dressed." Alexander closed the door.

§

When Peter finally made his way to the dining hall, he spotted Theo standing near his father who sat drinking fresh juice. The two were in the middle of a conversation.

"Ah, there he is," Alexander said. He motioned for the servants to assist Peter in sitting at the table. "Come eat all that you want. Try this juice. It is squeezed from a melon. You'll find it delicious, really."

Peter motioned for some juice. When he received it, he drank it down quickly. Then he picked up some of the biscuits and grapes. He gobbled them down almost without chewing. Next, he reached for the porridge.

"Slow down, son," Alexander said. "You'll get sick if you eat too quickly. We don't want it all to come back up."

Peter realized he was rushing to finish as if the prison guards would burst into the room at any minute and order him to the arena to fight again. He closed his eyes, exhaled, and sat back.

"Old habits, I guess," he said with no expression and slid the bowl of porridge aside.

"It's good to see you up and about, Peter," Theo said. He made his way to the boy and took out his dragon pipe. "When you are finished, we have much to discuss, so—"

"I'm finished," Peter interrupted. He leaned in and looked intently at Theo's pipe.

"But…there is still more food to enjoy." Alexander waved his hand over the food before them.

Peter wiped his mouth with the linen napkin, stood, and pushed his chair in. "No, I am finished. Where did you get that pipe?"

Theo looked at Alexander with a raised brow as though puzzled. The smoke from his pipe rose around him. Theo turned the pipe around so that Peter could see the details in the carvings.

"May I see it?" Peter asked. Theo handed it to him. When Peter took the pipe, he carried it to the window, and carefully studied it in the light. "This is amazing. Where did you get this?'

Theo narrowed his eyes. "It was a gift," he said, "from an old friend."

Theo looked at Alexander and raised an eyebrow. He seemed

concerned.

"Well, I really like it. How come you never showed it to me before at Illiath?" Peter handed it back to his former tutor. "You always used that boring pipe made of wood."

Theo scratched his beard. "That's good question, Peter."

Alexander cleared his throat. "And it's always a good to ask questions."

Theo smirked at Alexander.

"Because that's how we learn." Alexander stood and threw his napkin down in his chair.

"And I have some questions for both of you, that I'd like answered," Peter said.

Alexander motioned for the two to follow him. "Well, then, let's discuss things in the next room."

Peter followed Theo and the King into the adjacent room flooded with light coming in from the large windows. Peter walked over to the many book cases that lined the walls. He saw leatherbound books with strange Elfin titles that he couldn't recognize. In his mind raced all the questions about his mother, Peregrine, and Lord Bedlam that he wanted to ask Theo and his father. He turned to see them standing as though waiting for his questions.

"How did my mother die?" he asked without expression.

King Alexander turned to Theo.

Theo chewed on his pipe, studying how to answer. He blew some smoke and motioned for Peter to come sit at the round table in the center of the room. Peter obeyed, pulled out a chair, and sat. He leaned forward on the table.

"Well?" he asked.

His father sat next to him.

Theo narrowed his eyes as though trying to read Peter's mind. He mumbled something to himself while puffing on his pipe. His long white beard hung down to the middle of his chest and his grey eyes twinkled.

Then, a slight smile came across his face. "Your mother sat at that exact table many years ago, asking me some interesting questions herself," he said. "Did you know that?"

Peter squinted then turned to his father who looked down at the table surface, listening.

"Yes," Theo said as he paced before them. "She was slightly older than you are now." He chuckled.

"I had no idea," Peter said.

"Hmmm," Theo said. "There is so much you do not know about,

Peter."

Alexander looked up.

"I suppose it is time you knew the answers," Theo said. "Yes. It is the appointed time." He stopped pacing, placed his pipe onto the table in a gentle manner, and then he walked away from the table.

Peter waited in confusion. He looked at his father who stared at Theo, then nodded his approval.

When Peter's eyes turned to his former teacher, Theo took hold of his robe, raised his arms, and spun around. The room filled with powerful wind that caused Peter to turn aside. Instantly, before Peter, Theo transformed into the White Dragon right there in the middle of the large room.

§

Peter fell out of his chair, scooted across the floor away from the dragon, and hid behind another table. Chairs were overturned, books lay scattered on the shiny tiled floor, and papers fluttered to the ground. Peter imagined he was in the Great Arena at Rünbrior facing a fire-breathing dragon. He raised his hands to cover his face. "Nøel!" he yelled.

The White Dragon's talons clicked on the tile surface and its long leathery wings spread open. Instead of a growl, it let out a sort of squawk. The noise brought Peter out of his trance. He cautiously peeked around the table with sweat running down his temples.

Peter could see the White Dragon was a lithe Wyvern covered in glittering pearly white scales. King Alexander stood and made his way over to the large beast. The White Dragon lowered his snout to meet him.

Peter lifted his hand. "Father!" he shouted. "No! Stay away from it."

Alexander reached up and began to gently stroke the snout of the White Dragon. It closed its eyes as though it enjoyed the petting. "There is nothing to be afraid of, son," Alexander said. "It is still Theo, only in dragon form."

But Peter remained hidden. He peeked around the table and watched as his father continued to stroke the dragon. It folded his wings against its body.

"Peter," his father motioned toward him. "Come here."

Peter slowly stood and made his way over to his father. His eyes never left the White Dragon before him. As he approached, he gazed into the dragon's eyes. They were no longer the dull grey color of Theo's eyes, but were a sparkling crystal blue. They seemed to call to him. Peter felt a warmth wash over him as he stood before the beast. He reached out. The dragon lowered its head and met Peter's hand.

"Is it you, Theo?" Peter asked. He turned to his father who stood next to him.

Alexander nodded.

"But how can this be?" Peter asked. And as soon as the words left his mouth, the White Dragon transformed back into Theo. Peter leapt back from the sudden movement.

Theo stood panting before Peter and Alexander once again. He straightened out his robe, made his way to the table, picked up his pipe, and placed it back into his mouth. "Well?" he asked. "I suppose we should start at the beginning…"

§

"So, you see, Peter," Theo said after sharing the long story about Queen Laurien and the Dragon of Bedlam. "It was your mother who helped Bedlam, she helped him create the swords that were given to the ten rulers, and she was the one who made them as the secret weapon to end Lord Bedlam's power."

Peter looked away, deep in thought, taking in everything that he had heard.

Theo tapped the table with his finger. "And I tutored her here in this very room when she was a young girl," he said with a slight grin, looking around at the familiar surroundings.

But Peter didn't seem to be listening. His eyes grew trance-like as he made his way around the room.

"And that's why he killed her?" Peter asked.

Theo looked at Alexander. "Who?" he asked Peter.

"Lord Bedlam," Peter said.

"He deceived her into thinking she was safe," Alexander said.

"But Sir Peregrine," Peter said. "His name was written in the book about Théadril. I saw his name written in the margin when I read about my mother."

Alexander looked over Theo as if to ask for help.

"Why?" Peter asked. "Why was his name written there? What part did he play in all this?"

Theo puffed on his pipe and thought hard how to answer. He motioned for Peter to sit down.

"Peter, Lord Bedlam knew how to look into men's hearts. He still does. He can see who is weak and full of anger, rage, and jealousy. He searched Peregrine's heart and saw that the man was foolishly jealous of your father. So, Bedlam was able to deceive Peregrine into joining him to trick your father...and your mother."

Peter leaned forward in his chair.

"And so, he was used to hurt your mother," Theo said.

That far off look came across Theo's face yet again. Peter could tell he was thinking back to the time.

"I was speaking with your mother near her bedchamber. She was very concerned for your safety. She suspected Peregrine, but did not know how to approach your father with her suspicions," he said.

Alexander looked away.

"Once we finished conversing there in the hall, I made my way toward the secret passage," he said. "And that's when I saw Peregrine enter the hall. He did not see me, so I hid behind a pillar and listened..."

*"What is it?" Queen Laurien asked him. She folded her arms across her body. I knew she was uncomfortable. Deep down, she knew Peregrine was in love with her.*

*"Your majesty," Peregrine started. "Please, you must listen to me. You know what I have been ordered to do," Peregrine said to her. His face contorted. "But..."*

*"You have second thoughts," she told him. "Then leave. Ride away, if you must, far away. Never come back."*

*"He'll find me. He has ways." Peregrine turned away. "And you know he'll never stop until he has hurt you completely."*

*"Then do what you must," she said. Peregrine pulled out a vial of liquid and handed it to the Queen.*

*"This is for the boy to drink," he said as he placed the vial into her hand. He squeezed her fingers then pressed her hand to his chest. "I am to poison him, but I cannot do this." He looked longingly into her eyes, but the Queen pulled away.*

*"You and I know Bedlam's magic cannot kill the Prince as long as the Dragon lives." Laurien held up the vial. "And the Oath remains."*

*"This eilixir will only paralyze him," Peregrine said, "For the rest of his days. This way, Peter can never enter the Dragon Forest with the swords."*

*"And Bedlam wins." Queen Laurien said.*

*Peregrine lowered his gaze.*

*"That is not Bedlam's main plan," she said as she inspected the lavender potion inside the vial. "I was meant to find out. He knows I would gladly sacrifice my life for my son."*

*Peregrine nodded. "The elixir contains dragon blood."*

*"And that means death to anyone with Elfin blood in them. He would prefer that I die instead," she said. "That's been his plan all along."*

*"Will your death appease him?" Peregrine asked.*

*"For a time," she said. "But he will find other ways to attack Peter to keep him from entering the forest."*

*"There has to be another way," Sir Peregrine reached out to caress the Queen's cheek but she turned away.*

*"No," she said. "Leave me." She turned and walked down the hall into her chambers and Peregrine walked away into darkness.*

"Literally, and figuratively," Theo said. "Peregrine finally succumbed to the darkness and became pure evil in intent."

Peter studied Theo's eyes as they shone with tears. "And then what happened to my mother?" Peter asked Theo.

"To protect you and to ensure that you would live to enter the forest, she drank the potion instead," he said. "And over a few days, she became very ill." He gazed over at Alexander who was looking at the window as he listened. Theo knew it was difficult for the King to remember those final days of his beloved Queen.

"She called for me near the end of her life to tell me everything that Peregrine said," he continued.

She was frail and near death when I sat with her on her bed. She insisted that we be alone. She took my hand into hers.

*"I still had so much to teach Peter. You will have to teach him about the ways of the dragons and...the compass. But promise me," she said. "Promise me, dearest friend, that you will not tell Alexander about all this until the right time."*

*"Your majesty, please, I cannot keep such information from—"*

*"You must," she insisted. "You and I know what will happen. He will act rashly."*

*"So...I promised her," Theo said. He gazed down at the floor as though ashamed. "And then, she continued..."*

*"If Alexander discovers this, he will go mad with revenge. He will risk his life and go after Lord Bedlam," she tried to sit up, but in her weakened condition, she couldn't. "Don't you understand?"*

*"I begged her to get some rest, but there was urgency in her voice as if she knew she didn't have much time left," Theo explained. "She asked me to protect you and I assured her I would."*

*"It will be difficult for Peter to hear all this about his mother, but you must tell him everything at the appointed time. When he has shown that he is ready, then you must tell him, but not before that,"* she insisted. *"Because I am half Elf, I will be able to come to him even from the afterlife. I will be there for him even in death."*

Theo stopped talking and waited for Peter's reaction. He could see tears forming in the boy's eyes. Peter leaned back in his chair as he took in his mother's words.

"That's when she handed me the golden compass," Theo went on. "She begged me to give it to you. She explained that this little trinket would help you find me, find your way home, and always remind you of the Dragon Forest."

Peter's mind raced to when he first used the compass in his father's palace at Illiath to find Theo in his secret library.

"I returned to Vulgaard until your father sent for me," Theo said. "And then I returned as a tutor and remained hidden until I received the sign."

"What was the sign?" Peter asked.

"When you entered the Dragon Forest." Theo smiled. "That one act set off everything. That's when we all knew it was time."

Peter remembered back to when he first entered the forest and encountered the Dragon. Peter thought back to how Bedlam had used Lord Caragon as a way to attack his father, the Dragon of the Forest, and himself. He closed his eyes as he remembered his abduction in the desert and the torture of being alone in the dank prison cell at Rünbrior.

"You see, your father had entered the Dragon Forest when he was a boy, but the Dragon did not appear to him. Because he was the heir to King Aléon, his life was spared; however, your father was not the chosen one to usher in the time of man...the time of peace."

Peter nodded.

"That was you, Peter," Alexander said.

"But why," he asked. "Why didn't my mother just tell my father all this and throw the potion away? Couldn't we have escaped? Couldn't they have hidden me away? Why did she have to drink it? Bedlam continues to pursue me."

Theo sat with Peter. "My boy, her death was what Bedlam wanted all along, but he could never bring himself to kill her. He wanted everything around her to die in order to hurt her. He wanted to cause her great pain. Peter, Bedlam knows you are the prize...the heir to the throne...the only one who may enter in the forest and destroy him. You represent all that was good in her and Alexander. So, he commanded Peregrine to give you the potion. Bedlam could never get near you. The

Dragon has made sure of that. And, if you drank it, you could never enter the Dragon Forest."

"But Peregrine couldn't do it," Peter said. He ran his finger along the table. "He couldn't bring himself to harm a five-year-old boy."

Theo shook his head. "No, thank goodness."

"Peregrine knew your mother would take the potion instead, yet be able to come to you at certain times when needed," Theo said. "And he hoped that your mother's death would satisfy Bedlam's lust for revenge."

"Did it?" Peter looked up.

Theo shook his head. "When he was told of her death, his rage was seen and felt all the way from here at Vulgaard. Fire belched from Hildron for days, the rock below our feet trembled, and the rains poured. He blamed your father and the Dragon of the Forest for her death. He realized you were alive and could still enter the forest and sever the spell. His hatred grew even more."

"So, Bedlam had his revenge on my mother and because of her, I was spared..." Peter stood. "She gave her life for me, just as the Dragon gave its life for me once."

Alexander finally turned around and walked over to Peter. He placed his hands on his son's shoulders.

"Looking back, I can see why she did it," Alexander said. "In time, I came to understand. He would have hounded her all her life."

Peter looked into his father's eyes, gleaming with tears. "Did you get to say goodbye to her?"

Alexander nodded.

"Did I?" Peter asked with shiny eyes.

"Yes, son," Alexander said. "When it was time, we went to see her as she lay in bed. She held your small face in her hands. She whispered that she loved you and would always love you."

"She came to see me," Peter said. "In the prison."

Alexander smiled.

"She came to me in a vision." Peter blinked back the tears in his eyes. "She told me that she loved me and that she would always be there for me."

"And she will." Alexander sat next to his son. "Always."

Together, father and son sat, remembering the Queen. Theo puffed on his pipe.

"That is why you saw Sir Peregrine's name written in the margin of that book, my boy," Theo said. "When he heard of your mother's death, his heart blackened and he became more susceptible to Bedlam's magic spell. His anger toward your father grew. His hatred made it easier to follow along with Bedlam and eventually, with Lord Caragon. He was promised a great estate and power. He vowed to kill the Dragon for its scales once and for all."

Peter walked over to Theo. "So Lord Bedlam remains part man, part dragon?"

Theo narrowed his eyes. "Yes," he said. "Until those swords are brought together, the Anifornum spell remains."

"And if we gather the swords together in the Dragon Forest, then the spell will be broken and he will return to his true form?" Peter asked.

Theo nodded. "Yes, except..."

"Except what?"

"Except it is not *we* who must do this deed." Theo pointed to himself and Alexander.

Peter furrowed his brow as though confused. He looked at his father then back at Theo.

"Then who must do this deed if not us?"

"*You* must do this deed, Peter." Theo leaned forward as he spoke. "You and you alone must do this deed."

Peter's eyes grew large.

"That was the caveat your mother put into the spell when she forged those swords," he continued. "She warned that you, the heir, are the one and only, the Son of the Oath. The only one who can take the swords into the forest and end this reign of Lord Bedlam forever."

Peter's face grew pale.

"Me?" he asked. "Me *alone*?"

Just then, Peter heard the squawk of a bird. He turned to see the White Owl perched on the railing of the balcony outside the room. It flapped its wings and fluffed its feathers with its beak. Peter grinned when he saw it.

"You are truly never alone, Peter," Theo said.

"Yes, and we will be there with you in battle, son," his father said. "All of us...from here to the sea. We will join forces to ensure those swords reach their final destiny."

He placed his hand on his son's shoulder.

"That's why she sacrificed her life," Peter said. "She knew it had to be me."

Theo nodded. "And it will be you, Peter. You were born for this time. This is your time."

Peter gazed out the large window into the yellow eyes of the owl. He wanted to go to it, but it flew away. A sudden heaviness came over Peter as he thought about what was waiting out there for him.

# 19 HILDRON

The castle at Hildron, once a glorious palace carved from the Black Hills by Lord Hildron for his son, Ronahn. Now the home of Lord Bedlam's twisted magic spells. The servant navigated the darkened halls, carefully carrying the tray of refreshments. When he came to the door of Lord Bedlam's chambers, he paused, straightened out the contents on the tray, then slightly tapped on the wooden door.

"Enter," ordered the voice from behind the door. The servant obeyed.

Inside the room, the servant could see a figure standing near Lord Bedlam, but the shadows concealed the identity. The servant watched as the mysterious figure walked over to the window and exited the room. Whoever it was disappeared from view. Sir William approached from the other side of the room and took his place next to Bedlam. The servant shivered as though he felt a sudden coldness across his skin.

"Your refreshments, my Lord," he said.

"Set them down then leave us," Bedlam said. His voice was unusually low.

The servant did as he was told then made his way to the door.

"But now what shall we do?" Will asked as the servant shut the door.

Lord Bedlam made his way over to a bookcase, pressed one of the books, then stood back as the case swung open revealing a hidden passageway. He motioned for his protégé to follow him. Will obeyed and together the two headed down the labyrinth of steps. Finally, they stood at a doorway. Bedlam pushed open the door and Will saw, for the first time, Lord Bedlam's private wizard room filled with stacks of books, papers, and glass beakers of strange liquid. There were dragon skulls and dragon scales scattered along the floor.

A chill ran through Will's body as he entered the large room lit by torches and a massive fireplace with an opening at least seven feet high.

The heat was overwhelming at first, so Will removed his cloak and flung it onto a nearby chair. He watched Bedlam set his cane down and approached a black cauldron in a corner of the room.

"Come this way, Will," Bedlam said.

Will hesitated for a moment, then made his way over to the cauldron. He peeked into the liquid churning inside the cauldron.

"What is it?" he asked. Suddenly, the liquid boiled, and for a moment Will saw images in the liquid.

"The present," Bedlam spoke. He waved his hand over the liquid and it stirred even more. "And the future."

Across the liquid came images of many Baroks marching in unison across the plains. They carried torches and wore the thick black armor made in the dungeons of Hildron. And then came images of a great army heading over the plains.

"Is this the army you are building here at Hildron?" Will asked.

"Oh no, Will," Bedlam said. "You are mistaken."

Will studied the images closer still.

"For this is your army," Bedlam said.

Will looked at him.

"Yes. This is the army I have created for you."

Will listened intently.

"You will rule over this army and lead it into battle with none other than King Alexander himself." Bedlam waved his hand over the liquid yet again.

Will leaned in further, but then stepped back as an image came into focus. But this image was not of an army of Baroks. The image was of a giant creature that appeared to be part man and part creature. A mutant creature unlike anything Will had ever seen before.

"What is that?" Will asked with wide eyes filled with fear.

Bedlam grinned, revealing his small sharp teeth. "That is Magog."

Will studied his master's face for a moment.

"My most prized creation of all," Bedlam said.

In the image, the great horned creature roared and spewed fire at the armies of men many feet beneath it. It towered over the trees of the Dragon Forest leaning on its hind legs that resembled those of a bull steer. Its torso, massive in strength, was that of a man, but its horned head was shaped like a dragon's head. It razed the men with its massive arms as though they were but toys carved from wood.

Bedlam chuckled loudly at the sight of so many men falling to the creature's power. "Oh this will be a great day," Bedlam said as the liquid stirred some more. "To think we are only days away from the end of Alexander's line, the Dragon Forest, and the Dragon itself."

He turned to face Will.

"For this creature, Will, contains all my power…all the magic I have learned these many years," he said to his protégé. "This creature, Will, is the one."

Will narrowed his eyes. "The one?"

Bedlam nodded and walked away from the cauldron. He picked up his cane.

"Yes, the one to defeat the Dragon of the Forest forever," he said. And then he motioned for Will to follow him through another doorway. Will picked up his cloak and followed his master.

"This creature will stand guard at the entrance of the Dragon Forest to prevent Peter from entering," Bedlam said as he walked. He raised his cane high. "This creature will prevent Prince Peter from entering the forest. And, finally, I will see this creature burn the Dragon Forest to the ground."

Will looked away.

"As you can see, Will, we've much to do," Bedlam said as he walked down the corridor. "Worrying about a boy recently knighted in Vulgaard is futile at best. You have much bigger things to worry about, young Will."

Will listened.

"Peter's future is nothing to be concerned with. His time will soon come to an end." Bedlam once again turned to his protégé. "You have an army to lead, an enemy to battle, and a future kingdom to rule."

Will narrowed his eyes, infatuated with what he was hearing. "Yes, My Lord."

Bedlam led Will toward the dungeon where many Baroks continued to hammer steel into Bedlam's magic armor.

"I suggest you get to work," he said.

The Baroks stopped and looked up at their master when they heard his voice. Will stepped forward. He surveyed the area filled with hundreds of Baroks working feverishly side-by-side on the armor, swords, shields, and spears. They bowed when they saw him. In the back were the Zadoks chained to the rock wall. They growled their approval. Deep in the caves were many of Bedlam's dragons. Will could hear them roar from inside their caves. Will raised his arms high, sending a thrill throughout the room. The Baroks cheered and clanged the swords together in praise of their leader.

And, for a moment, Will realized Bedlam was right. Peter was nothing to be concerned with.

§

King Alexander entered the room where King Mildrir stood waiting. Mildrir rushed over and held out his forearm for King Alexander. "Mildrir, my old friend," Alexander said with a wide smile. The two grasped arms. Mildrir remained one of Alexander's dearest friends. Together with Theo and King Isleif, Mildrir helped Annika, Crispin, and Simon escape the Duke of Illiath and find security at Vulgaard. He was older than Alexander and it showed in the lines around his eyes and mouth and the grey in his beard and hair.

Nearby stood Alexander's old friend, General Aluein. "Aluein, you old smuggler." Alexander embraced him and slapped him hard on the back.

"I wouldn't miss this chance to fight with you again," Aluein chuckled.

"Here we are again, preparing for battle," Mildrir said. He lead Alexander to the large oval table in the center of the room and poured him a drink. "It seems that's all we kings do."

Alexander took the goblet filled with warm ale and sat down at the table. He drank down the warm liquid and felt relaxed. Mildrir sat next to him. Aluein preferred to sit on a large wooden chair near the wall.

"So what do we know of this young woman, Queen Esmeralda?" Alexander asked.

"Well, we know she is the daughter of King Eulrik," Mildrir took an orange off the platter resting on the table and began to peel it. "She was promised to Sir William before her father was assassinated. She believes strongly that it was the Duke of Illiath who sent the assassins to kill her father. So, we also know she is no friend of Will's nor of Lord Bedlam's."

Alexander leaned in. "So you feel we can trust her?"

Mildrir took a bite of the orange and nodded. He wiped the juice from his bearded chin. "Absolutely," he said. "Our knights have been working with her to devise a plan of attack. She has assisted greatly in the quest for the swords. She can be trusted."

Alexander took another drink of ale. Just then, the doors swung open and Queen Thordis entered along with Queen Esmeralda. Escorting them were Thætil and his nephew, Thurdin. Mildrir and Alexander stood and bowed as everyone took their places around the table.

"Please, be seated," Queen Thordis said. "Enjoy the refreshments."

King Alexander carefully studied Queen Esmeralda. She nodded her head toward him. Her hazel eyes reflected the light from the candles. Immediately, Alexander nodded back as though he felt at ease in her presence.

"Your Majesties." Queen Thordis slowly waved her arm. "May I present her Highness, Queen Esmeralda of Glaussier."

Alexander stood and bowed.

"My pleasure." Esmeralda nodded. "It is my pleasure to finally meet the great King Alexander." She shyly batted her eyes. "I have heard many great things about you and your kingdom for many months and was so overjoyed to learn that you were indeed alive and well again hiding, here in Vulgaard with—"

"Well, now." Mildrir cleared his throat as though uncomfortable with the flirtations. "Uh, shall we get on with the business at hand."

Everyone present sat down as Alexander prepared to speak.

"You must excuse my bewilderment," King Alexander began, "but can we truly trust that you desire to be one of our allies when not so long ago, your father's desire was to take my kingdom from me?"

Esmeralda looked down as though embarrassed. "Yes, that is exactly what I am asking. Although my father was King, a good King, he erred when he turned against you, your Majesty." she cleared her throat. "I do believe his anger was fueled by his pain and loss. He loved my brother Ryek dearly and, as you know, we still do not know where he is...or if he is still alive. My father took this loss very dearly."

Alexander nodded. "I understand. I recall the pain I had felt when I heard of Peter's death," he said.

"I always supported you, my Lord. And when my dear father was killed, well..." Her eyes welled up with tears. She swallowed, pushing back the emotion. A serious look came across her face. "I desire peace as much as anyone here in this room. But, I must also admit that, in addition to peace, I also desire vengeance for my father's brutal death at the hands of Sir William and Lord Bedlam."

She stood and placed her hand over her heart for effect. "I pledge all the resources of my kingdom and I pledge my loyalty to the Oath and to this cause. But I will never apologize for seeking vengeance for my father and my brother. Never."

"Here, here." Mildrir gently banged his hand on the table in approval. "There's nothing wrong with avenging your father's death, my dear."

Alexander stood. "As long as we all remember that peace is what we truly seek. The end of this evil presence is our main goal."

Esmeralda nodded as she sat down.

"Well, then," Queen Thordis said. "Shall we get down to planning our participation in this battle?"

"Absolutely." Alexander waved over an Elfin soldier who brought to the table many maps. He unrolled them on the table for the King. "Here we have the maps of the sea regions of Thorgest, the mountain regions near the south by Glaussier. As you can see, we will need soldiers to enter from the south and help lead the way to the Dragon Forest once Peter is able to enter in. We will move toward the Cornshire and protect him against Will's army of Baroks and other creatures."

Esmeralda lifted her hand. "But first," she said. "I have great news."

Everyone stared at her for a moment.

When Esmeralda could see that she had everyone's attention, she clasped her hands together with joy.

"The quest for the ten swords of the ten rulers has come to an end," she said.

Everyone present looked at one another then back at the Queen.

"It is true," she said. She turned to Queen Thordis who nodded.

"One of our Elfin soldiers returned not long ago with the great news," Thordis said. "The Sword of Niahm, the last of the missing swords, was discovered at Hildron and swiftly retrieved."

Alexander and the other rulers leaned back and exhaled. They murmured to one another in disbelief.

"But how? When…" Mildrir tried to fathom was he was told.

"Our scouts told us the location of the last sword. Lord Bedlam had kept the sword out in the open in the dungeons of Hildron where our spies infiltrated the area. Bedlam has been trying to replicate the steel for his own weaponry, but he has failed in his attempts. As a result, he grew careless. The location was easily discovered and so, Sir Roland and the Elfin soldiers went into Hildron to retrieve the sword," Esmeralda explained. "And there they succeeded. Eris brought me the last of the missing swords. I have it hidden away in my castle. It is safe and guarded day and night as we await the gathering of all the swords."

All the rulers applauded the news. Esmeralda laughed and clapped with joy.

"We are almost there, your majesties," she said.

"Great news indeed," King Mildrir patted Alexander on the back. "This is a day to be remembered."

Queen Esmeralda waved over her assistant who unrolled a map of the East Sea.

"Now, on with the planning," she said. "Here we have the regions where the sea dragons live. They will help us protect the shores from Bedlam's creatures. My dragons will fight for us and for the Dragon Forest no matter what. They have assured us through the language of the dragons that they will uphold the Oath and the Great Dragon."

Alexander studied the map of the sea, and then he studied Esmeralda's face. "You are certain of this?"

"I swear upon my life." She showed a certain fierceness in her eyes. "They will attack Bedlam's dragons and pirates on the seas. They will fight to the end."

With those words, Alexander believed the young Queen before him. He stood upright. "Alright then, it would seem all we need to do is arrive at Illiath, flank Bedlam's army, and then protect Peter as he makes his way toward the entrance of the forest."

General Aluein smirked. "Is that all?"

## 20 NIGHTMARES

Sir William, mounted on his beautiful steed, trotted over to the crowd of people in Illiath followed by a wagon filled with the usual baskets of fruit and bread. The people, as they always did, rushed to the wagon and began to distribute the baskets. Will dismounted and saw that this time Lord Byrén was there to meet him and Lord Bedlam.

"Where is he?" Lord Byrén stormed up to Will. "I demand to see him this instant!" Once a loyal ruler of the Crow Valley, Lord Byrén had fallen for King Eulrik's lies and Lord Bedlam's promises of wealth and power. The portly man with thinning grey hair had lost his title and his land when King Eulrik was assassinated and the stress showed on his wrinkled face. He had come to Sir William in desperation.

Will methodically removed his gloves and handed them to his squire who bowed and took the reins of Will's horse.

"I will not leave until I see him." Lord Byrén stabbed the air with his finger for emphasis.

"Oh, Sir William," a woman said as she parted from the crowd and approached the self-proclaimed Duke of Illiath. She knelt down at his feet, took his hand, and began to kiss it. "We are so grateful for this food."

Lord Byrén rolled his eyes at the sight of the woman kissing Will's hand.

"Get up you fool," he said to the woman.

"She is grateful for all that Sir William has done," came a menacing voice from behind Lord Byrén. "She understands what it means to be grateful."

Everyone turned to see Lord Bedlam, wearing his hooded cape as he entered the crowd. In the distance, his black dragon folded its wings and settled on the grass.

"Yes, she understands what it means to be grateful," Bedlam said as he removed the hood that covered his head. He sneered at Byrén. "Unlike you."

"I want a word with you Lord Bedlam," Byrén shouted. "And I will not leave until I have my chance."

"Friends of Illiath!" Lord Bedlam raised his voice over the crowd's murmuring and Byrén's bickering . "Once again, Sir William the Duke of Illiath has come to your assistance with food."

A local seamstress stepped out of the crowd. She held a basket of bread. "We grow tired of bread and fruit!"

"Yes," an elderly man spoke up. "We need meat and milk!"

Sir William lifted his hands to silence the crowd, but they ignored him.

"We need more than just fruit and bread!" Another shout came from the crowd.

"Friends," Will said. "Please. You must remember all that the land has suffered…"

"And I need the help with my livestock!" Another elderly man urged as he stepped from the crowd. He waved his hands. "All my cattle have scattered along with my sheep. I am too old to retrieve them. You took my sons and my sons-in-law. I need them back to help me work the land!"

"Yes! Bring back our sons!" More shouts came from the crowd. "We do not want war!"

Lord Byrén smirked and crossed his arms in defiance. "Well, Lord Bedlam, it looks like the masses have turned."

Lord Bedlam ignored Byrén's comments at first.

"It appears they are not as amiable as one thought," Byrén snickered.

At that moment, a farmer and his wife ran to the feet of Sir William and began to eagerly kiss his hands. They turned to the crowd.

"Have you forgotten all that Sir William has done for us?" the woman shouted as she held Will's hand. "How can you be so ungrateful?"

"But we need our sons! We need a King!" someone shouted.

"Yes! Where are all the rewards you promised us?" Lord Byrén asked loudly. He turned to the crowd. "We were promised land! We were promised bounty! And so far all we have are these baskets of fruit and bread!" He kicked one of the baskets over and spilled its contents. The crowd grew angrier and rushed forward.

Lord Bedlam stepped up. "Friends, have you forgotten the cause of all your woes?" he asked as he pointed his cane to the ruins of the palace of Illiath. "Remember what evil caused all this despair?"

The people quieted down and gazed over to the ruins of Alexander's castle.

"It was the Dragon of the Forest that did all this!" Lord Bedlam shouted. "Never forget! It was the Dragon that tore down the castle and with it all your hopes! It was the Dragon of Promise that deceived you all and now your hopes lie in ruins!"

Some of the people shook their fists and roared in approval, while others remained silent.

Bedlam pointed at the Dragon Forest to the north. The people turned their heads like a reflex and continued to listen.

"This is why we will storm the Dragon Forest and slay the Dragon once and for all. It is the cause of all our pain. Together, we will remove this evil from the land," he continued. "And then you will have your sons again. Only this time, the land will be yours. There is no longer a need for rulers or Kings." He pointed to Byrén. "You will all rule the land!"

More cheers and claps came from the people.

Lord Byrén shook his head. "And how are we supposed to trust you?"

The farmer's wife at Will's feet stood with reddened face. "How dare you question Lord Bedlam!" she shouted as spittle flew from her mouth. Her husband next to her let go of Will's hand and attacked Bryén as well.

"Yes, who are you to question our Lord Bedlam? You are one of the rulers who kept us all poor and starving!" He turned to the people. "He is one of the rulers who have kept us down all these years!" He rudely grabbed Byrén and motioned for the others to join him.

"You are the cause of all our troubles!" The farmer shouted. "Rulers like you ruined the land and kept all the wealth for yourselves!"

"No!" Lord Byrén shouted as he struggled with the man. "That is not true! Don't listen to these lies!"

Soon three more grabbed Byrén and began to haul him off. He turned to Bedlam for help.

"Stop this!" Byrén shouted, but Bedlam simply turned and walked away from the violent scene. He placed his hand on Will's shoulder.

"Look away, Will," he said. "There is no need for you to see this...violence."

The mob forced Byrén to a nearby tree.

"This is what we do to those who question Lord Bedlam!" the farmer shouted. "I need a rope!"

An old blacksmith took a rope off his wagon and handed it to the farmer. He grabbed the rope and tied it around Byrén's neck and then he used a piece of cloth to tie the hands. Against Bedlam's advice, Sir William stood by and watched the scene unfold.

Some of the women covered their faces and shielded their children from the scene.

The farmer tossed the rope over a tree limb and pulled. Lord Byrén's eyes grew large as the rope tightened around his neck. His feet soon left the ground.

"Pull!" the farmer shouted as he and the blacksmith pulled. They tied the rope around the trunk of the tree, leaving Byrén to hang until he died there in the Cornshire on the tree. His body swung in the background as the mob returned to where Sir William and the others gathered.

"Let it be known!" the farmer shouted and pointed to Byrén's body. "This is what happens to those who question Lord Bedlam. This is what happens to those who are ungrateful for all that the Duke has done!"

One elderly man lowered his gaze and shook his head in disgust. In silence, the women gathered their baskets and began to return to their homes in the Cornshire and the Cardion Valley. The sound of the Blue River was all that could be heard as the crowd dispersed. The farmer and his wife returned to Will's feet and continued to kiss his hands and murmur their endearments to him as the peasants walked away.

"Something needs to be done," one woman said as she walked off. "But what can we do?"

An elderly man heard her and gazed back at the scene of the farmer and his wife kissing Will's hand.

"It is hopeless," the old man whispered.

Lord Bedlam calmly surveyed the aftermath as the people returned to their homes and when it was clear, he waved his hand over the farmer and his wife still at Will's feet. They instantly changed into black crows and flew away into the afternoon sky.

Will watched them dart off and then his eyes found the body of Lord Byrén hanging from the tree.

"Did it have to come to this?" he asked as he stared at the dead man.

Lord Bedlam leaned on his cane. "Will, the people needed to see this. They crave justice. They needed to see that the time of Lords and Kings ruling over them has come to an end. Soon, they will realize that only one ruler is needed in the land. Only one ruler shall remain."

Sir William slowly nodded.

"And that one ruler is me." Lord Bedlam began his walk toward his black dragon.

Will's eyes widened as though shocked by Bedlam's declaration. The crows circled over Lord Byrén and soon many more joined them. The black birds descended upon the dead body there in the Cornshire that was once Will's boyhood home.

But Sir William dismissed the scene, mounted his horse, and ordered the wagons to return to Hildron.

§

Peter walked along a corridor at Vulgaard palace lit by sunlight shining through the windows. The corridor led to a large indoor training room for Elfin soldiers. There he would meet with Simon, Crispin, Annika, and Thurdin to begin their training with swords and on the backs of dragons. He entered the vast room and saw that no one was present.

"Hello?" he said only to hear his own voice echo back. "Anybody here?" The training room had dirt and saw dust on the floor. Peter bent down and ran his fingers through it. The dirt was fine and felt like powder. He was reminded of the arena. He could smell that familiar odor of dragon waste and knew that the beasts must be nearby. In his mind, he thought back to Rünbrior prison where he prepared to enter the arena to fight dragons wearing the heavy armor with a crude sword in his hand. Peter could feel the humid air once again and hear the roars of the crowds rise above him. "Death, death, death," he could hear them shout all the while shaking their fists in the air.

"Be prepared for anything!" Sir Nøel would always say to Peter before the battle began. And Peter would listen.

"Come in you fool," came a raspy voice from the opposite side of the room, startling Peter out of his trance. Peter smiled as he instantly recognized his friend's voice.

"Dangler!" Peter shouted to the old Dwarf he had known inside the arena. Dangler now leaned on a cane for support because of the wounds he had suffered inside the prison. As punishment, Lord Bedlam had tried to feed him to the dragons, but the Dragon Master escaped the snares of death thanks to his knowledge of dragons and to Peter who remembered him and carried him out of the prison.

Peter gently embraced him because he knew Dangler was still recovering from his wounds. "How are you my old friend?"

Peter saw that the wounds he had suffered in the prison had aged Dangler. His red beard showed specks of grey and skin sagged under his eyes and chin. In a rare show of emotion, Dangler squeezed his friend's shoulder. "I'm still here," Dangler sighed and pointed at Peter. "Because of you."

"Nonsense," Peter said. "We are here because of your excellent training."

Dangler chuckled. "Well, since we're both here now, let's get started with training."

Peter rolled his eyes. "I don't see why we need to train at all," he walked away. "I learned about fighting others in the arena. I know how to fight dragons and live. What other training do I need? We should be heading to Illiath in order to prepare for battle. Our time shouldn't be wasted with training here."

Dangler shook his head. "Being impatient won't help. There are still some things that need to be learned."

At that moment, several Eflin soldiers entered the room in mid-conversation. Each one made their way to the center of the room wearing Elfin armor made from thick leather and armed with a sword. Some pointed at Peter as their conversation died down. They all stood at attention, and then bowed out of respect. But there was one Elfin soldier who caught Peter's eye. A female Elf stood among the males. She wasn't very tall or opposing in form, but it was her face, her eyes, that Peter noticed. They were intensely grey and fierce with determination. Peter could tell she had seen battle and death. He knew that look and admired her steely resolve. Peter hesitated, and then bowed in return as though he had forgotten that he was now a knight of his father's realm.

He approached the Elves and one soldier handed Peter a sword. Peter took it and turned it over in his hand as he inspected the detail filigree of the blade. His eyes caught the female Elf's eyes again. She looked at Peter, then looked away, unimpressed. Intrigued, Peter noticed on her back was a quiver full of arrows. Peter returned his gaze to the sword in his hands.

"A beautiful sword," he said as he handed it back to the Elf.

"Made by my father long ago," Thurdin shouted as he entered the room. Behind him came Simon, Crispin, and Annika.

"He was a very talented sword smith, much like your mother," Thurdin said and bowed respectfully. "Forgive our tardiness, but we were inspecting the dragons we will be riding later."

"Peter!" Annika ran over to her friend. She hugged his neck. Peter awkwardly returned the embrace then pulled away embarrassed. All those weeks fighting in the arena, he never once was hugged by another fighter. He forced a smile and Annika giggled nervously when she realized her actions were not appreciated.

Peter inspected her clothes.

"I see you're out of the evening gowns and back in the trousers," he chortled.

"Yes," Annika narrowed her eyes, "and ready for training."

"Enough!" Dangler shouted and clapped his hands. "Come on, let's get started."

He waved at them to pay attention.

"Sit down," he ordered. They all obeyed and sat cross-legged before the Dragon Master.

"Now, as you know, we are about to head into battle on the ground and in the skies. So, it is imperative that we all are armed with the finest weapons known in all the lands," he clapped his hands again and a line of Elfin servants entered the room. Each carried an object that made Peter's eyes light up. He leapt to his feet.

"My crossbow!" he shouted and ran to the Elfin servant who held his weapon. Peter grabbed it and ran his fingers along it.

"Dangler!" Peter walked to his friend. "How did you ever retrieve this from inside the prison walls?"

Dangler tugged on his jacket. "I have my secret ways."

Peter patted Dangler's shoulder. "Well, I am most grateful. I didn't think I'd ever see this again."

Simon, Annika, Crispin, and the others were each provided a new crossbow. They sat admiring their new gifts.

"We'll practice using those later," Dangler said. "Fine weapons like these require thorough training and instruction."

"Oh, I've used one of these before," Crispin bragged. "No need for training because I—".

He accidently released the arrow that had been preloaded into the weapon. It whizzed by Simon's right ear and hit the wooden railing nearby.

Simon reached up and touched his ear, thinking he had been grazed by the arrow. When he saw no sign of blood, he sighed with relief. Then, he turned around to Crispin, reached over, and roughly took the crossbow from his hands. He shot Crispin a venomous look.

"Like I was saying." Dangler cleared his throat. "Fine weapons such as these require training and instruction."

"Peter chuckled, but he noticed the female Elf had a stern look of disgust on her face. She turned toward Dangler.

"Line up!" he ordered. "You there. You two will begin with swordfighting and stance."

The two Elfin soldiers stepped into the center and faced each other.

"You two will begin against Peter," Dangler added. The two Elfin soldiers looked at Dangler with wide eyes, then looked at each other.

Peter stepped up, drew his sword, and took a fighter's stance. He was reminded of training in the caves with Dangler so many months before and how he and Sir Nøel had fought against other fighters to win freedom from that dreaded prison. Now, he had his own sword and a more serious purpose: freedom for all the people. Freedom from Bedlam's evil.

"One man against two Elfin soldiers?" Simon whispered to Crispin.

"That's completely unfair." Crispin shook his head.

"Is it?" the female Elf said. She stood near Crispin. "A Royal Knight should be prepared to fight more than one opponent at any time in battle."

Crispin turned to see who was speaking to him. When he did, his eyes grew large. He traced her form with his eyes and then turned to Simon who was also inspecting the female soldier.

"Who's she?" Crispin asked and pointed.

"I am Eris," the Elf said, without looking at either of them. She drew her sword, which made Crispin step back with caution. She stabbed the ground with the blade and leaned on the hilt. Her eyes continued to watch Peter prepare to fight. "I fight for the Queen of Vulgaard as a soldier."

Crispin and Simon couldn't stop staring at her silken white hair braided down her back, her form-fitted leather tunic, and the quiver of arrows on her back.

"You *fight* for the Queen?" Crispin asked incredulously.

Eris slowly smiled. "Yes." She turned to him. "You'll see."

"Enough talking!" Dangler hobbled over to Simon and Crispin. "Pay attention and you might learn something!"

The two Elves took their stance before Peter with swords held out front. Then, one leaned in to attack Peter. But before he could, Peter swiped at him with his sword, striking the Elf's hand. The force sent the Elf's sword flying from his hand across the floor. Then, Peter turned and came at the unarmed Elf. His companion came to help, but Peter spun around and met the other Elf's sword with his own. The sound of metal clashing echoed throughout the room. Peter spun around again and sliced at his opponent's legs. The Elf leapt out of the way in time to miss the sharp blade. Peter grinned.

The Elf landed on his back with the tip of Peter's sword inches away from his eyes. He swallowed hard.

"Okay, so maybe it isn't unfair for Peter after all," Crispin said as he folded his arms across his chest. "Maybe it's unfair for the two Elves."

Simon chuckled then approached Peter who stood panting. He turned his sword over, inspecting the blade, and then slid it back inside its sheath.

"Peter, where did you learn all that?" he asked. But he could see a cold dullness in Peter's eyes. "Peter?"

Peter took a few steps back and blinked a few times, settling himself.

"Dangler," he said and pointed to his friend. "He taught me all I know."

"Bah!" Dangler shouted. "Not true." He approached Peter. "This lad was born to fight. He's a natural if ever I have seen one."

Again, Peter's eyes found Eris who stood off to the side. This time, she grinned slyly at Peter and nodded.

"Let's get on with it," the one Elf said as he stood and dusted off his suede trousers. He wiped the sweat off his red face.

Dangler grinned. "Well, they want more," he patted Peter on the back. "Shall we give it to them?"

Peter chuckled and removed his sword yet again. He sliced through the air with ease. Annika admired him from a safe distance. Simon and Crispin joined her.

"I always knew Peter was skilled," she said. "But I had no idea he had learned so much in that prison."

"He had to," Simon said to her. "In order to stay alive, he had to learn."

They jumped when they heard the metal swords clashing again as Peter fought off the other Elves. He showed them some of the footwork he had learned and soon his face was dripping with sweat. He wiped his face with his sleeve then removed his tunic. When he did, he turned his back toward his friends. Annika gasped at the sight. She turned away.

"What the?" Simon asked. "Peter? What happened to your back?"

Peter continued to wipe his face with his tunic. "What do you mean?"

His friends noticed the ghastly scar and healed cuts across Peter's back.

"That scar, those cuts and bruises across your back," Crispin said. He winced at the sight. "What happened to you?"

Peter frowned when he remembered. "Oh yes," he said coldly. "The scar...I was whipped for trying to escape."

Annika returned her gaze to Peter. The blatant scar across Peter's back was a long welt almost twelve inches across his young skin. There were other healed cuts and several purple bruises. Annika cringed as if she could feel the pain of the wounds herself.

She briefly looked away. "I am so sorry you suffered."

Peter casually threw his tunic down at Dangler's feet. "Yes, well, let's get on with training, shall we? We've not much time and we face a brutal enemy."

"Scars, bruises…" Eris said as she stepped forward. "They are all part of the life of a warrior."

Simon, Crispin, and Annika turned to see Eris approaching them.

"Wear them with pride," Eris said to Peter. "You earned them."

"Back to training!" Dangler shouted. "Eris, practice your shooting."

"As you wish," she said as she walked over and retrieved her bow from a servant nearby. It was a smaller bow than the others with an inlaid design on the polished wood. The three friends watched as she loaded the bow with an arrow from her quiver. She aimed it at the target placed forty feet away and released the bow string. Everyone watched as the arrow hit the target dead on center.

"Again," Dangler said and waved his arm. This time, a brave servant picked up the target and moved it along.

Eris loaded her bow, aimed, and hit the moving target with ease.

"Who is this girl again?" Simon asked no one in particular.

"She's one of the best warriors in the kingdom," Thurdin said and crossed his arms. "Watch and learn from her."

Peter sliced through the air again with his sword. Annika tilted her head as she stared at Peter. She watched as he prepared his stance. She seemed to be admiring his muscular torso in addition to his fighting skills. Annika walked over to a row of swords leaning against the wall and took one. She inspected the blade for a second or two, and then approached Peter. Without a word, Annika stood before one of the Elves and struck a fighter's stance.

At first, the Elf looked uncertain as to whether or not to engage with Annika. He tilted his head and shrugged as if to say, "Why not?"

Annika stood with feet apart and gripped the hilt of the sword with both hands. Her eyes narrowed to mere slits.

"Go ahead," she challenged. "I've fought off Baroks and Zadoks larger than you." She grinned.

The Elf raised an eyebrow and prepared to fight.

Simon spotted her. "Watch this," he nudged Crispin and nodded toward Annika.

Annika pretended to lunge toward the Elf and when he took one step toward her, she swung around and hit his sword with such force that the Elf stumbled backwards. But Annika regained her footing and swung her sword around in the opposite direction, coming at him hard with all her strength. He raised the sword and met hers near his chest. The two held their positions for a second and then the Elf pushed her back. Annika took her stance again.

"Not bad," the Elfin soldier said. He chuckled then looked at his companions. "She's strong."

"I've still much to learn," Annika lowered her sword and turned to Peter. "Will you show me more?"

Peter smiled and approached her. "Certainly," he said and raised her arms. "Here, hold the sword before you like this."

Simon noticed the look on Annika's face as Peter assisted her.

"Alright, then," he said to himself. He turned and realized he stood near the swords against the wall. Reaching out to take one, Simon found a thick bladed sword much too heavy to handle. But he stubbornly took it and, with a few grimaces, he lifted it. "Let's get started. Teach me what I need to know."

"Simon." Peter watched his friend struggle with the sword. "That one is much too heavy for you. Here, try this one." Peter grabbed a sword with a thinner blade and brought it to Simon.

"No thank you." Simon walked away from Peter. "This one will do."

"But you can't lift it above your head." Peter tried not to laugh. "Come, try this one."

Simon took his position in front of the Elfin soldier. "This one will do," he grunted. With the sword in front of his body, his arms shook and beads of sweat formed on his brow. His breathing grew heavy even though he hadn't yet swung at his opponent. He grimaced again. His muscles ached.

The Elf shrugged yet again and swiped at Simon with his sword. As the blades collided, Simon's sword flew out of his hands. He exhaled and bent over, relieved the heavy metal was out of his grip.

"Are you alright?" Annika asked. But Simon, still trying to catch his breath, said nothing.

Crispin chortled as he watched from the sidelines. "Well, that was entertaining," he said.

Simon, still bent over, shot him a harsh glare. Peter walked over to Simon and patted him on the back.

"We'll try it again, one more time," Peter said. "You'll get it."

Simon brushed off Peter and walked off without a word.

"Peter!" came a shout.

Peter turned in time to see his friend, Jason coming toward him.

The two friends embraced there in the training area.

"Jason, how are you my friend?" Peter said as he grasped his friend's forearms. "Getting stronger?"

"Every day," Jason said. "With all this fine Elfin food, I've gained weight and feel stronger."

"Come, let me introduce you to my friends from home." Peter walked Jason over to Annika and Crispin. "This is my friend from the mines...from Rünbrior. He and I have been through much together."

Crispin brushed aside the dampened hair from his eyes, reached out, and shook Jason's hand. Annika politely nodded to him.

"You fought in the arena, too?" Crispin asked.

Jason looked at Peter. "Well, yes, but not like Peter did. He was the best among the fighters."

"Is that true?" Annika asked Peter who simply shrugged.

"He fought valiantly and saved many lives." Jason placed his hand on Peter's shoulder.

"Really?" Crispin said. "What happened?"

"Well, after one last battle against the warden's greatest dragon, Scathar, Peter..."

"Where's Simon?" Peter interrupted the story and he looked around the room.

"Come now, all of you," Dangler shouted. "We've more training to complete. Bring the crossbows and let's practice with targets."

The group obeyed the Dragon Master and worked for many more hours training for the fight still to come.

# 21 BATTLE PLANS

*"Peter, how could you forsake me like this?" the voice asked. "Peter! Help me!"*

*Peter turned over in his sleep as sweat poured down his face and onto his pillow, soaking it through. He saw Sir Nøel reaching out for him on the arena floor. His blood leaked out of his wounded back. Peter tried to move toward him, but couldn't.*

*"Peter! Help me!" Sir Nøel shouted again.*

*"I'm coming." Peter tried to move his legs, but they wouldn't move.*

*He heard a laugh coming from behind the wounded Nøel. Peter could see it was Damon walking toward his friend. Damon's face was contorted into that same wicked grin Peter remembered so well.*

*"Stay away from him!" Peter shouted. Damon only laughed. Peter could feel his heart beating faster as he tried to move toward Nøel.*

*"I told you I would win in the arena," Damon said as he drew his sword from its sheath. "I always win, Peter!" He raised the sword high above the wounded Nøel.*

*"No!" Peter shouted.*

*Peter sat up in his bed. He clutched his chest and tried to breathe, but gasped for air as though drowning. The door to his bedchamber burst open.*

*"Son!" King Alexander shouted when he ran into the room to the bedside. "Are you alright? Is anything the matter?" He touched Peter's trembling shoulder.*

*"I...I can't breathe." Peter shut his eyes and continued to clutch his chest. He could see the rock walls and smell the musty air filled with moisture and dirt. He looked over at the empty cot across from his own. "Sir Nøel, he's...he's dead." Peter could feel the hot tears run down his cheeks.*

*Alexander leaned over his son. "Take in some air, slowly," he said. Peter opened his eyes and saw his father's concerned face.*

*"Father," he whispered.*

*"Everything's alright," Alexander said. "You're in the palace at Vulgaard—"*

*Peter saw a blade protrude from his father's chest and his father's body arch.*

*"No!" he shouted. His father's eyes widened and blood trickled from between his lips. "Father!"*

*Peter leapt out of bed and grabbed his father as he fell to the floor with the sword sticking out of his back. He heard the familiar laugh coming from the corner of the room and saw the shadow of a figure in the corner.*

*"I win, Peter," the voice came from the shadowy figure. "I always win."*

*"You." Peter gazed up from beside his father.*

*Damon came out of the shadows.*

"Go away!" Peter shouted, opened his eyes, and sat up in bed. He searched the room for any sign of Damon. He looked to the floor, but his father wasn't there. It was true. He was in the palace and it was just another nightmare. He inhaled deeply then exhaled.

Alexander knocked on the door. "Peter?"

Peter sat on the edge of his bed holding his head in his hands. "Yes," he sighed.

Alexander entered and saw his son, pale and frightened. He shook his head as he sat down next to Peter.

"You're safe now, son. No one is going to hurt you ever again," the King whispered and rubbed his son's back. "Everything is alright."

Peter pulled away. "I dreamed…of Damon killing Sir Nøel."

Alexander looked into his son's weary eyes.

"He died there in the arena," Peter said. He cringed and covered his eyes with both hands. "And I couldn't help him."

Alexander moved to embrace his son again, but Peter hopped out of the bed and reached for his velvet robe. He put it on then tied the belt around his waist.

"And then I saw Damon kill…" Peter turned away.

"It happens, Peter," Alexander said. He watched while Peter rubbed his forehead in an attempt to wipe away the scene from inside his head. "In battle, in war friends are lost. I have lost many—"

"I understand," Peter coldly interrupted his father. "It's over now. Time to get on with training. I'm hungry. Let's go eat breakfast." Peter forced a smile and walked toward the chamber door.

Alexander studied his son's reddened face. "Yes, well," he said as he approached his son. "I'm afraid there won't be anything waiting for us downstairs."

Peter stood in the open doorway with his eyebrows raised. "What? Why not?"

Alexander put his hand on Peter's shoulder. "Because it is just after midnight, Peter."

Peter closed his eyes, embarrassed. "Oh, I thought…"

"Son, you haven't been sleeping well. I think I should ask the apothecary for some lavender to put in a glass of warm milk. It really does help," Alexander put his hands into the pockets of his robe.

Peter turned away. "No," he said curtly. "I'm alright. It was just a nightmare, I mean a dream. Everyone has bad dreams, you know."

"Yes, but not everyone wakes up screaming in terror almost every night." Alexander remained in the doorway. "Are you sure you don't want something to help you sleep? Some chamomile tea? Anything?"

Peter removed his nightshirt and began to put on his clothes. Alexander winced when he saw the ghastly scar on Peter's back. Peter hurried into his tunic and trousers as though he knew his father was staring at his wounds. He sat down to put on his boots.

"No, I'm awake now. I might as well head downstairs and practice with my sword."

Alexander sighed. "Alright then," he said and turned to leave. "I worry that all is not well."

Peter stormed passed him. "Well, don't worry about me, father. I'm fine."

His father watched as Peter made his way down the darkened stairway disappearing into the blackness below. He could hear the footsteps and see a doorway open and close in the distance. He knew Peter had made his way outside into the courtyard. Alexander leaned on the bannister contemplating all that his son had experienced in Rünbrior. He scratched his bearded chin, turned, and crept toward his bed chamber.

§

Peter thought as he walked on alone. Seeing Jason again triggered more memories from inside the prison. He knew he had to rid himself of these nightmares if he was to be useful in the battle against Bedlam. He sighed heavily because some of the memories of his time in the prison he did not want to forget: Nøel, Jason, Dangler and his dragons, all these memories Peter wanted to preserve.

He walked until he found himself by the dragon caves. He could hear a few of the creatures in their stalls. Some were pacing while others slept. Peter cautiously entered the cave and found it lit with torchlight. He could see the emerald green eyes glowing from one stall and red fiery eyes from another. He didn't know how to approach them. One blew smoke from its nostrils, so Peter crept over to its stall. Its head barely reached to the top of the wooden gate that closed it in. The floor was covered with straw.

He carefully leaned over to see what type of dragon it was.

"Hello," he whispered. "A Wyvern, huh?"

The little dragon grunted then squawked. Its purple eyes blinked a few times then more smoke came from its nostrils.

"At least you can spew fire, right?" Peter asked.

The little dragon let loose a stream of fire that lit some straw and woke a few dragons. They growled and scratched at the ground.

"Shhh," Peter whispered and stroked its head as it stomped out the fire. "No fire. You need to be quiet now and get some sleep."

The little dragon curled up on the pile of straw. "That's a good dragon," Peter said.

"Peter?" came a small voice near the horse stables. Peter stopped petting the dragon, quickly left the cave, and searched for the source of the voice.

"Who's there?" he asked the darkness.

Annika appeared from inside the stables. She held a small brush in her hand. "It's me," she said. "I couldn't sleep, so I came out here to brush the horses for awhile. What are you doing out here this time of night?"

Peter began to speak, and then changed his mind about what he was going to say. "I couldn't sleep either."

Annika looked down at the sword attached to Peter's belt. "Oh, I see." She fumbled with the brush. "I'm not sure you'll find anyone to spar with in there." She nodded toward the practice yard.

"Doesn't matter," Peter said. "I can practice on my own. I practiced alone for many weeks inside the prison cell."

Annika raised her eyebrows in surprise. She walked toward him. "Really?" she asked. "What else did you do inside the prison?"

Peter looked down and kicked around a few small stones with his boot.

"I mean, you've never really told any of us what happened in there," she said as she stood near him.

"I haven't?" he said.

"No, and I'd really like to know." She walked over to a large rock and sat upon it. "What was it like?"

Peter looked up at her. His face had mellowed. Many images came across his mind. "I worked in the mines with my friend, Jason."

Annika nodded.

Peter looked at the palms of his hands. The calluses were still present. "It was boring monotonous work, but we had to do it or we'd be beaten and starved," he said.

Annika looked down.

"And then I was chosen to train with Dangler," Peter said with no emotion.

Annika grinned. "How exciting," she said as she leaned forward to listen.

Peter had a far away look in his eyes. "We took care of baby dragons."

"Really?" her eyes sparkled.

"Yes. That was the first time I had ever seen a baby dragon. And then I trained with adult dragons," he said. Annika finally spotted some life in Peter's eyes.

"They couldn't spew fire, of course, but they were still fierce," he said. He could see the young dragons' eyes glowing in front of him. "They were young, but very powerful, very beautiful. We were careful. One wrong move and..." He made a gesture across his neck with his finger. He chuckled and Annika smiled.

"Oh, Peter," Annika said. "I missed you." She chuckled.

Peter's face turned red. "And I..." He hesitated. "I missed you, too."

"What was it like in the arena fighting and everything?" Annika asked. "I mean, I know it must have been frightening, but also exciting, yes?"

Peter's face fell when he heard her words. Sir Nøel's face entered his mind. He could see his friend dressed in armor standing in the center of the arena waving to Peter to come circle around the dragon while the crowd chanted. Death, death, death, he could hear the chants. Peter closed his eyes, exhaled, and then turned to walk off.

"I have to train now, excuse me." The coldness returned to his voice.

"Peter?" Annika asked after him. She stood, but didn't follow him. Instead, she watched him walk off with hunched shoulders.

§

The next day, Theo browsed through several books on the bookshelf inside the Queen's library at Vulgaard. He adjusted his spectacles on his nose.

"Your father tells me you cannot sleep," he said and turned to face Peter who sank into a large comfortable chair nearby. He methodically tossed Theo's wooden pipe into the air over and over again.

"Is this true?" Theo asked.

He received no answer to his question.

Peter seemed to be ignoring the question. He thought about the many times he sat listening to Professor Theo's instructions years before in his father's palace at Illiath. Peter exhaled with frustration because he felt the times of questions and instructions were over.

"Hello?" Theo said. "Is anyone there?"

Peter caught the pipe and set it on the nearby table. He slouched deeper into the chair and exhaled again.

"He asked the apothecary to provide you with a sleeping agent." Theo leaned over to his charge. "I told him I didn't think it was necessary, but…"

"It isn't," Peter finally answered.

Theo stood straight. "Ah," he said. "Then you can hear me. For a moment there, I thought perhaps your hearing was damaged." He chuckled and pulled out a chair. He sat down, leaned forward, and stared at Peter who returned to fiddling with Theo's pipe.

"May I please have that back?" Theo reached out his hand. Peter reluctantly handed the pipe over. He sighed again.

"I like the dragon pipe better," Peter said with a smirk.

"Alright, what is the matter? It must be something horrendous because all I've gotten out of you are sighs and exhales and, well, annoying silence." Theo pushed the pipe aside.

Peter turned to face his former teacher. "Theo, I have read through all the history books here and much is written about my mother when she was here as a child," Peter said. "But I want to know more about what happened when she met Bedlam."

Theo gently pushed his glasses further up the bridge of his nose. "And that's why you cannot sleep at night?"

Peter leaned on the table and folded his hands together. "No," he said and looked down at the floor. "That's not it. My father worries too much." Peter stood and walked toward the books.

"Well, you are his only son. Not long ago, he was told of your death. And now he has a second chance. He wants to take care of you," Theo explained. He leaned back in his chair. "He feels responsible for what happened to you and desperately wishes he could have prevented it."

Peter stood with his hands clasped behind his back. "Yes, I know," he mumbled. "But it's over now. I'm here with him. I'm safe."

"And yet you have nightmares," Theo said.

Peter turned to face him. He nodded.

"About the arena?"

Peter nodded again.

Theo looked away. "I know it isn't easy to watch a friend die," he said.

Peter faced the books again. He could feel his eyes sting and the anger return. He blinked the rage away.

"To lose someone you care about hurts," Theo said. "There was nothing you could have done to—"

"That's not true!" Peter shouted. The loudness of his voice startled Theo who gazed at Peter intently. "That's not true."

Peter turned to Theo. "I could've... I mean, I should've..."

"What?" Theo tilted his head.

"I should've watched out for Damon." Peter felt his face grow warm. "I wasn't watching him and I should've been watching him. I could've stopped him from..."

"Peter." Theo stood. "Stop blaming yourself."

Peter wiped his forehead.

"You must stop blaming yourself immediately." Theo approached him. "And I mean it."

Peter looked up into the gentle face of his friend.

"Sir Nøel was a brave knight of your father's realm," Theo said. "He died doing what he was called to do: Protect you, his sovereign, at all costs."

"I know."

"And he did just that." Theo placed his hands on Peter's shoulders, "even though it cost him his life."

"It hurts," Peter whispered. His face contorted as he fought the tears forming in his tired eyes.

Theo studied Peter's face. "I understand. I truly do."

Peter listened.

"If you need to weep, then go ahead. No one here will laugh at you. You are among friends, here. Fighting back the tears does more harm than—"

Peter rudely stomped away. Theo watched his former student stand by the bookcases again.

"I don't need to cry," Peter said. "I'm too angry to cry."

"Well, then, come, sit down," Theo said as he walked over to the large chair. Peter obeyed and sat down. He swallowed back the anger.

"The pain will subside," Theo said. He sat down in his chair, took up his pipe, and spewed fire to light it. The sudden stream of fire shocked Peter but he liked being reminded that his dearest friend was a dragon.

Theo puffed on the pipe a few times, sending wisps of smoke into the air. "Believe it or not, the pain, the hurt, and the anger will eventually subside, Peter."

"He was a good friend." Peter stared down at the floor. "He taught me much. He helped me survive in that prison. Without him, I don't know if I would have made it. And now he's gone. I didn't get to thank him. I didn't get to tell him how much I appreciated all that he did for me."

Theo winced as he listened to the regret in Peter's voice.

"I sometimes wonder what would have happened if I had made it to Knight Training in the Crow Valley after all," Peter sighed.

Theo cocked his head. "You would have been taken prisoner," he said.

Peter looked at him. "What?"

"Peter, Lord Bedlam knew you were headed for the Crow Valley. He had his spies searching everywhere for you." Theo leaned closer to Peter.

"Around the time you were abducted in the desert," Theo explained. "Bedlam's men were instructed to bring you to him, but Valbrand's men found you first and took you to Rünbrior instead. Bedlam took all the men, women, and children of the Crow Valley and many other lands as his prisoners. Those who were killed were marched to Hildron where they remain to this day."

Peter's eyes widened.

"So, you see, Peter, had you arrived at Knight Training, you would have been captured and imprisoned, but at Hildron as Bedlam's prize."

Peter thought about what he'd heard. "And I wouldn't have been able to train, or fight, or learn about the dragons like I did in Rünbrior."

"Precisely. You probably would be rotting in that dungeon still," Theo said.

"And I never would have met Sir Nøel, Jason, or Dangler." Peter looked directly at Theo.

Theo pointed his finger for emphasis. "You never would have learned all about dragons imprisoned at Hildron."

"I will never have another chance to thank Nøel," Peter mumbled as he bowed his head. His shoulders hung low.

Theo smiled a sly smile like someone who knows something, a

secret, but isn't allowed to tell it. "Now, Peter," he said. "I promise you this...someday you will be able to tell him all that you long to tell him."

Peter looked up with shiny eyes. "What? How?"

Theo chuckled. "Do you trust me?"

Peter tilted his head to the side, confused by the question.

"Peter, do you trust me?"

Peter nodded.

"Alright then," Theo sighed and leaned back. He puffed on his pipe. "Lean on this promise. One day, soon, you will be able to tell him everything, just as you were able to tell your mother."

Peter's face lit up as he remembered the vision of his mother. He smiled. "Really?"

Theo laughed. "Have I ever steered you wrong?"

"No, never," Peter said and scooted the chair to the table. "So, tell me more about what happened to my mother and Bedlam?"

"Alright then, as long as you promise to try and sleep well?" Theo winked.

"Absolutely," Peter said.

Suddenly, the doors burst open. King Alexander entered with a concerned look on his face. He wore his silver armor and his scarlet cape flowed behind him.

"Father," Peter stood. "What is it?"

Alexander stopped in front of Peter and placed his hand on his son's shoulder. "Peter, how are you feeling?"

"I'm fine, father, but what is it?" As he spoke, several of Aluein's soldiers entered alongside Queen Thordis's Elfin soldiers. They each were armed and wore riding clothes. "What's happening?"

Alexander turned to Theo. "Queen Esmeralda has announced that the last of the missing swords has been found."

Peter stood. "What?"

Alexander smiled broadly. "It is true. The Sword of Niahm has been found and is hidden away safely. Queen Esmeralda has left for Glenthryst. I must now fly out to meet her and King Isleif. The planning for the final battle must begin."

"Yes, father," Peter said and approached him. "Do you need me to come along? I am more than ready to—"

"No, son," Alexander interrupted. "You stay here and finish preparing. Then, when you are ready, you will meet us at Illiath."

Peter huffed and clenched his fists. "But I am ready," he said sternly.

Alexander walked over to the Elfin soldiers. They nodded as though approving what King Alexander was about to say. He turned and faced

Peter.

"I am most pleased to tell you that all the swords are now in our hands." He smiled. He turned to Theo. "And now that we have all the swords, Theo, our time has come to put the plan into action and rid this world of Bedlam once and for all."

Theo narrowed his eyes and slowly nodded as he took in all the words.

"So, we will fly off on the backs of dragons, meet Queen Esmeralda and King Isleif, then plan the battle," he said. He looked at Peter with a most serious look. "It is your time, Peter."

"I understand," he said. And he meant it.

"Just know that you are not alone," his father said. "The Dragon is with us and it will be there in the forest."

"I find it hard to contain my excitement." Peter smiled as he pictured his old friend of the forest.

His father turned to leave with the others. "I'll see you soon, Peter!" he called out as he left the hall.

Peter stood there watching all the men leave. When all was quiet again, he turned to Theo who sat in his chair smoking his pipe again.

"How can you just sit there? Aren't you mad with excitement? This is amazing!" Peter paced back and forth wringing his hands. Theo watched with a smirk on his face.

"Maybe we should discuss how I will…I mean now that I am supposed to follow my mother's instructions…take all the swords into the forest," he suggested.

Theo let out more smoke and shook his head. "Yes, that sounds like a grand idea."

§

King Isleif, the younger King of Gundrehd of the north shore, paced the glossy floors of his palace with hands tightly grasping the scrolls his servants had given him. His unshaven face was contorted into a grimace of sorts as though his mind was deep in thought. His unkept brown hair rested on his shoulders and he blinked his red rimmed eyes, tired from lack of peaceful sleep.

A servant approached him. "Can I bring you anything, your Majesty?"

Isleif shook his head and rubbed the nape of his neck. "No, not now. Just tell me when they get here."

A trumpet blast interrupted him and he ran to the entrance of his grand palace of Gundrehd. The King raced across the courtyard ignoring all the peasant farmers who bowed as he passed by them. He ran until he reached the raised gate, but the bridge had yet to be lowered.

"Quickly!" he shouted. "Lower the bridge!"

On the other side of the enormous wooden contraption, a few screams could be heard coming from the peasants. Isleif raised his eyes toward the blue skies above in time to see several lithe dragons circling. He grinned and used his hand to shield his eyes from the bright sun.

His head flew back as he laughed heartily at the sight. "They're here!"

Finally, the bridge lowered and he made his way out to greet his arriving guests. He could see the frightened farmers running away from the approaching dragons as they landed nearby with the esteemed guests on their backs.

"Dragons!" one farmer shouted. "They'll burn us all!"

Isleif raised his hands. "Nonsense!" he shouted at his people. He walked over to a dragon along with his guards. He took the reins and stroked the beast's snout. It panted feverishly from the long flight. "You see? They are as gentle as that horse over there."

The eyes of the farmer grew wide as he watched his sovereign pet the dragon without any trepidation. Even after observing the King, the farmers took no chances. They quickly mounted their horses, turned their wagons around, and headed back home.

Isleif chuckled and lent a hand to his guest, Queen Esmeralda, as she dismounted the dragon.

"Your people are frightened," the Queen said.

"No worries," Isleif answered as he assisted her off her dragon. "And how was the journey, your Highness?" He bowed.

"Fast," she said, "and windy." She laughed.

"But much better than any horse, true?" Isleif said as he handed the reins to his guard.

"Indeed!" She straightened out her tunic. Dressed in suede trousers and a breastplate over her tunic, the queen seemed comfortable in the attire. Her auburn hair was braided into a single braid that cascaded down her back. She gazed at the surroundings and her hazel eyes studied the palace as it sparkled in the sunlight. "Your palace is quite spectacular, Isleif."

"Have you never been here before?" He walked with her for a moment.

"Not that I can recall," she said as she inspected the area. Her eyes followed the spires that seemed to ascend into the sky forever. "I do believe I would have remembered such a beautiful sight." In the distance, the crashing waves of the sea could be heard.

"There, go to the precipice. Guards, show your highness, Queen Esmeralda, the view of the sea," he ordered. He stood for a moment longer watching the queen reach the edge of the cliff overlooking the north shore. He could see her body react to the view of the waves hitting the rocky shore. She turned and waved with the enthusiasm of a young girl.

"King Isleif!" a shout came from behind. "You scoundrel."

He turned in time to see King Alexander approach wearing his silver armor and flowing cape.

"You old pirate." Isleif took Alexander's outstretched arm and grasped it tightly. "Glad you made it."

The dragons roared in the background as the guards led them across the bridge and into the courtyard. More screams from the peasants could be heard as the dragons entered.

"Quite the experience, isn't it?" Isleif asked. "Dragonflight."

Alexander nodded. "Aye, I can see why the Elves trained them for flight," he said. "They are faster and more powerful than horses. And they are very intelligent."

The two men stood watching the dragons being fed by the King's servants. Once all the guests had arrived, King Isleif hosted a bountiful luncheon in his dining hall. The guests enjoyed the food and drink, but there was much business to conduct and little time to accomplish all that needed to be done.

"Now that we are all together," Alexander said. "I have news of the swords."

King Thorgaerd, King Beatann, Lady Aemilia, King Baldrieg, Lord Ronahn, Lord Egamir, and Thætil, brother to Queen Thordis of Vulgaard, all sat around the impressive mahogany table at Isleif's palace. All listened intently.

"All the swords have been found and are safely hidden away," he said. His news was met with gasps of disbelief, sighs, and exhales of relief from all the rulers present. These men and women remained loyal to the Oath sworn by their forefathers so they understood the significance of the King's announcement. "There they will remain until it is time for my son, Prince Peter, to take them into the Dragon Forest."

"Escorted by General Aluein's men?" Egamir asked.

"And my soldiers," Thætil interjected. He stood and rested his long thin hands on the table. His braided white hair and his leather armor with purple cape made a profound sight.

Egamir bowed his head. "And we all know what capable warriors your Elves are, Thætil. I am certain the Prince will make it to the forest safely."

Thætil bowed and sat down.

"But once he arrives with the swords, what happens then?" Egamir asked.

Alexander made his way around the table as he spoke. "My men, along with Baldrieg and Mildrir's men will gather at Illiath when they arrive. Yes, we know Sir William and Lord Bedlam are already well aware of this plan. They have their spies all around. Bedlam has ways of seeing, but all our men are more than willing to fight to protect Peter and the swords as he makes his way to the Dragon Forest."

"And the Dragon?" King Beatann asked. "What of it? Will it be there to protect as well?"

"Always, in its own time and doing," Alexander said. "I have met with the Dragon. It has assured me that, although this is the time of man, the Dragon will be there to protect the Oath. It remains loyal to the covenant it swore many years ago in the hills of Vulgaard." Alexander thought of the time he arrogantly rushed into the forest after escaping the dungeon where Bedlam had imprisoned him. Alexander had rushed into the forest in anger, accusing the Dragon of allowing his son to be abducted to Rünbrior.

Alexander remembered the Dragon's body bursting forth in fury toward him and how he cowered in fear. But he also remembered the reassuring words the Dragon had spoken to him about Peter.

Now, here he was with all the rulers.

"The Dragon of the Forest will always remain faithful," Alexander said.

All the rulers nodded when they heard these words.

"And what of Lady Sillith and Godden?" King Thorgaerd asked. "What role do they play in this since we will be fighting on their lands?"

Alexander approached the table. "They have been in hiding deep within the forests since most of their people were affected by Sir William's conscription orders went out to the regions. The leaders feared for their lives. Many farms have been abandoned, women and children were either taken to Hildron as captives, or..." his voice trailed off.

King Thorgaerd waited for the King to regain his composure.

"I'm afraid there have been many casualties in this build-up to war," Alexander said as he sat down with a heavy sigh.

King Thorgaerd shook his head in disbelief. "When will it all end?" he said even though he knew the answer. "Why must there always be war?"

Lord Ronahn stood to speak. "As long as Bedlam remains, as long as his dark spell is cast over our lands, war will remain…slavery and death will continue to spread," he said. "We must endure to the end. Once Bedlam's spell is broken, only then can we return to our lands and reclaim what is rightfully ours." Lord Ronahn spoke from his experience. He remained the only rightful heir to the kingdom at Hildron. His face became red with fury. "And I will reclaim what is mine." He slammed his fist down on the table so hard it shook.

"Here, here," the rulers said among themselves.

"Rulers in the outlands continue to support Bedlam," Ronahn said. "As long as he supplies them with what they ask, they give him what he needs."

"He continues to lie to them and promise them land," Mildrir said. He lowered his eyes. "These fools have no idea what they have gotten themselves into."

"Then let us begin to discuss the details of this battle plan, shall we?" Isleif said. "So we can all reclaim the peace the land and our people so desire." He took his cup and raised it high.

"To the Oath!" he said.

Each ruler took their cups, stood, and raised their drinks high to toast the words.

"To the Oath," each ruler said before drinking.

"To Peter," Alexander said before he sipped his wine. "The Son of the Oath."

§

The black liquid churned in the cauldron with mesmerizing temptation. Will couldn't help but watch it with wide eyes hoping it would reveal more secrets. He was not disappointed.

"And here we see your friend, Peter," Bedlam said as the image of Peter appeared in the thick liquid. He walked with Theo across the grassy yard at Vulgaard. Will could see they were in a deep discussion of some sort. "Look how engrossed he is in conversation with his dear mentor and friend, Theodore Sirus III."

Will continued to watch the vision in the liquid.

"What are they discussing?" he asked as he leaned in.

Bedlam raised an eyebrow as he watched his nemesis in the vision. "Oh, they're discussing Queen Laurien, of course."

Will looked up at Lord Bedlam. He winced with confusion.

"Peter is obsessed with the history of the Oath and his beloved mother's role," Bedlam explained. "And that's to our benefit. His desire to have answers could very well lead to his downfall."

Will nodded.

Another image appeared in the liquid.

"I will deal with that later," Bedlam said. He pointed to the new vision. "This is what I am most interested in."

Will could see Simon, Annika, Crispin, Thurdin, and Jason practicing swordplay in the arena with the Elves of Vulgaard.

"The heart of a young man is easily darkened," Bedlam smiled, revealing his small sharp teeth. "We might be able to use this to our advantage."

Will straightened. He narrowed his eyes.

"Yes, I do believe we may be able to take full advantage of this time of preparation," Bedlam walked away from the cauldron, picked up his black cape, and swung it around his thin body. He adjusted it around his shoulders and clasped it underneath his neck. As Will watched his master, Bedlam put on his gloves, carefully adjusting each finger, and then walked to the table where his cane rested.

"You see, Will, there are always those so filled with hatred and jealousy that their hearts can easily be turned against those whom they love."

Will stood at attention and listened as his master turned to leave the room.

"It's the only way my work can be accomplished, Will, you know this. The weak minded will always succumb." Bedlam tossed his head back and let out a hearty laugh as he left the room leaving Will alone to take in the words.

Will turned to retrieve his sword which was leaning by the cauldron. As he picked it up, he leaned over and peeked into the black liquid one more time. Peter and Theo stood talking together in the courtyard of the palace. Will could see excitement in his former friend's face as he listened to Theo talk. Will placed his sword in its sheath attached to his belt. His eyes never left the vision of Peter.

Finally, he turned and exited the wizard room of Lord Bedlam.

## 22 THE MAZE OF THŒRGËN

Peter walked alongside his mentor, Theo, as he listened to the story of how his mother was bewitched by the black dragon of Bedlam.

"As you now realize, your mother's kindness toward Bedlam was abused. He could see into her heart as most dragons can, and he saw a pure innocence that he could twist and manipulate to get out of exile and begin his plan of revenge," Theo explained.

Peter nodded. "But why did you cast the spell? Why did you go forward with the transformation?"

"I sought the counsel of the Dragon of the Forest." Theo gestured to the north. "I flew to speak with it inside its realm. I saw the vision in the lake. It showed me the vision of the future. I felt I could trust the Dragon's vision. It knew this darkness must come in order to usher in the time of man, the time of light."

"At what cost? My mother's life?" Peter stomped off.

"Come now, Peter," Theo said after him. "You mustn't be angry."

Peter stopped and turned to face Theo. "How can I not be angry? The Dragon knew. It knew this plan, this spell, would ultimately cost my mother her life. It knew this plan would take my mother away from me and yet it counseled you to go forward with it. How can I not be angry about this?"

Peter walked away again.

"You can be angry about this, but your anger will not change anything. The plan was set many years ago. Your anger will only blind you to what is ahead of you, Peter. Just as your anger blinded you about Damon," Theo said. "And look how it cost Sir Nøel dearly."

Peter stopped walking, but he did not turn to face Theo.

"Your anger can only cause harm, Peter. No good can come from it," Theo said as he approached him and patted him on the back. He continued on, leaving Peter there on the gravel path. "I suggest you accept the past and let go of all the anger within you. Live in the present. That is where you are needed most."

Theo made his way over to a large hedge with an archway as its entrance. He stood and waited as Annika, Simon, and Crispin approached with Eris close behind. Peter stood alone for a moment longer, taking in all that Theo had said. Finally, he looked up and saw his friends waiting for him.

"Well?" Simon asked with arms crossed. "What do we do now?"

"I'm so very tired of all this training. We are needed in battle!" Peter complained

Theo ignored Peter's outburst.

"Fine," Peter exhaled loudly. "Let's get on with this."

Peter met them there at the entrance. He looked up and observed their surroundings. "What is this place?" he asked Theo.

Theo raised his hand to the entrance. "This, my dear friends, is The Maze of Thœrgën."

Annika stepped back to inspect one wall of the hedge. The hedge stood well over twenty feet high into the late afternoon sky and was trimmed to form dark green walls and archways.

"This…is a maze?"

"Yes." Theo clasped his hands behind him and rolled back and forth on his heels. "And it is part of your training."

Crispin looked up at the wall of the hedge. He smirked as though unimpressed. "Doesn't look like much to me."

Theo turned and waved for them to follow as he entered the maze. "Yes, well, that's because it isn't made of food, Crispin."

Annika chuckled as she followed Theo into the maze. Peter hesitated, and then looked over at Eris. She stood with a quiver full of arrows and her bow slung over her shoulder obviously ready to face whatever was over the hedge. Eris tilted her head and then walked ahead of Peter. Crispin and Simon came after her with Peter entering last. Theo stopped and turned to face them all.

"Why is she here?" Peter motioned toward Eris.

"Eris is here to assist you all. She has made it through the maze successfully several times."

Peter shook his head impatiently.

"You disapprove?" Theo asked.

"I won't need assistance here." Peter ran his hand through his thick brown hair.

Eris smirked. Annika watched her closely.

"Very well, then," Theo said. "Let's get on with this. The Maze of Thœrgën has a rich history, indeed." Theo paced before the entrance.

His students listened intently, but Peter only stared at the green hedge.

"Long ago, the young Elfin warrior named Thœrgën fought valiantly against the enemies of his people. This pleased his father, the King. One day, when he returned from war, he succumbed to the temptations of an old wizard named Olëon. This evil wizard tempted Thœrgën with great power and promised him a kingdom of his own. It was all a lie, but Thœrgën, in his weakness, began to fall for the temptation and was led astray," Theo explained. "As punishment, he was taken into a haunted forest by his father who then abandoned him there with nothing but the clothes on his back. Thœrgën watched as his father departed the forest. Alone that night, Thœrgën could hear the cries of the creatures that haunted the woods. The trees began to engulf him and he no longer knew the way out. He grew desperate and afraid. He cried out for his father.

His father's voice came from within the trees telling him the way out. If Thœrgën refused to listen, he would remain lost in the forest unarmed, forced to face many dangers. But if he listened to his father's voice, he would know the way out and leave the forest unharmed."

Annika, Crispin, and Simon listened with wide eyes. Peter crossed his arms in front of his chest, smirked, and ignored Theo.

"Young Thœrgën could hear the many cries of the ghosts that haunted the forest. They tried to mislead him and the trees continued to obstruct the way, but he obeyed his father, listened only to his voice, and made it out of the forest safely where he saw that his father had captured the wizard Olëon. Thœrgën was able to face the old wizard and see him taken to the prison at Rünbrior for treason."

Peter turned his head.

"Thœrgën learned his lesson and was given a second chance. As a gift to his son, Thœrgën's father, King Aidan, had this maze built and ordered that all Eflin warriors use it to teach themselves fortitude and the value of teamwork," Theo said.

"What do you mean?" Simon asked.

"Here in this maze, in order to find the end, you must use your skills of direction and perception along with your senses. You will be fooled into thinking you are near the end, no doubt about it. I know you are thinking it will never happen to you, but many Elfin soldiers who have entered here were fooled and they were far more experienced than you."

Simon tilted his head. "Fooled?" he asked. "Fooled by what?"

"Yes, what do you mean?" Annika asked. She studied the hedge. Crispin stood beside her.

"You will be fooled by your surroundings, tricked by your eyes, and tricked by your ears. Don't trust them," Eris interrupted. She gazed over at Peter who seemed to be deep in thought. "And don't trust your feelings either."

Simon, Annika, and Crispin nervously looked around as though suspicious.

"Is something going to...jump out and take us or something?" Annika asked. She leaned in near the hedge wall, poked it with her finger, and then she quickly moved away.

Theo grinned. "Possibly," he said coolly.

"What?" Annika asked as she stepped closer to Crispin.

"He's trying to intimidate us," Simon said with a sly smile.

"Well, it's working," Annika said. "Why are we doing this again? Haven't we proven we know how to use our sense of direction and everything by arriving here from Illiath in one piece...by our own doing?" Annika spoke of the journey she, Simon, and Crispin had made from Illiath to Vulgaard while Peter was held captive in Rünbrior. The three friends had faced many dangers along the way culminating with Crispin almost losing his life in a rushing river.

"No, you haven't." Theo walked passed them and exited the maze. "Were you not surprised by the trolls? Were you not fooled by the Dwarf, Toomley? Did that act almost cost Crispin his life? And what saved Crispin from the river? Was that of your own doing?"

Annika's face turned red. She remembered how they had mistakenly trusted one of Lord Bedlam's spies that turned into a killer wolf. Had it not been for the Dragon of the Forest, Crispin wouldn't have survived the journey.

"Listen to me, you must pay attention as you walk through the maze. The end is there, trust me. There is a way out, however, finding it is quite the task," he advised. "Do your best to stay together. Pride might take over and cause you to think you know the way, but beware of pride. Work as a team." He joined his hands together.

Theo turned to Peter. "Work as a unit. Help each other and you just might make it out before dark."

"This is ridiculous," Peter said. "Annika's right. Haven't we all had enough training? I have trained in the arena and they have learned much from their journey here."

Theo walked up to Peter. "Annika is right in that she, Simon, and Crispin have had a chance to work together," he said. "But *you* have not, Peter."

Peter looked at his friends. Simon took Annika's hand, and then looked at Peter.

"We endured much together, Peter," he said. "Our journey to Vulgaard and all that happened has brought us closer."

Annika nodded and grinned at Simon, but then she also took

Crispin's hand.

"We almost lost Crispin," she said. "Yes, together we have endured much."

"They had time to bond together, to work together, on their treacherous journey. But you haven't had your chance to work as a team...as a unit with them." Theo walked over to Annika and squeezed her shoulder. "Now is your chance to show them that you are ready to work with them."

Peter fingered the hilt of his sword dangling at his side.

Eris cleared her throat. "Because you do not want to be in here after dark alone," she said. "Trust me."

Peter rolled his eyes, took out his sword, and headed into the maze alone. Theo closed his eyes, shook his head, and exhaled in frustration.

"Peter, wait," Annika said. She took off after him, leaving Simon and Crispin alone with Theo.

"Well?" Theo asked them. He rubbed his bearded chin and gave them a stern look. "What are you two waiting for? Off you go."

The two ran after Annika.

Theo turned to Eris. "Good luck, my dear."

She smiled, nodded, and then ran into the maze.

§

Alexander found himself alone on one of the many balconies of Isleif's palace at Gundrehd. He leaned on the railing overlooking the sea as the waves crashed against the rocks below. The moist air mixed with the salty aroma of the sea as the sun sat low in the sky. On the sandy shore, the servants brought several of the dragons to the water. Some entered the water, playfully splashing around, while others flew over the waves. A smile came to Alexander. The beasts seemed to enjoy themselves.

"Amazing creatures, aren't they?" Isleif asked as he stood next to Alexander.

"Indeed," Alexander said. He turned to face his friend. "I wish I knew of their strengths long ago, but Laurien never spoke of her knowledge of dragons."

Isleif nodded.

"I suppose I know why," Alexander said.

"Oh I'm certain our fathers would have exploited their strengths somehow just as most men have," Isleif said.

"True."

"No, it's best that they are raised and trained by the Elves of Vulgaard. They understand the beasts, they speak their language," Isleif explained.

Alexander returned his gaze to the dragons below. Some swam in the water while others ate fish. The sunlight reflected off their scales. Alexander enjoyed the scent of the salty sea water in the air.

"We will need to rely on dragon strength and power if we are to win this war," he said.

Isleif agreed. "And we will."

"We accomplished much today, didn't we?" Alexander asked.

"Yes. All the rulers are in agreement," Isleif replied. He patted Alexander on the back. "Your father would be proud."

"Yours, too," Alexander said.

"You have done well, Alexander," Isleif said. "Peter is an amazing young man. He has proven to be most honorable. You should be proud."

Alexander looked at his friend. Isleif furrowed his brow because he could see concern in Alexander's eyes.

"What is it?" he asked him.

"I am proud, but..." Alexander's voice trailed off.

"Go on," Isleif urged.

"I'm afraid Peter's honor came at a great cost. I worry about him. His experiences in Rünbrior haunt him still. It isn't right for such a young man to have seen and experienced so much death," Alexander said.

Isleif pointed to the dragons below. "Look at those young dragons, Alexander," he said. "Look at their carefree ways. They have no fear of the water because they do not know what is in it. There are creatures in the water so large they could swallow all the dragons at once. I have seen them."

Alexander listened.

"Peter was once carefree, too, like those dragons," Isleif continued. "He lived unaware of all that could defeat him. But now he is experienced in the ways of battle. I can see why the Dragon allowed the capture to happen. Peter is a skilled fighter now, a knight of the Royal Realm. He is ready to face this task as a young man...as a knight."

Alexander nodded as he took in the words.

"Do not be concerned for him. He knows the enemy now. He knows what lurks beneath. He will approach with caution and he will be victorious. Just you watch, my friend," Isleif said and he patted Alexander on the shoulder. He said, as he turned to leave, "You're a good father, Alexander. Peter is blessed."

As he watched his friend leave, Alexander returned his gaze to the waves crashing against the rocks below. The dragons continued in their carefree manner.

"No, I am the blessed one," he murmured.

§

"Peter wait for us," Annika cried out as she caught up to him. "We must stay together."

Peter turned to her and paused only for a moment before he spotted Eris coming up from behind. "You go the way you want to go. I am going this way." He said to Eris then took off toward the right.

Annika sighed heavily as Simon and Crispin approached.

"Where is Peter going?" Simon asked. "Annika, are you alright? Did Peter say something to anger you?" He gently took her hand.

"He said he's going that way...alone. We were told to stay together. He seems upset about something. I'm concerned about him," Annika said. "He's been acting strange lately."

She looked at her hand wrapped in Simon's. "What do you think we should do?" she asked him.

Simon looked at Crispin who shrugged.

They all turned to Eris.

"What do you suggest?" Annika asked Eris. She let go of Simon's hand and walked over to Eris.

"Yes, what do you think we should do?" Simon asked Eris.

She blinked her grey eyes then reached up and pulled an arrow from the quiver. She loaded her bow and took a few steps into the maze. "Watch your back. Pay attention to everything," she instructed. "Things will happen that cannot be explained. Keep moving through the maze no matter what. Let's go." She walked off to the left opposite from the way Peter went.

"Well, there you go," Simon said with a shrug. He looked to his left and then to his right. The hedge looked exactly the same no matter what direction he looked. "I have no idea what she means by that, but alright. Let's go."

"Honestly," Annika sighed again. "I think we should go after Peter."

"Of course you do," Simon mumbled to himself.

"What's that supposed to mean?" Annika stopped and faced Simon.

"What?" he asked.

"Your tone," Annika said. "Is there something bothering you, Simon?"

Crispin pushed his way passed the two of them. "I don't have to listen to this," he said to Simon. "I'm going with Eris. You two do what you need to do. Go on, then."

Annika frowned. "What do you mean by that, Crispin?"

Crispin chuckled. "Never mind."

"That was strange." Annika watched Crispin walk off. She turned to Simon. "I'm going to look for Peter. Are you coming or not?"

"No," Simon said. Annika furrowed her brow. "You go on after Peter. That's what you want to do anyway."

"Simon?" Annika approached him. "What are you saying?"

"Come on, Annika," he said. "Everyone can see that you feel something for Peter."

"Yes, he's a dear friend."

Simon raised an eyebrow. "Really? That's all he is to you?"

Annika scratched her hair. "Well…"

"You have feelings for him even though," Simon's voice trailed off.

"What? Finish what you were saying," she said.

"I don't think he cares for you in the same way," Simon replied. He raised his chin with satisfaction. "There. I said it."

Annika frowned and looked down at her feet.

Simon exhaled and took her hand. "I'm sorry. Come on, let's forget all that nonsense get this task over with."

Simon waited for Annika's response. Finally, she jerked his hand away and looked at him.

"No, you go on with them," she said defiantly. "I'm going to find Peter."

Simon watched as she ran off into the maze toward the right.

# 23 THE TESTING

Peter continued meandering through the maze even though he knew he was alone, which was what Theo had warned against. But he didn't care. His anger fueled his pace. He could feel his face grow warmer and warmer as he thought more about his young mother being betrayed by her friend, Bedlam, and then by her tutor, Theo. He resented all the exercises he had to endure in order to prepare them for the battle. Deep inside, he was convinced he was ready and, in a way, he wanted to get it over with.

"I don't care what Theo says," Peter said to no one there. "It was wrong of him to cast that spell. He knew what would happen to my mother, yet he did it anyway as though he didn't care."

Peter gripped the hilt of his sword with white knuckles. He ran through the maze. "He knew it and so did the Dragon." He swung at the hedge, sending wisps of leaves to the ground. "That poison she drank was meant for me!" he shouted to no one. "I was the one who was supposed to get hurt, not her."

"And I don't need this so called training exercise!" He shouted to the sky. He ran ahead letting the hedge guide him left, then right, then left again until he found himself facing a dead end. "Oh great," he panted. "I'd better head back tell the others not to come this way."

He turned around and ran back the same way, still picturing his mother in his mind.

She was just a young girl. She didn't know what she was doing, he thought. Theo shouldn't have cast that spell.

His heart beat faster until it felt like his chest would burst.

Suddenly, he heard a sound that stopped him cold. The hairs on his arms stood up. He raised his sword.

"What was that?" he mumbled and took a few steps back. It was a growl, but not of a dragon or even a wolf. It was lower and raspier.

Peter remembered Theo's words about how he could be fooled by sounds. He ran off back to where he had come and stopped when he reached a dead end.

"The entrance of the maze." He looked all around. "It's gone."

He turned and gripped his sword even tighter. A gust of wind swept by his side and a he heard a ghostly laugh.

"What?" he leapt out of the way. "Who's there?"

He could see the wind sweep through the hedge ahead of him tossing a few dead leaves around. The low ominous growl came from ahead. Clouds rolled in above the hedge and blocked out the sunlight. It smelled of rain. Booming claps of thunder startled Peter.

"I'd better keep moving," he said to himself and crept further down the maze. Off in the distance, he heard Annika's voice calling out for him.

"Annika," Peter said. "I'd better warn her."

As he ran, he heard the sound of leaves rustling. He turned in time to see the dark green hedge wall close behind him like a curtain. "No!" he shouted. He touched the green leaves and his eyes followed up the hedge wall, but it was no use. "I see what this is now. It's a magic trick. It's probably just a game."

He fingered the hilt of his sword. "This is just a game of wits, that's all it is." He turned in a circle. When he saw there was nothing nearby, he continued on. He heard Annika's voice again.

You will be fooled by your surroundings, tricked by your eyes, don't trust them...

Peter began to realize the purpose of this maze. "Annika isn't really calling out," he mumbled to himself. "It's just an illusion." *But what if it's not?* He thought. *No, of course it is. There are no haunted forests and no haunted mazes.* He walked on with confidence. "I'll find my way out of this."

A few feet ahead of him was a turn in the maze. From around the corner, crept a creature Peter had never seen before. Its thick black fur was course like that of a winter wolf, but its eyes glowed bright red in the darkness and it stood much taller than any wolves Peter had ever seen. When it snarled, Peter could see its sharp teeth.

*I know he isn't real,* he thought. *This must be part of the illusion. I must keep going.*

§

Simon ran right behind Crispin and Eris.

"Wait up!" he shouted, but they seemed to ignore him and ran even faster until they turned a corner and disappeared. "Hey!" Simon shouted after them.

He stood alone in the maze catching his breath for a moment. And then he heard Crispin shout for help.

Simon ran after the voice, but saw no one when he turned a corner. Crispin and Eris had indeed disappeared. Or had something taken them? He turned around and no one was behind him either.

"Crispin!" he shouted. "Where are you?"

"Over here!" came the answer from the other side of the hedge. Simon leaned in close to the leaves and listened.

"Where are you?" he asked again. The leaves of the hedge rustled. "Crispin?"

Suddenly, the branches moved and grabbed him like arms would. He tried to jerk loose, but the branches pulled him into the hedge.

"No!" he shouted and struggled to break free. But his struggling only caused more branches to lurch out and take hold of him. He leaned back as much as he could and pulled on his arms, but the branches gripped even tighter and the hedge began to swallow him up.

"Help!" Simom screamed. Another branch reached out like a hand and began to take his sword from its sheath. His eyes widened at the sight and he    pulled on his arms with more intensity. "Someone help me!"

§

"Peter!" Annika cupped her hands over her mouth. "Where are you?"

She walked on and noticed the air had turned cooler. "Smells like rain," she said to herself. "Come on, Peter, where did you go?"

A rustling noise came from the wall of the hedge to her right. She quickly turned to see what caused the noise. "Peter?" she asked. "Is that you?"

She leaned in and saw something move deep inside the hedge wall. "Must be a squirrel or a bird," she whispered. A gust of wind swept by her back and she heard the sound of a woman laughing. "Who's there?"

Annika turned around and gripped the hilt of her sword. She suddenly felt very alone, which was what Theo had warned against.

She decided to walk on staying clear of the walls of the hedge. "This is only a test," she said to herself. "Don't believe what you see.

Don't be fooled. Just keeping walking."

Another gust of wind brushed her side and swept her hair into her face. A growl came from inside the hedge wall. Annika froze.

"Peter! Is that you?" she shouted. "Where are you? There's something inside this maze!"

She stood in the middle of the path waiting for someone or something to emerge from the hedge wall. The sudden silence unnerved her. Then, she felt the pressure of a hand on her shoulder. She exhaled with relief.

"Peter, I finally found you." She turned around and saw a silvery ghost had placed its bony hand on her shoulder. Annika screamed and leapt out of the way.

The ghost was of an old hag who tossed her head back and laughed heartily. The spirit of the dead woman dissipated into a gust of wind. Annika could hear the old woman's cackle move over the hedge.

"This place is haunted!" Annika screamed at no one then took off running back to the entrance of the maze. But before she turned a corner, a vine from the hedge wall reached out at her and took hold of her ankle. She tripped forward and hit the ground hard. The vine pulled her in toward the hedge. Annika quickly removed her sword and sliced the vine in two. She leapt to her feet and took off running down the maze path with a ghostly breeze following after her. She could hear the old woman's cackle behind her. She turned and sliced at it with her sword.

"Get away from me!" she shrieked and continued to run until she found a corner. She looked behind and saw no one was in sight. She could hear more rustling coming from the hedge and several vines leapt out at her again. One grabbed her wrist and another wrapped around her waist.

"Help me!" she screamed and tried to swipe the vine with her sword, but it had a hold of her wrist. "Peter!"

It squeezed her wrist so tightly, Annika dropped her sword. Two more vines took hold of her legs and she fell to the ground. The vines began to pull her toward the hedge wall.

Annika didn't know what would happen if that wall swallowed her up, but she had a feeling it couldn't be anything good.

§

A thick mist covered the ground at Peter's feet. His skin became moist. The air smelled of mold. The Zadok before Peter opened its jaws and thick drool oozed to the ground. Peter froze at the sight. He suddenly remembered the sight of the dead beasts on the fields during the war with Lord Caragon. This creature was much larger than what he had remembered. Its eyes glowed red, just like a dragon. It crept toward Peter cautiously with its sharp teeth showing and lips quivering.

Peter swallowed hard.

The sword in his grip trembled from the fear swelling up within his body. He tried, but he couldn't stop his hands from shaking. He knew the beast could sense his fear.

*Now what?* He thought. *Come on, Peter. Get ahold of yourself. You've fought dragons bigger than this creature.*

Peter narrowed his eyes, pursed his lips, and took a few steps toward the drooling Zadok, challenging it. He raised his sword and the beast roared so loud, it startled Peter.

Peter's eyes widened and he stepped back without taking his eyes off the Zadok. "Alright, bad idea," he panted. He continued to move away until, finally, he felt the hedge against his back. He was trapped.

"So this is it?" he asked no one. "This is how the test ends?"

The Zadok crouched down, preparing to lunge at its prey. Peter closed his eyes and waited for the end.

"I'm sorry I failed you, father,." Peter grimaced and turned his face away.

§

"Help!" Simon struggled with the branches that gripped his arms and legs. "Somebody!"

A vine snaked out from the hedge and wrapped around his mouth. His screams were muffled and he found it hard to breathe. Simon saw an opening in the hedge appear and his feet were pulled in, but he kicked and tried his best to scoot away from the opening all the while trying to wriggle free. He knew once inside that hedge, he was in big trouble.

A sword appeared from nowhere. Simon gasped.

It sliced one of the branches in two. Simon rolled over and tried to crawl away. The sword severed another branch and then another until

Simon was finally free except for the vine covering his mouth.

Then, the vine unwrapped itself from Simon's face and disappeared into the hedge opening which closed like a giant mouth.

Simon sat up and panted on the ground. "Thank you," he whispered. "…whoever you are."

"You're most welcome, my friend," came an unfamiliar voice from behind him.

# 24 THE SECRET OF THE MAZE

"Somebody, help!" Annika cried.

"Hold still!" Crispin ran up to her and tried to pry the vines off her wrists, but it was no use. He removed his sword and severed the vines. Instantly, they shriveled up and turned brown. Annika wrestled with the vine around her waist.

"Hurry, help me get this off!" she yelled as she tugged at the vine.

Crispin raised his sword to cut another vine, but before he did, he heard the sound of a woman's voice.

"What was that?" he asked with astonishment.

"It's a ghost!" Annika replied. "Of an old hag. I don't think she wants us here. Hurry! Cut me loose!"

Crispin cut another vine in two and helped Annika stand. She removed the vine from her body like it was a dead snake.

"Ugh!" She grimaced as she threw the vine down. "Thank you for helping me. Where were you?"

"Lost," Crispin said. "I heard your screams and then Eris heard Peter's shouts. She took off to help him and I found you."

Annika nodded and tried to catch her breath. "And Simon? Where's he?"

Crispin shook his head. "Don't know. We haven't seen him since we first took off into the maze."

A gust of wind swept between them almost toppling them over. The ghost's cackle rose all around them.

"Hurry! We'd better find him and from now on, we all stick together." Annika hurried off. "This maze wants us out!"

"I'm beginning to see that," Crispin shouted as he followed after her.

§

Peter winced as he waited for his death, but instead of the pain of Zadok teeth tearing at his flesh, he heard the beast cry out in pain.

Peter opened his eyes in time to see three arrows pierce the side of the Zadok. It jerked to the side then howled in pain. It ran off in a trail of blood. Peter grimaced at the pungent odor of Zadok blood and sweat. He looked up to the top of the hedge and spotted Eris. She jumped down off the hedge and landed a few feet away from Peter. She looked very disappointed.

"Well, I've lost those arrows for good," she said with her hands on her hips.

"And I, for one, am grateful." Peter placed his sword in its sheath. "Thank you for helping me."

Annika and Crispin came around the corner.

"There you are!" Annika shouted. She and Crispin came running up to Peter.

"Where did you two come from?" Peter asked. "I heard your voices but…"

"Never mind that," she said as she took his arm. "Let's get out of here before more monsters return!"

Peter and the others took off running down one passageway. They could hear the rustling of leaves behind them. Peter turned to his left only to be met with yet another dead end. Around his ankle, he felt the pull of a vine. It twisted and gripped his ankle like a hand would. Peter sliced it off with his sword, but another one shot out from the hedge.

"Not again!" Annika screeched.

"Watch it!" Crispin's eyes were wide with fear. "The hedge is alive!"

"More tricks." Eris waved at them. "Just keep going. Follow me!"

Together, they continued on and turned in a different direction. As they did, they could hear more vines coming after them. One grabbed Peter's arm, but he twisted free and continued to run alongside Eris and the others. Another vine reached out and grabbed his foot tripping him. He landed hard and the sword flew from his hand. Vines from within the hedge lurched at him and began to wrap around his body.

"No!" he shouted and reached for his sword, but the vines had already covered it. "Keep going!" Peter screamed to the others. He struggled to break free from the vines twisting around his frame, but each time he moved they tightened their grip making it hard for him to breathe. He could hear a witch-like cackle all around him. Finally, the vines covered his eyes, nose, and mouth. Peter stopped struggling, trying to breathe. But his chest was too constricted. He began to black out.

"Here! Help me free him!" Eris ordered the others. She pulled on the vines.

Annika pulled out her sword and sliced away at the vines coming for her and Crispin. Then, she turned and cut away the vines grasping Peter, freeing him. He wriggled and tried to breathe. Eris removed the vines from his face and helped him stand as he tried to catch his breath.

"Thank you all," he huffed. "This is all just a game, right?"

"Seems pretty real to me," Annika said. She pulled more vine scraps and leaves from Peter's tunic.

"Which way do we go now?" Peter asked Eris. "You've been in here before. What did you do to escape?"

Eris looked all around. "I ran and fought off whatever got in my way."

Peter nodded. "Sounds good to me. Let's go!"

Eris motioned for them to follow her down another path. This time, they heard footsteps approaching from behind. Peter turned and saw several of Bedlam's Baroks running toward them. They wore black leather armor and were armed with swords and shields.

"Don't look now, but we're being followed!" Crispin shouted.

"Then keep running!" Eris said without turning around, her braided hair flowing behind her.

The path seemed to go on without an end. Peter hoped they would find the way out of the maze, but something inside him knew that it was all another illusion.

He heard the whizzing sound of an arrow fly past his ear.

"They have arrows!" he shouted to Annika and Crispin.

Eris reached behind her and took an arrow from her quiver. As she ran, she loaded her bow. Instantly, she turned, aimed, and shot the arrow through the neck of a Barok as it ran at them.

Peter stopped and watched the sight with his mouth agape.

"Don't stop, you fool. Move!" Eris called to him as she ran off. The death seemed to only anger the other Baroks and they roared toward them.

But Peter decided to take them on. He stood with his sword raised high.

"Peter! What are you doing?" Crispin stopped. "We must go, now!"

One Barok reached Peter and sliced at his middle. Annika turned her head. Peter leapt out of the way and swung his sword around cutting the Barok's throat, spewing its thick blood all over the hedge. But the others had reached Peter, too. He swung around low and sliced the thigh of another Barok. In seconds, two more were fighting him.

Eris turned to see Peter fighting off the Baroks. She took out a knife from her belt and ran to help him. When she reached the fight, she sliced at the Baroks, sending their blood flying through the air. Finally, all the Baroks lay dead on the ground.

Peter and Eris stood over the carnage. "Fortitude and teamwork," Eris coolly said to Peter. She placed her knife back onto her belt.

He looked into her grey eyes and saw the fierce determination again.

"We'll need it to survive the final battle at Illiath, Peter," she said. "Understand?"

Peter nodded enthusiastically. "Absolutely," he murmured.

"Unbelievable," Crispin exhaled as he made his way over to them. "Where did you learn fight like that? In the arena? Amazing."

Peter ignored the questions and breathed deeply. He couldn't believe how real everything inside the maze was. The Baroks bled onto the ground. Their eyes remained open and dull as the life drained away. How could this all be just a trick? Peter remembered what Theo told him about his mother and how easily she believed that Bedlam was a man. Magic can seem so real, so believable, that it tricks the eye.

"And you!" Crispin turned to Eris. "Where did you learn to shoot arrows that way?" he asked. His blue eyes widened.

"Come on, we've got to find our way out of this maze before night falls and all the really strange happenings begin," Eris said. Crispin looked over at Annika, then back at Eris.

"You mean, it gets worse?" He winced.

"Much worse." Eris smirked. "Follow me." She retrieved her arrows and used her pant legs to wipe the blood off of them before she placed them back into her quiver. She stomped off in the direction they had come from.

"You must be frustrated with us," Annika said as she followed Eris. "I mean, we were supposed to stay together and follow you."

Eris kept walking.

"But instead, against all advice, we separated," Annika said to Eris's back.

"I suppose we broke the rules of the maze," Crispin said to Peter. "No wonder it attacked us."

"We were supposed to work together as a team. We aren't as prepared as we thought we were," Annika sighed. "Well, as prepared as I thought we were."

"You're right," Peter agreed.

"Pride, you know," Crispin said. "It snares the best of us."

"Yes, it does." Peter looked around as they walked. "Alright, we're together now, but I still don't trust this place."

"Wait a minute!" Annika shouted. Eris stopped walking.

"Where is Simon?" Annika asked everyone.

She looked at Peter who looked at Crispin. They all looked at Eris who rolled her eyes and shook her head.

"I'll go back and find him, you all wait here. Don't wander off," she ordered.

"But—" Crispin started.

Eris shot him a stern look that silenced him and then she jogged off. They watched her leave to look for Simon.

"I was only going to say that we were told before to keep moving." Crispin rubbed his forehead.

"I hope Simon's alright," Annika said. "Did you see him anywhere in the maze?"

Crispin shook his head. "No. The last time I saw him, he was with you."

Annika smirked. "Yes, well, we had a tiff and he went his own way. I went to look for Peter."

"Was Simon upset about that?" Crispin narrowed his eyes with curiosity.

Annika nodded. "Yes, why?"

Crispin chortled. "Just wondering."

## 25 THE LESSON AT THE FINISH

Bedlam tugged on the reins of his dragon as it landed at the palace of Hildron. Sir William met his master there in the courtyard. Two Baroks raced toward Lord Bedlam's dragon and assisted him as he dismounted.

Will bowed as he approached. "My Lord. Did all go as you expected with the boy?" he asked.

"Indeed. Exactly as I had expected." Bedlam removed his gloves. "His heart is definitely weakened by his hatred and jealousy. He can and will be used."

Will nodded. The two walked across the courtyard and into the entrance of the palace. "The weak have always served me well. Caragon helped me form the Baroks and Zadoks into an army and now you will help lead that army into one last battle. Tomorrow we shall assemble your men, Will. What an impressive sight it will be, my friend. You will have your army and begin the march toward Illiath to meet King Alexander there at the ruins of his palace."

"Understood," Will said.

Bedlam removed his cloak and set it on the table in the hall. He stood in front of the mirror admiring his image. "My plan is coming together just as I had hoped it would."

"But the swords, my Lord." Will stood next to him. "What of the swords?"

Bedlam shook his head. "With your army and mine combined with the soldiers of the rulers, there is no way a young boy will be able to enter the forest alone with those swords."

"But, my Lord, this same boy defeated dragons in the great arena of Rünbrior," Will said.

Bedlam grimaced when he heard those words.

"This same boy fought Valbrand's men and won," Will continued. "Are you certain that…"

Bedlam raised his hand to stop Will from speaking further. He took in all that Will had said. He was right. No matter what obstacles Lord

Bedlam had placed before Prince Peter, the boy had overcome them. As a result, Bedlam was weakened. He had suffered great physical pain when Scathar was slaughtered in the arena. He had used great magic to create the mutant dragon and so he had become connected to it. When it died, it took days for Bedlam's own body to recover. He was connected to every creature he created at Hildron and because of the Wizard's Code, his experiments with existing spells would continue to cause him harm. That was the secret he couldn't let anyone know.

His magic spells cost him dearly and would continue to do so. When a Zadok or Barok died, he needed to replace them immediately in order for his power to remain potent. And what if he could no longer replace them? Could it be that Peter could also defeat the army Bedlam had amassed? He considered the idea for a moment.

"I am most certain that my plan will succeed. For this same boy has yet to meet my greatest creation. No eye has seen a beast of this magnitude. No man, Elf, or dragon will be able to withstand the power of this creature. For all my strength and power goes with it," he exclaimed, jabbing his finger at Will. He grabbed his cloak off the table, turned to leave, but then paused.

"Do you understand? All my power is vested in this one creature. And with it, I have devised a way to prohibit Peter from entering the Dragon Forest with the swords. I have finally found a way to enter the Dragon Forest and kill the Dragon. No young boy can stop this now."

Will bowed. "Yes, my Lord."

"Trust me, Will," Lord Bedlam said. "Everything is set in motion."

Will remained silent as his master walked off down the darkened hallway.

§

"Hurry!" Eris shouted and waved for everyone to follow her. "This way! I have found the way out."

Peter, Annika, and Crispin ran after her. That's when they saw Simon running with them.

They sped down the path after Eris, turning left, then right, until they saw the exit and Theo standing there to greet them.

"We made it!" Annika cried. Crispin ran out of the maze and collapsed on the ground, exhausted. Above them, the darkened clouds cleared away and the late afternoon sun warmed the air.

Peter stopped and bent over, panting hard. "It's over, Theo."

Peter turned to Simon. "Are you alright, Simon? You look like you've seen a ghost."

Annika chuckled. "Don't mention ghosts. So, where were you, Simon?"

"Well, it's all over and we passed this test, right Theo?" Peter said.

"It's not quite over with," Theo said. Peter looked up at him. He could see concern in his eyes. Peter followed Theo's glance and realized that he was looking at Eris who stood with her bow loaded with an arrow pointing directly at Simon.

"What's this?" Peter asked. "Eris, lower your bow. What are you doing?"

"What is it, Eris?" Theo asked.

"Lord Bedlam," Eris said, her voice was shaky and her gaze intense. "He was in the maze."

Simon stared at the arrow pointing at him. He slowly raised his hands in surrender.

"What?" Theo said. His grey eyes widened.

Annika looked at Crispin who looked at Simon.

"What's happening?" Peter straightened up and glanced over at Eris then at Theo. "What's going on here?"

"Eris, why are you pointing your arrow at Simon?" Annika asked.

"Are you certain of this, Eris?" Theo asked. He furrowed his brow. "Are you certain you saw Lord Bedlam?"

"Yes!" Eris shouted, startling Annika and Crispin, who were both staring at the scene now with very frightened eyes. "I saw him. I saw him talking to Simon in the maze. I saw it with my own eyes!"

Theo looked at Simon whose face had gone pale.

"Lord Bedlam was in the maze?" Peter looked all around the area, almost expecting to see him appear.

"Are you certain it was him and not an illusion?" Annika asked. "I mean, we saw so many illusions that seemed real but…"

"It was him!" Eris interrupted. "I know it was him. I recognized his voice and when I turned the corner, I saw him standing before Simon."

"You have seen Bedlam before?" Peter asked her.

"Yes," she said, "at his fortress at Hildron."

"How is that possible? How could he enter the maze unseen, Theo?" Peter asked Theo who remained in deep thought as he took in the words. "Theo!"

"I do not know," Theo said incredulously. His eyes remained fixed on Eris. "It has never happened before."

"I suspected something before when we encountered the Baroks in the maze," Eris explained.

"Baroks?" Theo squinted.

"Yes," Eris continued. "I have never encountered Baroks within the maze before. Something seemed amiss. And when I went to find Simon, I heard Lord Bedlam's voice. I followed it and saw them talking together," Eris said.

"But why? Why was he in the maze?" Peter asked. "Why was he talking to you, Simon?"

"Lower your weapon, Eris!" Annika insisted.

"I will not. Tell us, Simon. Now!" Eris ordered Simon. She pulled back on the bowstring. "Tell us so we can know the truth."

Simon began to shake and he looked over at Peter and then at Theo.

"Tell us, Simon," Theo said calmly. "Tell us what he said to you."

Simon turned to Annika and Crispin. "It's true," Simon said. His face reddened. "Lord Bedlam appeared to me in the maze and I spoke with him."

Annika gasped. "What?"

Theo studied Simon's eyes.

"What did he say to you, Simon?" Theo asked.

"He…" Simon hesitated.

"Tell him or I will," Eris said angrily.

Crispin shook his head, clearly disappointed.

"He freed me from the vines that were hurting me. I couldn't breathe. I thought I was going to die. But he cut me lose and then," Simon explained, "he told me who he was and why he was there."

Theo took in the words and looked away as he listened.

"And you weren't frightened?" Annika asked Simon.

"No, I mean, yes, but…"

"How could this have happened, Theo?" Peter asked, but received no answer. He turned to Simon. "So, why was he there?" Peter asked. "What happened that has frightened Eris so?" Peter had never seen her so angry.

Eris' fingers shook from pulling on the bowstring so tightly.

Simon swallowed. "He promised me something if…"

Theo watched the boy carefully. "Go on," he said.

"If I followed him out of the maze, he promised me—"

"What did he promise you?" Peter asked.

Crispin closed his eyes as though he knew what Simon was going to say next.

But Simon didn't answer immediately.

"Go on," Theo said as he walked over to Eris. He gently motioned for her to lower her bow. She reluctantly obeyed.

"What was it?" Peter smirked. "Great wealth? Power, land, and a title?"

"Annika," Simon said.

Peter jerked his head around. "What?"

"He promised me Annika if I followed him out of the maze," Simon confessed.

*"Annika?"* Peter asked. He crinkled his brow and looked over at Theo. "Whatever did he mean by that?"

Crispin sighed.

"Oh, no." Annika covered he mouth with her hands. "Oh, Simon, no."

"He promised me that he could make Annika love me," Simon said. His eyes became shiny from tears. "He said he could make her love me as I love her."

Peter laughed slightly. "This is ridiculous," Peter said. "Make Annika love you as you…"

Peter realized no one else saw the humor in what Simon had said. "…As *you* love her. But you don't love Annika."

He looked over at Crispin.

Crispin looked as though he might be sick to his stomach.

Annika was crestfallen.

"Wait," Peter stood by Simon. "You love Annika?"

Simon nodded.

"And Bedlam said what else?" Eris cried out to Simon. "Tell him!"

Peter glanced at Eris then back at Simon.

"What else did he say to you, Simon?"

Simon avoided Peter's eyes.

*"What else did he say?"*

"He said that if I betrayed you, he could make Annika love me and we'd be together forever," Simon cried. "But Peter, I never said…"

Peter stepped back as though he'd been hit in the chest by an arrow.

"Peter, I never agreed to it!" Simon insisted.

Theo turned to Eris. "Is this true?"

"I tried to tell her!" Simon pointed at Eris then looked at Peter. "I told her that I never agreed to the deal. I would never betray you, Peter. You have to believe me!"

"What did you hear?" Theo asked Eris.

"I heard Bedlam make the deal ," she said, "But it was unclear how Simon answered. "And when I appeared around the corner of the hedge with my bow drawn, I saw it was Bedlam before he disappeared. That's when I asked Simon what he had vowed."

"And I told her I didn't agree to it," Simon cried. "Peter, I would never betray you."

Peter, still looking away, nodded.

"Oh, Simon." Annika wiped her tears. She ran over to him. "Look at me! Are you telling us the truth? Please tell me you didn't swear anything to Lord Bedlam."

"Annika, I swear to you all now, I did not accept his deal." Simon looked intently into Annika's eyes. She stared at him for a moment and nodded. His eyes hadn't changed. Wouldn't his eyes be deadened if he were struck with a spell? But his eyes were still gentle. Annika realized he remained the Simon she had known for many years. She turned to Theo.

"I believe him," she declared.

Peter turned to Crispin. "What about you?"

Crispin closed his eyes and groaned as though he'd hoped no one would ask him his thoughts.

"Well?" Peter asked.

"Yes, I've known all along how Simon feels about Annika," Crispin groaned. He looked over at Simon. "He loves her, the idiot. But I cannot believe he'd be so stupid as to enter into a deal with Lord Bedlam and betray you, Peter. He's stupid, but not *that* stupid."

"You see?" Simon pointed at Crispin. "He's right. I'm an idiot, but I would never be so stupid as to betray you Peter. For Annika or for anything in the world."

"Lord Bedlam goes after the weak minded. He knows the heart," Eris said sternly and pointed her finger at Simon. "He selected you for a reason!"

Peter studied Simon who looked down and wrung his hands together.

"Yes, I know," he mumbled nervously. "I was jealous of you, Peter. I admit that."

Peter listened.

"I know Annika loves you and not me," Simon continued. "I allowed my jealously to make me susceptible to Bedlam's temptations. But I swear, I didn't agree to anything. I would never betray you!" His voice cracked with emotion.

Peter studied Simon carefully and then he looked at Theo.

"Theo," he said. "I don't know…"

Theo raised his chin and nodded. "Yes you do."

In that instant, Peter remembered Simon from before all the madness with Lord Bedlam had started. He remembered Simon's face before and saw that he had indeed remained the same. He was still the same old Simon from years before. Peter felt the warmth of relief wash over him and that's when he knew it. He knew Simon was telling the truth. Peter smiled then embraced him.

"I believe you," Peter cried.

Annika wept and took Crispin's arm. "Oh, thank goodness."

The four friends embraced each other there at the end of The Maze of Thœrgën.

"Well, glad *that* adventure is over," Crispin sighed.

"And now we have all learned to work together, no matter what." Annika said.

As they held tightly to one another, the purpose of the maze became crystal clear to Peter. He realized that he had much to learn about his friends and himself at the start of the maze and had learned a powerful lesson at the finish.

They all had.

Peter realized that King Aidan was very wise to construct the maze for preparation of battle. He knew his Elfin soldiers needed to learn to work together if they were to survive. The four friends had learned that even Lord Bedlam's power was strong enough to penetrate the maze, but not their friendship. They had withstood evil with good.

When they parted, Peter turned to Theo whose eyes had softened.

"Thank you, Theo," Peter said as he took hold of Theo's forearm. "You were right and I was wrong. Very wrong. I learned a great deal here today."

He turned to his friends, still weepy with emotion. "I need them desperately," he said. "We will win this battle together."

Eris placed the arrow back in her quiver and slung her bow on her shoulder.

"I thank you, Eris," Peter said. He stood in front of her.

She looked at him. "I hope you are right about Simon."

"I am," Peter said. "And I thank you for your loyalty and honesty. We should have listened to you and stayed together. If we had, Simon wouldn't have been alone and then…"

She nodded.

"Come." Theo waved to them. "Let us return to the palace for a warm meal. You have earned it."

"Yeah," said Crispin. "Let's eat!"

"Tonight," Theo continued, glancing askance at Crispin, "you will rest and then you will head out to Illiath."

"When will we be leaving, Theo?" Annika asked.

"In the next two days," Theo said.

"So soon," Annika sighed as she watched Theo walk off. "I miss my grandfather and my home, but I will most certainly miss this place," she said as she glanced over to the palace of Vulgaard glistening in the late afternoon sun.

She started to walk off with Peter and Crispin.

"I'll miss all the food," Crispin said.

Simon started to follow and then he turned to Eris. "Thank you," he said. She raised her eyebrows.

"Thank you for helping us out of the maze," he finished.

She nodded and started to walk away.

"But..." he said. "Would you have really killed me?"

"Yes," she said without hesitation.

Her blunt reply startled Simon. She turned to face him.

"You see, Simon," she explained, "I have sworn to protect Prince Peter and the Oath made with the Dragon years before. I have sworn to protect it at any cost."

Simon listened intently as she spoke.

"And I am *very* loyal," she said coolly with no emotion.

"So am I," he said.

"I hope so," she said. "I hope we can trust you, Simon."

"Don't worry about that," he assured her. "Peter is one of my oldest and dearest friends."

"Lord Bedlam's powers are very strong," Eris said as she walked along.

"Yes, and today you saw how our friendship is even stronger," Simon said as she walked past her.

# 26 THE RETURN OF THE SWORDS

The Elfin blacksmith entered the dimly lit hall carrying the wooden box. Behind him followed several of his apprentices who were also carrying boxes. As they approached the table, each one gently placed a box down then stood by awaiting orders. Queen Esmeralda's servants quickly pulled the thick drapes closed over the large windows.

King Alexander rose from the table and made his way around until he faced the boxes. Across from him sat the other rulers with King Isleif and Queen Esmeralda. He could see the excitement in their faces.

"My Lords and Ladies," he said. "It is time."

At his order, the Elves raised the lid of each box revealing the contents. Inside each box rested the swords of the rulers.

Alexander could hear the gasps of the women and the murmurs as they walked around the table to get a closer look at the precious bounty. Queen Esmeralda stood before the sword of her forefathers. She reached out and took the hilt into her hand. As she raised the sword, the light from the nearby torch reflected off the blade with its intricate filigree design. The fire flickered when she moved the sword. A smile came to her face. She turned the sword over and back again until, finally, she returned it to the box.

"I cannot believe all the swords are finally here, together again," she said.

Alexander stood next to her. "Yes, amazing isn't it?"

"After all these years," she said. "To know that we have here the power to end Bedlam's reign of darkness once and for all...it is almost too much to take in."

"Now what do we do?" King Beatann asked.

Alexander turned and nodded to the Elfin guards. They approached and surrounded the swords. Then, they parted and Thætil walked alongside an elder Elf as he approached the table. King Isleif and Queen Esmeralda leaned in to see what would happen.

The elder Elf eyed each of the special guests present, and then touched one of the swords. In a strange Elfin language, he murmured something.

"Eloin el eloi," he uttered as he leaned over the swords. "Ilfendren eloi, ilféndren ur ilêl oli eloi."

All the guests remained silent as the elder Elf read the secret code of each sword placed there long ago upon the request of Queen Laurien when she was just a young maiden.

"Il Illiath ürunde il erriéndish üloi na nathrien elvin." the elder looked up at King Alexander and pointed. "Il Illiath rex üntis elilliëndirish il ëloi ün ti ilfendre ilf ürieundis il."

Alexander nodded to Thætil as though he understood.

"What is he saying?" Isleif asked Thætil.

"He is deciphering the message imbedded in the swords. He is reading the instructions for Prince Peter once he has all the swords at the entrance of the Dragon Forest," Thætil explained. "Peter, and Peter alone, must be the one to enter the forest with all the swords."

King Beatann shook his head. "It is too much," he mumbled. "It is too much to ask of the boy." He turned and paced near the window, rubbing the nape of his neck.

"Do not be afraid, King Beatann," Alexander said to him. He turned and nodded for the elder Elf to continue.

"Eismish il ilündriended il ëloi untis uliende ilféndre ish it. Illiénde il ne hethrëil oi elvin un Draco, un mein ëndiendre ish il üloi oi Bedlam." He nodded to each ruler in the room. "Ne il oi ëloi ün éndriende."

He waved his hand over the swords, stood straight, and then turned to King Alexander who raised his eyebrows, shocked by the mournful look on the elder's face. A shiver went up Alexander's spine. The elder Elf turned to Thætil, and then exited the room.

King Beatann returned to the table. "Well, what was all that about?"

The Elfin guards parted yet again. To everyone's surprise, Queen Thordis of Vulgaard approached the swords. Her silken white hair cascaded down her back in a thick braid revealing the intensity in her eyes. On her brow rested a sapphire and diamond crown. Thætil , Alexander, and the other rulers bowed with respect.

"It is a delight to have you here, your majesty," King Alexander said.

She nodded then looked sternly at King Beatann. "It was a warning to us all, your majesty. If Peter fails, all Elves, dragons, and man will suffer at the hands of Bedlam's power and control. His power has become that potent." She made sure to make eye contact with each ruler present. Her blue eyes sparkled like the jewels in her crown. "This war has now been elevated. The stakes are now that high, I'm afraid."

Alexander squinted and rubbed his bearded chin. He could see the resolve in her face. He turned to all his allies in the room. "I am aware of the costs. Are you my friends?" He reached over and closed the box that held the Sword of Alexander. "Now we wait. We wait until the appointed time."

He motioned for all the rulers to sit. Once they all acquiesced, he joined them in the dim room lit only by a few torches. They knew Lord Bedlam's spies were everywhere and they didn't want to take any chances. "The time approaches. My son is completing his training at Vulgaard and will begin his journey to Illiath where I and my men will meet him. We are certain Sir William will also meet us there to begin the battle. But we are prepared."

"And Bedlam?" King Beatann asked. "Where will he be?"

"At Hildron, no doubt," Alexander said. He waved his hand and a servant brought maps to the table. Alexander helped unroll all the maps as large gemstones of crystal, amethyst, and quartz were placed in each corner to hold them down. All the rulers stood to inspect each map.

"Here is where we will meet near the ruins of my palace. Here is where Queen Esmeralda and her men will meet for the battle of the seas." He pointed to the west. "My Generals will fight Bedlam's men here in the west near the Crow Valley."

All the rulers carefully studied each map with its battle markings.

"And here is the entrance to the Dragon Forest where the Dragon will wait for Peter to enter," Thætil said.

"And you are certain the boy can achieve this, Alexander?" King Baldrieg asked. "He has endured so much already. Are we not asking too much of him?"

The others murmured until Alexander raised his hand to silence them.

"Please," he said. "I know my son has endured much these last few months. I know the task before him seems almost impossible. But I also know my son. I know that he is ready to face this task."

The rulers listened intently.

"And I know that he is not alone in this," Alexander said. "I am with him, his mother will meet him there in the center of the forest, and the Dragon will be with him as well."

Esmeralda covered her mouth with her hands. "Such an exciting time to be alive," she said with tears in her eyes.

"If you believe this to be true, Alexander," King Baldrieg said. "Then I accept it as truth."

"Here, here," King Beatann said. "The time has come. We must finally fulfill the Oath and protect the Dragon Forest as our forefathers did. We will teach this to our sons and daughters."

"We will learn to live in harmony with the dragons, and we will once and for all ensure that peace reigns." Thætil said. He nodded toward Queen Thordis who grinned in return.

"An exciting time, indeed," King Isleif said as he nudged King Mildrir. Alexander motioned for the Elves to remove the swords from the room. As they carried the boxes out of the room, King Beatann approached Alexander.

"Can they be trusted?" he asked. "With the swords, can these Elves be trusted?"

Thætil narrowed his eyes.

"Of course," Alexander said. "They will secretly hold them here until Peter arrives."

Mildrir shook his head. "Is it too risky, Alexander?" he said. He pointed to the door. "How do we know Bedlam's spies have not penetrated these walls?"

Alexander approached his old friend. "Mildrir, my most loyal guard, Marek, will remain here and fly with the swords to meet Peter. I have trusted him with my life. I trust him now to protect those swords at all costs."

Mildrir raised an eyebrow as he studied his dear friend's face. "So be it. I trust you, my friend. If you say we can trust Marek and these Elves, then we can."

Alexander chuckled and patted Mildrir on the back.

## 27 PROMISES KEPT

"Lord Bedlam was able to enter into the Maze of Thœrgën," Theo said as he hastily entered the palace at Vulgaard. He gathered there together with several Elfin soldiers. "His power has reached levels of potency we did not predict."

"This has never happened before," one soldier said.

"Precisely," Theo said. "You must fly out tonight and inform the Queen. She is meeting with the other rulers."

The Elfin soldiers bowed and exited the room leaving a pensive Theo behind. He contemplated the significance of the event and was about to transform into his dragon form in order to join the Elves, but he heard Peter and the others approaching the entrance.

"And then I'll have bread pudding for dessert." Crispin had just finished listing all the food he was going to gobble up. Annika politely smiled as though she cared and then she saw Theo.

"What's the matter, Theo?" she asked.

Peter saw the concern on his former professor's face. "Did you tell the Elves about the maze?"

"Yes." Theo walked with everyone toward the dining hall. "The Queen must know. I have ordered the Elves to fly out this instant."

"Whatever does it mean, Theo?" Annika asked. "Lord Bedlam entering into the maze…"

"It means his power grows more and more," Theo sighed. "He has ways now of manipulating existing magic spells cast by other wizards." Theo inspected the room.

"What is it?" Peter asked.

"I grow more nervous," Theo said. "Bedlam's spies could be anywhere."

He turned to face Peter with intensity in his eyes.

"It is imperative that you all leave as soon as possible," Theo said. He made sure to make eye contact with each one of his former students. "Dangler has one more lesson for you in the morning, but then you must head out soon after that."

Theo stormed off leaving behind a group of curious adolescents.

"Should we follow him?" Simon asked. Peter shook his head.

"No, I think he needs to be alone. Come on, let's get some rest," Peter said as he turned to leave. "We've a big day ahead of us tomorrow."

§

The next morning, Dangler paced the arena floor back and forth as Peter, Annika, Crispin, and Simon entered. Already present were Eris along with many other Evles along with Jason, Peter's friend from Rünbrior.

"Well?" Dangler crossed his arms. "You're already late and you have the nerve to saunter in here like little girls picking flowers?"

Peter quickly jogged over to where the others were and sat by Jason.

"So you made it through the Maze of Thœrgën." Jason nudged Peter when he sat down. Peter grinned proudly.

"It was nothing compared to the arena," Peter said.

"Ah, the arena," Jason said. He chuckled. "There isn't much that compares to the arena."

Annika and the rest followed Peter and found places to sit while an impatient Dangler waited.

"You'll find that nothing makes me angrier than latecomers! Now that you all are here." Dangler cleared his throat. "Let's get on with it."

Theo walked in wearing his usual blue robe. He sat down on a stool in front of his audience.

"You have completed the testing of the Maze of Thœrgën," Theo said. "And now it is time for one more lesson before you leave."

"First, the healing paste." Dangler held up a leather pouch.

"But we already know about the salve," Crispin said.

Dangler shot him a most venomous look. Crispin crouched down.

"One more interruption and I'll feed you to the dragons!" Dangler shouted.

Crispin leaned over to Peter. "He wouldn't do that, would he?"

Peter shrugged.

"Now then, about this most mysterious healing powder ground from the horns of dragons. It has been used for generations." He put his hand into the pouch and removed the fine cream colored powder. "First discovered by wizards long ago, and to the chagrin of the Elves, dragon parts can be very beneficial to men. Wizards discovered that by grinding dragon horns or bones into a powder and mixing that powder with spring water from Vulgaard, honey, and one feather from a screech owl, this salve can heal outer wounds and, if ingested immediately after wounding, can heal inner wounds. But it must be used properly or sudden death can and has occurred."

Peter looked away. He remembered how the paste saved his life after he had been attacked by the Gizor in the arena. He reached over and rubbed his side, remembering his healed ribs. He forgot the cost involved in making the anodyne: the death of many dragons.

"But," Dangler said and pointed for emphasis. "Given to Elves it will cause death. Elves are more pure and can have nothing to do with dragon parts."

"Why not?" Crispin asked.

"Dragon blood," Dangler said. "There are mystical qualities in dragon blood. Some say, to drink a potion made of dragon blood, wine vinegar, and three hairs from a rare snow wolf, one can possess great wisdom. Elfin blood also has mystical qualities. They have known about the mystical qualities of dragons for thousands of years, but man only recently discovered them."

"What other potions are there?" Crispin asked.

"Oh, let's see, there are potions used for sleep, love, healing, and even death," Theo spoke up.

"So, what you're saying is that many dragons were killed in order to discover this secret healing salve?" Annika asked. Her face fell, saddened by the thought.

Dangler lifted his chin. "Yes, dragons have been killed and used in experiments by the wizards for many generations," he said and looked over at Eris and the other Elves. "And this is why the dragons came to despise man. It was the Elves who discovered the uniqueness of the dragons they encountered. They learned the language and respected the ways of the dragons and became one with them. It was man who slaughtered dragons for their own needs and paid dearly for this abuse over time."

Annika watched as Eris and the other Elves stood proudly as Dangler spoke.

Dangler glanced down at the pouch. "As a result of the harm done to dragons, the healing powder isn't used as much as it was used in the past. So, the Elves have agreed to allow each of you to be given a pouch to take with you into battle. Hopefully, it will help save some of you on the battlefield."

Annika stood and assisted Dangler in passing out the pouches to each fighter present.

"Not all those fighting in this battle will have this special powder. If you see someone in need on the battlefield, help them if you can," Dangler said. "So, use it sparingly and only when you believe it can help."

"So, it has limitations?" Peter attached the pouch to his belt.

"Yes," Dangler said. "All healing potions and salves have limitations. We do know it is capable of healing man, but we do not know all the dangers that can come of it. I have seen many wounds healed by the salve, but there are some wounds that are too deep for anything to stave off death."

Peter remembered how abused the dragons were inside the prison. He winced as he pictured Damon killing the proud young dragon in the cave for no other reason than cruelty and pride.

"When this final battle is over," Peter said. "Dragons will no longer be abused by man or anyone."

He looked over at Eris and the Elves who nodded to him.

"I promise," Peter said.

"Next." Dangler paced again. "About the dragons, as you know there are many variations of the creatures and, like each of you, some are more intelligent than others." He glared at Crispin.

Crispin noticed and turned to Simon. "What does he mean by that?" Crispin asked Simon. "Why is he looking at me?"

Simon chuckled.

"So, the legend has it that the weak minded ones were led astray by their leader, Bedlam." Dangler paced back and forth.

"They were led astray by a man?" Annika asked. "How could this be? Does he speak their language?"

Dangler looked over at Theo who nodded. Then, Dangler stood in front of the youths.

"Bedlam led the dragons astray because he is one of them," Dangler said.

Annika furrowed her brow. "Excuse me?"

"That's right! Lord Bedlam himself is a dragon. I take it you have not heard the entire story then?" Dangler said. He looked at Theo again.

"Proceed," Theo ordered. "It is time for them to know everything about the enemy."

Dangler inhaled deeply then exhaled as he prepared to speak. "Many years ago, there was a dragon unlike any other in the land. It was lithe and strong, but filled with venomous hatred toward man because of man's abuse of dragons and because of man's increasing power over the land," Dangler explained. "This dragon led other dragons on a mission to destroy man once and for all. And, as a result of that hatred, many men, women, and children were killed by dragon fire. The beasts swept down and stole livestock and destroyed crops. War loomed and this Dragon of Bedlam was enemy number one. Rulers of men plotted its undoing."

Peter, Annika, Simon, and Crispin listened intently.

"Until the prophecy was fulfilled," Dangler said. "And the Dragon of Promise came to bring peace between man and dragon. Bedlam foolishly tried to wage war against the Dragon, but lost. It was sent into exile with a death mark on its head. There it remained in the Mountains of Ranvieg alone and unable to do harm to anyone. Until, one fateful day, a young girl..." Danlger looked over at Peter. "A young girl befriended the dragon and desired to help it redeem itself by bringing it to her tutor, Sir Theodore Sirus III."

They all looked at Theo who took out his dragon pipe.

"And why did she bring the dragon to you, Theo?" Annika asked. The others nodded because they, too, wanted to know.

Theo stood. "Lady Laurien brought the Dragon of Bedlam to me because she knew I was once a wizard's apprentice and knew the ways of magic."

Annika's eyes widened. "You were a wizard?"

"But, you were our professor," Crispin said. "Weren't you?"

"I could explain it to you," Theo said. "But I shall show you instead."

He placed the pipe onto the stool and calmly removed his robe. Then, he proceeded to walk a few feet away from everyone. He stood alone with his arms held out, closed his eyes, and transformed into the White Dragon.

§

Marek dismounted his dragon and removed his helmet. He looked to his left and right, making certain that all was safe. Outside the palace, everything seemed tranquil and calm for the moment. The outer walls were lit with torches. The flames cut through the darkness. Even the air was still. As the other dragons landed, Marek made his way to assist the Elves who held the wooden boxes carrying the swords.

"All is clear," he said.

"Quiet for now," one Elf said. "Like the calm before the storm?"

Marek smirked. "A most violent storm," he said.

The Elves began to pick up the boxes one by one.

"Easy does it," Marek said to one Elf. "Precious cargo."

"Understood," said the Elf as he handed the box to Marek. He waved over some servants to assist him. Above him came a loud "caw" of a raven circling in the night sky.

"Here." Marek handed the box to the servant as he watched the raven fly. "Open the boxes! Hurry!"

The Elfin servant saw the raven and obeyed as quickly as he could. Marek motioned for the other servants to gather all the swords and place them into one box. They did and covered the swords with the velvet cloth. As they completed the task, Thætil ran out of the palace courtyard with dozens of his warriors. They each were armed with bows and arrows.

"Up there!" Marek pointed to the raven. Thætil loaded his bow and shot the raven through with an arrow. When it landed, it dissolved into dust leaving the arrow lying there on the ground.

Marek ran over to it. "One of Bedlam's spies?"

Just then, an arrow flew passed Marek's face just missing his cheek. Thætil grabbed him and threw him to the ground.

"Get inside!" Thætil shouted as more arrows shot out of the darkness. A few of his Elfin warriors were hit. They screamed from the pain, but Thætil kept urging them to run inside. He turned and shot two arrows into the darkness. He could hear the arrows pierce the hidden creatures. One of the dragons roared and startled Thætil. He could see it had been shot in the neck with an arrow.

"Hie! Eithrienden, al oi! Oi!" he shouted for all the dragons to take flight. They obeyed as more arrows shot out of the darkness and missed them.

"Hurry!" Thætil shouted to Marek and the servants. Marek followed him down the steps and entered the safety of the palace dungeon.

Once inside, Marek leaned against the wall, panting. He reached up and felt his cheek. He could feel the sticky blood.

"Are you hurt?" Thætil asked.

Marek shook his head. "It's nothing. Get the others some help."

The servants ran up the steps to retrieve assistance for the wounded.

"Now, what do we do with these?" He pointed to the box of swords being guarded by very nervous Elves and soldiers.

"We await the orders to take these to the battle," Thætil said. He ordered the box to be set in a special vault. The Elves obeyed. Marek watched the box of swords was placed inside the hiding place.

"Lord Bedlam knows where they are," Marek said. "He will come for them."

Thætil nodded. "Yes, in time he will try." Thætil turned and removed his sword from its sheath. He sat down to rest inside the dungeon. "And he will fail."

A few moments later, Marek followed Thætil up the stone steps and out of the palace dungeon.

An Elfin soldier ran up to his leader, Thætil. He bowed and then whispered, "King Isleif's palace has been discovered as the hiding place of the swords."

Marek nodded and pointed to his cheek. "Yes, we already discovered this."

"We must inform the others," Thætil said as he waved his arms high into the air. Suddenly, out of the south flew in several dragons. They hovered for a moment until they could see it was safe. They landed ever so quietly before Marek and Thætil.

"Ish ilendren noi," Thætil whispered to them as he approached. "Quickly, we must head to Queen Esmeralda's palace."

Before he mounted his own dragon, Thætil approached the dead dragon, angrily reached out, and yanked the arrow from his its neck. He inspected the crude weapon then broke it in half across his thigh in anger.

Marek knelt down by the dead dragon's body. "What a waste," he sighed.

Thætil inspected the arrowhead. "Poisoned," he mumbled. He turned to Marek. "The arrow tips were poisoned."

"Bedlam." Marek stood with clenched fists. He reached up and rubbed his cheek when he realized he had previously escaped death.

"Lord Bedlam, yes, and no..." Thætil said. He showed the arrowhead to Marek. "Look! This arrow is from the kingdom of Eulrik."

Thætil used his finger to trace the intricate etchings made on the arrowhead. "These arrowheads were made long ago by the Elves of Vulgaard for King Eulrik's guards."

Marek studied the etchings intently.

"What? It cannot be," he insisted. "King Eulrik is dead. His daughter is now one of the allies fighting *against* Lord Bedlam."

Thætil silently turned the arrowhead over in his hand.

"She is assisting in the attack. How could she possibly—" Marek said.

"I am aware of all this," Thætil interrupted. He clenched the arrowhead in his fist. "But I also know that the pattern etched into this arrowhead is that of Eulrik's kingdom. And it was used to slay this dragon and attack us."

Marek shook his head. "Perhaps there is a traitor within Eulrik's ranks?" he suggested.

Thætil turned to him. "Could be. Or Queen Esmeralda has joined Lord Bedlam."

The two men quickly mounted the dragons and flew off to warn King Isleif.

§

The White Dragon spread its wings and roared so loudly that Annika and the others covered their ears.

"What is this?" Simon shouted to Peter, but Peter simply smiled.

"How can this be?" Annika anxiously scooted away from the beast.

When Peter saw the fright in his friends's faces, he made his way over to the White Dragon. It lowered its snout and Peter gently rubbed it as it closed its eyes.

"Come now," he said to his friends. "There is nothing to be afraid of."

Annika slowly stood and cautiously made her way over to the dragon.

"Is this some sort of magic spell?" Jason asked as he pointed to the White Dragon.

"Yes," Dangler said. "The young girl brought the dragon to Theo so he could cast a spell that had been cast on him once many years ago."

Annika approached with wide eyes.

"So, you are really a dragon and not a man?" she asked.

The White Dragon snorted. Annika reached out and touched its snout. Then, she glimpsed into the crystal blue eyes and slowly smiled. Peter knew she recognized Theo.

"It's him!" she shouted to the others who were standing now. "It's really him! Come see."

Soon, Simon and Crispin were touching the White Dragon. Peter stroked its neck as Simon inspected its small smooth scales that sparkled.

"They're almost like pearls," he said.

"Alright, let's get back to the lesson on dragons." Dangler clapped his hands to bring everyone back to the center. "We've not much time before you head out."

Once everyone was seated again, the White Dragon transformed back into Theo. He walked back to the stool, put his robe back on, and picked up his pipe. He raised it up, nodded, and then shot a thin line of fire from his mouth to light the pipe.

Crispin's eyes grew wide. "Oh, how I wish you had shown us this years before!"

Everyone laughed.

"Yes, well, just imagine how much studying you would have accomplished." Theo smirked and sat down on the stool. "You were distracted enough already."

Crispin scowled. "What does he mean by that? Why does he look at me when he says that?"

Simon chuckled.

"Well, why didn't you tell us this years ago?" Crispin asked.

"I was ordered not to tell you until the appointed time," Theo said. "I promised I would keep the secret."

"So, Lord Bedlam was once a dragon. The Dragon of Bedlam," Annika said. "I was told by my grandfather that he was just a man exiled to the Ranvieg Mountains long ago."

"Same here," Crispin said.

"And, Theo, that's why Lady Laurien came to you? So Bedlam could be given the transformation spell?" Annika asked.

"Yes," Theo puffed on his pipe. "The young girl only wanted to help mend the relations between man and dragon, but unfortunately, that did not occur. The Dragon of Bedlam became Lord Bedlam and used his charm as a man to bewitch her and many others. His powers grew and now he is more powerful than anyone ever thought possible."

"How did the Dragon of the Forest allow this to happen?" Simon asked.

Theo heard the question and thought for a moment before answering. Everyone noticed he had a faraway look in his eyes. "Sometimes," he began in a soft voice. "It must become darkest night before the warmth of the morning light can truly be appreciated."

"Theo?" Simon asked. "Are you alright?"

"The Dragon looked into the future and saw the vision," Theo explained. He imagined the images in the lake the Dragon had shown him. "You see, in order for the truth about magic to be known and understood, in order for the people to truly understand what evil is, and for the Dragon of the Forest to show that it is the One to keep the peace between man and dragon, it allowed Bedlam to become a man and rise in power."

"But why didn't the Dragon of the Forest just come out and slay Bedlam once and for all and end all the darkness?" Simon asked.

"An excellent question," Theo said. He looked over at Peter. "When the Dragon died in the desert plains years ago, it ushered in the time of man. It went away so that Peter's rise could happen. Now is the time for Peter to show who he is and what he has to do. It is *your* time, Peter."

Annika smiled at Peter.

"The Dragon went away for a time to allow Peter to rise. Now, it is back because Peter is ready and when everything is said and done," Theo said as he paced. "Everyone will know the truth about magic, its failures and weaknesses. So, they will never rely upon it again. Everyone will know what the Elves already know, that we dragons are unique creatures with great intelligence and goodness that must be appreciated and not abused. And everyone in all the lands will honor the Oath and finally know that only the Dragon of the Forest can ensure the peace between man and dragon."

"There were many times I wanted to tell you everything. But I made a promise." Theo glanced over at Peter. "I was asked to wait until the appointed time."

"Well, you are very good at keeping promises," Annika declared. She folded her arms.

"Yes, very impressive," Crispin said.

"Alright," Dangler's raspy voice interrupted everyone. "Now you know about Lord Bedlam. Now you know more about the dragons and Theo's big secret. And now you know how magic spells work," Dangler said. "Magic is nothing but a lie. Manipulations with spells that fool the eyes...all lies. Everything about Lord Bedlam is a lie. Everything out of his mouth is nothing but a lie."

Simon nodded enthusiastically.

"Magic tricks the eye into believing what it wants you to believe. In his desperation, Bedlam continues to use his magic to create mutations of animals and men as he desperately tries to recreate the transformation spell that was used on him," Theo said. "You have already run into some of the beasts he has created."

They all nodded in agreement.

"Zadoks, Baroks, and the flocks of flying Gizor are all his failed attempts to recreate the spell. Well, because he is under a spell himself and because spells are only temporary..." Dangler walked over to Peter. "He can be defeated."

All eyes were on Peter as he listened to Dangler.

"Yes," Peter said with determination in his voice.

Dangler grinned at Peter. "You've been chosen for this task and I know you will succeed."

Simon and Crispin patted Peter on his back.

"The battle will be fierce and that's why you need to know about dragons," Dangler continued. His eyes met with each one of them. "You will fight against dragons in the air, on land, and in the sea."

"Sea dragons." Crispin grinned and whispered to Simon who smiled widely.

"You will need to know about dragon fire. Only some of the Dragon's scale shields remain. Many were lost on the quest for the swords. We will give you the ones we have. Some of the dragons remain loyal to the Great Dragon of the Forest, but others have been fooled into following Bedlam. He has lied to them about the shape shifter spell. They foolishly believe they, too, will be transformed into men one day and rule the land."

"How sad." Annika shook her head.

"Many of the rulers have believed the lies Bedlam has told them as well," Dangler. "And that's what makes his power grow."

"Bedlam's tactics have changed over the years," Theo said. "We now know he was able to enter the Maze of Thœrgën. We now know he is capable of making stronger weapons. He is working hard to destroy the one thing that keeps him under the spell."

"The Dragon Forest," Peter said. "If he destroys the forest, there will be no limitations on his power and, ultimately, he can become a man forever. But if the swords enter the forest first, the spell is broken, and he returns to dragon form."

"Well, that's the enemy you fight," Dangler said. "Any questions?"

Crispin raised his hand. "Theo, will *you* one day return to dragon form?"

Theo raised his eyebrows and puffed on his pipe. "We shall see what happens."

He regarded Peter. "Yes, we shall indeed see what happens," Theo said.

"Alright, let's continue," Dangler said. "To the crossbows!"

# 28 ONE LAST ITEM

"I've one last item to deal with," Lord Bedlam said. He leaned on his cane.

"What is it, my Lord?" Will asked.

Bedlam waved over a guard who carried something hidden under a cloth. Lord Bedlam reached out and removed the cloth to reveal a shield.

Will's eyes widened when he saw the iridescent shield glimmer in the fire glow. He carefully made his way over to the shield.

"This is…" he stammered. "This is a scale from the Dragon of the Forest."

"Yes. Yes, I know." Lord Bedlam allowed Sir William to touch the scale.

"It's been awhile since I have seen one," Will said. "Where did you get it?"

Bedlam walked away and stood by the large picture window of his chambers. He put on his leather gloves. "From one of King Alexander's Knights."

Will continued to admire its beauty.

"I will take it to the dungeon below and continue to work with it," Bedlam ordered. "Soon I will uncover the way to penetrate it with my weaponry."

"I understand," Will said.

"For now, I need you to ready your army." Bedlam strode passed Will. "King Alexander and Prince Peter are making their way to Illiath."

"Yes, my Lord," Will said.

"It is time, Will." Bedlam opened the door. "Are you prepared?"

Will bowed.

"Now, show me where your loyalty stands, Will," Bedlam said. "I trusted others before and they failed me. Show me your loyalty and I will greatly reward you." He closed the door behind him.

§

Will stood by fire pits as the Baroks brought a large bat before him. Next, they dragged in a man who had been captured from a nearby town and held prisoner at Hildron. His wrist was sliced open and blood was drained from the wound. When enough blood was in the jar, the man was taken away. Will raised his hands and uttered the incantations of the Aniformum spell Bedlam had taught him and sprinkled the man's blood onto the bat. The bat screeched and writhed in pain on the dirt ground. Will uttered the spell until the transformation was complete. Before him lay the newly formed Gizor creature, part man and part bat. Its thin arms and legs were weak at first, so it flapped its leathery wings in an attempt to stand. Will nodded to the Barok soldiers who took the creature away.

The transformations continued until Will felt he had enough creatures for the battle. He ordered the preparations to begin. At his orders, the Baroks rushed to gather their armor and weapons. He inspected each one as they passed, making sure they had all that they needed. Shields formed from the special blended metals, swords, spears, arrows, and armor were all created by Bedlam. The Baroks grunted and drooled as they ran by. Will grinned as though pleased with his army. Above him, he heard a screeching noise. He raised his eyes to see hundreds of Gizor flying by. The gangly creatures flapped their bat-like wings and flew out of the cave to prepare for the battle.

§

Peter stepped from his bedchamber dressed in a clean tunic. He stretched and smiled because he had enjoyed a warm bath and, even though still sore from training, he felt anew. He had slept peacefully for the first time in many months. He walked over to a window that overlooked the river valley below. He could see the sun's rays flowing over the Vulgaard Mountains. The beauty of the landscape made him forget all the previous nightmares and the details of the enormous task still ahead of him. For a few moments, he was just Peter again.

He left his room and ran down the stairs past several startled servants carrying breakfast trays to the Queen's many guests. Peter headed to the outer courtyard with its grassy precipice overlooking the Ranvieg Mountains to the west. He stopped and sat on the stone fence that lined the grassy area, took in a deep breath of cool morning air, and rested with his eyes closed. So much had happened since he escaped the prison of Rünbrior. All of the questions about the past he had wondered about inside that prison for so many months were now answered. Peter learned how, in an instant, all of life's plans that seemed to be firmly set in stone could change and without notice. He no longer felt anger inside, but anxiety about the future. He had always dreamed of being a knight, but now he began to understand about his destiny as King. Would he be able to rule as his father and grandfather had?

"You were born to be king, Peter," Dangler said.

Peter, startled by the interruption, turned to see Dangler standing off to the side leaning on his cane. "And you have become a fine knight. I know now, for certain, it is good that you did not go to the Crow Valley to Knight Training."

Peter made his way to his friend.

"Thank you." Peter turned toward the Ranvieg Mountains. "Yet, I can't help but wonder what Knight Training must have been like." His voice trailed off.

"Peter," Dangler hesitated. "Lord Bedlam came to me in the prison one day when he learned of your capture."

Peter's eyes widened when he'd heard the words.

"He bade me to keep you in there," Dangler said with sorrow in his eyes, "When he learned about Valbrand's plan to have you fight in the arena, Bedlam decided that he wanted you to die by his dragons."

Peter listened.

"But what he didn't know was what a gifted fighter you are," Dangler smiled. "Neither did I, neither did Valbrand. So, he tried to use his magic to destroy you."

"But he failed," Peter said.

"Yes." Dangler placed his hand on Peter's shoulder, "And he will fail again. He continues to underestimate your capabilities."

Peter returned his gaze to the valley below with the river dividing the land and the little thatched roof houses scattered along the river. The chilly wind brushed through his hair.

"It is no wonder, then, that I ended up at Rünbrior," he said as the images the Dragon had shown him in the lake appeared in his mind. He remembered the Dragon's words.

*You are the Son of the Oath, Peter. You are the one to save Illiath.*

"As hard as it is to understand," Dangler said as he turned to walk off. "It was meant to be."

Peter watched his old friend make his way across the grass area.

"What Bedlam meant for evil turned out to be for the good," Dangler said. Then, he turned and motioned for Peter to follow him. Peter did. Then, Dangler stopped and waved over some Elves. They led Peter and Dangler to a dragon munching on some grass. On its back was a polished leather saddle. The creature looked over at Peter with sparkling amber eyes and shifted its wings.

"This is my gift for you, Peter," Dangler said as he waved his arm to the dragon.

Peter raised his eyebrows.

"What?" he smiled.

"Yes, this dragon is my gift to you," Dangler said.

The dragon, a young male Draco with shimmering scales of dark forest green, continued to feed on the moist grass with relaxed composure.

"This is a good dragon with speed and agility." Dangler leaned on his cane. "I trained it myself. I have never given a dragon as a gift before. Usually, I have them select their owners, but this time I wanted to do the honors. I know you will find this is a good match."

"Of course!" Peter said.

"I cannot go into battle with you, Peter." Dangler looked down with regret in his voice.

"I know," Peter said.

"So, this is my way of assisting in the fight," Dangler said. "Hopefully, it will be the last battle."

Peter patted his friend on the back. "I'll take good care of this dragon."

"I know you will," Dangler said. "Never have I known someone who cared for dragons as you do...except for the Elves, and your mother."

Peter tilted his head. "Really?"

"To a fault, of course." Dangler winked and chuckled. "She was one with the dragons. She understood them. She knew there was more to them than just transportation into battle. No, she knew that they have kindred spirits within. She knew that each dragon has a special gift. They are kind and intelligent creatures. Fierce at times, yes, but also gentle," Dangler explained.

"I remember reading in *The Dragon Chronicles* about how much the dragons love the jewels and gemstones," Peter said. "That they receive power from them, I think."

"Yes, the dragons of the mountains make their nests out of the gold or gemstones found in the mountains. The Elves say there is a mystical power the gems give off." Dangler shrugged. "I don't know. All I know is that the Dragon of the Forest was the most special of them all. Its egg shell was made of diamonds. Only one of its kind."

Peter's eyes grew wide. "I agree."

Dangler nodded. "My father knew it was the prophecy fulfilled when he saw that egg. It had been found up there." He pointed to the Ranvieg Mountains.

Peter's face became crestfallen when he gazed over at the mountains that once imprisoned him. They seemed to loom over him. "It is sad how a once beautiful mountain range became so hideous," he said.

"Aye," Dangler nodded. "That's where your mother befriended the Dragon of Bedlam so long ago."

"She must have been heartbroken when so many dragons succumbed to Bedlam's lies as easily as she did," Peter said as he watched the dragon sniffing the air and stretching its wings.

Dangler's eyes softened as though he was remembering the young Laurien. "Yes, but she herself learned how easy it is to fall for his lies. Why should some dragons be any different?"

Peter listened.

"Now, Peter, remember all that you have read in *The Dragon Chronicles*, remember all that you have learned about dragons, and, when all this is over, you must write down your knowledge in the book for others to read as I did and as your mother did."

"I will," Peter assured his friend.

"All right, then," Dangler reached over and squeezed Peter's arm. "Your time at Vulgaard is nearing an end. We may never see each other again, Prince Peter, but if you ever return to Vulgaard, you will find me here with the dragons of the mountains and training with the Elves. Understood?"

"I understand," Peter said. "And I thank you, my friend, for everything."

Dangler turned and hobbled over to the dragon. He took it by the reins and motioned for Peter to mount it.

Peter grinned a wide-tooth grin and ran over to the dragon. He carefully reached out and touched its snout. The creature closed its eyes, sniffed Peter's hand, and then snorted. Some smoke shot out of its nostrils. Peter laughed and placed his foot in the stirrup.

"Temper, temper," Dangler said to the dragon. "Easy now. You'll find he's a bit temperamental at times."

"Alright," Peter said. "I'll remember that."

"I was talking to the dragon." Dangler chuckled and helped Peter mount his dragon.

"Peter, you will come to see that there is a time to ride a dragon for training," Dangler said as he led Peter atop the dragon toward the precipice. "And there is a time to ride a dragon into battle."

"Yes," Peter said.

"And then… there is a time to ride a dragon simply for the pleasure of it!" He handed Peter the reins, smacked the dragon hard on its hind leg, and watched as it leapt off the cliff with Peter on its back. "Enjoy the ride!"

Peter yelped as the dragon beneath him dove down the side of the mountain. The wind was so cold, Peter couldn't breathe for a moment. He tried to open his eyes, but was afraid to. Finally, the dragon spread its wings open and rose up higher and higher until together they flew through and above the clouds. When they leveled off, Peter opened his eyes and breathed. All he could hear was the wind and the occasional beating of his dragon's wings. They withstood the wind like the sails of a ship.

"This is incredible!" Peter screamed as they glided along the clouds. He laughed heartily then reached down and ran his hands through the misty clouds. He laughed with joy and gazed all around.

"I can't believe this!" he shouted. For miles and miles all he could see were the clouds. They spread across the sky like a cottony blanket so real that, for a moment, he thought he'd try to walk on them. The sun shone from high above them. Peter turned his face toward it, closed his eyes, and soaked in all its warmth.

His dragon squawked and turned to the left. Peter gripped the reins and squeezed the saddle with his thighs to hold on. They dove into the cloud cover and came out the other side to see the East Ocean nearby. His dragon flapped its wings and glided near the ocean surface.

"Yes!" Peter saw the white caps of the waves and a few spooked seagulls take off in flight as they approached. To his right, he could see a few dragons resting on the rocky cliffs along the shoreline. They flapped their wings and roared when they saw Peter fly past. "Hello!" he shouted and waved his hand.

"Whoa!" He felt the cold water on his feet. He looked down to see the ocean surface only inches away from his dragon's body. Peter reached down and put his hand in the water. It sliced through the cold water like a knife. He could smell the salt and see fishes swimming in the water.

"Look how fast they are!" he shouted.

He pulled back on the reins and his dragon shot straight up into the sky again. They spun around until they reached what seemed like the top of the world, and then Peter extended his arms out as the two fell to the earth as one. He closed his eyes and rejoiced in the feeling of weightlessness. The feeling of total freedom rushed over his body.

He opened his eyes in time to pull his dragon up before they hit the water. They soared over the ocean surface together and spied a few sea dragons swimming near the surface along with them. Peter could see the enormity of the snake-like creatures. Once in a while, the spikes along their backs would cut through the surface of the water. One splashed Peter with its gigantic tail. He laughed as he wiped the salt water off his face.

Peter turned his dragon toward the cliffs overlooking the ocean. There he spotted some trees growing. "I'm hungry," he told his dragon. "Maybe there's some fruit for us to eat!"

But his dragon ducked its head into the water as they flew and came up with several fish in its mouth.

"I see you prefer some fish instead?" he laughed. The two landed on the tender grass and sat there on the edge of the cliff watching the seagulls dive into the water occasionally frightened off by a few dragons. Peter sunk his teeth into a ripe fruit. He wiped the juice off his chin with his sleeve. His dragon gulped down the fish one at a time, spitting out the tails.

"Don't like the tails, huh?" Peter asked before he took another bite of the juicy fruit.

Finally, after breakfast, the two sat peacefully together. His dragon licked its feet clean and stretched out its wings. Peter tossed it a piece of fruit.

"Dessert?" Peter asked. It sniffed the fruit, and then gobbled it up in one bite.

Peter took in all the beauty around him. "I never knew it could be like this," he said. His dragon sniffed the air as the cool ocean breeze blew over them. "I had no idea beauty like this existed."

Peter stroked his dragon's side. "I must admit," he said. "When I was younger, I once thought dragons were cruel. Then, later, I met the Dragon of the Forest. I learned that dragons could be kind. In the prison, they were treated as terribly as the prisoners were. At Vulgaard, I thought they were only for flying into battle. Now I know better."

He sat and watched the dragons swim in and out of the ocean to the lull of the waves hitting the shore.

"How can there be war looming with such peacefulness like this happening all around?" Peter sighed. "It is hard to believe, isn't it?" He turned to his dragon.

"He'll need a name," a voice said. Stunned, Peter turned around. In the sunlight, he could barely see the outline of a woman coming toward him.

Frightened, Peter tried to block out the sun with his hand. "Who are you? What are you doing here?"

As the woman approached, a calmness came over Peter.

"You must name your dragon if you are to truly bond with it," the woman said.

Peter turned to her. "Mother?"

The woman came into view and Peter could see it was his mother in a vision. "Son," she said. She walked over to the dragon and stroked its back. She ran her hands over the spikes along its back, making her way to its snout. It munched on grass as she scratched its nose.

"You are learning more and more about dragons, Peter," she said. Her wavy brown hair was swept up by the breeze coming over the cliffs. She wore a long red gown. "They are such amazing creatures."

Peter sat on the grass listening and watching.

"Dragons will help you understand what peace, gentleness, and loyalty are. Even more than Titan did," she said.

Peter watched her.

"A dragon will die for you if you need it to," she said. "The Dragon of the Forest showed you this."

"Yes," Peter said.

"You must release all the anger inside, Peter," she said. "I hope you realize how dangerous it is to go into battle with all that rage inside."

Peter turned to the ocean. "I know," he mumbled. "It's just that—"

"It only weakens you, Peter," she said. "Anger only weakens. It will never make you stronger."

She sat down next to him. He looked down at his hand resting on the grass.

"There's no need to be angry with Theo or with your father. Nothing happened to me that wasn't supposed to happen," she explained. "I willingly drank that elixir knowing it would kill me. I did it to protect you."

Peter nodded.

"And there is nothing that happened to Sir Nøel that wasn't supposed to happen," she said. Peter looked up at her. "He died as a brave knight should die. He died fighting to protect his sovereign. He wouldn't have had it any other way."

Peter returned his gaze to the ocean, watching the dragons dive into the water for fish.

"It hurts," Peter sighed.

His mother placed her hand on Peter's hand and squeezed. "I

know," she said and nodded toward the dragon. "But learn more about these incredible beasts, Peter. They will teach you all about sacrifice and loss...and all about peace."

Peter looked at it and saw kindness in its amber eyes.

"Yes, they will die for you, Peter," she said, "and they will *live* for you, too."

Peter carefully studied its face. Strong jaws clenched and nostrils flared as it took in the scents around it. The sunlight bounced off each glassy scale and its sides expanded and retracted with each breath.

"Already, this dragon has shown me more than anyone or anything has ever shown me. I never knew such beauty before," Peter watched the dragons land onto the cliffs nearby.

The wind caressed his mother's face. She moved her hair away from her eyes. Her voice swept across his mind like the gentle ocean breeze carrying away the thistles of harmful thoughts that once held him captive. Now he finally felt free.

"I'm not afraid of this task ahead of me, mother," Peter said. "I know I can do it."

His mother smiled. "Good," she said, "Because you *can* do it."

She stood and looked down at her son. "And you will never be alone, Peter."

His dragon roared.

Peter opened his eyes and realized he had fallen asleep there on the cliff. He sat up and saw the sun was already low in the sky. Several hours had passed. He wiped his eyes and noticed his mother was nowhere to be seen. He felt a chill rush over his body as he realized the conversation was a vision in his dream again. The old familiar feeling of pain, loss, and regret came to him, or maybe it was simply the late afternoon air turning colder. He stood, brushed off his trousers, and prepared to mount his dragon.

"Come on," he sighed. "As wonderful as it is here, I suppose we'd better head back."

Together, Peter and his dragon flew off the cliff and headed west toward the palace at Vulgaard

# 29 THE PURPOSE OF THE BATTLE

Back at the palace, Peter made his way down the stairs and toward the dining hall to enjoy one last feast with his friends when he was stopped by an Elfin guard. The guard's face seemed stoic and Peter knew something of high importance had occurred.

"We've been looking for you. The Queen has arrived from her meeting with your father and the other rulers," the guard said. Peter's eyes widened. "She longs to speak with you in her library."

"Of course," Peter said.

The Elf turned and began to walk off. "Follow me."

Peter followed the guard down the hallway lit with torches. The sun was behind the mountains now, and torch flames reflected off the walls of polished glass mixed with diamonds. They sparkled like stars that lit up the night sky. *Annika was correct,* he thought. *It will be very difficult to leave this grand palace.*

They arrived at the large double doors leading to her majesty's private library. As the guard knocked, Peter could hear Theo's voice on the other side. When the doors opened, Theo turned to greet Peter. The Queen stood nearby her most loyal confidant. She raised her arm and waved Peter into the grand space with walls reaching thirty feet into the air. Each wall was lined with bookcases filled with thousands of leather bound books.

"Come, Peter," she said. He noticed her face was softer as though she were relieved about something. Peter bowed.

"Your majesty," he said as he approached. "What is it?" His eyes darted to Theo who stood grinning.

"Where have you been?" Theo asked.

Peter opened his mouth to speak, but the Queen stepped up. She took Peter's hand and squeezed it.

"I've just come from visiting with your father and the other rulers at the palace of Queen Esmeralda. Oh, Peter!" she clasped her hands and sighed. "I have seen all the swords. The elder Elf has read the secret message. Your instructions are set." She motioned for Theo to bring over something. Peter noticed there was a scroll in Theo's hand. He handed it to Peter.

"In this scroll are written your instructions for this mission, Peter," Theo said. "Read it. In the morning, you all will fly out with me toward the remains of the palace at Illiath."

Peter began to unroll the scroll in his hand, paused, and then he looked up at the Queen with raised eyebrows. "I'm sorry, your majesty, but did I hear you correctly? The *remains* of the palace?" he said. "My father's palace?"

The smile left Theo's face. The Queen stepped closer.

"Prince Peter," she said softly, almost like a mother comforting a child. "I'm afraid it is true. Your father's palace is yet another casualty of Lord Bedlam's war with all that is good."

Peter looked past her, as he took in her words. He stood in silence, deep in thought.

"All that is left of the once glorious palace of Illiath is…" She hesitated, "well, rubble."

Peter gazed into her troubled eyes.

"It's all so very tragic." She patted his hand.

"I'm so sorry, Peter," Theo said sadly.

Peter nodded and began to read the scroll all the while trying to forget the news of his father's palace.

"It says that the Elves of Vulgaard will guard me, along with my father's men, King Isleif, General Aluein, and many others, as I bring all the swords to the entrance of the Dragon Forest. There I will enter and take them to the lake in the center of the forest where my mother and the Dragon will instruct me further," Peter said. "When the swords are together, only then will the spell that controls Bedlam be destroyed."

"Peter, do you have any questions about the instructions?"

"How will the swords be carried in?"

Theo stepped forward. "It has been advised that all the swords be placed in one box and brought to the entrance of the forest. There you will remove all the swords from the box and carry them into the forest."

"Alone."

"Yes," Theo said. "No one else may enter into the forest at that time. Only you." Theo looked at the Queen then back at Peter.

Peter silently read the instructions again.

"It may seem impossible, this task that so many have asked of you, Peter, but I assure you that you are not alone in this," the Queen said. "So, please if you have any—"

"Did you have a say in the wizard's decision to turn you into a dragon, Theo?" Peter interrupted the Queen. She and Theo stood confused about the question.

"What? I'm not sure I understand what it is that you ask." Theo tilted his head.

"Years ago, when the wizard used the Anifornum spell on you," Peter continued. "Did you want to change into a man?"

Theo raised his chin and rubbed his long grey beard. "Ah, yes I see what you are asking. No," he said. "As a matter of fact, I was captured by soldiers to be used for flight. Because I was a rare white dragon, the wizard, being intrigued, asked to see me."

Peter listened.

"And it was then he decided to try his spell on me as he had done on my father and my father's father." Theo leaned forward.

Peter raised his eyebrows. "You mean he had tried it before on your father?"

"And my father's father, yes," Theo explained. "The spell failed and they perished in the attempt." In his head, he could hear the roars of the dragons inside the wizard Goyle's workshop. He could see them writhing in pain.

A look of horror came to Peter's face as he thought of the the dragons suffering.

"Because I was a pure white dragon," he continued. "The wizard felt the spell would surely work on me. It did and I was named Theodore Sirus III because I was the successful third attempt. I would remain in the palace as the wizard's apprentice and act as a liaison between man and dragon. For my work, I was knighted by King Aidan for faithful service as a wizard and as a tutor to his children long ago."

"*Sir* Theodore Sirus III," Peter whispered.

Theo nodded. "But Peter, why do you ask questions like these at such a time?"

"As a dragon, like so many others, you were used and abused by men." Peter rolled up the scroll. "Taken from your natural habitat and conformed to do a man's bidding. You were a slave!"

Theo squinted his eyes, studying Peter's reddened face.

"As I and so many others were inside that prison." Peter looked intently into the Queen's face. "Your majesty, you see, I remember what it is like to be a prisoner, taken from my happy life, and forced to do what others would have me do against my will. I dreamed night after night of one day returning home. And now, my only home has been destroyed."

She raised her eyebrows.

"I know this battle is to free many from this evil," Peter said. "But this battle is also to free the dragons and make sure *all* of us can live our lives in peace once again. That is the purpose of this battle."

Her eyes became shiny with tears.

"And so, if I have to suffer a bit for this cause, well, I believe it is nothing compared to what the dragons have had to endure for millennia. I do this for many people out there, but I also do this for you, Theo." Peter bowed. Theo grinned and wiped a tear from his eye.

"Your majesty, you are weary from your journey," Peter said and bowed to the Queen. "I will leave you to your rest."

He turned to Theo. "I will study the instructions further and inform the others." Peter turned on his heel and headed toward the door. Peter once again looked at the scroll in his hands then departed from the library, leaving the Queen and Theo alone.

As Peter strolled down the hall toward the dining hall, so many thoughts raced through his mind. He thought of his father's majestic palace destroyed. He thought of his friend, Theo, being captured as a beautiful young dragon full of hope only to be tortured by a wizard's spell. He thought of how magic spells and the vanity of man had caused so much pain for far too long. Lord Bedlam had destroyed so much, including his home.

Peter's bedchamber at home came to his mind, with all its toys and books on shelves lining the halls, his soft featherbed, and the window that faced the Dragon Forest all raced across his mind. It felt like years since he had slept in his own bed and felt its softness envelope him. He could see the candles illuminating the room in the ever so familiar soft glow sending the shadows dancing across the ceiling. He remembered it all so well: All the hiding places and secret chambers inside the palace, Theo's secret rooms where he and his friends studied and played chess, and of course the large mahogany table in the dining hall where he would often hide from his father's servants. Finally, he thought of the kitchen with all its wonderful smells. All these places were home to him. Peter staggered as he walked and used the wall to steady himself. He thought of his mother. *The portraits,* he thought. *My beautiful mother and the Dragon Forest...All those paintings. Gone. Forever.* The tears came to his eyes as he remembered staring up at her portrait on the wall. He swallowed back the tears, refusing to cry.

"And Titan," he softly whispered and closed his eyes. "My beautiful horse and old friend."

Peter leaned his back against the wall and closed his eyes as he thought about the only home he had ever known.

"If only I had stayed," he said to himself. "How could I know I would never see my home again when I left so many months ago?"

He shook his head and fought back the tears. He inhaled. *I can't think about this now,* he thought. *I have to prepare.* He rubbed his temples as he felt the anger return. His skin grew warm. He remembered his mother's words.

"No," he said. "I will not be angry."

Peter turned and continued on toward the dining hall until he found himself before its large doors. He could picture himself with all his friends in Theo's library chatting about so many things, plans they had made, and dreams they had. He grimaced when he thought about his father's palace lying in ruins while Will and Lord Bedlam resided in Hildron. Peter felt he had to mask his anger now even though he knew his friends would be more than willing to comfort him with condolences. *What use is it to tell them the news now?* He thought. *There's nothing that can be done and my anger will only weaken me.*

The screech of an owl was heard. Peter rushed over to a window and searched the branches of a tree nearby. There, resting on a branch was the White Owl. Peter grinned.

"My old friend," he said to the owl with its yellow eyes reflecting the sunset. Peter opened the window, lifted up his hand, and watched as the bird flew to him. It landed on his arm and Peter stroked its feathers. "I should have known you would come."

"Peter," he heard the familiar voice of the Dragon. "Now is the time. Do not reflect on the past. You are needed in the here and now."

The voice assuaged his fears and anger.

"But my home," Peter said to his friend. "My home is...*gone.*"

"Many homes are gone," the voice said. "Many lives have been lost. The people need you as their leader, not as a saddened boy Prince. You are much more than that now."

Peter understood.

"I am with you," the White Owl flew off. "You remembered me, Peter, and I will remember you."

Peter watched the owl fly away and he remembered all the times the Dragon was there for him.

Peter turned, stood tall, and then opened the doors of the dining hall to find his friends already feasting on all the delicious food. They were laughing and drinking together like old times. Peter entered the room with a forced smile. In order to be King one day, he realized he would need to mask his feelings. He would have to carry on no matter what his father and his grandfather had done before him. No, a King doesn't dwell on the casualties of war. There is a time and place for all that and Peter knew it.

"Peter!" Annika shouted and waved him over to the large table stacked with fresh fruits, breads, and meats. She held up some grapes. "Come join us for this last feast."

"What's that in your hand?" Crispin asked. Peter set the scroll down onto the table as an Elfin servant brought him a drink.

"We will get to this soon enough," Peter smiled. He took the goblet and raised it high. "First, a toast."

Each of his friends followed suit, raising their drinks high. As they did, Peter studied their faces. Simon, sat across the table grinning as he held up his goblet. Peter was very glad they made amends and were devoted friends again. Annika, with her crystal blue eyes reflecting the candlelight, smiled at him. Peter knew her beauty was more than outward. He could hardly wait to declare his true intentions for her to her grandfather after the war, after the mess. Crispin, patiently waiting for the toast, remained loyal even though war was not his calling. Peter knew he could trust in his friendship forever. Eris, raised her goblet with her serious eyes penetrating into Peter as though she could read his mind. He wasn't sure if she could read his very thoughts or not, but he was glad she was on their side. Finally, he could hardly wait to tell them of the ride on his dragon and all that he had seen earlier that day.

"To all of us," Peter said, "as we prepare to embark on this journey, this mission...this final battle over evil."

"Here, here," Annika said.

"May we endure," Peter continued. "May we be resolute. May we always remain loyal to each other and to the Oath of our fathers."

"To the Oath," Simon said as he drank.

"To Prince Peter." Annika smiled.

"To the future King of Illiath." Crispin said.

"To the Dragon Forest." Peter finished the toast.

Together, they all laughed heartily, drank more fruit wine, and ate one last meal at the palace of Vulgaard before they would depart for war with Lord Bedlam, Sir William, and all those who had joined forces with evil to try and destroy the Dragon Forest once and for all. He did not know if this would be their last time together, but, as he raised his glass, he did know with certainty that the life they once knew would never be the same again.

# Part III

# 30 THE GATHERING STORM

King Alexander watched the peaceful sunrise. The chilly breeze swept through his hair, longer than usual with more specks of grey in it. The lines in his face were more prominent from months of worry. But the sparkle in his eyes remained as he studied the glowing orb peek over the mountains, illuminating the sky with streaks of violet and grey. The wind swept over the rows of wheat the color of amber that covered the sloping hills of the Cornshire nearby. The little village with its hamlets in rows remained quiet and still that dawn. Only the baying of scattered sheep could be heard and the scent of the smoke from a few chimneys came to Alexander.

He breathed in the pleasant odor. Alexander knew the only remnants of people left in the villages were the elderly who refused to leave or couldn't leave due to illness. All the able men, young and middle aged, had joined the Duke of Illiath's forces weeks ago or they had fled for the forests to hide from the Duke's wrath. The women and children, who weren't convinced to follow Sir William's orders to journey to Hildron, knew their lives were in danger. They feared war was imminent. They took only what they could carry and abandoned the rest. Alexander couldn't help but notice the surrounding lands appeared forsaken, both literally and figuratively He sensed a void in the air as he watched the sun rise on this new era. He gazed downward dejectedly as he remembered the land in its former glory. Then, he turned to face the place where his palace once stood. His lungs filled with air and he exhaled his anger and sorrow away. The memories began to flood his mind. Memories of his father and mother, his son playing in the grass nearby, his wedding, and his beloved Queen's burial. But he shook them off. He knew there would be a time for all that and that was not the time. He heard footsteps approach from behind.

"My Lord," a knight said. Alexander blinked a few more times, enjoying the peace and quiet that comes before war.

"Yes," he said.

No answer. Alexander turned and found his knight standing with arms outstretched. On his arms rested a sword, its blade glistened in the morning light. The sight of the ivory hilt and intricate carvings on the blade almost took Alexander's breath away. He slowly reached up and took the hilt into his hand. He twisted it over and studied the blade for a moment. The knight bowed his head and backed away slowly. Alexander's eyes followed him as he joined the ranks of men awaiting orders from their King.

There on the hill, King Alexander stood alone holding the Sword of Alexander in his hand facing his men once again. It was here years earlier that they had fought off Lord Caragon's men in the battle that would lead to this war, this final war with evil. Alexander began to walk toward his men. He remembered the ground littered with the dead. He remembered the stench of death. His scarlet cape flowed behind him and the sunlight reflected in his silver armor. The faces of his men were steely and full of pride, but not arrogance. Many of them knew war; many had fought with their King before and had the scars on their flesh to prove it, and many had lost loved ones in the war. As he passed, their eyes followed the beautiful sword before him for he held it out knowing his men would want to see their King with the Sword of the Oath once again. He knew many had witnessed it taken by Baroks as they slaughtered the dragon in the fields nearby years before. On that day, the Baroks had taken more than just the sword. The wicked creatures of Bedlam had taken the people's hope. But now the sword was back together with all the Swords of the Oath ready to enter the Dragon Forest with Prince Peter to end the darkness that had scarred the land for too long. Hope had returned to the people.

Alexander stood there in the middle of the ranks of men and raised the sword high into the new morning sky. The whoops of the men were loud and sent a chill through his body. They shouted and clapped as a squire led the King's horse to him and helped him mount. The men raised their swords and waited for the words of their sovereign once again. But before he could speak, a cloud of dust rose from the desert plains in the west causing all the men and the King to turn and see what it was. Then, the sound came over the hills and they felt the tremors on the earth beneath them. The sound was too familiar. It was the sound of battle formations and that's when they knew.

"Prepare for battle!" the King shouted. Far off near the desert plains, the Duke of Illiath and his tremendous forces were on the march.

The men scurried into position. The knights mounted their horses while the soldiers took up their shields and swords, ready to march forward on their sovereign's orders. With the glittering shields, the very scales of the Dragon before them, they made an awesome sight and Alexander found pleasure in gazing over them. He raised his sword into the air once again. The men roared with an enthusiasm that spread over the hill. Alexander smiled.

"It is time!" he shouted and heeled his horse to gallop. He rode along the ranks of his men. "It is our time!"

The men shouted their approval.

He stopped his horse there for a moment. "As we enter into battle once again," he said, "we cannot forget all those who came before us."

He studied their faces. "Many have died here in these fields. Men we loved," he said. "But many men have lived here as well!"

Shouts rose again.

"Those of us who have survived now have the obligation to avenge our brothers, our fathers!"

The excitement filled Alexander's heart. He felt alive. "And it is now our time to end this evil once and for all. We are gathered here to strike down this evil that has taken over our land, our lives, and left us with nothing." He pointed his sword to where the palace once stood.

"No one can do this for us. No one *will* do this for us," he continued. "Only we can come together with those who desire good, with those who desire peace in all lands, to destroy this darkness that has plagued this kingdom for far too long. No, we cannot do this alone. We must join together with those who were once seen as our enemies but are now our friends. And together we will fight. Together we will endure. Together we will win this war!"

And with that came the roar of dragons as they swept over the hills with Elfin warriors on their backs. The men raised their swords and shields high into the air as the fierce creatures flew above them with the morning sun reflecting off of their scales. Alexander couldn't help but laugh with joy as he watched the beautiful dragons soar above. Deep inside his chest, his heart was full and the old feeling of the lion was back. For the first time in a long time, the hope he had known before had returned again.

§

"Peter, do you need assistance?" Thætil asked as he approached. He was dressed in his finest armor and white tunic. His long white hair was braided and pulled back to reveal his crystal blue eyes and chiseled face.

Peter smiled and placed one foot into the saddle stirrup. "Not at all," he said. His dragon, the lithe Draco, tugged slightly on the reins as though confused. "We're still getting to know each other."

Thætil grinned and grabbed the reins to steady the anxious beast. "You'll need to name it."

"So I've been told." Peter smiled. He thought for a moment and he stroked its neck.

"I need you to be strong and swift," Peter said. "I need you to be faithful and true to the end."

"In our language, *tavrith* is a word we use for speed and strength," Thætil said. "It was the name of a great dragon ridden by an Elfin king years ago."

"Tavrith," Peter said. "I like it. Tav, for short."

His dragon chewed on the bridle within its mouth. Thætil gently stroked the snout of the dragon and it closed its eyes as though it enjoyed the feeling.

"I think it likes that name," Thætil said as he nodded to Peter to mount.

Peter swiped his brown hair away from his eyes and obeyed. He sat high on his dragon, feeling its muscular body contract slightly. He adjusted his feet into the leather saddle and sighed with relief that the time to ride home had finally arrived. He then gazed around as all the Elfin soldiers also mounted their dragons. Some dragons were larger than his Draco and carried *two* soldiers. He remembered what his mother had told him about the faithfulness of dragons. He knew some dragons would die in the battle while others would make it home. It was the same for the Elves, men, Ogres, and Dwarves all headed into war.

"Better?" Thætil asked.

"Much," Peter said.

"You two will continue to bond along the way, I guarantee it. He seems a bit young and temperamental." Thætil looked at Peter. "But aren't we all?"

Peter chuckled. "Absolutely."

"Squire!" Peter shouted to his squire who ran over and handed Peter his crossbow and Dragon scale shield. He then assisted Peter in strapping the items onto the saddle. "Thank you."

The squire bowed. "Luck be with you, Sir Peter."

Jason sat atop his dragon. Together, they trotted over to Peter.

"Well?" he asked. "What do you think? Do I look like a dragonrider?"

"Most definitely!" Peter said. "Will you be flying with us?"

"No, I am to fly to the east and meet King Isleif's men." Jason beamed with pride. "I'll be fighting with the King!"

"Excellent!" Peter reached out to grab Jason's arm. The two friends grabbed arms then parted. "Goodbye, my friend!"

"I'll see you on the battlefield, Prince Peter!" Jason shouted as he flew off into the new sky.

As Peter watched his friend depart, behind him came Thurdin, Thætil's nephew. Peter realized Thurdin had been strangely absent from training over the last few days. He watched the young Elf approach his dragon. He was hastily putting on his leather gloves.

"Are you ready for the task, Thurdin?" Peter asked with a wide grin. But Thurdin mounted his dragon without a word. Peter shrugged. "I guess not."

Thurdin adjusted his saddle stirrups.

"I haven't seen you at training in a while," Peter said. "We certainly could've used your help in the Maze of—"

"That's because I do not need the training," Thurdin said, rudely interrupting Peter. "And I have passed the test of the Maze before."

Peter smirked. "Oh, I see."

Thurdin mounted his dragon and awaited orders from his uncle. Thætil ran over to his dragon, a Wyvern with glassy scales reflecting the morning sun. It gnawed on the bridle in its mouth and tugged as though it was eager to take flight. He easily hopped onto the saddle on its back, gently heeled its ribs with his boots, and held on tightly as it flapped its enormous leathery wings. Twigs and dirt spiraled into the air around the dragon and it lifted off the ground.

"Come on!" he shouted to the men and his fellow Elves. "Let's go!"

Peter raised his arm to protect his eyes from the debris, but he watched as Thætil and his dragon flew high into the fresh morning sky. For a second, Peter could hear the roar of the dragons and smell the damp air of the arena at Rünbrior. *I'm glad these dragons aren't chained and bound for death in the arena*, he thought. *These creatures are the warriors they were meant to be.* He turned to his own dragon, Tav, and stroked its scaly neck. He heeled it gently and nudged it forward. The beast shook its head and flapped its wings.

"I'm still getting used to this dragon riding," Peter said to Thurdin. "I'm not as good at it as I'd like to be."

"Yes, I know," Thurdin said. "Let's hope you improve in time to fulfill this task set before you or we're all in trouble, aren't we?"

Peter narrowed his eyes as though confused. "Is there something I've done to upset you, Prince Thurdin?"

Thurdin chortled. "Let's get on with this." He nudged his own dragon and the beast flapped its wings and raced off into the sky.

Soon, Peter and his friends were airborne on the backs of their dragons, some Wyvern and some Dracos, soaring through the misty morning air toward their destination: the desert plains outside of Illiath.

"Off we go, yes?" Crispin shouted to Peter as they soared side by side through the low lying clouds, the wings of their dragons almost touching.

"Yes!" Peter shouted, squeezed the dragon with his thighs, and leaned forward. Together, he and his dragon soared as one, cutting through the mist and sometimes hitting the tops of the trees with their feet as they flew, but Peter only laughed. The rush of air made it difficult to breathe at times, but he didn't mind. He was free and finally heading home. The grotesque Ranvieg mountains became smaller and smaller in the distance as they flew in the opposite direction. And that's all that Peter wanted. He had hoped deep in his heart to never see that mountain range again for as long as he lived.

"Far better than horses!" Annika shouted as she caught up with Crispin and Peter.

"I never thought I'd hear you say that!" Crispin answered. On his head he wore a leather helmet and mask the Elves had made for him. Annika chuckled at the sight.

"Why are you wearing that thing?" she asked.

"For protection," he mumbled.

"What?" she asked. "I can't hear you talk with that thing on your face!"

He removed it. "For protection!"

Annika rolled her eyes and pointed. "Well, look down there!"

Crispin glanced over the side of his dragon. Below his dragon, he could see the rugged mountain pathway he and his friends had to traverse in order to reach the White Forest, and ultimately, Vulgaard. Simon, Crispin, and Annika made their escape from Sir William while Peter was held captive in the prison of Rünbrior all the while facing Trolls, Ogres, and Lord Bedlam's wicked creatures. They had to overcome exhaustion, hunger, and fright but they prevailed and earned their rest at the palace of Vulgaard.

"Remember the horrendous journey out here?" she shouted as she looked below.

"How could I forget?" Crispin shouted.

"This is far better than riding horseback on those rugged mountain trails!" Annika smiled at Peter.

Peter gazed downward at the river slicing through the valley. He could see the white water gushing and a few deer scattering away at the sight of the dragons above.

"That's where the Dragon saved Crispin!" Annika pointed to the river.

Peter tried to fathom the idea of his friends making that journey on horseback...alone. But they weren't really alone. He knew the Dragon was watching over them always. And that's when he began to search the sky for it. He looked to his left and then to his right, but saw nothing, not even the white owl.

"Where are you my friend?" Peter whispered.

Suddenly, a shadow appeared on the ground. Peter smiled when he saw it. For the shadow racing along the landscape was the largest of all.

Peter looked upward and saw the Dragon as it burst out from behind the clouds and blocked out the sun for a moment.

"Look!" Thætil pointed to the silhouette of the Dragon in the sky. Simon watched the Dragon's shadow flow over the valley like liquid. "We're in the shadow of its wings!"

Peter smiled a wide tooth smile, raised his arm, and shouted with joy when he saw his friend flying with them. The dragon underneath him roared its approval and so did all the other dragons when they saw it, their leader.

The Dragon of the Forest.

The Dragon of Promise.

Immediately, Peter imagined himself back in the Dragon Forest as a ten year old boy, frightened out of his mind at the sight of the enormous Dragon towering over him. Peter laughed as he remembered thinking he could ever slay the dragon with a wooden sword. He remembered the voice that comforted him.

*"It is good that you are here," said the Dragon.*

As it soared high above, Peter was glad his friend was with them as they headed to Illiath to fight the final battle against evil. All those years ago, Peter thought possessing the scales of the Dragon would be the greatest achievement of his life. Only now did Peter truly understand why the Dragon was so pleased to see him in the clearing of the forest. Befriending the Dragon would become the greatest achievement of his life. The time had come for Peter to learn his destiny and, that night long ago, the Dragon of the Forest began to reveal to him what that destiny would be.

It began to lower itself until Peter could reach out and touch its underbelly. Peter laughed and the Dragon reached its head around. Their eyes met and Peter felt a warmth rush through his body calming him, giving him peace.

"I knew you would come!" he shouted. And he thought he saw the

Dragon grin before it soared off ahead of them all, its incomparable scales glistening in the new morning sun. Peter watched it ascend above the clouds as it headed to the north. He knew it was on its way to the Dragon Forest.

"I will see you in the Dragon Forest!" Peter shouted after it.

Whoops from all the Elfin warriors and the roars of all the dragons could be heard for miles and Peter knew he would remember this moment forever.

§

Sir William, mounted on his black steed, heeled the beast with his boots and nudged it forward to a gallop across the hills outside of Hildron. Together, they galloped as the Barok warriors ran with their swords held high. The battle cry of the gruesome warriors sent the sparrows fluttering into the sky. Will and his horse galloped feverishly until he spotted King Alexander's men waiting for them near the Blue River where the palace once stood. Now all that remained was a pile of limestone bricks stacked one on top of the other. The ruins seemed to call out to him as he rode, but he continued on toward his goal: King Alexander.

Behind him, the fires of Hildron castle continued to roar and the skies above began to darken. Alexander noticed it immediately. He knew what the dark presence meant.

"Lord Bedlam is near." He signaled to his captain.

"Yes, your majesty," the captain said. He turned and signaled to his men to take up arms and shields. "Dragons?"

Alexander nodded and gripped his shield. "Yes, be prepared. Be prepared for anything."

Above them circled the Elfin warriors on their dragons awaiting the orders to attack.

But Alexander wanted to see Will first. He wanted to see the former knight and look into his eyes for any semblance of the goodness he once knew.

"Should we begin our march, my Lord?" the captain asked. Alexander understood the question. He had once been an anxious soldier on the battlefield. He knew the men wanted to get this fight over with.

"Not yet," Alexander said as he searched the horizon. The roar of the enemy grew louder and he knew they were on the other side of the hill. The dust continued to rise into the air. But there was hardly any sunlight coming from the east as the dark clouds continued to block out the light making the air feel colder and smell of rain. Ah, the rain and darkness, Alexander knew Bedlam's tactics all too well. He had once fought in the darkened skies before and now he would do it again.

"There!" A soldier pointed to the hills to the west. "The Duke approaches!"

Alexander saw him, too, and nudged his horse forward. "Stay here and await my signal to advance," he ordered. He turned to his captain. "Understand?"

"Understood, my Lord," the captain of the soldiers said.

"At your command, my Lord," the head knight replied.

Alexander rode out to meet with Sir William there in the hills outside of Illiath.

# 31 THE BATTLE BEGINS

Alexander pulled hard on the reins as his horse slid to a stop. Directly across from him was Sir William, the self-proclaimed Duke of Illiath, dressed in black armor and mounted on his large stallion that dug impatiently at the ground with its front hoof. Behind him, a Barok held the banner of Lord Bedlam as it snapped in the wind.

"You take a tremendous risk riding out to meet me alone, King Alexander," Will said coolly through the visor of his helmet.

"I have no fear of you, Sir William," Alexander said.

"Your resistance, although admirable, is indeed futile, King Alexander," Will said.

Alexander raised his visor and sat quietly, inspecting the thousands of Baroks lined up in rows behind Will, all of them panting and growling like rabid animals. Drool seeped from their mouths. The grotesque creatures were mutant creations of Lord Bedlam and Alexander knew this. Part man, part beast, the Baroks roared and revealed rows of sharp teeth stained from years of feasting on flesh and bones.

"As you can see, I have amassed a great army that you and the other rulers cannot possibly defeat," Will waved his arm over the rows and rows of Baroks lining the hills with the fires of Hildron illuminating them from behind. "It will serve you best to submit to Lord Bedlam and surrender the swords."

"It is an impressive sight," Alexander said. "Remove your helmet."

Will cocked his head as though confused by the command. But he acquiesced and removed the metal helmet.

Alexander gazed deeply into the young man's eyes. He was caught off guard by Will's striking features. Although he worked for Lord Bedlam, Alexander could see that Will's physical appearance had not yet been affected by the evil presence. His face was hardened with cheekbones like chiseled marble and deep set brown eyes. His neck was thick and muscular from years of training and his shoulders remained wide yet strong.

"You once saved my life, Sir William," Alexander said. "You saved my son the Prince. I remember it well."

Will remained silent.

"And now here you are ready to take my life and the life of my son," Alexander continued. "And for what?"

"This battle is about the people, King Alexander, not you. This war is about the land and who controls it. The people have spoken. They have joined forces with us to take control of their land forever. The time of Kings is over. You are making this personal and—"

"My palace was destroyed!" King Alexander shouted. His horse became startled. "My son was abducted and taken to a prison where he fought for his life!"

Will said nothing.

"Of course I take that personally!" Alexander shouted. "Wouldn't you?"

"No matter. The fact remains, King Alexander, that the people are tired of Kings to rule over them," Will said. "They have joined my ranks and not yours. The people are now ready to rule the lands on their own. I will order my men to fight and they will fight to the death on the ground, in the air, and on the sea as ordered, King Alexander."

"For what? The promises of a man who isn't even a *man* at all?" Alexander shouted.

Will winced.

"Yes, that's right. You serve an illusion. You know we have all the swords, Will," Alexander said, "and you know Peter will enter the Dragon Forest."

Will said nothing.

"And when we do, that spell will be broken forever." Alexander squinted. He searched Will's countenance. "The illusion, as strong as it is, will be destroyed. If you align yourself with him, then you will be destroyed along with him and everything he has created."

Alexander nodded to all the snarling Baroks facing him.

Will stared at King Alexander.

"Perhaps, but the difference, O King, is this," Will said. "These creatures behind me have nothing to lose. And your men have *everything* to lose."

Alexander tilted his head.

"*You* have everything to lose, King Alexander," Will continued. "And my Lord's power, the true measure of his strength, has yet to be revealed completely. You may think his power is all an illusion, but you truly have no idea what he has achieved."

"Perhaps this is true," Alexander said, "But what I do know is this. His power is based on magic, a spell that was cast. And every spell has its limitations. Every spell is temporal, Will."

Will raised his chin and placed his helmet back onto his head. He lowered the visor.

"I admire you, Will," King Alexander said. "You were once a great knight in training and I am convinced you could have been my greatest knight, my greatest champion."

Will sat motionless.

"And what I saw in your eyes just now," Alexander said as he lowered his visor, "is hope that the Will I once knew…remains." He jerked his horse around. "And, yes, this is personal to me. I make no apologies for that." Alexander galloped off toward his men.

As he rode, he removed the Sword of Alexander from its sheath, signaling to his men to begin the advance. His captain, when he saw the signal, ordered the trumpet blast. The men roared and began their advance.

The war had begun.

§

Queen Esmeralda sat mounted on her large dragon, Daya, a Wyvern hatched long ago and raised as a gift for her. She stroked its neck as she searched the skies for the signal. She turned to the east as the sun rose from behind the sea. She squinted her eyes as she noticed more and more clouds building up in the western sky.

"Rain is coming," her captain said as he, too, inspected the sky above.

"No, it is Lord Bedlam," she said. "Remain steady."

Dressed in bronze armor, the Queen decided, against all advice, to fight alongside her men and the Elves. The war was personal to her, and the other rulers knew they could not stop her from participating.

A clap of thunder was heard from the west. Her soldiers along with the Evles sat mounted on their dragons, ready to join in the battle. All they needed was the signal.

"The sun rises higher." King Isleif bowed as he approached the Queen. "I fear something has gone wrong, your Majesty. We should have seen the signal by now."

"And there it is!" She pointed to the sky behind him. Circling high above them was an Elf on a dragon. The Elf waved his arms as he flew toward the Queen.

"It has begun!" he shouted as he headed out to sea.

"Ready the men!" Queen Esmeralda ordered.

She lowered the visor on her helmet and nudged her dragon. It flapped its wings and lifted the Queen high into the sky. She turned it and soared over the sea. Her task in the battle would be to stop all advances of Bedlam's sea creatures from attacking the kingdoms along the shores. Her men were prepared as they rode on dragons born from the seas.

"Be prepared for anything!" Isleif yelled to his men as he and his dragon flew with them over the hills. He would guard the eastern shores and meet Bedlam's warriors in the air. "He'll stop at nothing to defeat us all!"

The Elfin soldiers nodded as they flew alongside the King into battle.

§

"Peter! Look!" Annika pointed to the northwest. There, the dragonriders could see the fires of Hildron burning behind the Black Hills.

Peter knew they were close to their final destination. He turned to the north, hoping for glimpse of the Dragon Forest. He heard Tavrith roar. Then, he heard more roars, but they sounded high pitched, more like a wounded animal.

"Oh, no!" Annika shouted. Peter could see she was pointing to his dragon. It slowed down and they began to head toward the ground. Peter looked at its side and saw an arrow protruding from its ribs. Blood flowed. The beast tried to navigate through the trees, but several branches hit its wings sending it spinning to the ground. Peter was thrown from the saddle and skidded along the dirt. A tree trunk stopped him and he blacked out from the impact.

*"You can do this, Peter." He heard his mother's voice. "Hold on tightly to the reins."*

*For a moment, Peter was five years old again, riding his horse, Titan, in a field outside the palace. His mother held Titan's reins and led the horse through the field. Her dark hair flowed around her in the breeze.*

*"Hold on, Peter!" she said to him. "Are you alright?"*

He tried to speak, but couldn't.

"Peter!" he heard a voice. "Are you alright?"

He slowly opened his eyes and saw Annika leaning over him. He moved, but felt a sharp pain in his side. "Ow," he moaned. "Yes, I'm alright. Help me stand."

Soon, Thætil and the others were gathered around Peter helping him to stand.

"I think it's my ribs," he held onto his side. "Is anyone else hurt?"

Thætil nodded over to the clearing where several of the dragonriders had landed to fetch Peter and the others that were shot down in the attack.

"What happened?" Peter asked. His eyes grew wide. "Where's my dragon?"

Thætil looked away. Peter searched Annika's face. She frowned.

"Peter, it's severely wounded," she whispered. "I'm so sorry."

Peter ran over to where Tavrith lay. He knelt down by its head and began to stroke its snout. He removed the leather pouch from his belt.

"I'm sorry, my friend. I'll make the healing salve and you'll be fine," he whispered. "Bring me some water!"

Annika helped him make the paste and feed it to the dragon. Peter rubbed it on the wounds.

"No!" Thætil shouted and ran to Peter. "Don't give it the paste!"

"It will work," Peter said. "Come on, Tav, eat the paste."

"We do not give the healing salve to dragons!" Thætil said sternly.

"Why not? Will it harm the dragon?" Annika asked with a concerned look.

"We have never given it to the dragons. It may harm them," Thætil said.

The dragon did its best to obey its master. Soon, it rolled over onto its belly.

"There! You see?" Peter said. He looked at the arrow. The wound healed and the arrow fell to the ground.

Thætil scratched his head. "Unbelievable," he said. "I have never seen the healing salve work on a dragon before. I never knew it was possible."

Peter rubbed his dragon's snout and grinned at Thætil. "Well, Tav is different," Peter said. "Aren't you, boy?" Then, he eyed the arrow lying on the ground.

"Many have been killed in the attack," Thætil said. He motioned for Peter to follow him. "A few of my Elves succumbed to their wounds. I'm sending several Elves back to inform Theo about what happened.

He will send reinforcements, I'm certain."

"Attacked?" Peter looked at the wounded soldiers and dead dragons. "By what?"

Eris jogged over. In her hand was an arrow. She handed it to Peter. "By Bedlam's Baroks," she said. "These arrow tips are made from Bedlam's bewitched metal that he makes in the fire pits of Hildron. And, these arrows were poisoned. The dragons didn't stand a chance."

Peter inspected the arrow still stained with dragon blood. Then, he remembered.

"We cannot use the healing paste on the rest of the Elves who were wounded," Peter sighed.

Eris shook her head. "Do not worry about them. Use it on the men who were injured."

"Of course," Annika said. She ran off to make more of the paste. Eris joined her.

One by one, the wounded were given the paste to heal their wounds both outside and inside. Peter ate some of the paste to help heal his ribs. He moaned from the discomfort as the paste healed his broken bones until finally, he could stand on his own. Thætil patted him on his shoulders.

Peter stood amazed at how many of the Elves had regained their strength and were ready to proceed even without the healing salve. Eris made her way over to Peter.

"We are ready," she said proudly.

"Well done," Thætil said to his soldiers. "We know the Baroks are close by. They know we landed and will make their way to finish the job. We must begin our hike out of the forest immediately."

Peter agreed and helped gather all the men and Elves to hear Thætil's orders.

"Ride back on the dragons and get reinforcements," he ordered several of his Elfin soldiers. "The rest of us will double up on the remaining dragons."

"Will Theo and the others know where to find us?" Peter asked.

"Of course," Thætil said. "Remember, he's a dragon." He winked at Peter who grinned.

"Where will we go?" Annika asked Thætil.

"To the desert plains of Thèadron. We must stay clear of Hildron," he ordered.

"The Ogres." Annika turned to Crispin. "Perhaps they'll help us once again."

Peter tilted his head. "The Ogres?"

"Yes," Annika answered. "On our journey to Vulgaard, Crispin did a fine job of convincing them to hide us from the Duke's men months ago. We discovered the Ogres are very kind and generous. Perhaps they will help us again."

Peter raised his eyebrows. "Really?"

"I found it hard to believe at first, myself, but it's true," Crispin said.

"The Ogres long for peace in the lands," Simon said. "If we approach them, I am sure they will help us."

"Well, we can certainly try," Peter said.

They gathered all their belongings. Peter made sure he had his crossbow and Dragon scale shield.

"Make certain you have your shields!" he shouted to the others. "They are the only thing between you and dragon's fire."

Annika watched as Peter attached hers to her saddle for her. She smiled at him.

Soon, they all mounted the dragons and flew out behind Thætil as he led them out of the forest.

"I hate that I lost my dragon," Crispin panted as he sat behind Simon, "I had bonded with mine. It was my friend."

"I'm sorry, Crispin," Peter said as he flew next to him on Tav. Annika sat behind him. "Don't worry. Theo will send more to help us."

"Good because I despise hiking almost as much as I despise riding horses," Crispin said.

"Don't worry," Simon chuckled. "We'll be in Thèadron soon!"

"General Aluein and his men will meet us there," Peter said. "Just keep an eye out for Baroks on the ground." He slowed his dragon down and made sure all the others were following.

An hour later, the group landed at the foot of the Black Hills. The fires of Hildron belched into the darkened sky. The smoke made Annika cough.

"The darkness has returned," she said. The red sky reflected in her eyes. "I cannot believe this is happening again."

"Many rulers have joined forces with Bedlam," Peter said. "His powers grow as a result."

"His powers grow, but we have the swords," Thætil said. "Come, we must keep going."

"No wait." Peter stared at the hills and the fire. He had a distant look in his eyes. He turned to Thætil. "I need to know what is happening at Hildron."

Thætil furrowed his brow. "What?" he asked. "Whatever do you mean?"

Peter nodded toward the Black Hills. "Come with me," he said.

"We can sneak inside and see for ourselves what Bedlam is hiding in there."

Thætil gazed over to the fire rising into the sky.

"Thætil , listen to me. Theo and Dangler both alluded to the fact that Bedlam's power has grown and that he has secrets at Hildron, a secret weapon for my father," Peter explained.

"Peter, I don't know about this," Simon said nervously. "You are the only one who can enter the forest. Why do you want to put yourself and the whole plan at risk like this?"

"He has a point," Crispin said.

Peter nodded his head like he understood. "But it would help my father and the others if we knew Bedlam's secrets," Peter explained. Thætil, being a brilliant warrior, began to understand Peter's intent.

"I know it's insane." Peter walked over to Simon. "But if we could see for ourselves what Bedlam is hiding, we could use it to our advantage."

"If you make it out alive," Simon said.

"I'm in." Annika stepped forward.

"No." Peter shook his head. "This is far too dangerous."

Annika removed her sword from its sheath. "Excuse me. But I am going with you, and so is Crispin."

Crispin jerked his head to face Annika. "What?" he shouted. "Are you mad?"

Simon chuckled. "Yes, you go with her, Crispin. I think I will stay with Eris and head on."

Crispin stood with his mouth open.

Thætil looked at the hills again then back at Peter. He slowly smiled and put his large hand on Peter's shoulder. "You survived the prison inside the Ranvieg Mountains, fought dragons in the arena, and made it through the Maze of Thœrgën, and now you want to enter Hildron? Peter, you are your father's son," he said. "Let's go and see what Bedlam is hiding inside those hills."

He turned to his Elves. "El ëloin deir nüi il æs Thèadron. Ish iliündren," he ordered in their language and pointed toward Simon. "Na äl nathra un iél ündrien, Eris il Simon." They nodded and obeyed his orders.

"I have asked a few of my soldiers to take the dragons and head to Thèadron with Simon and Eris in order to meet General Aluein and inform him of our plan. Do not worry, Simon. You will be well protected." Thætil nodded.

Simon studied the tall armored Elves as they walked over to him.

"We will be alright." Eris adjusted the quiver of arrows on her back and held her bow firmly in her hand as she walked passed Simon. "Let's go before the Baroks return and find us."

The Elves and Simon mounted the dragons. Peter gazed at Simon and waved.

"Be safe!" Peter shouted after them.

Simon gulped and waved back.

Before Eris mounted Peter's dragon, he walked over to Tavrith and removed his crossbow and shield. Then, he stroked the dragon's neck.

"Take good care of Eris," he whispered. "Be safe. We will meet again soon."

Peter, Thætil, Crispin, and Annika watched the others fly off toward the desert plains,

"Come on, Peter," Annika said. "We've got to go on. You, too, Crispin. You're coming with us."

Crispin frowned, threw his head back, and groaned. "No," he said. "Not another adventure."

"You're coming with us and I don't want to hear another word about it," Annika ordered.

"Well, remember how we all craved adventure once?" Peter chuckled as he passed Crispin.

"Don't remind me." Crispin stomped off after the others. "Please, don't remind me."

# 32 THE SECRETS OF HILDRON

"Stay in the fight!" shouted Alexander. He swiped Baroks with his sword sending their blood splattering through the air. As he fought, he kept an eye on his men.

"More come from the hills!" replied his captain. He pointed behind Alexander.

"Never mind! Just keep fighting!" the King answered.

For many hours, the Elves riding on the backs of dragons, swooped low over the Baroks slicing at them with their swords. Limbs flew everywhere as the Elfin swords cut through them with ease. The Elves pulled up on the reins and circled the dragons back around again. This time, the dragons spewed their fire into the hordes of Baroks. They screamed in agony as the fire burned their grotesque skin. Soon after, hundreds of Baroks were nothing but burnt corpses on the desert plains near Illiath.

"Keep advancing!" Alexander ordered. His head knight ran up to him.

"Sire, there are no more Baroks coming from the west. I believe we have won this round." The man bent over, panting from exhaustion.

"Sir Rohan," Alexander said, "Well done. Well done. Have the men pull back to Lake Silith and find rest there. The second round will begin soon."

"Yes, sire." Sir Rohan jogged off and began to gather the surviving soldiers to begin their march to the lake.

Alexander stood panting as he watched his men assist the wounded. His mind raced to the battle against Lord Caragon years before. Although this part of the battle lasted only hours, he knew there were more battles to come. He made his way to the top of a hill to obtain a better view of the battlefield. There, covering the land, were hundreds of dead Baroks, men, and a few Elves as far as he could see.

Above him circled some Elves still on their dragons. He waved at them and motioned them to follow the others to Lake Silith. He knew Sir William was heading back to Hildron for reinforcements and he knew there would be even more fighters to come.

An Elf landed nearby and motioned for Alexander to mount the dragon with him. Alexander did and together they flew off toward Lake Silith. "When you drop me off, go and use the dragons to bring the wounded to the lake!" he ordered.

"Yes, sire," the Elf agreed.

Once everyone had made it to Lake Silith, they found rest for a few moments. The water was cool and refreshing. The wounded were given the healing paste to help them heal. Some food was prepared, but mostly the King and his men planned for the next attack.

"Any news of Peter?" Alexander wiped his face with a damp cloth. He handed it to a servant.

"Nothing yet, your Majesty," Sir Rohan replied. "We expected him hours ago. Something must have happened."

Alexander turned to one of the Elfin soldiers who nodded and ran to mount a dragon. When he flew off, Alexander's face relaxed as he felt relief.

"They will find him," Alexander murmured.

"Do not worry, my Lord," Sir Rohan said. "Here, allow this servant to apply the paste to your wound."

Alexander tilted his head. "My wound?" He noticed the knight was staring at the King's arm. His arm was cut open wide. He had been sliced open by a Barok's blade, but in the excitement, he hadn't even felt the pain. "Aye. I hadn't noticed I was wounded. What is that you have there?"

"It is a special healing salve Sir Theodore provided," Sir Rohan said as he applied the paste to the King's wound.

"I remember it now. I have not seen it in years. I did not know Theo still allowed it to be used." Alexander grimaced as his knight applied it to the wound. "It burns."

"Good." Sir Rohan chuckled. "That means it is working."

§

Eris walked with chin up, eyes darting side to side, with her fellow Elves at her side. She and the others landed to rest their dragons. They decided to hike on toward Illiath for a while. She turned to see the others falling behind.

"Come on! Stay with us. There is strength in numbers!" she commanded. Simon nodded.

Eris ran back. "You've got to keep up," she told Simon. "The others look to you as a leader."

Simon looked behind to see the other soldiers walking slowly. That's when he knew Eris was right.

"We must hurry." Eris turned to jog off.

Simon watched her jog on ahead with effortless ease. He admired her and the other Elves. They were in excellent physical condition and well prepared for such a hike. He knew he wasn't ready for this and felt ashamed. He turned to the men following him, "Come on, men, we've got to speed things up. Let's go!"

Simon jogged off and the others followed along.

They continued toward Illiath for a little longer, huffing and puffing along while keeping watch for Aleuin's men or the Baroks. Suddenly, an Eflin warrior the others called Thúris raised his hand and stopped hiking. The other Elves, including Eris, stopped too. Simon followed suit until all were quiet and still.

"What is it?" he whispered to Eris.

But she said nothing and only stared straight ahead. Slowly, she reached up and removed an arrow from her quiver and loaded her bow. Simon's eyes grew wide because he knew what that meant. He removed his sword and all the other men did the same.

He mouthed the words, "Steady now" to them and motioned for them to prepare. The Elves crouched down so the men did as well.

A loud scream came from the other side of the hill, sending several Baroks over the hill on the backs of snarling Zadoks. Eris immediately shot her arrow into the head of one of the Baroks. The creature fell to the ground, but the Zadok still charged ahead.

Simon took a stance, gripped his sword, and prepared. "Steady men! These things are brutal!" he shouted.

The Zadok, teeth glaring, jaws snapping, came hurdling toward him, but he waited until it leapt. Sure enough, the giant wolf-like beast leapt at him, so Simon instinctively thrust his sword into the chest cavity of the creature. He heard it yelp from the pain and watched it fall to the ground writhing in agony and shock. He ran and quickly pulled his sword from the dead animal, turned and prepared for another beast that was headed his way. He saw Eris shooting arrow after arrow into each Barok as it came up over the hill because her aim was true most of the men only had to deal with the Zadoks. But Simon knew the arrows would run out. And then what?

"Keep slicing at them, men!" he shouted. His arms became weak as the sword in his hands became heavier to lift. The muscles in his shoulders ached as he swiped at each creature. Soon his face was covered in the warm blood of the Zadoks, so he paused to wipe his eyes. That's when he heard it. A female's scream.

"Eris!" he shouted.

§

The sharp rocks were difficult to grip, but Peter did his best as he climbed behind Thætil who climbed without hesitation. He inspired Peter to keep going.

"Annika," he whispered. "Are you alright?" He looked behind.

"Yes," she answered. "Keep going."

She could hear Crispin struggling behind her as his misplaced footsteps sent smaller rocks tumbling down. "Crispin, you must be quieter," she said. "We're getting closer to the top. We don't know if Barok guards will be there waiting for us."

"Alright," Crispin muttered. "Don't be so bossy." He reached up and took hold of a rock, then used it to pull himself up, but the rock came lose. "No!"

Crispin slid down several feet until he was able to grab another rock and stop.

"I'll go help him, keep going," Peter said. Thætil continued on and occasionally reached down to help pull Annika up, but she made it to the top and the two crouched down peeking over the ridge. The heat from the fires coming from Hildron was almost unbearable. Annika's face was wet with sweat. Her hair was matted to her face. She wiped it away.

"The heat is making me dizzy," she said. "And the smoke…it's almost unbearable."

"Quiet," Thætil said. His eyes darted everywhere. "I cannot see any guards."

"Isn't that a good thing?" she asked.

"No." He crept closer. "It's better if we see them, so we can see if they spot us."

"I understand." Annika turned in time to see Peter helping Crispin up over the edge. The two crawled on their bellies over to where Annika and Thætil were.

"Do you see anything yet?" Peter asked.

"Nothing," Thætil said. He waved to Peter. "Let's go in further. You two stay here."

"Gladly." Crispin rolled over onto his back and panted. "My thoughts exactly."

Peter followed Thætil down the mountain which was much easier to descend. Once at the bottom, the ground turned into carved stone streets leading to the castle wall. The two hid in a crevice waiting for any of Bedlam's guards to make their rounds. But no one approached.

Thætil motioned for Peter to follow him up the side of the wall. Peter raised his eyebrows as he watched Thætil ascend the wall using only his hands and feet. Peter swallowed hard, and then gripped the stone as Thætil did and before he knew it, he, too, was climbing up the wall. *Don't look down*, he thought. *Just keep climbing.* Peter felt it a privilege to be with Thætil. He considered him and all the Elfin warriors the best of the best and he longed to be just like Thætil: a fearless leader.

Once they made it to the top, they crouched down along the wall until they could see guards marching into an opening that lead deep into the castle. "That's where we need to go," Thætil said. He smiled at Peter. "Still want to see what Bedlam's hiding?"

"Of course." Peter smiled in return then scooted along the wall with Thætil until they reached a point that they could jump off without hurting their legs. Once on the ground, they snuck into the castle and hid in crevices along the way. The searing heat was making it hard for Peter to focus. He rubbed the sweat from his forehead. *I feel dizzy. How can Bedlam stand this heat?* Peter thought. *Oh yes, I forgot. He's a dragon.*

Thætil stopped and raised his hand. Peter stopped, too, without a word. The hall they had crept down suddenly opened up into a large cavern. Peter realized that Bedlam must have gutted the old Palace hall and rooms to dig out this massive cavern for his work. *This is it,* Peter thought. *This must be where Bedlam creates all his creatures. His lair.*

Thætil turned to Peter and motioned for him to follow him to the edge so they could peer down into the cavern. Carefully, they were able to do just that. They crouched down and made their way over to the edge. There they peeked their eyes over the stone edge and saw several hundred of Bedlam's workers running amok as though in a hurry. They stoked the fires in the tremendous pits sending flames thirty feet into the air where a gaping hole opened the ceiling letting out all the smoke into the dark sky. Each Barok ran by the stacks of swords, took one, and then ran off.

"He must be preparing to send more fighters off to battle," Thætil said. Peter agreed.

The Baroks hustled about down below carrying swords and spears out of the cavern through caves that must have led out of the castle. Some carried the dark metal armor to waiting soldiers and helped them clasp it over their chests. Once armed, the soldiers marched out a side exit from the cavern. Peter searched the area, but did not see Bedlam anywhere.

"Do you see him?" Thætil asked.

Peter shook his head. Thætil nodded then motioned him to follow further into the cavern. At first, Peter hesitated as he saw the way was completely dark. But Thætil entered the darkness unafraid. Peter found the courage to continue on.

A loud roar unlike anything he had ever heard before stopped him where he was. Thætil stopped as well and turned toward Peter. His eyes were wide with fright. He ran over to Peter and the two crouched down.

"What do you suppose that was?" Peter asked. He swallowed hard.

The roar came again from one of the caves leading off of the cavern.

"That was no dragon," Thætil answered.

He and Peter peeked over the edge in time to see a tall thin man enter into the area followed by several guards. Peter realized it must be Lord Beldam. He wore his cape and black boots polished to a shine. One of the guards following him carried a shield.

Peter lifted his head to peer over the edge even more.

"Do you see that?" Peter asked. "That is a shield!"

Thætil nodded.

"That is a shield made from the scale of the Dragon." Peter pointed. "How is it that Bedlam has it?"

"Probably from one of the knights on the quest for the swords," Thætil said.

"The quest," Peter whispered. He had all but forgotten about the quest and how many lives it had cost. He thought of how Sir Nøel had been part of the quest.

Lord Bedlam had the guard place the shield against a rock. Then, Bedlam stood in front of the shield for a moment. He raised his hands and shot streams of green fire onto the shield sending the guards squirming away to avoid the flames. The fire simply reflected off the surface of the shield. Peter and Thætil could see the shield remained unscathed.

Lord Bedlam removed his cape and tossed it aside. Then, he motioned for a guard to bring him a sword from the stack of weapons nearby. Once he had the sword in his hand, he thrust it at the shield, but the black metal did not penetrate the Dragon's scale. Bedlam tried again and again with no success. A guard approached him, so Lord Bedlam swung around and cut off the guard's head out of frustration.

Thætil looked over at Peter. "Not a good sign," he said.

Peter chortled. "Nothing can or ever will penetrate those scales. No magic will ever change that."

"Come, let's go this way," Thætil suggested. Peter followed.

But before they moved, they heard the roar once again.

"You're right. That doesn't sound like a dragon," Peter said. "What could it be?"

"You wanted to find out, so let's go find out." Thætil crouched down and made his way further down the hall toward the caves. Peter followed.

Then, they peeked over the edge to see Lord Bedlam motioning his guards and Baroks to bring something into the open space. Peter and Thætil craned their necks in order to see what was happening. Finally, they saw it. Bedlam's secret weapon.

The giant creature entered the cavern from the cave. Before the beast came Lord Bedlam, strutting proudly. He smirked as the Baroks and servants screamed and scattered away from the giant creature that was part man, part dragon, and part demon with large wings protruding from its back. It stood on hooved feet but had a torso like a muscular man. Its hands were more like dragon claws with nails sharpened to a point and its head was shaped like a dragon's head, but with manlike features and the familiar red eyes glowing from the sockets. Smoke rose from its nostrils and fire was its skin. Scales covered its face and spikes ran down its back leading to a dragon-like tail that whipped around, sending Baroks flying through the air. Lord Bedlam cackled at the sight. The creature was easily forty feet tall, maybe more, and covered in flames, yet it was not consumed by the fire.

"There's your secret," Thætil said.

Peter nodded. "Yes," he muttered through lips dry from fear and from the heat.

"Do you want to see more?" Thætil asked.

"No, let's get out of here." Peter turned to crawl away, but when he did, he saw several armed Baroks sneaking toward him. "Oh no."

§

"Eris!" Simon ran toward the female Elf as she struggled with a Zadok. The beast was on top of her. She used her strong arms to keep its jaws from ripping into her throat. But her arms grew weaker.

Simon hesitated for a moment, unsure what to do. As he lunged toward the creature, an Ogre emerged from the bushes and used its club to knock the Zadok off of Eris. The Zadok was tossed aside like a rag doll. It lay dead nearby. Eris sat up panting and staring at the enormous Ogre that just saved her life.

Simon ran to her and helped her stand. He could see she had suffered many cuts and scrapes.

"Are you alright?" he asked. But her eyes never left the mammoth Ogre towering over them.

"Thank you," she said to it. It growled something in its own language. Eris and Simon turned to see many Ogres fighting off the Baroks and Zadoks with their clubs and axes.

"You see?" Simon said. "They want to help us win!" Simon swiped at Barok with his sword.

Eris loaded her bow and shot two arrows into the belly of an attacking Zadok. It roared and then transformed into a Barok before her eyes. Eris staggered back from shock at the unexpected change. The Barok attacked her so she grabbed the arrows still protruding from its belly and shoved them further into its body. It screamed from the pain, but continued to lunge toward her. It grabbed her neck before she could rearm her bow. She tried to struggle free.

Simon turned in time to see the Barok strangling Eris. Before he could help, the Barok he fought transformed into a Zadok. It growled and showed its sharp teeth. He swiped at it with his sword, but the Ogre came and clubbed the creature to death. Simon ran over to Eris and thrust his sword into the back of the Barok that held her throat.

He watched it fall to the ground and transform into a black crow. It died there on the dampened ground near his feet. Eris fell to her knees, gasping for air. She turned to Simon who reached over and helped her stand.

"Thank you," she panted.

Simon held her steady. "Are you alright?"

Eris nodded. Then, they both studied the dead crow. "I had no idea these creatures could transform," Simon said.

"Neither did I." Eris used her foot to nudge the dead bird. Simon was about to speak when he heard a noise from behind. Together, the two turned with weapons ready, but they were surprised to see General Aluein come from the bushes followed by his men.

"Fancy meeting you two here." He chuckled as he put his sword back into its sheath.

## 33 THE RETURN TO ILLIATH

Queen Esmeralda sat low on her dragon as it swooped down so close to the ocean she could smell the salty water. She reached out and touched the cold water with her finger. It parted the water like a cutlass. She could see the fish scatter beneath the crystal clear water. She yanked on the reins, sending her dragon climbing higher into the air with the ocean growing smaller and smaller below.

"We sighted several Baroks approaching on dragons!" an Elfin soldier who was flying next to the Queen said. "They're coming from the west!"

Queen Esmeralda turned to see, but when she did, an arrow pierced the Elfin soldier through his neck. Three more arrows pierced his dragon's side, sending it spiraling down to the ocean.

"No!" the Queen shouted. She yanked the reins and her dragon dove toward the water with three Baroks following close behind on dragons.

She could hear the arrows whiz by her head and she ducked in close to the neck of her dragon, but it was no use. She felt her dragon twitch and turn uncontrollably. That's when she knew it had been hit. It flew a few feet away from the ocean then skimmed on the surface of the water. The Queen dove off and disappeared into the blue green water. The Barok warriors cheered and turned their dragons toward the shore.

From deep within the ocean, Queen Esmeralda watched the Baroks fly away leaving her for dead. She held her breath and used her arms to keep from sinking. Once she felt it was safe, she turned to the ocean deep below, waved her arms, and waited.

"Do you think she's dead?" An Elfin soldier asked as he hovered above the ocean water on his dragon.

"I do not know," the other Elf answered. His eyes searched the water for any sign of the Queen, but didn't see anything. "I fear she is lost. Perhaps we should return to the shore and—"

As he spoke, the Queen emerged from the ocean deep on the back of a sea dragon. Together they broke through the water with a tremendous splash. The two Elves cheered as the water splashed them both. Their dragons roared when several more sea dragons emerged and flew through the air.

"Come follow me!" the Queen ordered. Her dragon was snake-like with no legs, only long shiny wings. Its body was covered with glassy purple and green scales and its eyes were golden. Long spines lined its back all the way to the tip of its tail. The Elves turned their dragons around, raised their swords, and began to fly off toward the Baroks.

§

"Run!" Will shouted to his men as they followed him into the desert plains near Thèadron. He whipped his horse, its neck wet with foam, and it galloped faster over the dry hills. The sky darkened above them, making the fires of Hildron even brighter. He knew retreat was the only way, so he returned to Hildron for reinforcements.

A scream of agony came from behind him. He turned in time to see several of the Baroks fall to the ground with arrows protruding from their necks. An arrow buzzed by his own head and he lowered his body closer to the neck of his horse, but it was no use. His horse had already been hit by three arrows. It collapsed to the ground, and Will skidded several feet to a stop. He rolled over, reached for his sword, and crawled to his dead horse. He used it as a shield until he could see who or what had attacked him and his men. More Baroks grunted and snarled as they came to their leader.

"Stand and fight!" Will ordered them.

They ran off down the hill while Will rose to his feet and steadied himself. That's when he saw his Baroks fighting General Aluein's men there in the desert plains.

§

The Baroks, armed with spears and swords, cautiously approached

Peter and Thætil. Peter reached for his sword, but one Barok lunged his spear toward Peter's throat. Peter swallowed and moved his hand away from the hilt of his sword. He raised his hands.

"Any suggestions?" he asked Thætil, who seemed rather calm considering the situation.

Thætil smiled at the Baroks. "Follow my move," he said to Peter.

The Baroks growled something in their language and one shoved Peter aside. "I think they want us to march," Peter said.

The Barok turned to Thætil and grunted, but before he could reach out to shove Thætil aside, he was met with a knife in to his throat. Peter saw what happened, reached for his sword, and thrust it into the side of another Barok. The others raised their spears to fight, but Thætil had already thrown his knife into the skull of one Barok and his sword into the back of the last one.

Peter didn't have the words to say. He just stood there with dead Baroks at his feet until Thætil grabbed him.

"Let's go! They'll be more coming!" Thætil shouted.

§

Annika nudged Crispin who rested with his eyes closed. "I think they're coming," she said. Crispin only moaned. "Wake up!"

He rolled over and rubbed his eyes. "Where are they?"

Annika crouched down and began to climb down. "Come on, gather all our belongings. They're coming," she ordered.

Crispin began to stand, but he fell to the ground when he saw Thætil and Peter running toward him. He clutched his chest. "You scared me to death!"

"That's nothing! Get moving or you'll be food for the Baroks following us!" Peter shouted. He quickly loaded his crossbow.

Crispin peered over the wall and saw several Baroks running and waving swords and spears. "Terrific!" He turned and passed Peter. He slid down the mountain screaming like a child.

"Run!" Thætil yelled. "I'll hold them off here!"

Peter grabbed Annika's arm and forced her down the mountain. "Go! I'm staying to help Thætil!"

"You can't hold them all off on your own!" Annika removed her sword and ran back to the wall where Thætil fought off three Baroks. She thrust her sword into the thigh of one of the Baroks, sending it backwards off the wall to its death.

"Well done!" Peter cheered. He released his crossbow and watched as the arrow struck a Barok deep into its chest. Then, Peter removed his sword and swung it around, slicing the neck of a Barok as it jumped onto the ledge. Then, he punched another one in the jaw and sent it flying backwards.

Thætil stabbed several more with his sword. Annika felt one grab her hair.

"Ah!" she screamed, reached into her belt, and pulled out a knife. She twisted around and jammed the knife into the temple of the creature. It fell back with a clump of her hair in his hands. She rubbed her scalp. "That smarts," she muttered.

The three fought off the creatures until finally there were no more. They stood panting on the ledge looking down at the castle.

"Let's go now before more come!" Thætil said.

The three slid down the rocky mountainside until they reached the bottom where Crispin waited. The three ran off into the darkness where several Elves awaited them holding dragon reins.

"Your Highness." One Elf bowed when he saw Thætil approach.

"Well done," Thætil said.

Out stepped Theo from among the Elves.

"Perfect timing, as usual," Thætil said as he climbed onto his dragon.

Peter and Annika joined him in the air on dragons. Theo quickly transformed into the White Dragon, rose, and flew alongside Peter. It winked at him. Annika laughed and cheered.

"Oh, yes, this is all just hilarious!" Crispin frowned from atop a dragon.

Soon the sun was completely gone behind the Black Hills and the first day of battle came to an end. Peter and the others landed near Illiath as the last bit of sunlight disappeared from the sky. The moon appeared from behind the clouds for a moment and illuminated the scene. Peter dismounted his dragon. He slowly made his way to where the palace had once stood.

Annika sat atop her dragon and gasped when she could see that the entire palace was destroyed. She covered her mouth. Crispin stared in disbelief. He watched Peter stand before a pile of limestone bricks and put his hands on them. Peter bowed his head.

The White Dragon landed and transformed into Theo. He stood by Crispin and Annika. No one dared to move.

"It's all so tragic," Annika wept. "Everything is…gone. Destroyed."

Annika began to take a step toward Peter, but Theo gently touched her arm to stop her. When she looked up at him, he shook his head. Annika understood.

Theo stood back for a moment and allowed Peter his time to comprehend all that had transpired while he was captive in Rünbrior.

Thætil watched the scene while he remained mounted on his dragon. He heard a noise from behind, so he quietly drew his sword and motioned for the other soldiers to follow him.

They dismounted and, with swords drawn, crept toward a pile of large boulders. But Thætil halted the others when he saw Eris emerge from behind the boulders with a loaded bow aimed right at his head. He grinned and she lowered her bow. Behind her came Simon.

"When did you arrive?" Thætil asked as he put his sword back into its sheath.

"Earlier in the day," she said. She placed the arrow back in the quiver and draped her bow over her shoulder. Simon stumbled over some of the stones. His eyes never left Peter as he came out of hiding.

"Poor Peter," Simon whispered.

"We were attacked before the Ogres and General Aluein's men saved us," Eris told Thætil. "He and his men are heading northeast to meet King Alexander. The Ogres are going to help after all. We were told to wait here until morning. The Duke and his creatures retreated into the hills."

Thætil nodded. "Good. We will all camp here tonight," he ordered. He looked over at Peter who remained alone amongst the rubble. "Poor boy."

"What happened?" an Elf asked Thætil as they watched Peter.

Thætil pointed to the piles of brick and boulders all around them. "This was once the great palace of King Alexander. This was the only home Peter ever knew."

The Elf nodded with sorrow in his eyes.

Peter choked back tears as he remembered his home filled with excitement and joy the day he left for Knight Training. He remembered Constable Darion and all his preparations. Peter ran his fingers along the smooth stone. Theo finally approached him.

"I cannot believe it, Theo." Peter rubbed his forehead. "It's all gone."

Theo only listened.

"My home," Peter said. "I mean, I knew it happened, but now that I'm here...I'm... it's almost too much to take in." He looked at his old friend.

The sound of the rushing water from the Blue River was heard. Peter turned and began to traverse the destroyed gate that led to the courtyard. He climbed over the remains of the wooden gate and entered the ruins that were once the courtyard where the peasants conducted commerce and Constable Darion would greet visitors. He walked on and saw the rotted carcasses of dead livestock. He saw the remnants of the Smith's shack. Some weathered swords and helmets littered the ground. He turned and saw the ladders that led to the curtain wall where his father's guards and soldiers once stood to protect all within the courtyard. Now those walls were gone. The area was thick with weeds and moss. Then, the stables came to his mind. *Titan*, he thought as he ran.

He came to the place where his father's stables once stood. He lifted up some wooden beams and threw them to the side. He struggled to roll over larger stones and bricks until, finally, he saw a leg. It was the remains of a horse's leg protruding from the pile of wood and stone. He followed the partial skeletal remains of the horse until he spotted the familiar reins and bridle. That's when he knew.

"Titan!" Peter knelt down beside the remains of his faithful horse. "Titan had made it back to the palace after that awful night in the plains when I was abducted." He could hear Theo's footsteps approaching him from behind.

"He had made it back," Peter sobbed. "Titan obeyed me that night and made it back home."

Theo rubbed his bearded chin as he listened.

"Titan was a good horse, Theo," Peter cried as he wiped away his tears. "He was a gift from my mother. He was my friend."

"Yes, I know," Theo said.

Peter reached over and took the bridle. He gently removed it from the skeletal remains and inspected it in the moonlight. "This was the bridle my mother gave to me."

Theo winced because he knew the pain Peter was feeling.

Peter stood and showed Theo the bridle. "He was my horse," Peter repeated. And then he began to sob again. "He was my horse. This was my home."

Peter screamed in anger and threw the bridle down.

"This was my home! Now it's all gone!" He shook his fists and screamed into the night. "Everything is gone!"

Theo quickly took Peter and held him as he wept, knowing it was probably a good thing for Peter to finally weep. It had been a long time since he had released all the pent up emotions he had inside since escaping the prison at Rünbrior.

"He was my friend," Peter said over and over again, but somehow Theo knew Peter was also speaking of Sir Nøel. He held Peter as he continued to sob. "He was my friend. Why did he have to die? Why did I leave? Why did I go so far away from home? I should have stayed here."

Theo shook his head.

"I should have stayed here," Peter said. "I never should have left."

"No," Theo said and parted himself from Peter so he could look into his eyes. "No, Peter. You were meant to leave home and go on your trials. This, all this, had to happen."

Peter pulled away and shook his head. He used his sleeve to wipe his eyes. "No, I should have been here to help. I could have saved Titan. I could have—"

"Nonsense," Theo said. "All this would have happened had you remained here at Illiath."

Peter tilted his head. "I know, but…"

Theo stepped toward him. "Peter, had you stayed, Lord Bedlam still would have come here. He was searching for you. Had you made it to Knight Training, he would have found you there."

Peter looked away. In his mind, he could see himself in his bed chamber gazing out the window at the Dragon Forest.

Theo exhaled and rubbed his temple, searching for the right words to say next.

Peter looked to the west and saw the fires of Hildorn light up the sky surrounding the Black Hills. He ran his fingers through his hair as he walked to where the entrance to the palace once stood. He said as he climbed over the stones and entered the space where the grand hall had been.

Theo followed.

Peter stopped and looked around, remembering the details of the grand hall. He could see the polished mahogany paneled walls reaching up to where the crystal chandelier had hung for so many years. He visualized the intricate tapestries depicting the famous battles his grandfather had fought hanging on the walls with the statues of his forefathers guarding them. He looked down and visualized the shiny marble tiled floor that once reflected the burning torches that lined the hall leading to the staircase. Peter walked over to the remains of the staircase. All that was left were a few banisters protruding from the dirt like an old skeleton. Peter's eyes rose to the balcony that had once led to his bedchamber. All of it was gone. Destroyed by Bedlam.

Theo stood by him, gazing upward to where the bedchambers once were. "I'm so sorry, Peter," he said, shaking his head.

Peter jerked his body then suddenly took off, "My shield!" he cried. He hopped onto a pile of limestone bricks and wooden beams and began frantically sifting through it, tossing bricks aside and lifting the large pieces of wood, grunting as he did.

Theo rubbed his hands together as he watched the boy in the moonlight desperately trying to find his lost shield. "Your shield?"

"Yes!" Peter yelled as he continued the search. "It must be here."

Theo exhaled and removed his robe.

"It's impenetrable. I know it was not destroyed." Peter struggled to lift the larger pieces of wood.

Theo could hear the desperation in Peter's voice. "Surely, Sir William discovered it and took it with him," he said.

Peter hesitated for a moment. "Impossible." Peter grunted as he tossed another heavy limestone brick aside.

"What do you mean?"

"I mean, I hid it," Peter exclaimed. "Before I left for training, I decided not to take it with me. For some reason, I felt the need to hide it away. And so, I made a place for it."

Theo raised his eyebrows. "Impressive." He rolled up his sleeves. "Well, then, I suppose we must find it."

With that said, Theo transformed into the White Dragon and used his massive jaws and legs to help remove the large stones and pieces of wood. Together, they were able to dig out and sift through much of the rubble.

# 34 A PALACE IN RUINS

"Finally!" Peter shouted. He lifted up one of the books from his bedchamber. He turned to the White Dragon, "A book from my room. You see? My shield has to be here."

Annika climbed over the piles to where Peter and the White Dragon stood. "What is happening?" she asked. "What are you two doing?"

Peter threw some books and they landed by her feet. She lifted one up and used the moonlight to try and read the title.

"This is a child's book," she said.

"Yes," Peter said. "It was my book. It was once on my bookcase in my room."

The White Dragon turned its head to Annika and blinked its blue eyes. She rubbed its snout. "Perhaps we should light some torches?" she asked.

Later, several Elves came to assist Peter in the search for his shield. Crispin held up a torch as Peter worked. Everyone helped in the search. Annika handed Eris a torch and climbed out of the rubble. Together, they sorted through the rubble looking for the special shield made from the scale of the Dragon of the Forest.

Simon exhaled as he tossed aside a brick. "Where did you hide it, Peter?"

"I found a space under the floor panels. I used a knife to lift out one panel and that's when I saw that the space could hold my shield. So, I removed enough panels and slid my shield into the space." Peter dusted off his hands. "So, it has to be around here somewhere!"

"I believe you, but I need some water." Simon hopped down from the pile and made his way to his dragon. Eris followed him. She removed her water pouch from the saddle on her dragon. She motioned for the beast to lie down. When it did, she stroked its neck and gently scratched behind its ears. Its eyes began to close.

Simon watched her.

"I think your dragon likes that," he said to her.

"Yes." Eris smiled. "Most dragons do."

Simon approached her. "I think that's the first time I have ever seen you smile."

Eris looked up at him. The moonlight reflected in his large brown eyes.

"I was schooled here you know." Simon pointed to the remains of the palace. "All four of us were. Crispin, Annika, Peter, and I were tutored here."

Eris continued to pet her dragon and listen to Simon.

"We were tutored by Professor Theo." He turned and motioned to the White Dragon still helping Peter in his search. "Before we knew his secret, of course."

Eris turned and watched the Elves help Peter. Then, she turned to Simon. "You have many wonderful memories of this place?"

Simon nodded. "Three years we were together here," he sighed. "Three years of studying, laughing, and playing around the grounds. Peter knew of so many excellent hiding places. This palace was a childhood playground! We would play tricks on the servants and steal food from the kitched." He laughed out loud. "We even played tricks on Theo."

Eris grinned.

"Some days we would sit on the edge of the lake and make plans. We dreamed of finishing school so we could leave this place and be on our way." He took a gulp of water from his pouch. "Oh, this is all silly. You don't want to listen to stories like this."

"No, go on," Eris said. "To where? What places did you want to visit?"

Simon chuckled. "To where? Why to grand adventures in far off lands of course!" he raised his hands in the air. "What fools we were!"

Eris tilted her head as she watched him become animated as he spoke.

Simon looked down and kicked the dirt with his boot. The somber tone returned. "What fools we were," he muttered. "We had no idea what would happen."

Eris studied his face.

"Or how we all would change." He looked over at Peter and the others.

Eris followed his eyes and saw Simon watch Annika help Peter.

"Things must change, Simon." Eris stood next to him. "That's how we grow and become who we are meant to be."

"I suppose you're right." He glanced over at her. "Did you have dreams of your own, Eris?"

She jerked her head toward him as though shocked by his question. "Surely, you do." Simon leaned over to her.

A slight grin slowly crept across her face.

"Ah, so you *do* have dreams," Simon said as he folded his arms across his chest. He seemed proud to have discovered something new about her. "I knew there was more to you than being a soldier."

Eris averted her eyes. "Well..." she hinted.

"It's important to have dreams to reach for," Simon said.

Eris examined his face.

"That's what makes all this worth it." He smiled warmly at her.

"I found it!" Peter shouted startling Simon and Eris. They ran over to the place where Peter sat hunched over.

The White Dragon transformed into Theo again. He put on his robe and climbed over the debris. There he found Peter reaching under splintered wooden floorboards.

"It's still here," Peter grunted as he reached in. Several seconds later, he pulled out the desired shield made from the scale of the Dragon of the Forest. He held it up.

Annika, Crispin, and the others raised their torches high in order to see the scale.

"There it is," Annika breathed. "It's so beautiful."

The scale reflected the torch light and sparkled before them all. Peter gently slid his hands over the surface.

"Not a scratch on it," he whispered. "It's just the same as the last time I saw it."

"Peter, you already have a shield made from the scales, remember?" Crispin asked.

Peter slowly stood being careful not to drop the shield. He shook his head.

"No," he said with a voice gruff from exhaustion. "No, you don't understand."

Theo tilted his head.

Peter hopped out of the pile of rubble. He slid his forearm into the grip on the back of the shield. "This," he said with shiny eyes from emotion. "This is the scale the Dragon gave to me that night."

Crispin and the others listened intently.

"This is the scale it removed from its shoulder and handed to me there in the forest." He lifted the shield up for everyone to see. "I was the first to have the scale shield. It saved me...it saved my life."

Annika nodded.

"Well, then I am glad that you found this most special shield. Now we can rest," Crispin sighed.

"Thank you all for your help," Peter sighed. He watched the others begin to make their way out of the piles of stones and rock. Peter remained near the site of his former bed chambers. He glanced over the torn books and damaged shelves. He shook his head.

"I may not have anything left of my home." Peter turned toward the ruins of the palace. "But I still have this."

Theo scratched his beard and grinned at Peter.

"I still have this." Peter said to him.

"Yes, and much more than you know," Theo approached him.

Suddenly, Will's face came to Peter's mind. The coming battle loomed over him like the ruins of the palace. He waited until he and Theo were alone.

"I have to face him, don't I?" Peter asked in a voice barely above a whisper.

"Who?" Theo asked.

Peter looked over at him with regret in his eyes.

"Sir William?" Theo asked. "Yes, of course you do."

Peter winced. "I don't know if I can, Theo. I don't know if I can...*kill* him."

Theo furrowed his brow. "After all that he has done to you and your father?" He motioned to the piles of stones surrounding them.

Peter threw his head back and groaned with frustration. "I know, but—"

"After all that he has taken from you?" Theo asked incredulously.

"Yes, but, as you said, he is under a powerful spell." Peter tilted his head.

"Aye," Theo took a few steps away from Peter.

"And he once saved me and my father," Peter said after him.

Theo raised an eyebrow. "True."

Peter narrowed his eyes. Calmness suddenly came over his face as he remembered the Will he knew. "It would be like killing my own brother," he said quietly.

"Yes," Theo said and turned to Peter.

Peter closed his eyes. "Is there any good left in him?"

"That remains to be seen," Theo said.

Peter nodded slowly. "There has to be good left in him." He remembered the day Will left for Knight Training.

Theo clasped his hands together behind his back. "Like there was in Lord Caragon?"

"Lord Caragon never loved my father," Peter answered.

"Well, you will have to forgive Will if you are to spare his life," Theo said, "before you can trust him."

Peter nodded. "Can this spell be broken?"

"Of course." Theo raised his chin.

"But how?" Peter came toward him with wide eyes.

Theo smiled. "Peter, you must remember your time in the forest with the Dragon."

Peter did so. In his mind, he pictured the moment he met the Dragon.

"Remember everything about it," Theo said. "It spoke to you and showed you something about its power."

Peter closed his eyes tightly trying to remember everything the Dragon ever said to him.

"The spell Bedlam used on Will was an affecting spell and it goes against the Wizard's Code," Theo squinted. "It is a forbidden spell and he knows it."

Peter opened his eyes and saw Theo's face illuminated by the full moon. "And so it can be broken?"

"Yes, by the Dragon itself." Theo nodded his head toward the Dragon Forest. "If it looks within Will's heart and sees the good in him, the Dragon may sever the forbidden spell."

"May, or may not," Peter sighed.

"Exactly." Theo placed his hand on Peter's shoulder. "But that is for the Dragon to decide. Your task is to face Will. Hope, Peter. Never lose hope in this fight for good."

Peter tried to smile. His eyes grew more and more weary. "I won't," he answered. "And I do remember everything the Dragon did in that forest."

"That's good, Peter." Theo squeezed Peter's shoulder. "Always remember." Peter watched as Theo started to walk away to where the others were camped.

"And we both know Bedlam will do anything to keep you from entering the forest," Theo said as he walked away. "We both know what he is capable of." He stopped walking and turned to face Peter. "It would be best if you tried to anticipate his every move." Theo tapped his temple with his finger.

A chill ran through Peter's body. Yes, he knew exactly what Bedlam was capable of and he knew Theo was right. Did Bedlam already know of the plan the rulers had developed? Peter's eyes darted everywhere as he searched the area. He knew Bedlam's spies were all about. He thought of the swords of the Oath.

"We've a most toilsome day ahead of us," Theo shouted a reminder. "You'd be wise to get some rest."

Peter, his mind engaged, did not respond. He looked down at his shield and ran his hand across the smooth surface. *I entered the Dragon Forest to slay the beast for its scales,* Peter thought. *And instead I was provided a scale for protection.*

Just then, the White Owl appeared out of the night sky and landed on the branch of a tree nearby. It screeched and startled Peter.

He grinned when he saw it.

And then, Peter's mother entered his mind. "She knew of the Dragon's power and its protection. She knew I would be safe inside that forest," he said to the owl.

He thought of the strongbox that carried the swords of the Oath.

"She made the swords and set the plan in motion all those years ago," he said. "But then, she took them to the Elves." He turned his face toward the encampment. Then, he gazed upward into the brightness of moon.

"Why did she take the swords to the Elves?" Peter exhaled. "Not because of magic. The Elves didn't use magic." The owl flapped its wings as it positioned itself on the branch.

Peter shook that thought out of his head. He began to pace the area as he thought about the swords over and over.

"She took the swords to the Elves for help, didn't she?" he asked the owl. Peter grabbed his shield. "She understood what Bedlam would ultimately do with the swords. And she also knew she could trust the Elves to protect them."

He spotted Thætil at the camp. "If she trusted them," Peter exclaimed. "Then, perhaps I should trust them as well." The owl took off.

With that Peter walked off into the darkness, but not to his bed. He headed to where the Elves were camped with the White Owl flying above him.

# 35 DRAGON BATTLES

The sun rose over the ocean horizon sending the streaks of yellow light shimmering into the sky. Annika rolled over when the light hit her closed eyelids. She opened one eye and saw a sleeping Peter lying on his side. She lifted her head and noticed he was asleep on a tattered quilt. His head rested on a dirty pillow that must have once been snowy white. Annika smiled because he looked like a little boy asleep in his bed.

She nudged Crispin who lay nearby. He just groaned and rolled over. Annika tried to sit up. "Ow." she grabbed her back. "I hate sleeping on the ground."

She saw Theo sitting on a broken chair smoking his dragonhead pipe and thumbing through a dust covered book.

Annika slowly stood and stretched. She dusted all the dirt off her trousers. "Where is everyone?" she asked Theo.

"Thætil and his Elves went to meet King Alexander in the Cardion Valley," Theo said.

"Oh." Annika made her way to Theo and peeked over his shoulder. "What book is that?"

Theo puffed on his pipe and wisps of smoke rose around him. "A history book," he said. He slammed the book shut revealing the title, *The Illiath Chronicles.*

"Fascinating," Annika said. "Wherever did you find it?"

"Amongst all the ruins," he said.

"Where is Simon?"

"Hmm? Oh, he went with Eris to find some food around back by the pond." Theo stood and motioned to Peter. "Better wake him."

Annika blinked the sleep from her eyes and stood over Peter. He slept surrounded by some of his broken toys made of wood and a few books partly destroyed by the destruction and weather that he had found during the night. "He looks so peaceful sleeping like that. He looks like a little boy," she said. She bent down and nudged his shoulder. "Peter, time to wake."

"The pond," she said as she stretched upward and yawned loudly. "A dip in the pond sounds wonderful." She nudged Peter harder and then looked by his leg at the glistening scale on its side.

He slowly stood up and dusted himself off. Still dazed, he stumbled over the stones and bricks until he made it over to Theo who simply puffed on his pipe.

"Come on, Peter! Let's go to the pond for some berries and a bath!" Annika urged. She used her foot to shove Crispin until he finally sat up and stretched.

"Come on Crispin!" she yelled as she ran off into the morning sun.

"In a minute." Crispin smiled as he watched her run off. "Where does she get the energy?" He said as he hobbled off toward the lake.

Peter chuckled and stretched his stiff back.

"Oh!" He winced and rubbed his back, and then turned to Theo. Peter could see Theo was interested in his pipe, so he walked off toward the grassy area. He turned to face the sun rising over the tree tops in the east and let the light warm his face. With his eyes closed, he could hear Theo's approaching footsteps.

"I never grow tired of being free." Peter exhaled. "Away from that dank prison cell and the lice and the disgusting porridge."

Theo released more smoke into the air.

Peter gazed around at the grass bending in the breeze and rested his hands behind his back. "Nothing from General Aluein yet?" Peter asked with his eyes still closed. He inhaled the crisp morning air deeply.

"No, nothing yet." Theo turned to the west. "But we'll know something soon."

Peter opened one eye and looked at Theo. "I have a feeling you already know something."

Theo grinned.

Peter turned to see a familiar sight off in the distance. He smelled the jasmine growing nearby, and then exhaled all the night's frustrations away.

"My mother's favorite vine," he said. "Jasmine."

"You remember that?" Theo chuckled.

"Of course," Peter pointed to a partial wall that remained. "It grew along the walls by the kitchen."

Theo grinned with his pipe between his teeth.

Peter turned to face north. "There it is," he said with a sigh of relief. "The Dragon Forest."

Its trees remained as tall and green as he had remembered in his dreams in that horrid prison cell. The breeze animated the trees and their silver leaves twisted and danced. A flock of white doves burst from the treetops and glided away into the turquoise sky almost like spirits. Peter began to walk toward it in a trance-like state. He could hear the rush of the Blue River nearby.

"So peaceful," he said. "You know, the very thought of that forest helped me survive in the prison."

"I can only imagine," Theo said quietly.

Peter glanced around at the grass bending in the breeze. "Hard to imagine a war will be fought here soon, it's so tranquil."

"Hmm," Theo chewed on his pipe.

"And the villagers?" he asked without turning around. "What happened to them?"

Theo shook his head and clasped his hands behind his back. "The men are now part of Will's army. The elderly and the women ran off to hide in the woods or to seek shelter at Gundrehd. Some defiantly remained."

Peter looked to the east. "It's so far for them to hike to Gundrehd with their children," he said.

"Yes, but they had no choice." Theo rocked back and forth on his heels. "The Duke ordered all to swear allegiance to him or be imprisoned for treason."

Peter shook his head and kicked the dirt in frustration. "How can this be? What happened to Will? How could he do this to his people? How could he do this to my father?"

Theo furrowed his brow. "The spell is very powerful."

Peter returned his gaze to the serene land before him

Theo watched the breeze dance through the trees of the Dragon Forest in the distance.

"And what of my father?" Peter asked. "When will I see him again, Theo?"

Theo used his pipe to point north. "In the Cardion Valley. He and his men were victorious in causing Will to retreat. Sir William was forced to head back to Hildron for reinforcements. The Cornshire is scattered with the remains of Will's troops."

Peter chortled. "I can imagine, knowing the fighting skill of my father's soldiers and knights." Peter turned to Theo. "But Bedlam isn't finished yet."

Theo faced the sun slicing its way through the treetops in the east. "No, he isn't," he said.

"And he has a secret, Theo," Peter said with concern in his voice. "A beast unlike anything I have ever seen before—"

"But we have the Dragon of the Forest," Theo interrupted. "Don't we?" He smiled and waved a finger at Peter.

Peter returned the smile, patted Theo on the back, and laughed. Suddenly, a group of dragons flew in from the east. Peter pointed to them as they glided over the trees. Their shadows were long in the morning sun. "Look, Theo!" he shouted. "Who are they?"

"King Isleif and his men, I presume." Theo turned to meet them in the grassy area outside the castle ruins. He paused and turned to Peter. "Go to the pond, eat something, bathe, and then meet us here for battle plans."

Peter nodded, turned and ran off to meet the others.

"Please remember to bathe!" Theo shouted after him.

"I will you old dragon!" Peter laughed as he ran.

§

Thætil dismounted his dragon and hastily made his way to the waiting King. He reached out his arm.

"Your majesty." he grabbed King Alexander's forearm and squeezed.

"Thætil, it is so good to see you again." Alexander led him to where the others waited for the orders to march. "I trust all is well with my son and the others?

"Yes, my Lord," Thætil said. "He waits near the palace at Illiath…near the ruins, well, near the…" Thætil looked away.

"It is alright, Thætil," Alexander said.

"I am so very sorry, my Lord," Thætil said with regret in his eyes.

"There is no need to be sorry," Alexander said as he adjusted his armor. "My son is alive, we have been victorious in the first battle, and now we are all here with the swords ready to defeat this enemy once and for all."

"Yes sire." Thætil bowed.

"Palaces can be rebuilt." Alexander shifted his gaze to the Dragon Forest. "We fight for what cannot be rebuilt."

"Your majesty!" came a shout from behind. An Elfin soldier pointed to a gathering of ominous clouds coming in from the west.

Alexander looked up at the sky. "Bedlam's darkness comes."

The dark clouds formed in the sky over them, blocking out the sun, and covering the earth with long shadows. Thunder echoed from every direction and the wind whirled by them with such force, Alexander had to shout his orders to Thætil.

Thætil gazed at the phenomenon with wide eyes. "What magic is this?"

"Never mind, keep focused on what is real, on what is true." Alexander pointed to the Dragon Forest. "Prepare your fighters now!"

Thætil watched as Alexander jogged down the hill to where his own men were waiting. He waved his arm and an archer sent an arrow set aflame high into the air so that Isleif and his men would see it.

Alexander mounted his horse and galloped over to where Thætil sat with his Elves mounted on their dragons. The beasts gnarled on their bridles and dug into the damp earth with their claws. They seemed anxious to fly.

"Fly and circle above, wait for the signal!" he shouted.

Thætil nodded and flew with his Elves into the darkened sky. Although it was morning, the sky was almost as dark as night.

§

"Peter, where are we going?" Annika ran as fast as she could to keep up with Peter. She looked up at the ominous clouds rolling in. She felt a few icy cold rain drops hit her skin.

"Come on!" he shouted as he ran. Once they arrived at the palace ruins, Peter saw all the dragons in the air with King Isleif. Theo stood nearby with four Dracos waiting for their riders. Peter saw his dragon, Tav, waiting for him. It nodded its head as though eager to take flight.

"What took you so long?" Theo asked. The wind blew his long white hair and beard all around his face. "Your father awaits you near the Cardion Valley! Ride!"

"Yes! We ride!" Peter hopped onto his dragon and attached his shield to the saddle. Once he was ready, he tugged on the reins. "Let's go Tavrith!"

Tav flapped its leathery wings hard to fight the wind. Soon they all were airborne searching the heavens for any signs of Bedlam's fighters. Peter look down at the valley below. He could see the Blue River snaking toward the sea. He looked to the north and spotted his father's men marching through the Cardion Valley. He swooped his dragon low and waved to his father. But his father, trotting along on his horse, paid no heed. He sat with his helmet visor down, prepared for battle.

Peter swung his dragon around and faced Hildron. He saw Annika and Crispin flying nearby. Eris and Simon were on his right. Not too far below were Thætil and his Evles soaring on their dragons. More Elves marched along arming their bows with arrows. Peter estimated at least six thousand men and Elves marched below and he knew even more were coming from the north, south, and east. *We will do this*, he thought. *We have to.*

"Coming in from the west!" a cry came from the Elves. Peter looked to the west and saw hundreds of Baroks flying toward them on Bedlam's mutant dragons. These beasts were thicker and stockier than the other dragons with grotesquely shaped heads. One by one they spewed their fire into the dark sky.

"Here they come!" Crispin shouted. He removed his sword from its sheath. "I hope we're ready for this!"

"Of course we are!" Annika removed her sword.

"Steady and make sure you protect your dragon!" Peter shouted. His friends knew that meant maneuvering through the air away from the poisoned arrows that would whiz by them. He heeled his dragon's side, nudged it forward, and together they soared into the fight.

As Peter approached the flying creatures, he gripped his sword with one hand and the reins with the other. His shield was tied to the saddle just in case he needed it later. There, before him, flew a Barok, snarling and drooling. *I loathe these creatures,* Peter thought.

He sliced at the creature as it flew by, severing its arm. The creature screamed and tumbled off the dragon, but the dragon spun around and spewed its flames at Peter who ducked out of the way. He yanked the reins and turned his dragon into a downward spiral with the mutant dragon only a few feet behind. So, Peter sent his dragon into a spin only a few feet off the ground. He felt the sting of the grass as it hit his face. The mutant dragon roared and spewed more of its fire, just missing Peter and his dragon. Peter pulled up on the reins and his dragon bolted into the sky heading straight up with such speed that Peter couldn't breathe for a moment. When they soared high enough, he stopped the dragon and together they hovered in the air for a second. The mutant dragon had followed them and as it approached Peter took his sword, swung it, and hit its snout. Blood sprayed the air like a mist. Peter nudged his dragon to fly away. It obeyed and soon the mutant dragon was flying after them again, roaring and spewing fire just missing his dragon. Peter tugged the reins and his dragon soared left then right over and over again causing the mutant dragon to miss every time. But Peter knew his dragon was growing tired so he sent it into a dive to rest its wings. The mutant dragon dove behind them with jaws open trying to bite at Tav's spiked tail. Peter turned and swiped at the mutant dragon but missed. When he turned back, he saw the earth coming toward them, so he pulled up on the reins just in time. He felt his stomach rise within him and he felt nauseous, but the dive worked. The mutant dragon did not pull up in time and it crashed into the ground to its death.

Peter stroked his dragon's warm neck, damp with sweat, and let it glide for a second or two. Peter turned and saw Annika swerving her dragon away from a mutant dragon's fire. Peter turned Tavrith toward the fight and came up behind the Barok riding the mutant dragon. Peter stabbed the dragon in its hind leg causing it to roar. It turned toward Peter and snapped at his dragon. Annika got away and turned her dragon around. She came up along the other side and used her sword to slice at the Barok. It fought back, cutting a slash in her dragon's hind leg.

"No!" Annika screamed. She pulled her dragon back and swung at the Barok's dragon, hitting its tail. The Barok turn in the saddle and tried to stab at Annika, but it lost its balance and fell off the dragon. Peter's dragon spewed fire and blinded the mutant dragon. It fell to its death in the fields below.

"Thank you, Peter!" Annika shouted.

"Well done!" he said to her. "Keep going!"

He heard an arrow whiz by his head and he ducked. He waved at Annika to fly away and she did. Peter turned to see another Barok shooting arrows at him from atop a mutant dragon. Peter turned his dragon around and flew off toward the Elves lined on the field below. He could see them kneel and arm their bows with arrows. As he swooped by, the Barok followed on his dragon, but several of the Elfin arrows struck him and his dragon. They hit the ground and rolled several feet. Soon, several Elves were upon it to make sure it died there in the field.

"Yes!" Peter cheered. He landed his dragon in the field near the Elves. He dismounted Tav and stroked its neck hot with sweat. "You're a beauty," he said to it while rubbing its snout as it panted and chewed on the bridle in its mouth.

Peter removed his shield from the saddle and his sword from its sheath. He marched off with the Elves to where many Baroks were approaching.

"Peter," Thætil shouted. "Look over there!"

Thætil pointed behind them where Marek was walking alongside a large dragon. Strapped to the back of the beast was a wooden box. Peter knew that inside that box must be the swords. All of them, except his father's sword. He looked all around for his father, but couldn't see him.

He ran to Marek.

"These are the swords?" Peter asked. "Is this the dragon the Prince will ride?" He reached out and touched the mammoth dragon's side. It turned its head to see what was touching it. It squawked at Peter. He took hold of the bridle in its mouth walked alongside it with Marek.

Marek narrowed his eyes as though he didn't recognize the Prince. "Yes, now go on! Don't bother us with questions!" he shouted and waved Peter aside.

"But I am the Prince. *I am* the Prince." Peter pointed to his chest. "Where is my father, King Alexander?"

Marek's eyes widened and he bowed nervously, "You Highness, I had no idea," he said.

"It's alright, where is my father?" Peter looked all around.

"He fights over there!" Marek pointed to the north. Peter turned and saw his father mounted on his white horse. His father's silver armor sparkled and his scarlet cape flowed behind him.

Peter took off running toward his father with shield and sword in hand. He leapt through the thick grass never taking his eyes off his father. That's when Peter heard it: The familiar high pitched scream he hoped never to hear again.

"Oh no," he grimaced. He stopped running and turned around to search the sky. There, hurtling toward him was a flock of Gizor with their fangs glaring and claws out ready to attack.

# 36 THE SPELL AND THE SWORDS

King Alexander swung around in time to thrust his sword into the chest of an advancing Barok. He pulled the sword out and watched the life drain from the creature's eyes. His sword was covered with the thick black blood of Bedlam's mutants. A rain drop hit the blade, then another, and another. Alexander heard more thunder echo from the west. He pulled tightly on his horse's reins. He knew the animal was nervous. Thick dark clouds hovered over the Dragon Forest, but he felt no fear. He sensed what was coming.

"Fight on, men!" He ordered. He turned to his left and saw several Elves fighting off the Baroks. "Ish Elöin ères ülrienden!" he shouted to them. The Elves looked at one another and then at the King. They raised their swords high and cheered when they heard their language. Alexander smiled because he knew they had understood him when he urged them to fight bravely.

Several arrows flew by Alexander's body and he ducked out of the way.

"Archers!" he warned his men. Alexander held his shield higher to protect his body, and then he dismounted his horse. He advanced to where three Baroks were fighting with his knights. A sudden high pitched scream made them all search the sky for its source.

A knight thrust his sword into the chest of a Barok, retrieved it, and then turned to his King. "What is that hideous sound?" he asked.

"A flock of Gizor!" Alexander answered. "Continue fighting, but they will attack from the skies. Be ready!"

Alexander kicked a Barok as it ran toward him. It collided with Alexander and sent him to the ground. The creature roared as it stood over Alexander. It raised the spear in its hands high, but Alexander rolled out of the way before the spear pierced him. He rose to his feet and thrust his sword at the Barok, but it used its spear to block the sword. The two fought back and forth until Alexander spotted one of his knights running up behind the Barok. It snarled, revealing its grotesque teeth between thin lips. Alexander used both arms to shove the beast back where it met with Sir Rønnik's sword in its back. When the creature fell to the ground, Alexander inserted his sword into its belly.

Before they could celebrate the kill, a group of Zadok hurtled toward Alexander and Sir Rønnik. They leapt out of the way. Alexander rolled over onto his back as one of the beasts jumped on top of him. He used the hilt of his sword to keep its jaws from chomping down on his neck. Its putrid breath made Alexander sick. He tried to get his legs underneath the belly of the beast to push it off, but he couldn't. It growled and snarled spewing drool all over the King's face. He took a deep breath and pushed the monster back with all his strength and when it tried to leap on him again, Alexander successfully stabbed the creature in the neck. It whimpered and clawed at the sword in its neck. Alexander quickly rose to his feet, retrieved his sword, and helped Sir Rønnik fight off the other creatures. Together, they sliced at each one, sending them to the ground with deep wounds to their legs and chests.

Finally, when all the creatures were defeated, Alexander lay on the ground trying to catch his breath with the bleeding mutant creatures dying nearby.

"Are you alright?" he asked Sir Rønnik as he sat up.

"Yes, sire," Sir Rønnik said as he hunched over. Alexander could see blood drip from the young man's mouth.

"No, you are not. You are wounded." Alexander stood and assisted the knight to where the Elves were assisting the wounded. They took him from the King and helped him sit.

Satisfied that the knight would receive the help he needed, Alexander turned to inspect the battle before him. He could see many Elves fighting Baroks alongside his knights and soldiers. Alexander looked down at his sword, wiped the blood off the blade, and then headed off to fight.

§

Peter turned around in time to see the flock of Gizor diving toward him. He raised his sword and sliced at their legs when they flew past. He successfully injured two of them and when they landed on the ground with a thud, he ran over to finish the job. But the other Gizor swooped down to attack him. One clawed his arm with its talons. Peter screamed from the pain.

"Peter!" It was Simon who came running with his sword. "I'll help you!"

Peter smiled at him. "Good!" he shouted. "I need all the help I can get!" When he pulled his hand away from the wound, he saw much blood. Simon took a stance with Peter and prepared to fight off the creatures as they swooped down. Sure enough, two more came in fast from above. They hovered above the boys using their claws to scratch and their teeth to try and clasp onto arms or legs. Peter's blood splattered all over his tunic.

Peter took his knife from his belt and stabbed one creature's arm. It winced from the pain, so Peter sliced at its wings. The creature fell to the ground and Simon fatally stabbed it with his sword.

"Thank you, my friend," Peter panted and winced from the pain. He covered his wound.

Simon grinned.

"There's another one!" Peter pointed to the flying creature, but it came too fast and kicked Simon to the ground. It scratched him before Peter could get to it. A Gizor grabbed Peter's arms and pulled him back. It flapped its wings and began to lift Peter off the ground.

"No!" Peter tried to wriggle free, knowing that if it flew off, it would drop him to his death. Just then, Peter felt heat from behind. The Gizor screamed and released Peter. He tumbled to the ground and rolled over to see his dragon, Tavrith, standing over the Gizor. It breathed its fire onto the creature and killed it. Smoke rose from the burning carcass.

"Thank you!" Peter laughed. The dragon roared and shook the rain off its long neck.

Peter turned to help Simon fight off the remaining Gizor. When finished, the two stood panting, waiting for more to attack. "I think that's it for now," Simon huffed. He looked up to let the rain wash his face and wiped it with his sleeve. The cold wind sent a chill through him.

"Fighting in storms," Peter said. "That's all we need."

"Peter! Look out!"

Peter turned and saw Thurdin flying toward him on a dragon. His sword was drawn and he was ready to attack Peter. Simon shoved Peter out of the way in time, but was cut deeply by Thurdin's sword.

"What's this?" Peter shouted at Thurdin. "What are you doing?"

"He has fallen to Bedlam's spell!" An Elf ran over to help Simon stand. The blood flowed from his wound. "Simon is cut deeply. I will take him to where the other wounded are. We will use the powder to heal him. Go, Peter! You must run to your father now! It is time to take the swords into the forest."

"But Peter is hurt as well," Simon shouted to the Elf. "Help him first."

The Elf stood helpless, unsure how to act.

Peter ripped off a part of his tunic and wrapped it around his wound, tying it using his teeth and other hand. "That will do for now. Go on, now!"

Simon, gripping his bleeding arm, nodded to the Elf.

"Peter, you must go." Simon winced from the pain. "No matter what, you must keep going!"

Peter looked at the Elfin soldier. "What happened to Thurdin?"

"We discovered that he was tempted by Lord Bedlam. He has fallen under the spell," The Elf said, "We do not know when this happened, but he told Thætil he now fights for Lord Bedlam and ran off to attack our Elves and soldiers."

Peter shook his head in sorrow as the rain pelted his body. "Go, take Simon and give him the powder." Peter helped the Elf walk off with Simon. Then, he turned to see Thurdin hovering over him still mounted on a dragon. Peter waved Tavrith over and mounted it. He yanked the reins and took off to meet Thurdin in the air.

§

"Where is the Prince?" King Isleif shouted from the air.

"Near the Cardion Valley!" the Elfin soldier shouted back as he glided on his dragon.

Isleif turned his dragon around and inspected the thousands of Baroks on the ground fighting the men and Elves. He looked at Hildron with its fire rising into the air. He shook his head. "This is no good," he said. "Bedlam will come soon. He will send more of his magic to fight us!"

"Yes, sire!" the Elf shouted.

"Go, tell General Aluein that it is time to have Peter enter the forest before Bedlam comes!" he watched the Elf fly off and land on the ground where Aluein fought alongside his men. Isleif flew over to where he saw the General and the Ogres fighting the enemy in the fields. He ordered his dragon to spew fire over the Baroks. It obeyed and the fire spread over many of the Baroks. General Aluein and his men stood by and watched. The Ogres raised their axes and clubs into the air. King Isleif turned his dragon around for another pass. When it appeared that most of the creatures were burned or dead, he hovered over the General.

"Not bad, eh?" he chuckled as his dragon flapped its mighty wings.

"Aleuin raised the visor on his helmet and waved to Isleif. "Not bad at all!" he shouted. "But I still won't ride one of those things!"

Isleif smirked then shook his head in disbelief. He flew over to where he saw Peter. His eyes widened when he noticed Prince Thurdin fighting Peter in the air. "What's this?" he said to himself.

"Why are you doing this?" Peter shouted to Thurdin.

Thurdin threw his head back and laughed. "You and your kingdom are finished, Peter!" he twisted his sword in his hand, slicing the blade through the air. "Lord Bedlam has seen to it. He has promised that I will rule the land and you will die! Come now, let's finish this once and for all."

Peter furrowed his brow. He thought of Damion. "I do not wish to fight you, Thurdin. I have more important tasks at hand." Peter yanked on the reins and flew off on his dragon to meet his father, but Thurdin flew close by. His dragon shot out bolts of fire and hit Peter's dragon, sending it spiraling down to the ground.

"Oh no!" Peter shouted as he tried to pull up, but it was no use. Tavrith landed hard, throwing Peter off. He rolled in the grass and blacked out for a moment.

"Peter!" he heard a voice and felt someone turn him over. The rain pelted his face and he tasted the grass in his mouth. He spit it out.

"Are you alright?" Annika shouted.

Peter nodded. He opened his eyes and saw Annika's face flushed red. A rush of peace came through him. "Yes," he muttered. "I think so. It's good to see you." He touched her cheek then sat up.

She smiled. "Your dragon is alright. A bit shaken up, but it will make it. Hurry! You have to get to your father." She helped him stand. Peter adjusted his armor and moaned from the ache in his back. He looked up and saw Thurdin running toward him. Peter reached for his sword, but it was not in its sheath. He took Annika's sword, pushed her out of the way, and met Thurdin's sword in the air. The metal blades collided. Annika gasped when she saw the struggle and rolled out of the way.

Peter grimaced from Thurdin's strength, but he remembered what Sir Nøel had taught him. He fell to the ground and rolled Thurdin up and over his body. He landed hard, so Peter regained his footing and pointed his sword at Thurdin's throat before the Prince could find his own sword.

"Enough!" Peter said. "I don't have time for this." Peter handed the sword back to Annika, found his own sword lying nearby in the grass, and then he ran off to mount the dragon. Thurdin turned to Annika who had her sword pointed at his chest. "Run off, now Thurdin," she narrowed her eyes. "Before I kill you."

His eyes widened as he saw the seriousness in her face. He quickly got up and ran off.

Simon came running to her side. "Are you alright?" he watched Thurdin run off to his dragon and fly away. "Was that Prince Thurdin? What happened to Peter?"

"He flew off to meet his father." Annika placed her sword in its sheath. She ran over to her dragon and mounted it. The beast pulled at the reins. "We must get over to the Cardion Valley. It is time for Peter to take the swords to the Dragon Forest!"

A look of shock came to Simon's face. He turned and ran off to find his dragon. Together with Annika, they met King Isleif and Thætil in the air.

"Your nephew has had a change of mind!" Simon shouted to Thætil.

"Yes, I know," Thætil said. "He has tragically fallen for Lord Bedlam's temptations. I will see to it that he does not interfere with this mission any longer. Go help Peter!"

Annika and Simon soared through the air on their dragons. Crispin met them and they landed in the Cardion Valley where most of the fighting had stopped. Dead Baroks, Zadoks, Gizor, together with dead soldiers and Elves littered the wet ground. Puddles of water mixed with blood formed everywhere. The sky darkened but was lit occasionally with bolts lightning that struck near to the ground. The wind blew the rain sideways and it stung when it hit exposed flesh. The scent of death permeated the air.

"What do we do now?" Crispin asked.

Annika pointed. "There!" All turned to see King Alexander coming toward them. Behind them was the dragon carrying its precious cargo. The three ran over to meet the King. They bowed when they faced him.

"Where is Peter?" Alexander asked.

"Father!" he heard Peter's voice through the wind. Alexander ran to meet his son in the field. They embraced. "I made it, father! I made it!"

"Peter!" Alexander studied his son's face. "We've not much time. You must begin the ride to the Dragon Forest. I fear Lord Bedlam is coming to stop us all!"

He pointed to the dragon with the box of swords on its back. Peter swallowed hard. He knew the time had come.

"Take this dragon, fly to the forest, and enter," Alexander led Peter to the waiting beast. Much larger than his own dragon, Tavrith, it panted and snorted as though impatient, but it crouched down low to allow Peter to mount. Alexander helped Peter place his foot into the stirrup then climb into the saddle. Once atop the saddle, Alexander's eyes welled with tears as he looked at his son. "You look so small atop this large beast," he said.

"Father, please," Peter said sternly as he took the reins. "I am no longer a child. I am ready for this."

Alexander blinked back the tears, cleared his throat, and adjusted the stirrups. "Yes, I know you are. You will be fine. All of us, the Elves, knights, and soldiers, will ensure you make it to the entrance." Alexander pointed to everyone awaiting the order to move.

Peter spied the Dragon Forest in the distance. He nodded and reached into his pocket to remove the golden compass. He opened the lid and saw the words *The Dragon Forest* appeared on the rim. The arrow pointed and showed him the way. Peter closed the lid and felt his mother was with him.

"Once you enter, do you know what to do?" his father asked.

"Yes, I take the swords to the lake in the clearing," Peter said. "There I will receive further instructions."

Alexander nodded. "Good," He stepped back. "You have your shield, you have the swords. Here, take mine. It is the last one."

King Alexander handed the ivory handled sword of his fathers to his son. Peter reached down and took it by the hilt. He held onto it tightly.

"You have all that you need, now. Go on then, ride!"

Peter tugged the reins and gave his father one last look. "Don't worry, father," he said assuringly. "I will make it. The spell will be broken."

Alexander grinned. "I know you will, son. Now ride!" He swatted the hind leg of the dragon and it flapped its long wings sending wind, pebbles, and rain flying all around. Alexander raised his arm to protect his face, and then he saw his son fly off toward the forest.

"Mount up!" General Aluein shouted. "Time to move!"

As Peter flew on the back of the dragon, Jason, Thætil, Annika, Simon, and Crispin flew alongside him. Below, all the men marched with weapons drawn, ready for Bedlam's next wave of attack.

# 37 THE DUKE OF ILLIATH

"He is here, he is here!" Marek approached King Alexander who motioned for his squire to bring him a new sword and his helmet. He placed the sword into the sheath on his belt and the helmet onto his head.

"Who is here? Lord Bedlam?" he asked Marek as they walked to the top of the hill.

"No, my Lord," Marek said as he pointed to the West. "It is Sir William, the Duke of Illiath. He has returned with reinforcements."

In the distance, Sir William rode in on a black stallion. Behind him stomped large mutant Ogre-like beasts. Some held banners displaying Lord Bedlam's emblem. Others held long spears. They grunted and roared as they marched.

"Send for our reinforcements!" Alexander ordered his Captain who signaled the archers to send their flaming arrows high into the sky.

§

Queen Esmeralda, mounted on her dragon, hovered over the East shore surrounded by her soldiers mounted their dragons.

"Keep an eye out for ships!" she shouted to them. All eyes were on the thick layer of fog that had formed over the sea. She knew it was only a spell by Lord Bedlam, yet she also knew the rulers from other lands who joined Bedlam's fight were sending men to the shore to battle for her kingdom. The fog would hide their approach. She yanked the reins, turned her dragon around, and glided over to her captain.

"Send in the first round," she ordered. He bowed his head and raised his hand. When he lowered his arm, thirty of his men flew into the fog on the backs of dragons and disappeared from view. The Queen soared over the shore and waited. Her men flew back and forth along the shoreline. She sensed they were nervous.

A strange ominous roar was heard coming from the fog. More roars of dragons followed. Bursts of flames could barely be seen through the fog, and that's when Queen Esmeralda knew her men were battling the enemy.

"Now!" She raised her arm. "Let's go!" Together with the remaining men, she entered the thick curtain of fog, unaware of what they would find. The air was dense with moisture and difficult to navigate, but she heeled her dragon to make it fly faster. In her hand, she held her sword ready to strike.

A man's scream came from her right. She turned and saw nothing but fog. Another scream came from her left, but still she saw nothing.

"Keep going!" she shouted. She felt a tug on her leg and looked down to see a tentacle had caught her foot. Her dragon stopped in midflight and reared up from shock. It roared and frantically flapped its leathery wings. Esmeralda struggled to hold onto the reins as another tentacle grabbed her and began to pull her off the dragon. She swiped at the creature with her sword and severed its tentacles. She heard the roar of the beast as it lowered its bloodied tentacles.

She decided to fly low near the ocean surface and risk being attacked in order to see what enemy she and her men faced. When she yanked the reins, she was met with resistance. Her dragon sensed something and did not want to fly out of the fog.

"Move!" she ordered it. She heard more screams of her men in the distance. Her dragon reluctantly obeyed and together they flew out of the fog and near the ocean surface. Once in the brief clearing, she saw several ships headed toward the shore. Some of her soldiers were flying over the ships while their dragons spewed fire onto the sails.

"Let's go! Now's our chance!" She leaned in close to her dragon's neck as it flew even faster to join in the fight, but another tentacle grabbed her leg and this time pulled her off her dragon. She plunged into the water and blacked out for a second. Her dragon sped away.

§

Once the flaming arrows flew through the air, more dragons flew in from the east with King Isleif's men atop. The ground trembled as fighters from the southeast came crashing through the treetops with Ogres leading the way. They pushed down the trees making way for the soldiers from King Beatann's land. Grauble, the leader of the Ogres, wore leather armor and carried a large battle axe like a child holds a twig. Alexander stood in awe at the sight of so many fighters coming to assist.

"My heart is full, Aluein," Alexander said as his friend came to his side. "This is quite the sight."

"Aye, it is." Aluein took out his pipe and lit it, but the rain made it difficult. "But do not celebrate victory just yet. Sir William is headed this way."

"Yes," Alexander sighed. "I suppose we must face him."

Aluein placed his hand on the King's shoulder. "Don't worry about Peter. We will make sure he makes it into the forest."

"Thank you, my old friend." Alexander removed the sword from its sheath, lowered the visor on his helmet, and began the long walk to where he would meet Sir William. "To battle, once again."

"One last time," Aleuin replied.

§

Peter felt secure atop the mammoth dragon. He could feel its sinewy muscles contract underneath its scaly skin each time it flapped its wings. Below, Peter could see the battle formations and hear the combat between men and Sir William's Baroks. Before him was the Dragon Forest. *We can do this,* he said to himself. *All of us together, we will do this. And when it's all over, we will celebrate there at the entrance of the forest.*

Behind him came a squawk like that of a dragon. Peter turned to see his own dragon, Tavrith, flying along like some sort of escort. He smiled at his friend. A sudden jerk came from the dragon he rode on, so Peter turned to see its hind leg had been hit by fire. He turned in his saddle and saw Thurdin coming at him on his dragon from behind. In his hands was a loaded bow.

"Oh no!" Peter shouted. He feared for his dragon. "Tavrith! Go on! Get out of here!"

The dragon obeyed and flew off.

"I've got this!" Simon shouted and steered his dragon toward Thurdin. Peter pulled the reins and swerved his dragon out of the way toward the south and away from the forest. The beast roared from the pain and began to descend.

"No," Peter said. "We've got to keep going!" He tried to force the dragon to fly off, but the dragon landed in a patch of tall grass near the ruins of the palace at Illiath. Peter dismounted and ran over to the hind leg of the dragon to inspect it. When he saw that it was badly burned, he looked around for assistance knowing how vulnerable he was to be alone with the swords.

Annika, Crispin, Eris, and Thætil landed nearby, dismounted, and quickly ran over to Peter.

"Peter!" Thætil shouted. "This is no good. We've got to get you out of here. You are not safe here with the swords. It is too risky to—"

An arrow shot through the air and hit Thætil in the upper arm.

"No!" Peter shouted and ran to his friend. He turned to see where the arrow came from. Several more shot out from the air and hit the grass. "Take cover!"

Thætil pushed Peter aside and raised his sword. "Peter, your shield," he said. "Get it and hide behind me!"

Peter obeyed and unhinged his shield from the dragon. It roared as three arrows hit its chest. Peter ran off and stood behind Thætil. Annika, Eris and Crispin shot arrows into the air hoping to hit the enemy still unseen.

"To the ruins!" Thætil ordered. "Cover us!"

Annika and Eris shot more arrows and heard a few grunts from the bushes. "Over there!" Eris shouted. "Baroks! We struck them!"

Peter helped the injured Thætil over to the ruins where the Elfin commander loaded his bow with two arrows and waited. "Stay here," Thætil ordered Peter. "Elöishni, ildriénden oi! Oi!" He shouted to their dragons and they took flight away from the danger. Then, Thætil made his way to a tall stack of larger stones. Eris, Crispin, and Annika made it to the ruins.

Peter watched as the Baroks raced out of the bushes over to the now dead dragon. They began to unhinge the box that contained the swords.

"They're taking the swords!" He shouted to the others. "We've got to do something!"

"We will!" Thætil shot his arrows into the Baroks. They struck the necks of the creatures. Peter watched as they fell over dead. But three more Baroks ran out of the bushes to retrieve the swords.

"Cover me!" Peter shouted to Eris. She loaded her bow.

Peter raced across the grass with his sword held high. He swiped at the Baroks. One kicked Peter back and he landed with a hard thud. The Barok stomped on Peter's hand causing him to release his sword. The Barok kicked it away and pointed his sword at Peter's face. Peter watched as three arrows hit the creature's chest, but it only grimaced and pulled out the arrows. It roared with pride and lunged its sword at

Peter. His eyes grew wide.

Behind the creature, Peter helplessly watched as the box of swords was hauled away by the Baroks.

"It is over, your highness," came a voice from behind the dead dragon.

The Barok grabbed Peter by his tunic and yanked him to his feet. Peter struggled with the creature, but it overpowered him. The creature forced Peter to stand. He saw that Annika, Eris, and Thætil had been captured. The Baroks held them with swords pointed at their throats. Peter swallowed hard.

He looked up and saw Sir William, the Duke of Illiath, mounted on his horse staring down at Peter. "It is all over," Will said. He raised the visor of his helmet.

Peter struggled with the Barok. "Let me go, Will!" he shouted. The Barok threw him to the ground. Peter tried to regain his footing, but the creature kicked him down.

"Take the swords back to Hildron," Sir William ordered. He shook his head at Peter. "I expected more from you, Sir Peter."

Peter looked up at Will. "You can't do this!" he shouted.

"Peter!" Annika shouted, but Peter ignored her.

"I can and will do this, *Sir* Peter," Will said. He dismounted and walked over to the Prince still on his knees with the Barok standing over him. The rain pelted them both. "Sir Peter. Well, well. You are a knight now."

He walked over and picked up Peter's sword. He held it up and turned it over, inspecting the blade. "I was saddened to have missed your dubbing ceremony."

"Peter!" Annika shouted again. Peter turned to her.

"Ah, the Sword of Alexander," Will said. He walked up behind him. "I will make sure it is destroyed at Hildron along with all the other swords. Very nice."

"Peter, look!" Annika shouted again. She pointed up. Peter searched the sky as Will spoke and finally saw what Annika was pointing at. In the grey sky Peter saw the white owl circling above. He grinned and felt a surge of power come over him.

"Take hold of him," Sir William ordered. The Barok grabbed Peter's shoulders as Will came up behind him. "It is fitting that you should be killed by such a splendid sword…your *father's* sword."

Peter watched the white owl descend. As he watched, he remembered his time in the Dragon Forest when he held his wooden sword in his hands before the Dragon. He remembered how the extraordinary blue flame hit the sword and changed it into metal within seconds. *The extraordinary blue flame,* Peter sneered as though he knew what was coming.

Sir William raised Peter's sword high, but as he brought it down, Peter stood up and hit the Barok in the jaw with his head. The creature fell back. Peter turned and struck Will in the face with his hand then used his leg to push him back. Will stumbled and dropped the sword. Before the Barok could regain its footing, Peter grabbed the sword and sliced the creature's throat. Its blood mixed with the rain on the ground.

Sir William removed his sword from the sheath and swung it at Peter who blocked it with his own sword. Peter used his weight to shove Will back. The white owl screeched.

"Release us, Will, and I will spare your life!" Peter shouted.

"Kill them! Kill them all!" Will waved at the Baroks holding Thætil and the others, but Thætil used his elbow to strike the Barok in the face. It fell back, so he grabbed its sword and stabbed it in the chest. Eris and Annika fought with the Baroks holding them. Thætil struck the creatures and allowed enough time for Eris to shoot arrows into the skulls of the Baroks.

Annika ran over to Peter who held his sword at Sir William.

"I said, let us go, Will," Peter said.

"Never!" Will moved to strike at Peter, but met with his sword instead. Peter tried to shove Will back again, but he was too strong. Will swung around and sliced at Peter's leg. Peter leapt out of the way in time and lowered his sword on Will's arm cutting it deeply. Will screamed from the pain and thrust his sword at Peter's belly. Peter jumped back and swiped at Will's sword again. The sound of metal clashing echoed. Annika looked up at the white owl as it circled above.

Will removed his helmet and threw it to the ground. His eyes were wide and fierce with anger. Peter could see his old friend was indeed under a powerful spell. Will leapt at Peter again, but he moved away in time. He kicked Will in the back, but Will swung around and barely missed Peter's throat. Peter fell back to the ground. Will pointed his sword at Peter's throat.

"No!" Annika shouted. She held up her sword at the back of Will's neck.

"One move and I'll end your life," she hissed.

"One move and the Prince dies," Will panted as he stood over Peter. His hair, soaked from the rain and from sweat, dripped down his face.

"You can't win, Will," Peter said, trying to catch his breath. "The spell will be broken."

"We'll see," Will laughed and thrust the sword into Peter, but before it entered his flesh, a stream of blue fire hit the blade and threw

Will down to the ground. Annika leapt out of the way.

Will covered his face from the intensity of the blue flame. Peter stared at the flame as it came from behind Will. The white owl had transformed into the Dragon of the Forest and landed a few feet away. The earth shook when it landed and sent the Baroks flying back onto the ground. It stomped on them with its massive clawed feet, making them forever one with the muddied ground. Eris, Annika, and Thætil ran over to the Dragon and stood by its broad legs.

Will rolled over still covering his face from the blue flame. "My eyes!" he screamed.

The Barok guarding Peter lay dead. Peter could see that it was consumed by the icy cold flame. Its body froze solid. Peter reached out and took back his sword from Will. He held it up and the Dragon stopped spewing the flame.

"I remembered!" Peter said to the Dragon, holding his sword high. It nodded at Peter, lowered its head, and sniffed the sword.

"So did I," the Dragon answered.

Peter grabbed Will's shoulder and turned him over. He helped remove Will's hands from his face. They were stiff from the cold and his face was pale with shock.

"Will," Peter said as he shook him. "Are you alright?"

Will's eyes were no longer glazed over as though under a spell. He looked at Peter and then at the Dragon. He screamed and scooted away from the Dragon.

"No!" he shouted and placed his arms over his face. "No! Don't let it kill me! Don't let it kill me!"

Peter took his friend by the shoulders and shook him. "Will, it's alright," he said. "Don't be afraid! There's no need to be afraid. The Dragon is not going to kill you."

Will looked at Peter. His face softened as calmness ran through his body. He seemed to be recognizing his friend's face and remembering their time together.

"Peter?" he said as he squinted his eyes. "Peter, is that you? Is it really you?"

Peter smiled and looked over at his friends. "He's alright," he told them.

Will stared hard at Peter's face, studying it carefully.

"Yes, Will," he said. "It is me, Peter, your friend. Welcome back."

Will looked around at the dead Baroks and at Peter's friends who stood by cautiously with swords drawn.

"What happened? Where am I?" Peter helped his friend stand. They could hear the deep breathing of the Dragon. Will stumbled out of the way of the mammoth claws.

The Dragon lowered its head by Peter. "It won't hurt you, Will," Peter stroked its snout. "So long as you are on our side."

Sir William gazed over at the ruins of Alexander's palace with the many piles of limestone and the remains of the tall spires that once reached into the sky, but were now destroyed. The outer curtain walls were flattened and the gate was nothing but scattered wood. He looked over at the Black Hills with the flames of Hildron still rising into the dark sky. He felt the cold rain on his face and closed his eyes. Peter knew Will was hoping the rain would wash everything out of his memory.

"You were under Lord Bedlam's wicked spell, Will," Peter walked up to his friend. "We all knew it, but there was nothing we could do. Thanks be to the Dragon, it is all over now. You are free again, Will. Free from Lord Bedlam's spell."

Will hunched over exhausted and heavy with weariness. "Oh, Peter," he said as he ran his hands through his hair. "Did I cause all this?"

Peter looked over at Eris who was helping to wrap Thætil's wounded shoulder. Thætil raised his hand to his mouth.

"Draconian!" he shouted to the sky. "Nieründriendén! Ish undriendén!"

Several dragons, including Tavrith, flew in from the south and landed in the grassy area.

"Yes, Will," Peter said. He placed his hand on Will's shoulder and surveyed the ruins of the palace. "Through Lord Bedlam, many people have lost everything. We will rebuild. There is much to rebuild."

Will looked at Peter with eyes wet from tears and rain. "Please forgive me, Peter," he said.

The Dragon spread its wings signaling that it was time to return to the mission while Annika stroked its leg. It seemed to assuage her fears.

"I forgive you, Will," Peter said as he watched all the dragons land. "But I do need something from you.

"Anything." Will straightened up. "Anything at all. What can I do?"

"I need your help. *We* need your help." He motioned at the Dragon and his friends.

Will nodded as Peter walked over to the box of swords. "I need to get the swords of the rulers to the Dragon Forest, Will. Once there, the spell of Lord Bedlam will be destroyed forever."

Will furrowed his brow as a look of determination came to his face.

"I need your help because—"

"Say no more." Will walked over to the box of swords. He studied its size and then compared the dragons. "Can your dragon carry this heavy load?"

Peter inspected Tavrith. It shook its head and sent rain splattering all around. Peter walked over to it and thought for a moment as he looked at the creature's legs.

"What do you think?" he asked the dragon. It blinked in the rain.

Will approached. "It will have to carry the box in its talons as it flies," he suggested. "Do you think this smaller dragon can—"

"Yes," Peter said as he took Tav's head in his hands and gently scratched its chin. "We will do this together, right?" The dragon's amber eyes shone.

Will patted Peter on the shoulder. "You are still as determined as ever, Peter. I have missed you," he said. Peter turned to Will and the two embraced.

"I have missed you, my friend. I only wish…" Will said. "I wish none of this—"

When they parted Peter knew what Will was going to say.

"I know," Peter said. "But all this has happened for a purpose."

Will looked toward the Dragon Forest. "Alright then," he said and he ran to his horse and mounted it. Eris brought him his sword. He took it and raised it high.

"But you're wounded!" Peter pointed to the slice in Will's arm. "You need a bandage or something."

"There is no time! We must go now. No one knows the plans of Lord Bedlam better than I do. Come, there is no time to spare. We must get you and the swords to the Dragon Forest!"

"Yes!" Annika ran to the grassy field and mounted her dragon. "This is so exciting!"

"Let's go!" Thætil shouted. "Everyone! To the Dragon Forest!"

# 38 TO THE FINAL BATTLE

Sir Rohan ran to King Alexander as he approached the top of the hill. "The Prince!" he shouted. "His dragon was struck down by Baroks!"

Alexander turned to his Head Knight. "What? When?"

"Soon after he left, my scouts saw him land near the ruins of the palace," Sir Rohan said.

Alexander winced and removed his sword. "And Sir William?" he asked. "Where is the Duke of Illiath?"

Rohan shook his head. "We are not certain," he said.

Alexander smirked and looked toward Illiath. "Well, I am certain," he said.

"He approaches!" came a shout from a soldier running frantically toward the King. "Sir William approaches!"

Alexander turned to Sir Rohan and Marek. "Ready your men," he ordered. They bowed and headed toward the waiting soldiers.

Will galloped on his horse to where Alexander stood ready to fight with his soldiers near. He leapt off the horse and ran to King Alexander who raised his sword in defense. All the King's men drew their swords and pointed them at Will.

"Your majesty." Will fell to his knees before his King. "I beg your forgiveness."

Alexander cocked his head and stood perplexed before the kneeling knight. "What..." Alexander gripped his sword. "what did you say?"

Without looking up as the rain pelted them both, Will spoke again. "Your majesty, I beg your forgiveness."

Alexander ordered his men to stand down. They obeyed.

"Look at me, Sir William," Alexander said.

Will hesitantly raised his chin. He knew Alexander had every right to kill him there on that hill in the pouring rain. He swallowed and gazed into the eyes of his King.

"Please," he said as he raised his hand toward Alexander. "Have mercy."

Alexander stepped back. "The spell," he said, "It has been severed?"

Will blinked in the rain. "Yes, my Lord," he said. "The Great Dragon of the Forest severed it and set me free."

"Yes." Alexander grasped his hands together and raised them high. "I knew it would happen."

Will, still on bended knee, shivered in the cold rain.

"Please, my Lord," he said as he removed his sword. "I am here to serve you, my King, once again. Let me help Peter enter the forest. Let me help you defeat Lord Bedlam this day."

"Rise, Sir William," Alexander said.

"I have much to repent for," Will said as he stood, "and I know Lord Bedlam's plans better than anyone. I know what his next move will be."

Alexander could sense Will's rage. He reached out and took Will's arm.

"I will fight for you and for Peter," Will said. "If need be, I will sacrifice my life."

Alexander nodded. "Let's hope it does not come to that, Will," he said. "I knew the good in you remained. Now, go!"

Will ran to his horse, mounted it, and rode off toward the entrance of the Dragon Forest.

Sir Rohan watched as Will rode off. He ran toward him.

"Are you one of us again, Will?" he shouted.

Will pulled back on the reins and his horse reared up. Will raised his sword high and made sure Sir Rohan saw him. "For Illiath!" he shouted and smiled.

Sir Rohan waved his sword back and laughed in the rain. "For Théadril!"

Will heeled his horse and rode off toward the Dragon Forest.

§

Esmeralda swam to the surface of the ocean and gasped for air. She treaded water and looked for any sign of her men flying on dragons nearby. Before she could summon help, the tentacle of the sea creature wrapped around her waist and dragged her under the water again. She tried to struggle free before it took her into the deep, but it was no use.

The grip of the creature was too tight. She could feel herself begin to black out.

A sudden rush of water and bubbles rose around her and she saw a sea dragon with jaws open wide swimming toward her. It sunk its teeth into the tentacle then dragged the Queen to the surface where a dragon awaited her. Although weak, she tried her best to climb onto the saddle of the dragon as it hovered over the water. The ocean waves made it difficult. Each waved splashed her face and the salty water stung her eyes. She gripped the saddle horn and pulled herself into the saddle. She sat, panting from exhaustion, on the dragon. Below the surface of the water, she could see the enormous sea dragon swimming in the clear ocean waters toward the ships.

"Beautiful," she whispered. The sea dragon's scales glistened in the water. Its turquoise and pearl colors were mesmerizing. It used its enormous fins and tail to glide through the water with ease followed by several more dragons of the deep. Ahead were the burning ships with dragons of all kinds attacking them. The Queen smiled and gratefully stroked her dragon's neck as it took flight and made its way to the shore.

"Your majesty!" She heard someone shout after her as soon as they landed on the sand and pebbles. She turned to see one of the Elfin warriors speeding toward her on a dragon.

"I am alright," she huffed. "We cannot allow those ships to disembark. We must keep them from—"

"All is well, your majesty." He raised his hand. "The ships have been destroyed. The soldiers are ready along the shore to march toward the Dragon Forest. We have been told General Aluein needs reinforcements."

She nodded. "Yes," she said. "To the forest. Send all the men and Elves!"

The Queen leapt out of the saddle and knelt on the sand. She turned to see that the fog over the ocean had lifted and all the burning ships were sinking into the sea. The fire glow reflected in the water. She sat for a moment and rested.

"It is almost over," she sighed. "Almost over…"

§

Simon turned his dragon around and prepared to swipe at Thurdin again. Thurdin ordered his dragon to dive at Simon. He hovered in the air and gripped the reins and waited for Thurdin. He raised his sword, and turned his dragon away as soon as Thurdin's dragon spewed fire.

"Whoa!" Simon shouted as his dragon dove toward the field. A few arrows flew passed them, so Simon nudged his dragon and the two soared higher in the sky. Simon leaned right and the two of them spun around causing all the arrows to miss them. Once they straightened out, Simon grabbed his belly as dizziness overwhelmed him.

"Let's not do that again." He covered his mouth. Thurdin and his dragon caught up to Simon so he ordered his dragon to dive. Finally, a few Elves approached from behind Thurdin sending dragon fire at him. Hit by the flames, his dragon spun out of control and landed with a hard thud below. Simon pulled up and could see Thurdin roll along the ground.

Peter flew across the gloomy sky on the back of his dragon with several Elves escorting him. Below he could see the enemy fighting off Aleuin's men as they tried to make way a path for Peter to take when he landed near the entrance to the Dragon Forest. Many bodies littered the landscape as they flew over. Peter's heart sank at the sight of the tremendous sacrifice of all sides. He tugged on the reins, nudged his dragon forward. It held onto the box and flapped its wings as best as it could.

"Hang on, Tav!" Peter shouted. "We're almost there."

Annika and Crispin along with Thætil flew at his side.

"To your left!" Thætil shouted. "Bedlam's men are marching!"

Peter and the others could see the rows and rows of torches lighting up the ground as the Baroks and men of Will's army marched on toward the Dragon Forest.

"We're almost there," Peter shouted. "Should we fight now or—"

"Peter, you get to the forest entrance!" Thætil ordered. "We will fight them off."

Peter nodded and heeled Tav's ribs and the dragon flew faster finally making its way to the entrance of the forest. Peter landed with his dragon, inspected the area for the enemy, and ordered it to put down the box of swords. Then, Peter prepared to dismount when he heard the shrill of several Gizor coming from above. Peter hopped off the dragon and ran to its side.

"Wait for it," he ordered the Tav. It turned its head toward the approaching Gizor and when they bore their claws to strike, Peter shouted, "Now!"

The dragon spewed out fire, hitting all the Gizor. Their wings were aflame and they spun to the ground. Peter ran over and stabbed them with his sword. Then, he ran to Tavrith and the box of swords. He began to open the box, when he heard another sound coming from the west. A dragon roared and dove in to attack. On its back sat Thurdin.

§

King Isleif flew in from the northeast atop his dragon, a Wyvern with long thin wings. He and his men had successfully stopped the enemy from reaching the shores near his kingdom. Now he was ready to help King Alexander's men fight off Lord Bedlam. He searched the ground below for signs of the enemy, but only saw the scattered corpses of the dead.

"We missed the battle!" he shouted to his head knight.

"Down there, sire," the knight pointed to the fighting below. King Isleif pulled back on the reins and nudged his dragon to descend toward the battle. His men and the Elves with him all followed along.

"This way!" Will shouted. General Aluein jerked his head when he heard the galloping horse coming toward him and his men. "Follow me!"

Aluein turned to his captain. "Was that Sir William?"

The captain shrugged. "I believe so," he said. "Perhaps he is on our side now?"

"It would appear so," General Aluein raised his sword and galloped after Will followed by hundreds of his men. They ran over the hill and immediately clashed with Lord Bedlam's Baroks and Will's former army.

Will leapt off his horse mid gallop, drew his sword, and challenged an approaching Barok. He screamed a primitive scream and lowered his sword deep into the shoulder of the creature nearly severing its arm. Another Barok came from behind and tried to stab at Will, but Will turned around in time, ducked, and thrust his sword into the lower belly of the Barok. It fell backwards. Will advanced toward two more Baroks racing toward him with spears raised. One released the spear and it whizzed by Will's head, the other released the spear and Will caught it, turned it around, and thrust it into the Barok, lifting it off the ground.

General Aluein watched the scene from atop his horse. When the General's men saw Will coming toward them, they didn't know how to react. Will, covered in Barok blood, carefully approached the townsmen turned soldiers.

"Brothers," Will exclaimed to the men staring at him with frightened eyes. "I fight for King Alexander now."

One man turned to the other in confusion. "How can we trust you Sir William after all that has happened?"

Will shook his head. "I don't know," he said, out of breath. "But follow me and you will see many of Lord Bedlam's evil creatures die at my sword!"

The men watched as Will ran off toward the creatures. True to his word, he continued fighting the Baroks left and right. The men of the Cornshire and Cardion Valley saw severed limbs and heads fly to the ground one after the other.

"He speaks the truth!" one man shouted. "Let's go!"

The men ran after their leader clashing with the Barok swords. Will led the way swiping his sword at anything that came at him.

General Aluein, his eyes wide open, turned to his captain as they watched Will race off. "I do believe he is the greatest knight I have ever seen," the General said.

§

Peter swung at Thurdin when he came for him. He could see the hatred in Thurdin's eyes. He thought of Damon yet again. Their swords clashed amid the flames and Peter swung around. He sliced at Thurdin's thigh sending his blood into the air. Thurdin screamed and staggered back.

"I will kill you," Peter told him. "Now back off!"

Behind him, Peter could see the Baroks charging toward him. He ran to his dragon again and the beast began to inhale. Thurdin's eyes grew large and he ran off down the path with the dragon's fire flowing behind him. He leapt out into some tall grass, safe from the flames. Then, Thurdin rolled over, stood, and found himself facing Sir William.

Peter could see that Will would handle Thurdin for him, so he turned to the box of swords but instead he found a two Gizor, with the box in their claws, hovering in the air.

"No!" Peter shouted as the creatures began to fly off. Peter climbed into the saddle of his dragon and ordered it to fly off after the Gizor. Soon the two were flying through the night air after the Gizor as it weaved back and forth. Arrows from below flew past Peter and he turned his dragon around to miss the poisoned arrows. He nudged it to spew flames onto Bedlam's archers below. They ran off into the desert to escape the flames.

The Gizor hurried as fast as they could toward Hildron. Peter knew the creatures would drop the swords into the fire pits destroying them once and for all. He kicked Tavrith to make it fly faster, but to his amazement, Simon and Annika raced toward the Gizor on their dragons. They easily caught up to the flying creatures. Annika leaned over and hit one with her sword. It stopped flying, turned in midair, and headed in the opposite direction. The other one continued to fly off with the box of swords. Annika and Simon had to do some quick maneuvering with their dragons in order to catch up to the one, but soon they flew alongside it again. The creature dove to the ground where the Baroks were arming their bows again. Annika's dragon spit fire all along the rows of Baroks while Simon and Peter chased after the other creature with the box still in its claws.

"I've had it with this thing!" Peter shouted. He took out his knife from his belt and put it between his teeth, nudged Tavrith to fly faster, and then reached over to the Gizor as it flew. He swiped at it with the knife, but missed each time. The wicked creature laughed at him as it flew. Simon growled and looked below. He could see they were over some soft grass, so he did the unthinkable: He leapt off his dragon, grabbed ahold of the Gizor, and together they landed on the grass, tumbling and rolling to a stop. The box of swords went flying from the creature's grip and landed nearby still holding its cargo safely inside.

Peter landed his dragon and ran over to Simon. "Are you alright?" he rolled his friend over. Simon's face was covered in mud and he spat out grass.

"Yes, I think so," he groaned, wiping his face with his sleeve. Peter heard the Gizor make some noise, so he ran over to it and slit its throat with his knife. He grabbed the box of swords, but it was too heavy to carry on his own.

"Simon, can you help me?" Peter asked. Simon slowly sat up and rolled over. He tried to stand.

"Not sure if I can," he said as he tried to stand, but he stumbled backwards.

Alone, Peter dragged the box of swords over to Tavrith. It flapped its wings and took the box into its claws. Once secure, he mounted the dragon.

"Thank you." He gently rubbed the snout of Tavrith. It blinked its eyes. Peter remained in awe of the gentleness and bravery of these creatures he once feared. "Let's go again!"

Peter nudged his dragon, turned its neck, and they both headed toward the Dragon Forest.

§

Will sprinted toward Thurdin whose eyes grew large when he saw the brave knight coming toward him. He raised his sword, but it was too late. Will's rage and power overwhelmed Thurdin and he fell to the ground. Will sat over him and pointed his sword at Thurdin's throat.

"Prince of Vulgaard, I give you a chance to surrender!" Sir William said. "You are under the spell of the Bedlam. Surrender now and I will let you live!"

"Never!" Thurdin spat at Will's face. Will turned and saw a torch burning on the ground nearby. He took it and waved it in front of Thurdin's face. The flames scorched Thurdin's eyes and he rolled over from the pain.

Will waited to see if the spell had been broken, but Thurdin rolled over and struggled to attack Will. He shook his head in disbelief.

"I'll give you one more chance Prince of Vulgaard!" Sir William knew he might have to kill the Queen's son. "Surrender now or die!"

But there was no change in the Prince's eyes. They were as black as the sky all around him. "Never! I follow Lord Bedlam and no one else!" he yelled so hard the veins in his neck bulged.

Sir William again shook his head with regret knowing how it would destroy the Queen's heart to know her son was dead. "So be it," he took his sword and thrust it into the boy's neck. Thurdin's eyes rolled back and he gurgled in his own blood. Will blinked back tears as he watched the boy die. It was as though he realized how lucky he had been to be freed from the spell of Lord Bedlam. He stepped over Thurdin's body and prepared to assist Peter by facing Lord Bedlam one last time.

Will heard the whoops and hollers of Bedlam's fighters and he knew what it meant. The evil Lord himself was approaching the scene since Peter had almost made it into the forest. Will ran to the nearest hilltop and saw the source for the joy in Bedlam's creatures. There, in the desert plains, marched Lord Bedlam's men escorting the demon creature Will had seen Lord Bedlam create in the fire pits of Hildron. The beast stood forty feet high and walked on hooved feet. Its dragon–like tail swished along the ground. Fire engulfed its body and burned anything in its way, except Bedlam who walked in front of it with a proud scowl across his face.

Will turned to see the creatures celebrating while racing toward the forest. He knew he could face Bedlam without resistance since the evil Lord thought he remained under the spell, but Will decided not to risk it. He had promised the King to help Peter, and he intended on keeping that last promise to his sovereign on the battlefield.

# 39 MAGOG

Alexander and Sir Rohan successfully fought off a few remaining Baroks in the Cardion Valley. They raced to a dirt road that led to the Dragon Forest. There they spotted Lord Bedlam's demon creature, Magog, making its way across the grassy fields toward the forest.

"What power is this?" Alexander cringed and shook his head.

"I never knew such evil magic existed," Sir Rohan said.

"It has been said that many of the rulers and outlying leaders have entered into pacts with Lord Bedlam causing his power to grow more and more," Alexander explained. "Now I see that it is true."

"Is it stoppable?" Sir Rohan asked.

Alexander grimaced. "That I do not know."

"Above us, sire!" Rohan pointed to the sky and spotted King Isleif's men soaring through the air on dragons.

"There are so many of them!" Alexander shouted.

"My Lord." A familiar voice came from behind Alexander. He turned to see it was Sir Ryek, the long lost son of King Eulrik, walking toward him. When his eyes met those of Ryek, Alexander couldn't believe it. King Eulrik had never known if his son had been killed during the quest for the swords or if he had lived. Alexander and all the rulers had mourned for him.

"Can it be?" Alexander reached out. "Sir Rohan, can you believe it? It is Sir Ryek back from the dead! Is that really you Sir Ryek?"

Sir Rohan stood with mouth agape as though he were seeing a ghost.

Sir Ryek did not respond at first. That's when Sir Rohan noticed the sword in the young man's hand.

"We had feared the worst," Alexander said as he excitedly came toward the knight. "Does your sister know you are here? Come, we must find Queen Esmeralda and—"

"No!" Sir Rohan tried to come between the King and Sir Ryek, but it was too late. Ryek had already thrust his sword deep into the King's lower abdomen where the armor left his flesh exposed. He retracted the sword and raised it at Sir Rohan.

"As you can see, King Alexander and Sir Rohan, I am very much alive," Sir Ryek said as he watched the King fall to his knees. "And, like my father before me, I serve Lord Bedlam now!"

Sir Rohan swiped his sword at Ryek and the two stood facing each other. He shoved Ryek back and lowered his sword down, but was met with Ryek's sword.

§

Peter and his dragon soared through the sky at high speed toward the forest, but his dragon reared up when it saw Magog in the clearing. It roared a high pitched roar and Peter knew Tavrith was greatly afraid.

"It's alright!" Peter yelled and stroked its neck. "We must keep going! The swords, remember we must get the swords to the forest!"

Peter's eyes studied the fearsome creature as it ambled through the fields spreading fire all through the brush. Its body was completely engulfed in flames. The smoke from the many fires began to rise and becloud the area, yet Peter knew he needed to make his way to the entrance no matter what obstacles were placed in his path.

Together, he and Tavrith weaved back and forth in the muddled air, trying to avoid any more arrows shooting toward them. The box attached to the saddle banged against Tav's body. The Baroks were too busy marching alongside Bedlam's prized creation to notice the dragon flying past. Finally, Peter decided to land his dragon a bit to the east of the entrance where the shadows of the trees hid them from the creature and the fires burning nearby. Peter dismounted and peeked through some trees.

"Bedlam's creature," Peter murmured to no one. "How could it have made its way to the forest so easily?"

He watched helplessly as Magog approached the forest entrance with Baroks racing alongside it. Its tail swished back and forth setting brush aflame. It roared in triumph as did the many Baroks at shrieking its feet. Then, it opened its mouth and spewed out fire onto the forest trees igniting them and sending flames high into the night sky.

Peter stood there panting and sweating, thinking about what to do next. He could feel the fear begin to rise inside of him when he considered that he might not be able to complete the task.

"No!" Peter shouted when he saw his beloved forest set aflame. "This can't be happening!" He ran back to the Tavrith, unstrapped the box from the saddle, and carefully set it down. He could hear the raucous celebration of Bedlam's creatures rise with the flames. Peter looked into his dragon's amber eyes.

"I hope the others are alright," he said to his dragon. Peter covered his ears so he could think for moment. Tavrith squawked and tilted its head. "What if they didn't make it? Should we go find them?"

Peter raised his head and shouted. "Please tell me what to do!" he called to the Dragon of the Forest, but he knew it was no use. This mission was his and his alone. Stay calm, he thought. This is your purpose. You can do this. He paced for a few moments turning his thoughts over and over in his mind desperately. The roar of the fire could be heard nearby. The heat grew in intensity.

"There has to be a way to stop this creature!" He yelled into the air. "There has to be a way."

§

"How on earth is Peter going to get past this madness?" Annika asked as she sat atop her dragon. She wiped the rain and sweat off her forehead.

"I had no idea a creature such as this existed," Crispin said. His face was pale with fear. The trees of the Dragon Forest burned a bright yellow in the dark sky.

"We've got to keep going. Come on! We've got to help Peter." Anika flew through the air as the others watched Bedlam's creature, Magog, ignite more of the forest.

"Come! Follow me!" King Isleif shouted at them. Behind him were hundreds of men and Elves flying atop their dragons.

"Amazing!" Simon shouted. He motioned for Crispin to turn and see the help.

Crispin turned and saw the sight of so many coming to their aid. "Excellent!" he yelled. His eyes lit up with joy when he saw so many coming to help in the fight. He spotted Jason, Peter's friend from the prison. They waved at each other as he flew by.

"Let's go find Peter!!" Simon shouted. As he and Crispin soared by the Baroks below, their dragon spewed fire onto the enemy fighters. "Careful not to hit King Alexander's men!"

Their attack was successful in sending the Baroks running for cover.

The fire set all the brush aflame making it even smokier and harder to see, but Isleif's men made a second pass over the enemy spewing more flames. From the bush, the Barok archers shot their arrows into the smoky air. Magog, the giant creature, paid no attention to them and continued to spew its fire onto the forest trees.

"Arrows!" Annika shouted as she swerved her dragon away. The arrows raced past her. "Watch the arrows!"

She turned around to see that Simon and Crispin had safely avoided the arrows. She turned her dragon around for another pass. Just then, she felt a tug on her dragon. It roared from the pain. She turned in her saddle to see a Gizor had taken hold of her dragon's tail. It grinned a sickly grin revealing its small sharp teeth. Then it sunk those teeth into the dragon's tail sending it spiraling down. The dragon whipped its head back trying to bite the Gizor. When it did, it accidentally hit Annika and she fell backward, but her boot stayed in the stirrup. As her dragon spiraled down, she desperately tried to hold on. The Gizor flapped its wings and sped off. Annika, dizzy from the spinning, reached up and grabbed the saddle horn. Finally, her dragon leveled off and she was able to land it in the grass.

Peter's friend, Jason, landed and ran toward Annika.

"Are you alright?" he asked.

"Yes," she moaned. "A bit dizzy, but I'm fine." She nudged her dragon to take off and Jason followed after her. They met Simon and Crispin in the air.

"More arrows are coming our way!" Simon shouted in the air. Jason joined in and jetted across the sky on his dragon.

"Jason!" Simon shouted. "Be careful!"

Peter's friend effortlessly commanded his dragon to fly alongside Simon. "Don't worry about me. Dragon riding comes naturally."

"Quickly! Everyone follow me!"Thætil exclaimed. He turned his dragon and soared across the grasslands.

"Where is Peter?" Jason asked. "Did he make it into the forest yet?"

Simon looked over at him. "We don't know, but we've got to find him. He has the swords and those creatures want them at any cost!"

"King Isleif's men are attacking the enemy from the skies as we speak. The ogres are fighting alongside us," Annika shouted to Simon and Jason. "And Queen Esmeralda and her men are on their way. It is far from over."

Jason nodded his head. "Trust me, Peter will do this. He will enter the forest. I've no doubt about it."

Annika nodded and smiled.

Thætil pointed below.

"Sir William," he said. "I must find him. He will know what to do about the creature. You must find Peter. Go!"

General Aluein's men remained in the area watching the giant creature. Simon, Annika, Crispin flew on to find Peter while Thætil along with Eris and a few Elves landed in the brush to assist Sir William. When they landed, they quickly dismounted and ran to General Aluein's soldiers.

"Sir William?" Thætil asked one of the men. "Where is he?"

The soldier pointed to Will mounted on his horse surrounded by men awaiting his orders to fight. Thætil and his Elves ran over to him.

"Sir William," he said, "what is the plan?"

Will turned and saw that Thæil and his Elves were ready to enter the fight, he nodded. "We wait here for Lord Bedlam's grand entrance. We will allow him his final bow," Will smirked and held up his sword, "and then we will join in the celebration in our own way."

Thætil understood. He turned and studied the creature Magog as it raised its arms in triumph, causing an even more frenzied reaction from the Baroks at its feet. Behind it, the Dragon Forest burned.

"Will, can it be defeated?" Thætil asked.

Sir William, staring intently at the beast, slowly nodded. "Oh yes," he answered. "As with all magic, it is only temporary. Therefore, it has a weakness. We just have to find what that weakness is."

Thætil could see that Will's eyes had found what he had been waiting for. Lord Bedlam had finally made his grand entrance into the sickening celebration at the feet of his creation.

"Oh yes, it can be defeated," Will raised his sword, signaling all his men to take up arms and prepare to advance. "But only with a sword of truth and honor."

Thætil watched as Will threw down his sword to the grass as though it were diseased. He knew the sword had been created by Lord Bedlam's Baroks in the pits of Hildron, therefore, it was tainted with magic and evil. So, Thætil removed his own sword and handed it to Sir William.

Will bowed to the thoughtful gesture, reached out, and took the sword. He understood the Elves of Vulgaard refrained from magic in their blending of metals. Their swords were of the purist mix of metals.

"May its aim be true," Thætil wished. "May it bring you victory over evil."

Will gripped the hilt, raised the sword high, and grinned widely. "It will, my friend," he said, turning to all the Elves in the knowledge of how honorable they had been for millennia. "Indeed it will."

§

"You may stop me, Rohan, but you'll never stop Lord Bedlam," Sir Ryek hissed.

Sir Rohan could see the deadness in Ryek's eyes. He used his foot to trip Ryek and send him back to the ground. He rolled over and tried to regain his footing, bit Sir Rohan stabbed him in the back with his sword. Ryek screamed in agony from the pain.

Sir Rohan grabbed King Alexander who slumped over. The grass turned red from the blood. "Hang on, sire," he cried as he searched the area for help. He spied a soldier running ahead, so he waved him down.

"Sir Rohan," the soldier said with eyes wide. "What has happened?"

"Go and get some help," Rohan ordered. "I need assistance for the King! Bring some soldiers to take this knight prisoner. Move!"

The soldier stood in stunned silence at first, then rushed off to find help. Rohan held King Alexander and placed his hand over the wound. The King winced. With trembling fingers, Sir Rohan took the small bag from his belt and removed some of the healing powder. He gently placed some of the powder into Alexander's mouth.

"Take this, my Lord," Sir Rohan pleaded. "It will help you." He then gave Alexander some water.

"Peter," Alexander whispered. He sipped some of the water. "Find Peter."

"He will make it into the forest," Rohan said. "Don't worry, my King. He will make it. Now, drink." Rohan frantically searched for any sign of the soldier returning with assistance.

# 40 THE GHOST KNIGHT

Peter took Tav's bridle and lead him away from the forest. "I've got to keep going. We've got to get the signal out to—"

A gust of wind interrupted Peter. He looked up at the treetops and could see the flames had spread in the wind. Then, directly in front of him, he spotted Annika, Simon, and Crispin along with Jason landing their dragons.

"Peter!" Jason shouted as he approached. "You made it."

"What are you doing here?" Peter ran to him.

All of them removed their swords.

"We're here to make sure you can enter in even with that creature still standing," Simon said.

Peter jerked his head around when he heard the Magog's roar.

Suddenly, a green mist appeared everywhere surrounding them. Peter looked at his friends and then back at the mist. He quickly ran to the saddle and removed his shield and crossbow. He tossed both to the ground.

"No! You don't understand!" Peter shouted to the others. He waved his arms. "You've got to get out of here before it's too late!"

"But Peter, the swords," Simon ran over to the box on the ground. "You've got to get them to the forest!"

"No, you have to trust me. You must get out of here and hurry!" Peter shouted. He saw the mist swirling at their feet.

Then, Peter took Tav's face into his hands. "Tavrith, fly away!" Peter ordered. "Find the Elves. Bring them here. Go, now!"

Peter watched his dragon fly off. That's when he remembered what his mother had told him. *A dragon will die for you, Peter.* She said. *But it will live for you, too.*

"Peter, what is happening?' Annika asked. "Where is all this mist coming from? What do we do?"

The baffling mist grew thicker and swirled around their feet. Peter removed his sword and prepared for whatever would come from that green mist.

"Annika, you and the others must leave, now," he said sternly. "Go and help Thætil fight off the Baroks. Go!"

But before they could obey his order, an ear-splitting shriek came from above them. When they all turned to see the source of the sound, they watched as arrows hit their dragons in the chest and neck. The beasts roared from the pain and slumped to the ground.

"Oh no!" Annika shouted. When she and the others ran to their dead dragons, they spotted several armed Baroks swoop in on mutant dragons and land on the ground nearby. They quickly dismounted and came at the group with swords drawn.

"Stop them!" Simon ordered his friends.

Peter picked up his crossbow and aimed it at the approaching Baroks. Suddenly, he heard a low ominous sound come from the mist. He turned in time to see a horrible sight. His eyes watched carefully then widened in fear and disbelief.

"Unbelievable," he mumbled with his mouth agape. "It cannot possibly be you again."

There, in the green mist, appeared Damon. He reappeared as one of Lord Bedlam's green knights that had once been used to fight against his father's men during the battle with Lord Caragon.

Damon wore the armor of Bedlam and gripped his sword as he stepped toward Peter.

"How can this be?" Peter said to no one.

Damon swiped at the air with his sword. "Time to die, Sir Peter," he sneered, "once and for all."

Peter studied Damon's appearance. Although a ghost, he was not the rotting corpse that Peregrine had been when his spirit rose from the dead. This ghostly knight was still whole with striking eyes that had haunted Peter's dreams for so many months. Damon's ghost was all that stood between Peter and his goal of entering the forest and he was not about to let a ghost stop him now.

Thætil gathered with his Elves near the melee of Baroks. They stood watching the scene knowing the Baroks were too busy celebrating to notice them.

"Look! In the sky to the east," an Elf shouted to his leader. "Dragon fire!"

Thætil turned in time to see Tavrith's fire light up the sky to the east of the creature Magog.

"What does it mean?" the Elf asked.

"Peter's dragon! It is the signal. Go! Find Peter!" Thætil ordered them. "Go now!"

§

"There is no way you can win this, Peter," Damon hissed. "Lord Bedlam's powers are far too great. Greater than the Dragon itself."

Peter gripped his father's sword, the Sword of Alexander, in his hands and waited for the ghost knight to strike.

"The forest will burn to the ground," Damon continued, "and the Dragon will soon be dead. Lord Bedlam will have its scales and forge weapons no man can destroy!"

Peter winced when he heard the words. He turned around to see his friends fighting off the Baroks, but he knew he needed to stay and face Damon.

"Come then," Peter replied. "Let us begin."

Damon chortled. "You are no match for me. Your pitiful weaponry cannot withstand my—"

"Enough of your girlish talk!" Peter shouted. "Fight me!"

Damon glared at him, raised his sword, and lunged at Peter. But when he lowered his sword, it struck the Sword of Alexander and stopped right at Peter's face. Peter grinned.

"You see?" Peter asked as he shoved Damon back. "My mother knew how to stop Bedlam's magic when she forged these swords so long ago."

Damon growled and lurched at him again, but Peter leapt out of the way and stabbed Damon in the back. He screamed from the pain as Peter withdrew his sword. When Damon screamed, so did the creature Magog.

Peter noticed this instantly and he remembered how the land and his father, King Alexander, are connected. He wondered if the two creatures were similarly connected somehow by Bedlam's magic.

Damon turned around and swung at Peter. He slashed open Peter's shoulder. Peter thrust his sword, but Damon quickly moved away and brought down his sword again striking Peter's sword.

Peter realized Damon's strength had waned since being stabbed. So, he kicked Damon back. Damon staggered a bit, but kept coming back at

Peter. The two fenced back and forth until their swords grew so heavy they grunted each time they struck. After a while, Peter had Damon just where he wanted him.

Behind him were Annika, Simon, Crispin, and Jason battling the Baroks with their swords. They fought valiantly. Striking down creatures with ease, but it was no use. More Baroks landed and soon, the hideous creatures outnumbered them and out maneuvered them. Finally, they held Peter's friends at bay. The Baroks pointed their swords at them while the other Baroks made it to the box of swords lying nearby. The Peter's friends helplessly watched as the Baroks took the swords and carried them to the mutant dragons clawing at the ground impatiently.

"Stop them!" Simon shouted. "The swords!" He lunged at a Barok and hit it in the jaw with his fist. Crispin did the same, but another Barok grabbed Annika and held its sword at her throat.

The boys froze.

The Barok sneered at them and its lips curled into a distorted grin revealing rows of sharp yellow teeth. Drool oozed from its mouth.

"You harm her," Simon threatened through clenched teeth, "and so help me."

The creature began to take Annika with it toward the waiting dragons.

Annika tried to struggle free.

"What do we do now?" Crispin asked Simon.

"Don't give up yet. Look over there!" Simon pointed to the sky. The Baroks turned their heads to where Simon pointed.

When they did, arrows hit their chests and their swords fell to the ground. Eris swooped in on her dragon, leapt off it, and shot more arrows into the Baroks, killing them all.

"Get to the swords!" she shouted.

Simon and Crispin ran to the box, but four more Baroks landed their dragons directly in front of it. The creatures cackled as one of their dragons lifted the box of swords with its talons. It spewed fire at Simon as it flew away.

"Watch out!" Simon cried out. He leapt out of the way in time.

Eris jerked around and saw Annika being taken to a dragon by the Barok. Annika used her elbow to strike the creature and it dropped its sword. That was the opening that Eris needed. She aimed an arrow and shot the creature through its neck.

"They have the swords! This can't be happening!" Crispin yelled as the rest of the Baroks jetted through the sky.

"Stop them!" Simon shouted as he and the others ran after them.

Eris leapt onto her dragon and jetted off after the creatures. Simon aimed his crossbow at the Baroks and released the arrow. It hit one Barok, and it fell off its dragon. Crispin shot his arrow, too, but it was too late.

As she soared after the Baroks, Eris reloaded her bow and aimed at the Baroks speeding through the air. She released the arrow and it struck the back leg of the dragon carrying the swords, but it continued to fly off. Below, Eris spotted the melee of Baroks near Magog. Sir William's cadre of soldiers stood in line. They appeared to be waiting to advance. Just then, a mutant dragon appeared from nowhere and struck Eris's dragon. It roared and whipped around. Eris yanked its reins to turn it away from the scene, but more mutant dragons followed after her.

"Simon!" Annika pointed to the sky. "It's Eris!"

Simon turned to see Eris atop her dragon as it descended to the ground.

"Go help Peter!" Simon ordered as he ran off to help Eris.

Eris's dragon landed hard on the ground and sent her rolling off the saddle. She lay motionless as Simon approached her.

"Bedlam's creatures successfully escaped with the box of swords," Crispin said to Annika and Jason as they watched Simon run off toward Eris. "What do we do?"

"Help Peter, just like Simon said!" Jason grabbed his sword and headed to where Peter fought with Damon.

# 41 THE SWORDS OF THE OATH

"Where is Peter?" King Isleif shouted to his captain. Isleif pulled his sword from the chest of a Barok. It fell back and Isleif used the grass to wipe the thick blood off his sword. He and his men fought their way toward the brawl, successfully slaughtering the Baroks left behind.

"He has made it to the forest!" his captain shouted as he marched with his fellow soldiers and Elves across the field toward the melee. "We saw him fly off toward the east to land there."

King Isleif looked at the demon creature guarding the entrance to the forest with its body aflame. "Peter could not possible have yet entered, not with this monster standing guard."

"No, your majesty," the captain said as he watched King Isleif motion for his men to follow him to a clearing outside the Cardion Valley.

"We have learned that Sir William is up ahead," a soldier explained. "He fights for the King now and is waiting until the right moment to attack Lord Bedlam."

Ahead, Sir William remained mounted on his horse as he watched Lord Bedlam approach with his minions.

"When shall we strike?" one of the soldiers asked him.

Will shook his head. "Not yet," he answered. "But ready the men to begin our march. When Lord Bedlam sees us, he will think we are still under his command. Go, tell the others to march forward and attack at my signal only."

The soldier bowed then ran off to inform the rest of the soldiers in rank. Will never took his eyes off his former mentor. He watched as Bedlam meandered his way through his ranks of monstrous creatures all bowing down to him as he passed. Magog kept guard at the entrance of the burning forest.

Soon, the ogres marched alongside King Isleif. They had advanced enough to attack Bedlam's men when they saw the signal from Will. At the bottom of the hill, they remained well out of sight of the menacing

Lord Bedlam.

General Aluein stood with his men in the grassy plains. Together, they watched from nearby as Sir William patiently waited to attack.

He turned to his own captain. "How much longer is he going to wait? Until Lord Bedlam is directly in front of him?"

"I do not know, sir," his captain answered.

Isleif continued to search the area for any Baroks. "Wait. And be ready for anything!" he ordered his men. "You never know when—"

"Sire, look!" one of his men shouted. He pointed toward Sir William.

"Ah," Isleif said. "Lord Bedlam approaches his young protégé at last."

§

Peter turned to see his friends running toward him gripped with fear. Sorrow and confusion covered their faces. His heart sank for them.

Peter returned to face Damon. He came at him hard and kicked him to the ground, but Damon disappeared into the green mist. Peter looked all around for him, but Damon was gone. Just then, Peter was thrown to the ground by an invisible force. He landed on his stomach and rolled over only to see that Damon had reappeared with a ghost dragon. Peter saw his shield and crossbow nearby.

The ghost dragon inhaled then spewed its fire at Peter.

"Hide yourselves!" he shouted to his friends. They saw the dragon's fire and hid behind some large rocks just in time.

Peter leapt to his scale shield while the fire hit a tree behind him. He knew the dragon would not miss again. Sure enough, the dragon inhaled and sent its fire at Peter again. This time he raised his shield and deflected the fire. The dragon did not relent. The steady stream of fire was strong and began to push Peter back. Peter yelled through the scorching heat and leaned into the stream of fire until it stopped. The ghost dragon was very powerful. Peter was glad Tavrith had flown away. He knew the little dragon would've been no match for this bizarre creature.

"We've got to help him," Jason suggested. He and the others ran to assist Peter, but the dragon's fire stopped them again.

The dragon roared and flapped its wings in anger, fanning the flames which spread over the grass. Damon laughed and came at Peter with his sword. Peter rolled out of the way in time to miss Damon's attack. Instead of piercing Peter, the sword hit the scale shield and slid off onto the ground. Damon yelled with anger and frustration, pulled his sword from the muddy ground, and faced Peter again.

But Peter was there with his sword and stabbed Damon in the chest. Damon screamed from the pain. Simultaneously, Magog roared and clutched its chest. It staggered back a few paces. Peter could hear it roar. He tilted his head when he realized something. It is true. Damon and the creature are connected by Bedlam's magic.

"You and that creature," Peter shouted. "You are connected!"

"We are all Bedlam's creations!" Damon shouted and pointed to his chest. "We are all one with Lord Bedlam!"

"Good to know," Peter replied.

Damon raised his sword again, but Peter used his shield to ram Damon in the face. He staggered back and disappeared. The ghost dragon tossed its head back and roared before it, too, disappeared. Peter threw the shield down and removed his sword.

"You have become weakened," Peter shouted to the air. "I know you can hear me!"

Damon reappeared and rushed Peter from behind.

"Peter! Watch out!" Annika warned him.

Peter turned around in time to stab Damon one last time.

Damon's eyes grew wide and his mouth remained open. Peter knew it was not from the pain. The ghost knight, mortally wounded by a noble sword, began to dissipate into the abyss as Sir Peregrine had done years before. The ghost dragon disappeared forever.

When they saw it was safe, Simon and the others ran up to Peter.

"Peter, the swords...the swords of the Oath are gone," Annika wept. "They've been taken by the Baroks!"

"And the forest is still aflame," Jason said. "What do we do now?"

"All is lost." Crispin sighed. He put his hands to his head and groaned. "The swords are gone. The forest burns. It's over."

§

"My Lord," Sir William said and bowed to Lord Bedlam as he sat mounted on his steed.

"Sir William," Lord Bedlam replied. He leaned on his cane and stared at his protégé. "I have the swords, Will. It is finished."

Will frowned when he heard the words.

"It is finally finished," Lord Bedlam said. Several of his Baroks flew in on dragons and landed nearby. Lord Bedlam waved his arm toward them and the cry of victory that came from his soldiers rose into the air while Magog roared and sent its flames high into the night sky.

"No," Will murmured to himself. "This cannot be true."

"At long last, the time has come! This is indeed a great victory." Bedlam clenched his fist. "A victory for all who follow me, Will."

Will raised his chin as Lord Bedlam came toward him with eyes glowing red.

"I have waited so long for this moment," Bedlam continued. "And now the day has finally come. I will destroy the swords with my power and then destroy the Dragon Forest!"

More cries and shrieks came from the Baroks as they banged their swords and spears together.

"But…" A serious look crept across Bedlam's face. "I had rather hoped you would be joining me in the victory."

Will clenched his jaw.

"Alas, it was not meant to be." Bedlam raised his cane and shoved it at Will. "You have failed me!"

Will looked away when he realized Bedlam knew he was no longer under the Affecting Spell.

"You know all my powers reside in that creature, Will," Lord Bedlam said as he turned his glance toward Magog. "And it will not fail me as you have failed me. I will be victorious!"

Bedlam jerked around to see that his creatures hastily carried the box of swords with toward him.

"Here they are!" Bedlam waved his dragonhead cane toward the arriving Baroks.

Will grimaced at the sight.

"My Lord," one Barok soldier said. "Here are the swords."

Lord Bedlam kicked the corpse of a soldier out of his way and stood in front of the box of swords on the ground at his feet. He studied the strange design carved into the lid. His Baroks bowed in humiliation as they waited for their Lord to open it.

Lord Bedlam studied his creatures bowing before him. He used his thin hands to slick back his hair away from his sallow face and slowly turned toward Will.

"The time has finally come, Will. I will destroy the swords here at the entrance of the Dragon Forest and destroy the Dragon while you and all of Alexander's men watch," he hissed.

# 42 THE RUSE

General Aluein stomped through the ranks of his men as they waited nervously for the signal.

"Nothing has been seen yet, sir," his captain said. His eyes were fixated on the scene near the forest entrance. Off in the distance, they could see Will mounted on his horse.

Aleuin grimaced when he saw Magog roaring and spewing its flames over the brush. "We cannot wait much longer. Peter cannot enter the forest with that thing guarding it."

"Yes sir," his captain said. "What are your orders?"

Aluein reached up and scratched his bearded chin. He sighed. The battleworn general knew that timing was everything when it came to attack. He knew he'd have to trust Sir William. "We wait," he ordered. "We wait a little longer."

§

Sir William watched cautiously as Lord Bedlam leaned over the box of swords. The evil Lord released a bolt of green fire from his fingertips, splitting the box open. He thrust out his chest and triumphantly approached the swords which were still covered with the red cloth.

"And I think I shall kill you first, Will, with the Sword of Alexander," he sneered. "Yes. How fitting it will be to slay you, one of King Alexander's greatest knights, with his own sword!" Bedlam cackled and jerked the cloth that covered the swords away with his long bony fingers. When he did, he gasped and stepped back.

Will craned his neck to see what was the matter.

Underneath the red cloth lay not the swords of the Oath, but just nine ordinary swords.

"What's this?" Bedlam reached down with his bony hand and quickly picked up one of the swords. "No!" He threw it to the ground as though it were poisoned. He gazed upon it with his reddened eyes.

"What is this!" he screamed. "This is the box that held the swords of the Oath!" Several spikes rose on his back and scales rippled across his face. "Where are those swords?"

"We do not know." One of the Barok soldiers whimpered as it backed away.

Bedlam roared, grabbed another sword, and lowered it onto the neck of the Barok, severing its head. "Where are the swords of the Oath?"

A slight grin crept across Will's face as he realized the ordinary swords were a decoy.

"You fools!" Bedlam threw the sword to the ground and kicked the worthless swords across the muddy ground. His Baroks scattered with fear. "Where are those swords! I must have them. Find them and bring them to me! Now!"

Lord Bedlam slowly faced Will. His voice lowered to a throaty ominous growl. "What have you done?"

Sir William realized the end had come. He leapt off his horse, raised his sword, and lunged at Lord Bedlam.

"Your plan is not as secure as you thought it was, Lord Bedlam!" he yelled as he thrust his sword at the evil Lord. "Neither are you!"

Bedlam swerved out of the way. He released a vicious roar of a dragon and spikes appeared along his back for a second or two.

"You dare attempt to strike at me, Sir William?" Bedlam shrieked. He raised his hands and shot green flames from his fingers that struck Will in the chest and sent him flying backwards several feet. This was the signal Will's men needed.

"You had your chance, but you betrayed me!" Bedlam roared. "Now you will die along with the others!"

"Attack!" Isleif cried to the men and Elves once he saw Will fall to the ground. His men immediately obeyed and stormed the ranks of Baroks, squirming to escape the creature Magog.

They raised their swords and spears and raced toward the unsuspecting Baroks striking them down where they stood. Lord Bedlam saw the squads of men and Elves coming toward him. He raised his arms and waved them in front of his body. Suddenly, from the ground arose hundreds of his ghost knights ready to fight King Isleif's men.

"Where did they all come from?" Isleif asked no one.

Lord Bedlam began to shape shift into a crow, but Will threw his sword and it struck Bedlam's arm. He fell to the ground and his dragonhead cane was tossed aside.

Will picked himself up and ran after his sword. Lord Bedlam shot fire at Will again and sent him to the ground. Magog began to stomp on Isleif's men, its giant hooves crushing them into the damp ground. It opened its mouth and spewed fire down onto the helpless men scampering to get out of its way, but few escaped its intense fire. The ghost knights attacked the confused soldiers of the King.

Will regained consciousness in time to see Lord Bedlam reach his black dragon. "No!" he shouted. "Stop him!"

A soldier tossed Will a spear. Will took it and ran after Lord Bedlam but he saw he was too far away. Will spied his sword lying on the ground, so he picked it up and inspected it, remembering it was once Thætil's sword.

"Honor and truth," he whispered.

Then, he looked up and saw Magog was rapidly approaching. Magog roared with pain and clutched its chest. Lord Bedlam watched the beast stagger backwards. Sir William noticed this as well. As Bedlam's power waned, his creatures weakened.

"The creature has been wounded!" Will yelled out. "Somehow, it has been wounded."

Will gripped his sword by its blade and aimed it at the giant demon as it roared before him. Magog noticed Will on the ground at its feet aiming his sword. It opened its mouth to spew fire on him, but Will released the sword and it flew through the air settling deep within Magog's side. It clutched the sword, but could not remove it.

King Isleif watched the scene with wide eyes. The sword of honor and truth sunk deep into Magog and began to overpower it. The Baroks roared with great fear at the sight of the dying creature. They began to run off, but Thætil's Elves stopped them with their swords and their arrows. Instantly, the ghost knights dissipated into the air.

§

"What do we do now, Peter?" Annika wept. "The swords? What can we do?"

But Peter remained oddly silent for a moment. He made his way past his shocked friends and spotted Tavrith landing in the grass behind them. When the dragon landed, Peter ran to him.

"Peter, where are you going?" Crispin asked with confusion.

But instead of answering, Peter walked Tavrith over to the edge of the forest. Crispin's eyes widened and he stepped back when he saw that Peter was not alone.

Behind Peter and Tavrith came nine of Thætil's warrior Elves walking in unison. When they reached Peter and his friends, they stopped and bowed respectfully. Their crystal blue eyes shone and they were dressed in their battle armor.

Even though they had sprinted across the fields with great haste, all the Elves stood tall at attention, barely out of breath. Peter turned to face them and when he did, they all removed their swords at the same time.

"What's this?" Jason asked with raised eyebrows.

In their hands were not ordinary swords of the Elves. Instead, they held the swords of the Oath.

Peter stepped toward them. "Come now, we don't have much time."

Annika, Crispin, and Jason stared at the glistening swords. Their eyes filled with wonder.

Peter led the Elves to the edge of the forest and each Elf handed him the sword of the Oath he had vowed to protect. Peter stretched out his arms and they placed each sword one on top of the other. He grimaced from the weight of all the swords.

"Can you perform this task, Prince of man?" one Elf asked, with eyes so clear, they seemed to be made of crystal.

Peter nodded. "I have to," he replied. He could see that the fires at the entrance had almost burned out, but many more trees remained aflame. The creature, Magog, was no longer guarding the entrance.

"Sir William's men are fighting off the Baroks in the grassy hills to the west of the forest," the Elf said. "Now is the time."

Tavrith squawked.

The Elves bowed toward Peter once again. Peter's friends watched the scene with mouths agape.

"Our thoughts go with you, young Prince," another Elfin warrior said and he placed his large hand on Peter's shoulders.

Peter started into the trees, paused, and then turned to the mighty Elves of Vulgaard.

"Thank you, my friends." He bowed toward them. "I knew you would not fail me...or my father."

The Elves grinned, then, one by one, they jogged off to rejoin the fight.

When the Elves had departed, Peter's friends gathered around him. They stared in awe at the extraordinary swords in his arms.

"But how, Peter? How did you...And when?" Annika asked. She

cocked her head to one side. "When did this happen? I thought the swords were in the box. We thought they were lost for good."

Peter smiled awkwardly.

"We saw the box being taken," Crispin said.

"It was a decoy," Peter explained. He winced with embarrassment. "I made a plan with Thætil and his Elves back at the ruins of the palace. I sensed that Lord Bedlam knew of my father's plan and I had to do something."

They listened intently.

"I'm sorry I didn't tell you. I couldn't take the chance. I figured, the less you knew, the better it would be."

His friends all looked at one another then back at him.

"I knew I needed help so, like my mother did many years before, I asked the Elves to help me save the swords." Peter gazed down at the bounty in his arms. "And, once again, the Elves of Vulgaard came through."

He looked up at his friends' concerned faces.

"That's why I didn't want you here at the forest. I feared you might get hurt if the Baroks came for the box."

"Peter," Crispin began, "I understand why you did it."

"Brilliant plan, Peter." Jason squeezed Peter's shoulder.

"Yes," Annika said. "We all understand."

"Now, that you've got the swords," Crispin said. "Can you get them into the forest?"

"Yes," Peter said as he adjusted the heavy swords. Beads of sweat formed on his face.

"Alright, then," Jason said as he turned to the others. "We've got to find Simon and Eris. We'll finish the fight, Peter! Don't you worry!"

The group came together one last time and gripped arms. Annika wiped her eyes and smiled at Peter.

"Thank you, my friends" Peter said. His eyes glistened. "Be safe. When this is all over, we'll…"

"Yes," Crispin interrupted. "We will. Now go!"

Peter watched his friends run off and disappear into the grasslands toward the battle.

§

Will stood watching the creature Magog stumble back. He raced toward it, grabbed a sword he saw lying on the ground, and picked it up.

When he reached the creature, he sliced at its leg that no longer burned with fire. It roared from the pain. Will ran toward and sliced its other leg and the demon fell to its knees. Isleif's men shot arrows into its marred flesh. It raised its mammoth hands and tried to stop the sharp arrows from hitting its body. Will climbed onto its back and raised his sword high. Before the creature could reach around and grab him, Will lowered his sword into the neck of the demon creature.

It roared one last time and began to fall to the ground. Isleif's men scattered to avoid its falling body. They could see its glowing eyes grow dim and roll back into the sockets. And then, Lord Bedlam's demon creature finally fell to the ground and diminished before the men as many frightened Baroks scattered about like frightened insects.

"Come on!" Isleif shouted. "Let's finish them off and be done with this already!"

Above them came hordes of Queen Esmeralda's men flying in on dragons from the east. They dove down and spewed their fire onto the remaining Baroks as they ran.

Will rolled out of the ash heap that was once Bedlam's greatest creation and retrieved Thætil's Elfin sword. Then, he headed over to where he saw General Aluein and King Isleif's men fighting off the remaining Baroks and soldiers of Bedlam's realm. He raised his sword and lowered it into a Barok. He turned and stabbed two more as they advanced toward him. More came at him with teeth glaring and eyes glowing, but none survived Will's blade that night.

§

"It's dying," Peter said as he stood panting and holding the swords of the Oath in his arms. He could hear the creature Magog's cries of agony. "Finally."

Peter turned to his dragon.

"Will you help me my friend?" he asked Tav. The creature blinked its amber eyes, flared its nostrils, and snorted. Peter grinned as the dragon flapped its wings. Peter motioned with his head for it to follow him to the entrance of the forest. Together, they passed the old wooden signpost that stood near the path. Beware the Dragon Forest it read.

The rain pelted the ground and the flames crackled and popped. The area smelled of burned wood soaked in rain. Soon, everything became eerily quiet.

Once they entered the forest, Peter hesitated. He knew only the chosen could enter the forest realm. He hoped Tavrith could enter along with him. Once Peter felt it was safe, he continued to lead the dragon into the trees. The strong odor of smoke permeated everything. Peter coughed and gagged from the thick smell. Tavrith lowered its head trying to avoid the branches that blocked its way, but a few times its wings became snared in the web-like branches.

Finally, the two saw the clearing ahead. "There it is!" Peter nodded to where the trees thinned and the mist covered the lake in the middle of the forest. Once they were close enough, Peter ambled to edge of the water with the cluster of swords in his arms. He set them down and stood mesmerized at the sight of the beautiful swords before him. For a moment, Peter remembered the first time he had ridden off alone on his quest to enter the Dragon Forest. His mind raced back to when he first had seen the Dragon of the Forest all those years ago.

*There, from between the branches of the trees moved a set of glowing yellow eyes, each one about the size of Peter's head. They stared right at Peter and his horse unblinking in the moonlight. Peter's mouth was open and he turned to see if Titan was experiencing the sight as well. Titan's eyes were large and his nostrils flared as his ears were pointed back. Together they stood, staring at the yellow eyes glaring back at them. The dark pupils were vertical slits that reached from the bottom to the top of each glowing eye.*

*Then they heard it.*

*A low ominous growl penetrated from behind the trees as the eyes rose from a few feet above the wet earth to just near the tops of the trees. They blinked as they rose. The growl grew louder still. Then a hot mist from between the trees shot out toward the Prince who was near tears in his fright. His body shook. The short blast of mist warmed Peter's skin and made him and Titan take a few steps back.*

*"Do not move," A low voice hissed. It seemed to come from the glowing eyes which were nothing but slits now peering from the tops of the trees. "It is important that you are here."*

The White Owl landed on a low branch near Peter, waking him from his trance. Standing there, Peter remembered the last time he had been in the forest all those months ago.

*"The time has come, Peter," the Dragon said with seriousness in its voice. "I have watched man these three years from my home here within the trees. I have observed the comings and goings. And what I have seen brought me back," it said. It turned its head toward Peter. "You have brought me back."*

Peter carefully set the swords down. He stepped back and waited, trying to catch his breath. A breeze animated the trees near the lake and removed the smoke from the air for a moment. As he glanced around the familiar place, he remembered the choice he had to make and how he never realized how that one decision had changed his life forever.

*"You must save Illiath, Peter," the Dragon said.*

*Peter raised his eyebrows.*

*"Save Illiath? Me?" he exclaimed, pointing to his chest. "Surely you must mean my father."*

*The Dragon shook its head.*

*"Your father has fought his battles. He faced his trials on the battlefield and fought valiantly," it said. "And he was rewarded with a son."*

*Peter felt his face grow warm.*

*"Now it is your turn, Peter," it said. It nudged Peter's side with its snout. "You are the Son of the Oath. You are the one to save Illiath."*

*Peter sighed. "I should've just trusted and obeyed you. But it was a choice I had to make, wasn't it?"*

*"You do have a choice to make, Peter," the Dragon said as it stretched out its mammoth wings. "You can choose to be the king you were meant to be."*

"I wasn't meant to be just a knight," Peter whispered to himself. "I was meant to be King of Illiath."

The White Owl flew over to another branch and perched itself there. Peter grinned when he saw the familiar yellow eyes glowing softly. The cool blue mist rolled in from the other side of the lake in the middle of the forest. Peter watched it unfurl like a soft downy blanket until the entire lake was covered. He remembered how he and Titan had ridden out into the middle of the lake when Sir Peregrine was after him. He remembered how the Dragon had saved him there and, together, they had flown over the trees as one. Peter looked up to see the moon appear from behind the clouds. It illuminated the clearing. He looked down at the mist covered lake and that's when he heard it: A soft voice rose like a whisper carried by the wind.

"Peter," said a voice.

Peter blinked a few times. He searched the mist, but couldn't see where the voice was coming from.

"Mother?" he hesitated to say it.

"Peter," his mother said. She appeared inches away from him. He jumped from the shock of seeing his mother so close. She seemed so real. She reached out her hand to him. He took it, and for the first time in many years, Peter felt his mother's hand squeeze his own.

He gazed down at their hands intertwined together. Her hands looked so small and delicate. His eyes stung with tears. He looked up into her light green eyes as the mist was reflected in them. She wore a long red gown and her thick dark hair tumbled graciously around her shoulders. She smiled the warm smile he treasured from his youth.

He knelt down and kissed her hand. "Mother, is this real?"

"Yes, Peter," she chuckled. "Rise, my son. It is time."

## 43 THE BROKEN SPELL

Thætil finished off one of the last of Bedlam's soldiers then ran to assist King Isleif.

"Your majesty!" Thætil found the King removing his sword from the belly of a Barok.

"It is finished!" Isleif shouted and laughed as he waved his sword into the air. "They are defeated!" Thætil grinned. He inspected the battlefield and saw Will running toward them.

"Sir William," he held out his arm. Will took Thætil's hand and handed him his sword.

"Here," he replied. "I believe this belongs to you." Thætil laughed heartily and received the sword with gladness.

"A job well done, Sir William!" King Isleif shouted. "Well done indeed."

"Any news of Peter, your majesty?" Will asked.

Before he could answer, Isleif grotesquely arched his back and cried out in pain. Will's eye widened when he saw the King's chest. A spear had penetrated his body from behind. Will ran to him in time to catch Isleif as he fell to the ground. Will gently laid him down and ran after the Barok that threw the spear. The creature growled at Will who removed his knife from his belt. Sir William growled back at the Barok who titled its head, confused that a man would growl. Then, Will lunged at the beast and sliced its middle. He swung around again and this time sliced at its neck, and, finally, with one last move, he kicked the mutant fighter to the ground. Its head rolled in the opposite direction from its body. Will smirked at the sight, and then winced with pain. He reached down and noticed blood flowing from a wound in his side. He hadn't realized that the creature had stabbed him. Will hunched over and put his hand over the wound. He turned to find King Isleif lying on the blood soaked grass.

"Sir William," Isleif whispered through blood stained teeth.

"I'm here, my Lord," Will said as he knelt over the King. He lifted

Isleif's head.

"Will, find Crispin," he ordered. "My nephew…"

"Yes, my Lord," Will said. He looked up at Thætil who simply held the King's hand.

"Find him," Isleif begged as he tugged on Will's tunic. "Please, you must return him to his mother, my sister."

Will blinked back tears. "I will, your majesty."

"Tell Alexander," Isleif whispered. "Tell the King that…"

"Anything, King Isleif," Will replied.

"Tell him…" But before he could finish, King Isleif closed his eyes.

Will knew the wound was fatal. He could see the life begin to drain from King Isleif's face.

There on the hill, King Isleif of Gundrehd died. Will gently laid his head down on the grass and bowed his head as he knelt over the King's body.

"He was a great King," Thætil said and bowed his head. Will nodded in agreement. He raised his eyes to the Dragon Forest and stood. He picked up his sword and limped off. He grabbed his side and noticed his trousers were soaked with his own blood. Will ignored the pain, gripped his sword, and ran off to find Peter.

"Sir William," Thætil ran to Will and grabbed his arm to stop him. "Stop! You are wounded."

"It is nothing," Will walked off. "Go and find Crispin. Make sure he is safe. I must find Peter."

§

"It is your time," Queen Laurien whispered to Peter. Then, she waved her hand over the lake. "Remember what you must do here in the forest realm."

Peter bent down and grabbed all the swords. He stepped toward the lake, but a loud roar unlike anything he had heard before, stopped him. It seemed to come from the entrance of the forest. He quickly turned with frightened eyes. His mother turned to see what it was as well, but something told Peter his mother already knew what it was. She looked at the White Owl, but it remained quietly perched on the branch with a soft breeze combing its feathers. Sensing his mother's concern, Peter continued toward the center of the lake.

"When you reach the middle, you will set them down onto the surface in a circle. The tip of each blade touching the others," Queen Laurien said with urgency in her voice. She used her fingers to show

Peter what to do. "The blades must touch."

Peter nodded to her, and then began to walk out onto the lake that was now solid as ice. "Trust me. Do not be afraid," she said.

Her voice calmed him as he walked. He could still hear the uproar of battle outside of the forest. Peter exhaled. He was glad the demon creature Bedlam had unleashed to stop him was gone. He kept walking along the slippery surface. His body ached from the day's battles and his arms grew weaker and weaker from the weight of the swords. The thought of his father made him continue on.

Queen Laurien turned to the forest entrance. Nothing could be seen. She turned around to see that Peter had made it to the center of the lake. She closed her eyes and sighed. "Good. Now, lay the swords out onto the surface, leave them, and come to me."

Peter carefully set down all the swords and then arranged them into a circle in the middle of the lake. The tips of each blade touched. But one was missing. Peter felt fear rise inside him until he remembered he had his father's sword in the sheath attached to his belt. The Sword of Alexander.

He removed it, held it up, and admired its beauty. For a moment, he regretted how he would never wield it himself as King of Illiath. The clouds parted and the moonlight peeked through. It reflected off the blade and shimmered. Peter set it down with the other swords. As soon as the blade touched the others, the filigree of each sword began to glow from within. He stepped back from the strange phenomenon and looked into his mother's face. The blue light from the swords reflected in her wide eyes. The mist over the lake increased and covered their feet.

"What is happening to the Swords of the Oath?" Peter asked as the mist enveloped them.

His mother reached out her arms.

"Come to me, now," she said.

Peter could see the concern in her eyes as she continued to look back at the entrance then back again at the glowing swords. Peter saw that the White Owl was no longer perched near her. He walked toward his mother. Then, he hesitated.

"I don't have a sword," he said, gripping his belt.

"And you won't need one. Come to me." She waved him toward her.

Once he reached the shore, she hugged him close to her. He could smell the familiar scent of jasmine in her hair. He wrapped his arms around her shoulders and hugged her close. She parted and moved him away from the lake. He turned to see the water begin to ripple and the mist churn as though the water was suddenly boiling. Peter cautiously stepped back.

"Is the Elfin message working?" Peter asked. He remembered what was written in the scroll.

"Yes," she answered with hands clasped before her. "It is working." Her eyes remained on the water. Peter's dragon flapped its wings and reared up with fright.

"Tavrith is nervous about something out there," Peter said.

Queen Laurien nodded. A tear rolled down her cheek.

"It's alright," Queen Laurien said. "We must stay here. We are safe here."

§

"Any news of Peter?" King Alexander panted.

"No, my Lord, please hold on," the Elfin guard said. He had provided the King with more of the healing salve to digest and he applied a portion to the open wound, but Alexander continued to decline. "You must hold on until we hear some news."

A soldier ran over to Sir Rohan as he paced near the King.

"The demon creature has been destroyed," the soldier reported to Sir Rohan.

King Alexander nodded when he heard the words. "And my son?" he asked. His face turned pale and his breathing became labored.

"He has entered the Dragon Forest," the soldier answered. Alexander was barely able to grin.

"It won't be much longer, my Lord, and we will see the sign that the spell has been broken," Rohan said as he knelt down by Alexander and took his hand. He gazed toward the forest and saw billows of smoke rise into the night sky.

Over the hills came the surviving fighters with their wounded. One by one, they limped over the fields, assisting their friends as they came. Sir Rohan ran over to them.

"What has occurred?" he asked. A weary soldier looked into Sir Rohan's eyes.

"Sir William," he said in a raspy voice. "Sir William saved us all. He killed the creature and helped us fight the enemy away."

"Indeed!" he exclaimed. Sir Rohan closed his eyes and nodded in relief. He patted the young man's shoulder. "Thank you for the most excellent news?" He waved over an assistant. "Here, get this man some water," he ordered.

Rohan walked to the top of the hill and felt a rush of cold air. The rain had stopped, but to the west the fires of Hildron continued to burn. Lord Bedlam remained alive. Above him, he could see many of Queen Esmeralda's dragon fighters circling. To the north, the Dragon Forest stood as elusive as ever.

§

Peter stood next to his mother by the edge of the lake in the middle of the Dragon Forest. They watched the water churn and the swords glow with a blue light. Suddenly, everything became still.

"Is it over?" Peter asked. His mother remained silent.

Peter turned to her for an answer, but she continued to stare at the lake with large eyes.

"Watch," was all she said.

A streak of brilliant blue light shot out of the swords and reached high into the sky above the forest sending Peter to the ground in shock. He sat back and raised his hand over his eyes to shield them from the light.

"The blue light!" he shouted. "Where is it coming from?" But no answer came. He carefully stood and uncovered his eyes, but the light was so intense it hurt to look at it. Peter followed the stream of blue light as it reached far past the treetops and illuminated the forest like an enormous torch. His mind raced back to the time when, as a small boy, he had stood at his bedroom window staring at the forest. He remembered seeing the blue light shine from within the trees, but thought he had only imagined it. Now he knew it was not his imagination.

He turned to his mother who trembled and grinned like a young girl excited about a gift.

A booming roar came from behind them, ending the stillness. Tavrith flapped its wings, sending twigs and pebbles into the air.

"Is it time to go?" Peter asked her. "Is the spell broken?"

Laurien turned to Tavrith. She could see the dragon was concerned.

"You know what's out there, don't you?" Peter asked her.

She nodded.

"He is coming for you, isn't he?" Peter touched his mother's arm.

She looked down at his hand.

An explosion of light came from the swords and, this time, it knocked both Peter and his mother to the ground.

"Mother!" he shouted. "What is happening?" They looked at the light and in its center were the ten swords hovering above the lake.

Laurien pointed to the swords. They began to spin furiously until they came together.

Peter observed the scene and shook his head. "One sword," he murmured.

In the center of the stream of blue light, the ten swords came together to form one sword. One glorious silver sword remained. It hovered inside the blue light directly above the lake.

"Mother, are you seeing this?'

"Yes, my son," she sighed.

"Amazing! You did all this so many years ago. You made this possible!" Peter stared at the sword hovering above the waters.

"No, son." she turned her face to him. "This is of the Dragon."

Peter furrowed his brow with confusion.

"I did not do this. I had much to atone for. I knew Bedlam was so powerful. I knew his power would grow and no one could stop him. No one, except the Dragon of the Forest."

"But how? Is all this done with magic?"

She earnestly shook her head and stood. "No. What you see before you is not magic, Peter" she explained. He came to her side. "The swords were not forged with magic. This is of the Dragon."

The sword continued to hover inside the gleaming blue light.

"This Sword of Truth came from the Dragon itself," she explained. "Magic comes from without. The Dragon's power is from within. Its power is inherent. It is a part of the Dragon forever...inseparable. That is what Bedlam could never understand, Peter. Lord Bedlam could never attain such power no matter how much magic he used or how many followed him."

Peter tilted his head. "But when you made the swords—"

"I had the swords taken to the Elfin elders in secret. They knew what to do. They sought the Dragon. Its power was secretly ingrained into each sword." She turned to him.

"Including your father's sword." She smiled. "That is why I was glad when you took the swords to the Elves, Peter."

"But you sacrificed your life." Peter looked down. "For me. For all of us."

"It was the only way." She turned to him and took his face into her hands. "Only because I knew that one day, here in the Dragon Forest, I could see you again. I knew one day we would have a chance to be together one more time."

Her green eyes sparkled as she smiled. Peter felt a warmth rush through his body.

"If only for a moment, I could see you again," she sighed. "I knew it had to be me to leave first."

Peter understood.

She swallowed back tears and turned her son around to the entrance. "Now you must go," she ordered. "You must find your father and tell him all that has happened."

They heard the roar again.

"But Lord Bedlam," Peter said. He could see the blue light reach into the sky. "He is still out there. He can see this light, too."

"Yes," she murmured. "It is the roar of the Black Dragon."

"How can that be?" Peter asked. "Mother, do not be afraid. He cannot enter this realm. The Dragon will not let him!"

She shook her head. "Peter, go now. You must find your father."

"But—"

She gently shoved him and motioned for him to leave. "Tavrith will help you. The Dragon of the Forest will protect you and me both. Now go!"

Peter cocked his head in confusion. "Will I see you again?"

"Yes," she nodded. "Now go!"

Peter ran and mounted a very nervous Tavrith who snorted fire from its nostrils. He nudged his dragon and together they soared out of the forest. He could feel the icy cold from the blue light as they flew close to it. Once above the forest, Peter could see the effects of the blue light. All the burned trees were healed as Peter and Tavrith soared above them. The trees were as green as ever. In the sky, the dark clouds began to dissolve and reveal the deep purple hues of the dawn.

*The Dragon will always be with you*, Peter heard his mother's voice near him. There is nothing to fear.

The White Owl flew past his right shoulder and circled above the trees. Peter felt no fear. He knew the Dragon would always be there for him. He knew all would be well.

# 44 THE BLACK DRAGON OF BEDLAM

"Over there!" Crispin pointed toward the forest. "Lord Bedlam!"

His friends turned to see the Black Dragon landing at the entrance of the Dragon Forest.

They looked at each other with wide eyes.

"Now what will happen?" Crispin asked.

Peter and Tavrith flew toward the Cardion Valley when Peter saw the Black Dragon near the entrance of the Dragon Forest. It roared and immediately transformed into Lord Bedlam. He leaned on his cane and began to make his way toward the entrance of the forest.

"What is he doing there?" Peter asked. "How can this be? The spell is broken. All the swords were placed into the lake. It is over!"

Peter narrowed his eyes. *Maybe it didn't work after all,* he thought. *Could it be true?* Peter pulled on the reins and ordered Tav to land. Peter sat atop his dragon for a moment. He covered his eyes with his hands. *No, it can't be true,* he thought. *The plan had to have worked! If not, all is lost. I have lost everything. The land will be in Bedlam's hands forever. We will all be his slaves.* He imagined Lord Bedlam destroying the Dragon Forest. *How can this be? Where is the Dragon?* Peter ran and followed Bedlam into the forest, but Peter hid within the thick of the trees so as not to be seen. He watched from behind a tree as Bedlam made his way further down the path to where the forest opens to the clearing. Peter could feel his own body tremble.

"Where is she?" Lord Bedlam demanded as he surveyed the trees. The sword inside the blue light slowly rotated above the lake. A few sparrows fluttered away.

"Here I am." Queen Laurien appeared feet away from Lord Bedlam. Peter watched the evil Lord's eyes. He could see a sudden calm appear on the man's face as soon as he saw the lovely Queen appear.

Bedlam took one step toward Laurien, and then stopped himself. His eyes traced her form. "I..." he hesitated. "I wanted to see you one last time."

Peter could see his mother's chest rise and fall as she stood before Lord Bedlam's powerful and almost hypnotic stare. He feared for her safety.

"I *needed* to see you one last time," Bedlam said.

The two stood in silence. Bedlam raised his arm to her, but Laurien remained still. Her eyes never left his face.

"You are as beautiful as I remembered," Bedlam said almost with regret.

She remembered the words of Theo from so long ago…

*"A very powerful magic spell will be cast while you and I live,"* Theo said. *"And a great number of rulers will succumb to its temptation."*

"I am much wiser than the young girl you once knew." Laurien narrowed her eyes.

Bedlam raised his chin and spread his arms wide. "As you can see, your plan did not work, Queen Laurien. I remain a man standing before you." He arrogantly bowed.

Peter watched his mother and grinned as though proud she did not fall for Bedlam's nonsense.

"And your son will now become my prisoner forever." Bedlam raised his dragonhead cane. He twisted it in his hands. "I told you, your majesty, that I would live to see everything that you love dearly succumb to my power and be utterly destroyed."

Peter turned to see his mother's reaction. He was startled to see her staring directly at him hiding there behind the tree. A slow smile came to her face. *I told you all is well,* she said to his thoughts. *There is nothing to fear.* And then her gaze returned to Bedlam as she remembered all that had happened…

*"What if you discovered tomorrow that all you knew to be real, wasn't?"* Theo asked Laurien.

*She squinted and searched Theo's face. "I would be…well, I would be devastated," she said.*

*"Exactly," he said. "And that is magic, my dear."*

"I did this," Laurien said to Bedlam. "I am the cause of all this death and destruction…all this devastation."

Bedlam narrowed his eyes and the skin on his face rippled like water. Some scales appeared then disappeared under his skin and his eyes glowed red.

"I did this because I trusted you," she said.

"You came to *me*, remember!" He thrust his finger at her.

"Because I thought you were wounded and needed my help!" she cried. "I didn't know your true intent was to harm me and many others."

"You weren't meant to drink the poison!" Bedlam yelled.

"I know," Laurien said.

"Then why? You knew the boy wouldn't die if he drank it!" Bedlam furrowed his brow. "You knew I couldn't kill him as long as the Dragon remains."

"No, he wouldn't die, but he wouldn't *live* either," she said. "And I wanted him to live and not remain in some stupor unable to feel anything or experience anything!"

Bedlam winced.

She pointed at him. "I wanted Peter to grow into the man who would one day defeat you," she said. "I wanted to see him become a great King, husband, and father."

Bedlam shook his head.

"And I knew if I drank the elixir, I would die, but I could still see him grow." Peter saw the tears stream down her face. "I could see it all from here." She raised her eyes and lifted her palms to the sky.

Bedlam growled. Peter could see the spikes of a dragon appear along his back.

"I knew because of the Dragon, I could remain here in the forest realm and still see Peter live." Her eyes returned to Peter. "And I did. I have seen him live his life!"

Peter watched her, realizing all that she did for him.

"No!" Bedlam roared, startling Peter.

"I caused all this!" Laurien yelled back, "I know this now. But it was because I trusted you as a young girl." She blinked back tears. "But I have learned my lesson about magic. Yes, I have learned and now it is time that *you* learn. That is why I needed to see *you* one last time as well, Bedlam."

He tilted his head.

"To say goodbye..." Laurien took a step back. "Forever."

Peter raised his eyebrows as he continued to watch the scene from behind the trees.

"No!" Lord Bedlam shouted and jabbed his finger at her. "It isn't over!"

"This is how it has to be," Laurien said, remembering Bedlam's words to her long ago.

"No! I won!" Lord Beldam rushed toward her, but the Dragon of the Forest appeared from behind Queen Laurien.

It stomped through the trees, sending them crashing to the ground like twigs, as it trampled toward Lord Bedlam. He staggered back at the sight of the mammoth Dragon.

"You dare enter into my realm, Bedlam!" The Dragon roared. Peter hid behind the tree and covered his ears.

Instantly, Bedlam transformed into the Black Dragon. Laurien disappeared into the mist and Peter ran to another tree, far from the fight he knew was coming.

"You have no place here!" The Dragon roared again. The Dragon of Bedlam flapped its wings and flew high above the Dragon Forest. The Great Dragon followed it.

§

"There! Above the trees!" Crispin pointed.

"Yes, I see them!" Annika watched as the two dragons flew out of the forest and landed on the ground near the entrance. The Dragon of Bedlam spewed its fire at the Dragon of the Forest, but it was to no avail. The scales of the Dragon were far too powerful. Bedlam jetted off and came at the Dragon from behind with its talons out to strike.

Annika covered her eyes with her hands.

But the Dragon swung its tail around and hit Bedlam sending it to the ground. It rose and flew off just missing the line of fire coming from the Dragon. Sir William stood by watching the scene, wondering where Peter could be. When he had a chance, he ran through the trees of the forest.

"Peter!" he cried out. Peter peeked out from behind the tree and ran toward the voice.

"Will!" he yelled when he saw his old friend. "What are you doing here?"

"Peter, come with me," Will motioned with his hand for Peter to follow him.

"The battle? My father? What has happened?" Peter asked.

"The battle is over, Peter!" Will took him by the shoulders. "But we need to get you to your father."

"Thank you, Will," Peter said.

"Come, we've got to get you to a safe place," Will turned to leave. They ran out of the forest to a clearing nearby.

Sir William and Peter stood by and watched as the dragons battled. Peter noticed Will was limping.

"You're wounded!" Peter said to him, but Will ignored him.

"Never mind me," Will insisted. "Come on!"

Thætil spotted Sir William leading Peter to safety.

The Dragon flew after Bedlam as it twisted and weaved through the air. The Dragon spewed its fire and blinded Bedlam. It hurtled to the ground, rolling several feet. The Dragon landed on top of Bedlam and held it down with its massive claws. Bedlam struggled to get free, but could not.

Peter and Will ran closer to the scene. The Dragon lowered its snout to face Bedlam once and for all.

"Surrender now," it said in that throaty but ominous voice. "Surrender to me now and join forces with the other dragons to live in peace with men."

Bedlam opened its jaws and roared. His eyes glowed.

"Join me," the Dragon repeated. "And I shall spare your life."

"Never!" Bedlam roared and his body flinched. "I'll never join you!"

The Dragon slowly shook its head with disgust.

"Still? After all you have endured? After all the pain you have caused, you refuse to relent?" the Dragon asked.

The Dragon of Beldam hissed and scoffed while he tried to claw at the Dragon holding it down.

Finally, the Dragon gazed around at the many knights, Elves, and soldiers gathering nearby with eyes filled with fear. Queen Esmeralda stood with Annika and the others, observing the entire spectacle. The Dragon returned its gaze to Bedlam, who struggled beneath it.

"All your powers are gone," the Dragon said. "You are but a dragon now. You can no longer transform into a man."

Bedlam's eyes widened when he realized what the Dragon meant.

"The spell has been severed forever," the Dragon continued. "All your fighters are scattered and lost. Your creature, Magog, has been destroyed."

Bedlam stopped struggling.

"You have nothing left," the Dragon said. "So, I ask you once again. Will you surrender to me, join forces with the other dragons to live in peace with men...or must I destroy you here and now?"

*Do it, Bedlam*, Peter thought to himself. *Surrender and live in peace as a dragon.*

"You want to destroy me!" Bedlam hissed. "You've wanted it all along!"

"I obtain no pleasure in the death of any dragon...good or evil," the Dragon said.

The Dragon of Bedlam's face contorted as it took in all that the Dragon had said. Peter couldn't breathe as he watched. Those nearby waited for Bedlam's answer.

But when Bedlam saw Peter standing by, its eyes glowed dark red once again and it sneered at him with rage and fury.

"Never!" Bedlam struggled to break free from the Dragon's grasp. "Never!"

The Dragon turned to Peter and their eyes met there in the field. The Dragon wanted Peter to know it gave Bedlam a chance to repent. Peter nodded that he understood. It was no use. Bedlam would never relent. Its hatred was too deeply ingrained.

The Dragon opened its jaws and bit deeply into the Dragon of Bedlam's throat and severed its head.

Annika gasped and turned her face away. She saw Peter far off and ran to him. He met her there and held her close. When they parted, they, along with everyone else, watched Bedlam's blood cover the ground. The fires over Hildron burned no more. The shrieks of the Gizor were heard as, one by one, they pummeled to the ground.

Peter closed his eyes with relief because he knew it was finally over. Evil...the darkness that had plagued their lands for so long... had finally been defeated there in the grassy hills outside the Dragon Forest.

Peter opened his eyes and looked up into the heavens as the dark clouds dissolved and the morning sun spread its new rays over the hills. He exhaled as he stood there with his friends and the Great Dragon of the Forest. Now everyone both near and far would know the truth.

The Dragon of the Forest had defeated evil once and for all. It remained loyal to its Oath.

# 45 THE SECRET OF THE DRAGON FOREST

Thætil ordered his Elves to stand at attention when the Dragon of the Forest trudged by. Its mammoth head reached high into the sky and the light reflected off its scales. Its tail swished along the ground. General Aluein came running with his men close behind. Queen Esmeralda approached the remains of the Dragon of Bedlam, the one that had her father killed, and tossed her father's ring on its headless carcass. She approached its severed head.

"Good riddance," she said. She kicked the severed head, turned on her heel, and walked away. Peter and Annika observed the act.

"It's so tragic how many lives were ruined by Bedlam's lies and trickery," Annika said. The two began to walk toward their friends when they saw Will collapse.

"No!" Peter cried as he ran to his friend. Peter knelt by Will and took his hand. It was wet with blood.

"Peter," Will whispered. Blood seeped from the corner of his mouth.

"Hold on!" he said. He squeezed Will's hand. "Simon! Bring me the healing powder, quick!"

Simon removed the leather pouch from his belt and handed it to Peter.

Will closed his eyes. "Peter," he said in a weak voice. But Peter placed some of the powder between Will's lips.

"Hold on, Will," Peter motioned for Annika to bring him some water. "You'll see. Drink this water and it will help you—"

"Peter," Will muttered again. "…your father."

Peter leaned in to hear. "My father?"

"Find him," Will said. "Tell him that I beg his forgiveness for…for everything."

Peter looked up at Simon and Crispin with desperate eyes. They understood the silent order, nodded, and then ran off to find King

Alexander.

"We will find him and bring him to you," Peter said to his friend. "Hold on, Will. We'll get you to the surgeon. You'll be—"

"No," Will interrupted. "Peter..."

"But..." Peter thought of the death of Sir Nøel. He shook his head. "Please don't go," he said. "I need you to be my Head Knight. I can't do this without you. I can't rule a land without your help."

Will coughed up blood. "You will be a great King of Illiath, Peter."

Peter closed his eyes. He knew the life was leaving Will's body.

"Please..." Will's voice was barely above a whisper, "tell my father that I love him. I pray he can forgive me for all that I have done."

Peter nodded. "I will," he said. "I will find your father and tell him everything."

"Peter, forgive me for—"

Peter looked into his friend's eyes and squeezed his hand. "Will, rest easy, my friend. You have proven to be one of my father's greatest knights here on this battlefield."

Will closed his eyes and smiled. "Thank you, Peter."

Peter buried his head in Will's chest and sobbed as his friend breathed his last breath.

Annika wiped the tears from her eyes with her hand. She turned to see Crispin and Simon running toward her. She could see the shock on their ashen faces.

"Peter," Simon knelt by his friend and gently placed his hand on Peter's shoulder. "Peter, you must come with us."

"Did you find my father?" Peter asked Simon. Then, he looked over at Crispin who had tears streaming down his face.

"Peter," Crispin wept. "Please, you need to come with us. Now."

Peter's eyes grew large and he looked over at Annika.

"My father!" Peter shouted as he took off running across the fields. He could see Sir Rohan standing and waving to Peter. Peter couldn't breathe as he ran to where Sir Rohan beckoned. With everything that had happened, he never once feared for his own father. Peter froze when he saw Sir Rohan kneel down by the King's weakened body. The grass was stained red with his blood. At first, Peter thought he was too late, but then he saw King Alexander extend his trembling hand toward him.

"Father!" Peter grabbed it and squeezed it tight. He could see the light in his father's eyes begin to dim. "I'm here now. I'm here, father. All is well."

"Peter...your time in the forest...tell me all that happened," Alexander asked his son.

Peter leaned in and told his father about how he had made a pact with Thætil and the Elves to protect the swords at all costs. He explained how he had used the box as a decoy to fool Bedlam. Peter went on to describe how he had made it to the center of the forest where he saw his mother and how he had placed all the swords onto the surface of the lake as instructed and how they had formed the one magnificent sword, the Sword of Truth, which would guard the forest forever.

Alexander closed his eyes and sighed as he listened. Finally, Peter went on to tell his father how the Dragon had defeated Bedlam and peace had been returned to the land.

"It is over, father," Peter said. "War is finally over."

"Finally," Alexander whispered. Then, he opened his eyes and tried to sit up. Sir Rohan helped him. Alexander took Peter's hand. "Son," he said. "You did well."

"Yes, father," Peter said. "I couldn't allow Bedlam to intercept the swords. And then I remembered how mother had trusted the Elves by taking the swords to them, and I knew I had to do the same."

Alexander tried to smile. "I am so proud of you, son. I knew you could do this task."

Peter bowed his head.

"Now, Peter," Alexander said.

Peter leaned in. "Yes, father," he replied.

"I want you to listen carefully to me." Alexander nodded to the Dragon Forest. "Peter, now that peace has come to the land and the spell is over; it is time for you to learn everything about the Dragon Forest."

Peter narrowed his eyes in confusion. "Everything about the forest?"

Alexander nodded at his son. "Look, Peter, look now all around you..."

Peter blinked a few times, and then turned to inspect the scene around him. There, in the fields of battle, Peter saw the spirits of his father's men rise from their remains. Peter's eyes widened. Each of his father's knights who had died in battle rose in spirit, dressed in the finest golden armor with capes flowing in the breeze. They greeted one another with laughter and headed to the Dragon Forest where Peter saw them walk inbetween the trees, disappearing from view.

Peter turned to his father whose face was gleaming.

"This could only have happened once the darkness was completely gone, Peter," Alexander told him. "Thanks to you, Peter, the day has come."

Peter understood.

"Turn around, my son," Alexander said.

Peter obeyed and watched as Sir William's spirit rose from his remains. Peter's mouth dropped open. Will stood and gazed down at his arms and legs covered in the golden armor. He looked over and saw Peter. He waved to him. Peter raised his hand to wave back, but froze in shock at the sight of his friend's spirit. Will stepped over his dead body and joined with the other knights dressed in the similar armor. Together, they turned to walk off. Peter watched them as they entered the Dragon Forest. Peter laughed through his tears.

"Father! This is amazing!" Peter shouted as he watched the spirits head toward the forest.

Finally, Alexander gently tugged on Peter's shoulder. Peter turned his face toward his father again, and, when he did, he gasped. Before him stood the gleaming spirit of Sir Nøel dressed in golden armor. Peter slowly stood and faced his long lost friend one last time. Sir Nøel grinned just as he always had done when they were together at Rünbrior prison.

"I hoped we'd see each other again," Sir Nøel said. Peter laughed and wiped his tears. "I always knew you were meant for more than dragon battles in the arena, Peter."

"Sir Nøel...I can't believe it's you here again," Peter wanted to touch his friend, but hesitated. "There's so much I wanted to say...I wanted to thank you for all that you did for me in that prison."

Sir Nøel looked behind Peter at the Dragon Forest. "I know I said I didn't believe you about the Dragon, Peter," he said. "But I did. I guess I was just too proud to admit it."

Peter grinned.

"This is the secret of the Dragon Forest, Peter," Alexander said to him. Peter knelt down beside his father and took his hand once again. "Only those chosen may enter its realm. These few are the guardians of the forest." Peter saw many Elves also rise in spirit and walk side by side with the spirits of his father's soldiers and knights as they entered the forest realm. "They have given their lives to defend it. Peter, you have been chosen as its protector," his father said.

Peter swallowed back tears.

"I have been chosen, too," Alexander said. "And now, it is time for me to enter."

"No, father!" he shouted. Peter's face turned pale and he shook his head. He squeezed his father's hand. "We can give you the healing powder and get you to the surgeon. You will be well again! You'll see. You will be well again and stay here with me! Together we—"

But Alexander sighed. "The wound is far too deep. I fear nothing can save me now."

But Peter frantically took some powder from his pouch and carefully placed it onto his father's dry lips. "Here, father. Try this," Peter cried.

Alexander smiled at his son and feebly moved Peter's hand away. Peter closed his eyes in defeat and bowed his head. He wept as his father spoke.

"I have lived my life as knight and as King and I was rewarded with a noble heir. Now, it is time for me to go so that you can rule as the King you were meant to be." He rubbed his hand through Peter's thick brown hair. "I love you son, more than you will ever know." He gently kissed the top of Peter's head and breathed deeply.

Peter looked into Alexander's teary eyes. "I love you, father."

Alexander sighed when he heard the words. "I am so very proud of you," he said. "You will be a great King. Far greater than I ever was."

Peter winced. "No, don't say such things."

"Rule with fairness, Peter," Alexander looked at Thætil standing nearby, "and your people will respect you. Work together with all men, Elves, and dragons to live in peace."

Thætil bowed to the King.

"For that's how it was meant to be," Alexander said. Peter agreed.

"I will," Peter cried. "Please don't leave me."

Alexander touched his son's chin and traced his face with his finger.

"I'm afraid," Peter said. "I'm so afraid. I can't do this without you."

Alexander smiled. "You can do far more than you think you can. Don't ever be afraid, Peter. You will never be alone. And when you are uncertain, come to the Dragon Forest. That is where you get your strength. Always keep it in view."

Peter remembered what his mother had told him.

"I will, father. I will."

"The Dragon is the defender of the weak. It will give you strength when you think you cannot go on. It never grows tired or weary," Alexander said.

"Yes, father," Peter kissed his father's hand. "I understand this now."

"Good," Alexander sighed. "Now I can go rest in peace."

And with that, King Alexander, great ruler of all peoples of Illiath, closed his eyes forever. He took in one last breath and died there on the battlefield with his son by his side. Peter felt his father's hand go limp and then fall to the ground.

"No, father," Peter lay his head on his father's chest and hugged his body close. "No, don't leave me."

Annika knelt next to Peter and rubbed his back. General Aluein bowed his head and even wiped away a tear. Marek, Sir Rohan, Thætil, and his Elves knelt down in respect. One by one, all the King's soldiers knelt down in the grassy field outside the Dragon Forest as the grass shimmered in the sun.

"Long live the King," one soldier cried.

"Yes, long live the King," Aluein said.

The land around them grew silent. No one dared to move as Peter continued to hold his father.

"Don't leave me, father," Peter whispered again. "Please don't leave me. I'm afraid. I don't know if I can do this without you. Please don't go."

Annika wept with him.

"Please," Peter cried. "Not now. I need you. Please stay with me."

"I will never leave you," he heard a strong voice say.

"What?" Peter looked up and saw his father's spirit standing next to Sir Nøel and many of his knights. King Alexander wore the golden armor with his golden crown resting upon his head. His scarlet cape waved in the breeze.

Peter blinked in amazement then looked deep into his Alexander's bright eyes.

"We will always be here for you, my son." King Alexander turned and pointed to the entrance of the Dragon Forest. Peter stood when he saw his mother's frame at the entrance. She waved to him. Her long red gown danced in the breeze. Peter watched as his father made his way toward the Queen. Surrounding her were the past rulers: Théadron son of Ulrrig, Byron son of Gundrehd, Hildron the Mighty, Niahm son of Egan, Glaussier the Brave, Queen Ragnalla and King Aidan of Vulgaard. They stood by to escort Alexander into the forest.

Peter took a few steps to make sure he could see them both clearly. King Alexander made it to his bride then abruptly stopped before he reached her. He studied her face for a moment. Queen Laurien was crying and laughing at the same time. She raised her hand to her mouth and shook her head in disbelief. Alexander knelt before her and took her hand into his.

"My Queen," he said.

They were still for a moment, remembering each other's faces. Alexander kissed her hand, then rose and embraced his Queen, lifting her high off the ground and twirling her around. Annika laughed tears of joy while she watched. Peter turned to her and took her hand.

§

Alexander put Laurien down and the two kissed deeply. When they parted, they started to walk toward Peter who ran over to them with Annika. When they reached his mother and father, Peter and Annika bowed their heads.

Alexander lifted his wife's hand to his lips and kissed it once again. He turned to Peter. "My son," he said. "We will always watch over you."

"Yes, Peter," Laurien said with shiny eyes. "Always."

Peter understood.

Above them came the White Dragon swooping down. It landed and abruptly transformed intoTheo. He approached the scene grinning. He sighed as he remembered Laurien as a young girl scampering through the palace at Vulgaard, not yet knowing what her role would be in her own future.

Queen Laurien grinned at him. "Theo, you old dragon," she chuckled.

He bowed then looked up at her with eyes brimming with tears. "You have done well, my Queen," he nodded at Peter. "Very well."

"And when you become King, Peter," Laurien continued, "rule as your father did with all fairness and dignity."

Peter listened.

"And when you marry…" Alexander looked at Annika. "Lead your wife and children with all love and patience."

Peter turned to Annika and nodded.

"Oh, Peter. You will be a wonderful father one day," his mother said. "I look forward to watching you become the man you were meant to be."

"Never forget all that has happened, my son," Alexander said. "Learn from the past but do not dwell on it. Theo will remain to instruct you and Darion will assist you for as long as he can."

"Yes, father," Peter said. He squeezed Annika's hand. "I understand."

"Now go," Alexander said. "There is much work to be done. Much healing remains."

Peter stepped toward his parents. The Queen raised her hand to stop him. "One day, we will all be together again." she smiled as she turned to the King. "But not yet."

"Good bye, my son," Alexander began to walk off. "We will always love you."

Peter felt his eyes burn with tears again. "Goodbye, mother and father."

He watched them as they made their way, arm in arm, toward the Dragon Forest with all the rulers of the past surrounding them. Near them appeared the spirit of King Aléon, Alexander's father. They watched as Alexander once again lifted Laurien up off the ground and twirled her around. She threw her head back and laughed like a young girl. And then, Alexander carried his Queen into the Dragon Forest where they disappeared from view. A flock of white doves burst from the treetops and flew off into the morning sun.

Peter stood there in silence with Annika for a moment. He turned to her and met her eyes with his. Her lovely faced calmed him.

"Annika, I cannot do this great task alone," he said.

Annika nodded to him. Her blue eyes shone.

"But with you by my side, I know I can do anything." He knelt before her and took both her hands into his own. "Will you be by my side as my wife, as my Queen, and help me rebuild this kingdom?" He kissed her hands.

Annika wept and nodded enthusiastically. "Yes," she giggled. "Yes, of course I will!"

Peter rose and embraced her in his arms. "I love you so," he whispered into her ear. When they parted they heard applause behind them. They turned to see Simon, Crispin, Thætil, and Eris, along with many of the Elves of Vulgaard, Queen Esmeralda, and the surviving soldiers clapping for Peter and Annika. Annika covered her mouth in embarrassment. Theo turned toward them. He had a sheepish grin on his face as he placed his hand on Peter's shoulder.

"Well, done, my boy," he chuckled.

"Thank you, my old friend." Peter touched Theo's hand. "Will you be transforming into the White Dragon again?"

Theo shook his head. "Of course!" he sighed. "The Dragon has allowed me to remain as both dragon and man."

Simon and Crispin approached as Theo made his announcement.

"What's this?" Simon asked with a serious tone.

Theo turned to face his former students. "It is true." He looked at the youths standing before him. "The Dragon has allowed me to remain as a dragon and a man."

Peter raised his eyebrows. "Really?"

"Yes." Theo stepped back and moved his thin hands over his robe. "I am forever at your service." He bowed.

Simon, Crispin, Annika, and Peter all gathered around Theo and congratulated him with pats on the back and the shaking of his hand. Theo appeared to be overwhelmed at first.

At that moment, the White Owl took off and circled above them all. Peter was the first to see it. "Look there, in the sky above," he said, pointing to the sky.

When everyone gathered to see the White Owl flying, it changed into the Dragon and continued to circle above them all.

"So beautiful," Annika said.

The morning sun reflected on the Dragon's mystical scales and made them sparkle.

The Dragon landed in the field, snorted, and folded its wings onto its body. Its long tail swished along the ground as though waving Peter over. He made his way to his old friend and gently rubbed its snout. Thætil took the reins of his dragon and walked it over to the Dragon of the Forest. Many of his Evles did the same with their dragons. Soon, the Great Dragon of the Forest was surrounded by grateful people, Elves, and dragons, all eager to hear what it had to say.

"On this somber day after war," it said, "I renew my promise to live in peace with all who respect the Oath I made with man."

All present looked at one another and nodded in agreement.

"It was here that your forefathers swore to protect the Dragon Forest at all cost," it said. "And I swore to protect them."

Peter watched its eyes as it spoke, remembering how saddened he had been when it had died in the fields. Now, the carcass of the Dragon of Bedlam lay nearby because of the Dragon of the Forest and its faithfulness to its promise. Peter leaned in and put his head against the Dragon's body as it spoke. He closed his eyes and listened to its massive heartbeat. It once gave him great comfort as a child and he found that it still continued to do so.

"Now we must come together and restore the peace that was lost," it said. "All must come together to help."

The dragons reared up, flapped their wings, and roared when they heard the Dragon speak. Their eyes glowed and their nostrils flared. Some thrust their chests out and dug at the ground with their claws.

Peter sensed the dragons' joy. His thoughts scattered. He was too excited to think at the moment.

Thætil, with his deep blue eyes gleaming, turned to his Elves then approached the Dragon. He lowered his head respectfully.

"Il illiëndren ünd ish èl Elöin," he said in his language. "Théadril, Théadron, Illiath, Vulgaard, I ülrigg Thætil intriënde ül illiésh dür ünd örguen illündrén dir."

All the Elves applauded and whooped loudly when Thætil said the words of his people. He had sworn to all the surviving rulers of the lands that he and his Elves would uphold the Oath forever. Peter nodded and felt the warmth of joy throughout his body. Everything was becoming more and more real to him. He knew it was time for him to speak to all present. He swallowed and exhaled through his mouth.

"The scales of the Dragon are more powerful than any weapon forged by man," Peter began. "Many men will try to obtain those scales. But we must continue to protect the Dragon. As the Dragon has always been faithful to the Oath, so must we remain faithful."

Everyone stared at Peter and then moved their glances to the Dragon.

"We've much to do," Peter continued. "And I promise that when I am King of Illiath, I will uphold the Oath as my father did." Peter's voice cracked.

Annika stepped toward him and extended her hand.

"Together," she whispered.

Peter took her hand and gently squeezed it. He mouthed the words *thank you* to her.

All the people applauded and the dragons roared as the sun rose that new morning. The looming fires of Hildron no longer burned in the distance. The Dragon changed into the White Owl and flew to the waiting arm of the Elf who had helped raise it and risked his life for it long ago in the forests of Vulgaard. The Elder Elf, Thuriel, his son, Eliel, and his youngest son, Oliel, all stood by in spirit form. They ambled off together into the Dragon Forest and disappeared from view.

Peter stood with his arms around his friends as they watched the new day begin. Many lives had been lost, many lives had been shattered, but peace had come to the region once again. Peace that no one would ever take for granted again.

# 46 THE CORONATION OF THE KING

The time had come for the many funerals honoring the fallen who had given their lives to defend the kingdom of Théadril against Lord Bedlam. The somber villagers from the Cornshire held their funerals and memorials in the rolling green hills near where the palace at Illiath once stood. Lady Silith and Lady Godden returned to their lands to rule over the peace. Lord Byrén did not survive to return to the Crow Valley, but General Aluein's son, Sir Roen, took over as leader. Constable Darion made his way back to Illiath and was grieved when he heard of the passing of King Alexander.

King Beatann of Beamoor returned to his land in the south east region, but he sent workers to assist in the rebuilding of the palace at Illiath. King Isleif was buried in a grand procession to his palace at Gundrehd in the north. King Mildrir mourned Isleif even though they rarely got along. He hated to see the brave King die so young. To everyone's amazement, Isleif had named Crispin to be the heir to the throne in a testament he had signed before he went to battle. Soon, Crispin would join Peter as a newly crowned King.

Queen Esmeralda returned to her palace at Glaussier in the south by the east seashore. Although she cared for King Isleif deeply, they never declared their love for one another. But she chose never to marry after the war with Bedlam, choosing instead to love her people as her children.

King Ronahn, the true heir of Hildron, gladly made his way back to the palace where his father and grandfather had once ruled before Lord Bedlam took over the land. His brother, Sir Rohan, served as his Head Knight. All were glad to never see the fires burning at Hildron again and the people of the Crow Valley felt safe.

King Baldrieg of Glenthryst happily met with Peter to secure his granddaughter, Annika's hand in marriage. She would be crowned as Queen Annika soon. He also sent assistance to help rebuild the palace for Peter.

Finally, Thætil returned to Vulgaard with his Elfin warriors with the grave task of returning Thurdin's body to his mother, the Queen. Thætil dreaded the thought of informing his sister, Queen Thordis that not only was her son dead, but that he had fallen to Lord Bedlam's spell and turned against the Oath. But before he departed, he did promise to send assistance to Peter to rebuild the palace. He also promised many Elfin warriors to serve as guards for Peter's castle. The Elves of Vulgaard were known throughout the world for their honor and excellence in fighting. Peter knew this was a most impressive gesture of trust and confidence Thætil could have ever bestowed upon Peter. Dangler, the Dragon Master, was to remain at Vulgaard to help train dragons. Peter missed his old friend, but understood.

A proclamation went out through all the lands announcing that Prince Peter would immediately be crowned King so that Illiath would finally have its ruler. This proclamation was greatly received and anticipated by the surviving rulers.

§

A late autumn breeze swept across the golden fields of barley that afternoon. Peter, dressed in his finest armor with the scarlet cape of his father snapping in the breeze, stood at the gravesite of his mother and father. He raised his face to the warm sun and breathed in the scent of nearby lavender. He could hear the sound of footsteps approaching him from behind.

"Prince Peter," Constable Darion said. "It is time."

Peter nodded without facing him. His eyes returned to the headstone of his father, King Alexander, chiseled out of limestone.

"He was my age when he became King, wasn't he?" Peter asked.

"He was slightly older," Darion replied.

Peter bent down and placed a bunch of wildflowers he had picked onto his mother's grave.

"She loved wildflowers," he said as he carefully adjusted them.

Darion looked up at the pale blue sky and then back at Peter. "Yes. Yes, she did."

Peter stood and stepped back, admiring the graves side by side. "I like that they are together again."

"Yes," Darion smiled. "So do I."

"That's how it should be," Peter said and turned toward the Dragon Forest in the north. Even at a distance, Peter could see the dark green trees bending in the breeze.

Darion nodded.

Peter came toward his old friend and placed his hand on Darion's shoulder. "Alright, Constable," he sighed. "I believe I am finally ready."

§

The trumpets sounded and all the guests turned to face the entrance of the grand hall of King Mildrir's palace. Since the palace at Illiath was being rebuilt, Mildrir offered his palace at Thorgest in the east for Peter's coronation ceremony. It was a most thoughtful gesture. One that Peter knew was meant more for his father than for him since Mildrir and Alexander were very close.

A red carpet ran along the floor of the Chapel and ended where the newly made gilded throne of Illiath sat surrounded by dozens of candelabras. The throne was a gift from King Beatann of Beamoor since Alexander's throne was destroyed by Bedlam. Dozens of burning candles illuminated the room. The glistening light reflected off the polished marble floors and gilded molding all around the room.

Annika stared dreamily at the lit candles flickering. The partially lit nave of the Chapel lined with several marble statues of previous Kings took on a somber tone.

"What are you thinking?" Crispin leaned over and whispered to her.

She turned to him with a wide smile. "About how Peter will soon be a King."

"Is that really what you were thinking?" He smirked at her.

Annika shrugged. "Alright, I was also thinking about my wedding to Peter that is to come."

Crispin nudged her. "Thought so."

"I hope that the Chapel at the palace at Illiath will be ready for our wedding ceremony," she said.

The doors swung open, silencing everyone in the room. Kings and rulers from the outer lands stood alongside the red carpet ready to watch Prince Peter enter the room for his coronation. Each wore their ceremonial robes representing their lands. Queen Thordis and her brother, Thætil stood opposite Annika, Crispin, and Simon, regally adorned in their royal robes. Eris attended as well, but instead of leather armor, she wore a silvery linen gown with her long white hair loose on her shoulders. Annika grabbed Crispin's arm and hopped up and down.

"Everyone is here. This is so exciting," she said.

"Calm down," he whispered.

The drummers played their drums and the trumpets blared signaling the procession was beginning. First, King Mildrir entered the room dressed in his armor and cape. In his hands, he held the scepter of Illiath and the crown King Alexander had worn. All eyes were upon him as he made his way to the throne. He stood on the left side of the throne and then turned to face the entrance. When he did, all guests then turned to see Peter enter the grand hall.

The trumpets blared again to announce Peter's arrival. He stood in the entrance in his armor with the royal scarlet robe of Illiath with its train trailing behind him. Around his neck lay the necklace Queen Thordis had bestowed upon him after he was knighted at her palace. Peter wore it as a reminder that he will always remain the link that unites the Royal Knights in his kingdom. He swallowed hard when he saw so many eyes staring at him. He inhaled, and then took his first steps toward becoming King.

As he walked toward the throne, he saw Annika beaming with pride next to a snickering Crispin who had bet Simon a few gold coins that Peter would trip over the long train of his robe. Peter remembered the bet and consciously watched where he placed his feet until he was finally in front of the throne. At his feet was a stool for him to kneel upon. A squire came to his side to take his sword. Peter removed it from its sheath and handed it to the boy. The Sword of Peter left his hand as a sword of a prince, but would return to him as the sword of a king.

Peter then knelt on the cushioned stool and winced. It was difficult to kneel in the stiff armor, so Peter hoped the ceremony wouldn't take too long. King Mildrir smirked as he approached Peter carrying the scepter and crown.

"Your majesties, Lords, and Ladies," Mildrir began in a loud voice that echoed throughout the hall. "I present before you King Peter of Illiath, your undoubted King. You who are present are here to pay homage and service to the King. What say you?"

"Long live the King," the people proclaimed as one voice.

"Your majesty." Mildrir turned his countenance toward the kneeling King. "Are you prepared to take the oath?"

"I am willing," Peter said.

"Will you govern your people according to their lands and customs?" King Mildrir asked.

"I solemnly promise to do so," Peter said. He swallowed as he remembered his father dubbing him a knight at Vulgaard.

"Will you cause law, justice, and mercy to be executed in all your judgments?"

"I will," Peter answered.

"As King, will you swear before all peoples present from the outer lands this day that you will uphold the Oath made with the Dragon of the Forest sworn by your forefathers?"

Peter looked up at the tapestry that hung behind the throne. It depicted the day the Great Dragon of Promise swore the Oath with all the people near Vulgaard.

"I will," he said.

Annika wiped a tear away as she squeezed Simon's arm. He gently patted her hand.

"Rise and be seated," King Mildrir stepped aside to allow Peter to take the throne. Peter rose, took the Sword of Peter from his squire, and placed it back into its sheath. It was now the sword of a king that would be handed down to generations.

Peter exhaled and walked toward his throne. He sat down as two peasant maidens from the Cornshire adjusted the long train of his robe. King Mildrir stepped in front of Peter holding the scepter and crown. He handed Peter the scepter and he took it. Then, Peter gazed out into the crowd of people staring at him and cleared his throat.

"These things which I have sworn before the presence of witnesses, I will faithfully perform and keep as King," he said.

Mildrir raised the crown and stepped toward Peter until the crown hovered over his head. Annika held her breath as she watched King Mildrir lower the golden crown onto the head of Peter. It rested perfectly right above his eyes. Mildrir stepped aside.

"Having sworn these solemn oaths, know that I, King Mildrir of Thorgest, by right of arms do crown you King Peter."

Peter stood and waited.

"Your Majesties, Lords, and Ladies, and the people of Illiath, I present to you your King. The King of Illiath," he said. The trumpets blared again.

"Long live the King!" the crowd proclaimed again and then applauded vigorously throughout.

Constable Darion wiped a few tears away. Theo turned to him.

"Emotional, Darion?" Theo asked.

"I've waited so long for this day," he wept. "From the day he was born, I imagined it." Theo hugged Darion's shoulder.

Peter began his procession down the red carpet carrying his scepter. The two maidens adjusted his robe as he walked by the spectators.

Annika clapped and cheered as Peter strolled by. "You see?" she said. "He didn't trip."

"He did during rehearsal," Crispin smirked.

"You owe me ten gold coins," Simon whispered to Crispin who nudged him away.

"Now we go eat," Crispin said as he rubbed his hands together.

Annika rolled her eyes. "That's all you think about."

"At my coronation next month, there will be so much food," he said as he headed toward the dining hall, but Annika stopped him.

Crispin, Annika, and Simon rushed to the entrance hall to greet their friend as King. Peter handed the scepter to Constable Darion for safe keeping and then waited as the maidens removed his long robe.

"Oh, thank goodness," Peter sighed. "That robe was cumbersome."

"Peter!" Annika ran up to him. "I mean, your majesty." She humbly curtsied before him.

Simon and Crispin bowed with respect then vigorously shook his hands loosening the crown on his head. Peter grabbed it before it fell off.

"Good catch," Thætil said. He helped adjust the crown on Peter's head. "You'll grow into it, your majesty."

Peter and his friends laughed as more of the guests came to congratulate him. Afterwards, everyone enjoyed the food and wine well into the next day. Peter and his throne traveled back to Illiath where he would oversee the construction of his palace.

# 47 THE WEDDING OF THE KING

Over three years had passed and Théadril began to heal. The palace built for King Peter rose south of the Blue River and sat majestically on top of a hill of Illiath facing the Dragon Forest. The limestone bricks shone in the morning sun and could be seen from miles around with its many tall spires reaching high into the sky. Many parts of the palace remained incomplete, but Peter was able to settle into the castle to rule.

It was proclaimed that on his seventeenth birthday Prince Peter was to marry his beloved Annika in the Chapel of his palace. Constable Darion overlooked the planning of the festivities. After a harsh winter, the people were more than ready to enjoy the warmth of springtime that had finally come.

People of the Cornshire and the Cardion Valley anticipated the grand celebration after they had suffered so much loss and pain. Darion planned a weeklong celebration of Peter's wedding and also his triumphs over Lord Bedlam with games, jousts, and fireworks. The Elves of Vulgaard flew in on dragons and allowed the peasant children to ride the young dragons around the courtyard.

It was a bright clear afternoon as Annika stood nearby, observing the little children atop the young dragons being led by the Elfin trainers. A newly crowned King Crispin came alongside her followed by Simon. Crispin munched on a fire roasted turkey leg.

"Your majesty." Annika curtsied before Crispin.

Crispin bowed in return.

"It is fitting that these children learn to respect and not fear the dragons," Annika said. "One day they, too, will ride on the backs of dragons over Théadril."

"Absolutely," Simon replied.

Crispin mumbled something. Annika turned to see him chomping into the turkey leg.

"Honestly, King Crispin." Annika rolled her eyes. "Is eating all you do anymore?"

He shook his head and swallowed. "No, of course not. I am also learning to cook!" He rubbed his full belly. He inhaled deeply. "Just smell all the delicious food."

"Oh, wonderful." Simon smirked. They turned toward the palace courtyard. Simon lifted his eyes. "I see that the outer walls of the palace are complete."

"Yes, Peter has been working hard with the builders to make sure every part of the palace is finished on time," Annika explained. Little children raced by her with kites. "It is wonderful to have the courtyard open for the people again. It has been too long."

Once inside the grand entrance hall, the three friends found a frantic Constable Darion commanding the servants.

"And make certain food is on the tables at all times!" he shouted. They could see the light in his eyes.

"Excited for the wedding, Constable?" Simon asked.

Darion rolled his eyes. "It cannot come soon enough," he sighed. "Whose idea was it to have these celebrations last all week?"

Simon raised his eyebrows.

"Oh yes." Darion squinted and rubbed his forehead. "It was my idea, wasn't it?

They all laughed together.

"And where can we find Sir Peter?" Crispin asked as he placed the now meatless turkey leg onto the tray of a passing servant.

§

As the three friends made their way down the staircase of the secret passage, they were amazed at how familiar it was to them. Peter used his memory to construct all the secret hidden rooms underneath the castle.

Simon removed a burning torch from the sconce and led them down the remaining steps to where they saw the light from a room cutting through the darkness. As they approached the doorway, they could hear Peter laughing.

"What's happening in here?" Simon asked when he opened the door. He pretended to be upset. Peter sat with his feet on the large wooden table polished to a shine. Bookcases lined the walls and Professor Theodore Sirus III sat in a chair across from Peter.

"Welcome!" Peter turned in his chair and waved his friends into the room. "We were just reminiscing about our time here at the palace."

Crispin walked over to the table and picked up the pitcher of wine.

"Some wine your majesty?" he asked Peter. He bowed.

Peter lifted his glass of wine. "I have all I need, thank you, your majesty."

"Do tell, what stories were you sharing this time?" Crispin asked. He poured some wine into a crystal glass and sat at the table.

"The time when Peter was late to class?" Simon asked as he sat down.

"Which time was that? There were so many." Annika sat down next to Peter.

Crispin poured a glass of wine for Simon. "Or, perhaps the time Peter tried to beat me in chess," Simon said as he took the glass of wine from Crispin.

"No, that was me," Crispin said. He raised his glass in a mock toast to Simon.

"We were discussing the time when we all went fishing that last summer and we all were late for our lesson," Peter said.

"I beg your pardon!" Annika sat straight. "But I was on time that day."

"This is true," Theo said. He removed is dragon head pipe from his robe and tapped it onto his palm. "From what I remember, it was only you boys who were ever late to my lessons." Theo cleared his throat and leered over at Annika who grinned with approval.

They all laughed at that and drank more wine together in the room. Peter searched the bookcases with a somber look on his face. So many books were missing from the shelves. The emptiness was a glaring reminder of all that was lost. Theo could see the sorrow in Peter's eyes.

"Don't worry," Theo said as he searched for a match in his pockets. "Books can be rewritten with time."

Peter agreed. "You are correct. I will ensure the history of Théadril is preserved and all that we have endured will be recorded."

Peter watched as Theo searched his pockets. "No need for a match old friend. Remember?"

Crispin chuckled. "Yes, simply spew your dragon fire and light the pipe on your own, eh?"

Simon chortled.

Theo spewed a thin line of fire and lit his pipe. He puffed a few puffs of silvery smoke into the air and grinned in triumph.

"I'll never grow tired of seeing that!" Crispin laughed.

"Ah, vanilla," Annika said once the scent reached her.

Theo nodded to her. Another long snake-like wisp of smoke rose from the pipe.

"I'm glad I do not have to use matches again," Theo said. He raised his pipe and nodded to his former students. "Now, when is the grand ceremony, Sir Peter?"

Peter looked at Annika who beamed with pride.

"Day after tomorrow," he said.

"Are you excited?" Simon asked.

"Are you petrified?" Crispin leaned in. "I would be."

Annika frowned. "So would I if I had to marry you!"

Crispin tossed his head back and roared with laughter.

"I'm terrified enough of being King, but marrying?" Crispin admitted. "I never planned on ruling the people, marrying, and fathering children." His face contorted as though in agony.

"None of us ever really thought about one day ruling our lands," Simon said, "except Peter."

"Yes, Peter was always well aware of his destiny," Annika said.

"I suppose I should be a little hesitant," Peter said. He ran his fingers along the smooth table top until he found Annika's hand. He caressed it. "But I am at peace about everything now."

"Good," Theo stood. "You should be at peace. All of you will make excellent leaders one day."

Crispin grinned sheepishly.

"Even you, Crispin." Theo chortled as he gave Crispin a stern look.

"Why did he say that?" Crispin asked Simon who shrugged.

"Come now, let us rejoin in the wedding festivities. I look forward to the ceremony, King Peter. I have looked forward to it for many years," Theo said.

As they all left the room and began to head up the stairs, Peter hesitated in the doorway for a second.

"What is it, Peter?" Theo asked.

Peter gazed up the stairs that disappeared into the darkness of the passageway. "I'm trying to take it all in, Theo."

"And?"

"Crispin's right. I should be terrified. In a few days I shall not only be King of Illiath, but a husband," Peter held his breath.

"Aye, and you will be a great—"

"And one day a father," Peter interrupted. He wiped off the sweat that had accumulated on his forehead. He gazed into the darkness ahead.

"Peter." Theo turned toward him. "As you gaze into the dark passageway, the unknown can appear to be frightening. Yes?"

Peter gulped and nodded.

"To us all, the unknown is frightening." Theo furrowed his brow,

"Much like standing at the entrance to the Dragon Forest as a young boy, or standing in the grand arena at Rünbrior about to face a fire breathing dragon."

Peter continued to stare at the darkened steps ahead. Theo hugged his shoulder.

"And yet, you faced the unknown before with strength and courage," Theo said as he scratched his long white beard. "Yes, the unknown is terrifying sometimes. But, trust me, you are ready."

Peter crinkled his face. For a moment, he resembled the small boy Theo remembered from years before.

"I am completely certain that you are ready to rule Illiath, to be a husband to Annika,"

Theo said, "and one day you will be a loving father to your children."

Peter exhaled with relief. "Thank you, Theo."

Theo grinned that familiar grin, turned Peter toward the stairs, and gently shoved him up the first steps. "Now, go!"

Peter laughed.

§

The day had finally arrived and Annika stood in the center of the Queen's chambers as her ladies in waiting helped her dress for her wedding. Her golden hair, much longer now, was braided and layered with tiny white flowers from the meadows. Her veil was lowered onto her head and secured with a thin crown of braided silver. Constable Darion lightly knocked on the door and opened it. Annika turned to see her grandfather, King Baldrieg, standing by the Constable, ready to escort her to Peter, her King. His deep set eyes welled with tears at the sight of his beautiful granddaughter dressed in the finest white silk gown stitched with silver thread and embroidered with delicate roses around the bodice and down the train. He combed his grey beard with his fingers, cleared his throat, and approached her.

"You are stunning, my dear," he said before kissing her forehead.

Annika smiled and reached out her hand. "I'm ready, grandfather," she said. Baldrieg took her hand and led her down the hall.

"So is Peter." He winked.

Annika and her grandfather made the stroll toward the Chapel. Many guests stood at attention when she appeared in the doorway. She grinned a wide tooth grin as her blue eyes sparkled. At the end of the aisle stood her nervous groom. She winked at him and he smiled back.

The Chapel at the palace of Illiath was filled with the scent of jasmine and lavender in the air. Eris, dressed in a full length silver gown embroidered with flowers, wore her long white hair loosely down her back and adorned it with flowers from the hill country. Annika had asked her to be her maid of honor. Simon was chosen to be Peter's best man.

Simon approached Eris. "You look beautiful," he said softly as he held out his forearm.

Eris smiled nervously and wrapped her hand around his arm and the two made their way down the aisle. "I'm much more confident in my armor," she replied.

The guests lined the walkway and watched as they took their places at the nave of the Chapel where Peter and the Chaplain stood.

A flute played a song that Annika requested. She remembered it from her childhood. Peter wore leather armor over his tunic. The armor had been a wedding gift from Thætil and the Queen at Vulgaard. On his head rested the gold crown of Illiath.

King Baldrieg escorted his granddaughter to her waiting groom and gently kissed her cheek. He gave Peter a stern look of warning and Peter swallowed hard. And then, Baldrieg playfully patted Peter on the back.

"Relax," the King joked. Peter chuckled anxiously.

Before the many noble guests, friends, and family, the Chaplain placed Annika's hand into Peter's. He turned them to face one another where they promised their fidelity to each other and the people as King and Queen of Illiath.

Before Peter spoke, he gazed at his hand wrapped around Annika's and Theo words of reassurance came to him. *Theo is right. I am ready,* he thought. *With Annika, I can face the unknown and all will be fine in the end.*

"I, Peter, King of Illiath," Peter began. He swallowed hard. "Do take thee, Annika, as my Queen and my Wife."

Annika smiled.

"I, Annika, take thee, Peter, King of Illiath, as my King and my husband," she said in a soft voice.

As Peter and Annika spoke, Simon stared longingly at Eris. When she turned to meet his eyes, he slowly grinned. Eris reached up, awkwardly stroked her hair, and shyly looked over at Peter and Annika.

"Annika," Peter said, "when I first saw you, all those years ago in Professor Theodore's library, I knew that I loved you and that one day we would be here together." Peter squeezed her hand as he gazed into her light blue eyes. "There was a time when I didn't know if I would ever make it out of prison. I thought all was lost. So when I saw you waiting for me there on that hill, well, I knew everything would be alright."

Peter gently rubbed the fingers of her hand with his. "And so, today, in front of all these guests, I promise to honor you, protect you, and be faithful to you all the days of my life as your husband and lifelong friend."

Annika coyly lowered her gaze and inhaled to keep from weeping. "And, Peter, when I first saw you in Theo's library with that scraggly brown hair atop your head, I knew I loved you and would love you forever," she sniffed and wiped a tear. She raised her eyes to meet his. "The hope of seeing you again was what kept me going on that long horrible journey to Vulgaard. I would look up at the moon and hope that it would show me the way to you. The thought of you was what made me brave. I pictured you inside that prison fighting for your life and I knew I, too, had to keep going."

Peter felt a tear run down his cheek as she spoke. He remembered gazing at the same moon from the prison window.

"And so, Peter," Annika concluded, "I promise that I will honor you, support you, and be faithful to you all the days of my life," she said.

Crispin looked around to make sure no one was watching him before he quickly wiped the tears from his eyes.

And then, when the vows were complete, Peter gently took Annika's face into his hands, leaned in, and kissed her waiting lips. When they parted, all the guests applauded. The new couple turned to face everyone. Cheers of joy and whoops of approval rose from the crowd. The land of Illiath had its King and Queen once again.

§

*In the end, the people had learned the uniqueness of the dragons and the purpose of the land. Man had once taken what was given and used it for evil. They had abused the dragon, twisted reality with magic, desired power, and scarred the land as a result. So, man had to suffer the consequences: the light was removed. Only by removing the light can one truly see the emptiness and feel the heaviness of the Darkness.*

*The Dragon of the Forest understood this. Its plan was to set in motion the time of great testing...the Time of Man. This painful time began when the young Prince of Illiath had entered the Dragon Forest for the first time all those years ago.*

*He had entered in and lived.*

*Now, the light has returned to the land and man clearly sees what the Elves had always known: We are to live as one with the dragons, take care of the land, water, and sky, do away with all magic, and turn to the Dragon for counsel.*

Peter read the words he had written in the section he titled *The Dragon Forest*. He had entered his portion into *The Book of Théadril* that his forefathers had started so long ago. He chronicled all that he had experienced as Prince and as a new King. He remembered his rebellion and the Dragon's mercy toward him when he had brashly entered its realm when he was ten years old.

He thought back to the Oath his father had honored as King. And he thought of how the Dragon of Bedlam had succumbed to the lust for power and hatred toward man. Peter saw with his own eyes the power of magic spells on the weak minded.

*The land thrives and man lives peacefully with the dragons. The purpose of this evil time of testing was to bring those faithful to the Oath together and drive those opposed to it away forever.*

When he had finished writing, Peter recognized his father's handwriting in the margins. He carefully traced his fingers over it. Alexander had written many notes to his son long ago. Peter grinned when he noticed how similar his own handwriting was to his father's.

He spotted some of the notes his mother's had written even before he was born. He was amazed at how she had seemed to know she would have a son and that he would be named *Peter.*

*He will be the foundation of this kingdom,* she wrote. *And he will rule with fairness and dignity pointing all his people toward the Dragon Forest.* Peter slowly closed the book, sat back, and pondered all that had been chronicled. He laid it atop the other book in which he had recorded his experiences and knowledge: *The Dragon Chronicles.*

"Well, it's good to see you working on such a fine day as this," a voice came from behind. Peter smiled when he recognized it. "I thought for sure I'd find you strolling in the fields outside the palace walls, fishing somewhere, or riding dragons."

"Actually, I was just about to gather the family up to go visit to the Dragon Forest." Peter turned to see his old friend, Theodore Sirus III standing in the doorway with a pipe in his mouth. Peter ran over to him and embraced him. "What brings you here to Illiath my old friend?"

Together they walked down the hall. "Well, it seems I've been asked to assist King Crispin in mapmaking, so I thought I'd stop by on my way to Gundrehd and visit," Theo said as he walked down the corridor with Peter.

"I am glad you are here. I have completed my part of the story in the Book of Théadril." Peter began. "It feels good to reflect on all that has happened."

Theo puffed on his pipe. "Hmmm," he said. "Perhaps that is because all turned out well and the Dragon Forest remains?"

Peter shrugged. "I suppose," he said. "It certainly helps that all ended well."

"Ah." Theo released a few wisps of smoke. "A wise King learns from the past, Peter. Remember that."

Just then, a little girl ran down the hall toward Peter. "There she is!" Peter shouted. He scooped up the little girl into his arms and kissed her cheeks. She had long golden curls atop her head and crystal blue eyes that twinkled.

"She is the image of her mother." Theo chuckled and gently touched the child's cheek. "Thank goodness."

"Nøel, can you say hello to my friend, Theo? You remember Theo don't you?" Peter asked his daughter.

"Hello, Theo," Nøel said in a voice as tiny as she was.

"Hello, my dear." Theo bowed. "Princess Nøel."

"Theo!" Annika appeared around the corner and ran to her former tutor. "What are you doing here? It's so good to see you again!"

Theo held her tight and when they parted, he patted her pregnant belly. "You look as lovely as ever, my dear."

Annika rubbed her belly. "Why thank you."

"You two have been very busy these last three years as King and Queen," Theo teased.

Annika blushed. "Yes, and I believe we are going to have a son this fall," she said. Theo looked at Peter and raised his eyebrows.

"Wonderful. And what shall this son be called?" Theo asked.

Annika looked at Peter who grinned.

"Well, if it is a son," he said to Theo. "Then we shall name him, William Alexander."

Theo nodded his approval. "A most noble name," he said, "A name that befits a prince."

"Come, join us for our flight to the Dragon Forest!" Peter nudged Theo as they spotted two dragons being brought into the courtyard. "It is Nøel's first visit."

"Ah, and so it is." Theo gently touched the girl's chin. He faced Peter. "I remember your first time entering the forest."

Peter chuckled. "So do I. Then you'll join us?"

But Theo had to decline, so Peter, Annika, and Nøel made their way to the palace courtyard. Peter spotted Tavrith champing at the bit in its mouth.

"Hello, old friend." He nuzzled the dragon's chin and looked into its kind amber eyes. "It is good to see you again."

Peter assisted Annika onto her dragon and he mounted Tavrith with Nøel. Together, the little family flew off waving goodbye to Theo as they departed into the afternoon sky.

They landed in the grassy fields just outside the entrance to the Dragon Forest. As they headed out, Peter placed Nøel onto his shoulders while Annika picked flowers and walked alongside. She sang the song she had sung on the journey to Vulgaard so long ago...

*Of dales and hills stretching far and wide,*
*Of paths leading homeward bound,*
*I cry for home as I ride singing*
*Filled with eternal love ringing.*
*In my deepest heart.*
*Oh, for the sun and the hope that it brings,*
*I ride on to hope's ending,*
*Of paths leading home*
*I come singing.*
*In my deepest heart.*

She placed the flowers to her nose and inhaled the mellow fragrance as she thought of the long journey back home. Nearby, she observed her husband and daughter laughing together. "I am home," she sighed. "Finally, home."

§

"Is this the forest, Daddy?" Nøel asked. She gazed up at the trees towering over them.

"Yes, my love," Peter said as they approached the entrance. "This is where the Great Dragon of the Forest lives."

"Really?" she asked.

"When I was a little boy, I had entered the forest alone," Peter said as he studied the path.

Nøel reached out and touched a leaf. "Were you frightened?"

"I was very frightened." Peter could see the glowing yellow eyes of the Dragon in his mind. "But then I realized that I was safe with the Dragon."

"You were safe?"

Peter smiled. "Yes. I was completely safe." He watched the sunlight peek through the tree branches as they walked.

"And this is where the Dragon of the Forest saved the people of Théadril," Peter continued as they walked by the old sign post.

"How?" Nøel asked.

Peter told her the story of how the Dragon laid down its life to save his kingdom. He spoke of how the Dragon returned to protect the people again. High above them, Peter noticed the White Owl circling.

"Look!" he pointed.

Nøel stared at the beautiful bird gliding above. "Pretty!" she said as she pointed.

Annika shielded her eyes from the bright sun with her hands as she watched Peter and Nøel walk on.

As Peter spoke, the White Owl suddenly flew away with the wind catching its wings causing it to gently glide its way over the tall trees. The owl flapped its wings with more effort in order to ensure it reached its final destination of security, rest, and solitude unlike any other place in the land.

"Tell me more about the Dragon," Nøel asked.

Peter watched the White Owl fly away. "Well, it is the Dragon of Promise... the great defender of the weak," he said as he thought about what his father told him. "And it will never forsake them. It does not grow faint or weary and its understanding is unsearchable. It gives power to the weak ones and faith to those who are uncertain. Even young men like me grow weary, but not the Dragon, Nøel. It will always remain faithful... even when we are unfaithful." Peter's voice trailed off.

As the White Owl approached its destination with the ease of familiarity and placidity, it circled the treetops once around, but not to inspect them as a general inspects his troops, looking for any sign of weakness or vulnerability. No, this time, it was completely satisfied with its surroundings. The Owl finally and gracefully entered its realm.

"Really, Daddy?" Nøel asked.

"Yes," Peter said as he lifted her off his shoulders and set her down. "Just when you think you cannot go on, the Dragon will be there for you."

"No matter what, Daddy?" Nøel reached out and tried to touch the sunlight.

"No matter what," Peter said as they walked along the path holding hands. His voice cracked with emotion. "The Dragon of Promise will always be there for you, Nøel. Never forget that."

A few white doves burst forth from the treetops.

"Always, Daddy?" Nøel asked as she entered the Dragon Forest for the first time, hand in hand with her father.

Peter smiled. "Always."

## The End

## ABOUT THE AUTHOR

When she isn't drawing dragons, award-winning author, R. A. Douthitt, is the author of *The Dragon Forest* trilogy and *The Elves of Vulgaard: The White Wolf* (Book One), an action/adventure series for children of all ages. *The Children* series won the 2017 Moonbeam Children's Book Award Bronze Medal for Best Book Series.

R. A. Douthitt lives in Phoenix with her husband Scott and their little fat dog. For more information on R. A. Douthitt, visit: www.thedragonforest.com

Made in United States
North Haven, CT
30 September 2024

58105693R00205